MW01681234

Anya Knows...

Fulton Wirt

Copyright © 2026 Fulton Wirt

All Rights Reserved. No portion of this book may be reproduced, stored in a retrieval system, or transmitted in any form or by any means, including electronic, mechanical, photocopy, recording, scanning, or other except for brief quotations in critical reviews or articles, without the prior written permission of the publisher.

Cover design and typesetting by CoverKitchen

ISBN Number 979-8-234-03105-1

Honey, you can't kill bad grass.

— Kirksey Nix
One-time roustabout for the Dixie Mafia

People do things for power that they would never consider doing for money…

Power is truly something different.

— Arthur Mitchell
Kirksey Nix's scam protege

BIENVENUE

CHAPTER ONE

1984

New Orleans

"It always starts with a little voodoo," is what the lady at the tarot table said as I wandered by one day. Those words, in that order, may not squirm through books of higher learning, but they sure as hell stir the souls abiding in the rough of dirt, cradling scarred and bruised fruit, in what certain folks in certain circles would call vulgar fingernails.

"Fuck'm!" might be heard around the campfire. "Fuck'm! We got too much on our shoulders to waste time worryin' about crap behavior behind gilded walls."

Which is true, but what happens behind those gilded walls does bleed through. It'll forever infect their little fire-lit world without any announcement.

The first time I saw Becca, she was still alive. In a stumble, she spilled her ice-cold hand grenade down my leg. That weekend, she had come down, like all the others, escaping *every fucking thing* for just a fraction of a moment in time.

When she looked up and found my badge, she apologized in one of those sweet Southern accents that make you wish for tree shade and a glass of cool, hand-squeezed lemonade. Raising a hand to rest on my shoulder, pretending I was her big brother, she asked if I could promise to be her guardian angel—a half-joking flirtation, touched with an awkward seriousness. I smiled and said of course, I'd be happy to. She slid her hand down my arm, letting me know she sensed she could count on me. We talked about things she would like to do while she was down. She smiled, bought herself another drink, and wandered back into the crowd, slipping from my thoughts.

The thick heat of a French Quarter summer quickly pushed the cold of the ice from my mind as I continued my patrol. I picked up a hot sense that Becca was here contemplating relationship revenge.

The next time I saw her face in real time, it was in a Polaroid being shown to me by her suffering mother. Her mother's eyes were the same storm grey as the girl who reached for my shoulder, except the neon lights made the mother's color rings spark and dance like frantic lighting in a sixties anti-psychedelics program. She had come down begging us to help find her missing daughter, Becca. And now, Becca's face had begun forcing its way into my dreams, whispering the same thing each time: *You forgot to look after me*. Then her lips would begin to mime the counting of numbers backwards, starting with ten. Becca always faded when she stretched her mouth for six, slipping away with a smile.

She wasn't haunting me because of the Polaroid time stamp; Becca was spookin' *me* because *I* was the one who found her severed hand lying on the ground. Then *I* lost it. Becca floated through purgatory, worried I'd let her soul slip into an abandoned file.

Her vision counted backwards, tugging me into her time. It made me ponder why the mind invested extra energy in refracting light during dreams. Fuck if I knew, but my best guess was the universe liked to keep us floating in a salty brine of horror and ecstasy. My skin turned cold when I became suspended in her animation.

I slipped into a back booth at Brother's Three Tavern and closed my eyes to let her count down to six again. I needed to move beyond her to let my mind recount the steps through that night's horror. The night, I discovered her hand lying on the ground like a slice of unwanted pizza. I needed to remember someone out of place. A pair of eyes peeking through curtains, maybe. My toes curled and unfurled to the edges of my shoes as I listened to roustabout voices choke on cigarettes and cheap liquor over at the bar.

Ten, nine, eight, seven, six, the Quarter *was* merry the other night, until a certain hour rang.

My mind took me to the middle of that patrol, to the naked incandescent bulb under the dipping, hundred-year-old veranda of the Gold Mine Bar, flushing straight to the ground, exposing just the small area under the old, crooked beams. Darkness curtained everything else. That was when Leda and a fella, who I've spotted slinking around town lately, pushed through the squeaking doors, landing directly under the porch light. The light stuck to the outer ridges of their features, while shadows looked pasted onto the other spots. She was pushing his hands back down to his side with grit in her jawline. He turned his nose up at her words and spotted me making my way toward the corner, as my patrolling brought me to this area throughout the night. The fella quickly fumbled his hands into his pockets, said something through a forced smile, and quickly moved off in the opposite direction. Little did I know I'd be forced to shoot him in the gut just a few minutes later.

I shouted, but she turned and walked down Burgundy, unaware that I was near, so I quietly crossed the street to get a bead on the slimeball giving her shit. I got past the back of a parked panel truck and caught his shadow shrinking down the wall of a hotel, headed toward Canal. I wasn't in the mood to chase unnecessary trouble and leave her vulnerable again, so I turned and made my way back to the porchlight to find Leda. I secretly wanted to watch from a distance. I needed to impress myself with her natural gait, so I stealthily followed her red leather soles, fading from the porchlight into another slick October night.

A cab pulled to the curb just in front of her, and the Couvillions, a family that lives on the block, paid their fare, and she stopped to talk. They shared some of a joint as I slipped into a curve in the wall line. The rumble of a city bus crossing Canal toward us told me it was nearing three-thirty in the morning. I kept a close eye on them and our vicinity as they laughed, hugged, and parted.

On one side of the coin of mythology is beauty in stride. On the other, it's a dark and messy world.

What was out there that night? I kept asking myself as I wandered, hoping for clues in this dream state.

I wasn't ready to intrude into her personal space, so I remained a guardian angel, so to speak. Back here on this dark neighborhood street, it would get eerily quiet; you'd expect sacrificial spirits to move in to inspect your intrusion. With enough absinthe in your gut, the long, shadowed corridor ribbed with wooden houses resembled the passage Job slid through after being gobbled by the massive, unwavering whale. According to the Good Book, gettin' right with God again was a tough chapter in a bumpy life. Leda sauntered through it as if it were her own personal, yellow-bricked road.

Generally, when I was in her company, I was under her employment, keeping her and her friends safe on nights out. I was obliged to throw in a freebie that night: making sure she safely made it to her gate as she smoked a joint, taking in some night air. It had been a long night shift, but I happily admitted to myself that it was my best effort of the day.

The first time I laid eyes on her, I thought I saw the place where gods vacationed. A place where hawks and butterflies mated and bred irresistible peril.

She detoured into Fahy's to buy a shot, and I crossed to the opposite side of the street so I could keep an eye on her through the open doorway. A smaller-sized U-Haul panel truck drove slowly up Barracks toward the river. It was the same one the perp was hoping to haul Leda away in.

I'll be damned. This fucker had watched her walk this path home before. He was ready at different points. *Homework.* He must have missed me hanging against the wall, because he chose to execute his plan.

She exited the bar and crossed back to *my* side of the street, something I hadn't expected; she usually walks on the right side of the street, as the inside curve makes a shorter walk to her home, which piqued my curiosity. She was usually with a gaggle of girlfriends. Why was she all alone?

I stayed in the shadows; for some strange reason, I wanted to slink and remain invisible. I guess I wanted to reveal myself closer to her place. Hell, I can't say why, but that's what I did. Maybe I didn't have anything I wanted to declare.

I was watching her do her thing two and a half blocks down. She'd saunter under a streetlamp, then slip back into darkness, heels tapping on concrete. I still can't recall anything out of the norm up to that point. Then I saw it: the white shape of a hand, lying in the pit of the curb.

From a distance, it didn't raise my suspicion, as an occasional mannequin part or Mardi Gras prop will stick out from a trash can more often than you'd think. I approached it with little concern until I caught sight of the wrist end of it.

Saw marks had ripped through the flesh. It was set with rigor; a large flap of mangled skin had sagged and hardened over the sawed end. No blood, though, not even in the wrinkles of the knuckles; it had been scrubbed clean. Lime sherbert-green fingertips with the pinkie filed to a rounded point, and a thick scar curved just under the nailbed on the ring finger. I pulled my flashlight and pinched my fingers into it. The skin was morbid and cold, but it wrinkled a little, telling me it was the real thing.

A cloud of despair infected me. The sunken voice of Becca's mother echoed that I should compare the Polaroid to the hand.

I stood to pull the picture from my rear pocket. Could Leda have been leading me to this side of the street? She *had* just walked past the hand. The marijuana could have pushed her head up to the stars. Maybe she'd assumed it was a showpiece, as I initially had. I kneeled again, matching the hand to the picture. I could faintly make out a scar on the hand resting on her hip. The cloud of despair turned into a heavy blanket, weighing me down.

I looked around so I would know which building I was standing in front of as I raised my radio to call it in. But I was distracted by a sudden struggle just around the corner on Chartres Street.

Leda. I quickly glanced back at the hand, then ran like hell to her.

I rounded the corner. A man was pressing a knife against the side of her neck. He slowly walked her backward toward the U-Haul I had dismissed earlier. She was facing in my direction, and as I unsnapped my holster, she must have spotted me. Leda dug her heel into his shin twice, making him loosen his hold, and twisted herself downward. Blood poured from her neck. I yanked my pistol, aiming at his guts, just around the appendix, and pulled the trigger.

He grabbed his wound, but still made another attempt toward her with the knife. I put another bullet in his leg, blowing his kneecap off. He fell to the ground. I ran to her, removing my belt and shirt to make a tourniquet.

The gunshots woke up this side of the Quarter; lights were turned on, doors opened, and the streets began to fill with concerned folks. I called for two ambulances and backup as I worked to slow her bleeding. My heart was thumping, seeing Leda covered in her own blood. It was the weakest I'd felt since the night I watched my mother break down after hearing the news of my father's murder. My knees wanted to collapse under our weight for a second. I held Leda tight and told her that I had her. She looked up without much concern.

"Just a flesh wound, Officer Fremeaux, I'm gonna live. Keep that asshole alive for me, please."

Nothing like a little contempt to keep the pain away. We loaded her into the ambulance and whisked her off to safety. I began to wonder when I should break the news about the severed hand. I scanned the area, trying to record as many faces in the area as I could, then walked over to my supervisor, Captain Barlow, and asked him to follow me. I didn't say what it was for, for some odd reason. I said I had seen something interesting, and we should take a look.

As we approached the scene, I was stunned to find that the hand was no longer there. It had been swiped from the scene. I immediately searched the shadows and windows for eyes. I looked through car windows to see if any drunks had passed out, or if an overnight worker was taking a catnap.

I swallowed and told Captain Barlow I must've just seen a ghost. I apparently didn't have anything to report.

"What did you think you'd found?" he asked.

"Just a stage prop of a hand, I guess."

"Hand?"

"Yeah, now that I think on it, it looked plastic. Somebody probably dropped it and returned to discover it after the shots were fired."

"Most likely, Fremeaux. You look like ya tired and stressed. Go home. Get yaself rested, Paw Paw. We got a lot of paperwork on this one. A shit ton of questions to answer for. Leda's mother will raise hell—be ready."

He shook his head and turned away. "A hand," he stated in a tone you'd use to make a child feel gullible on purpose. The tone was fuckin' odd and out of place.

He left me standing there. I searched around every corner, retracing our steps through this side of the dark Quarter. I walked the blocks again. I couldn't remember seeing shit. Somebody had outwitted me. There was another murderer close by, and I'd found and lost the goddamned evidence. Jailhouse confessions say you never return to the scene of a perfect crime. I had probable cause to believe I'd just witnessed a return; somebody somewhere foiled their part in a crime.

Ten, nine, eight, seven, six… Becca's eyes kept reminding me I'm not allowed to forget.

Fuck me.

CHAPTER TWO

Whenever the Steamboat Natchez tooted its calliope, the music was heard all over the French Quarter. Whenever a rich and powerful woman flushed her toilet, it washed all the way down through trailer parks. The air told me there was gonna be another toilet flush soon.

I asked Leda to meet me for an early mimosa or cocktail. I needed to hear that she didn't see Becca's hand, and I figured she might've witnessed someone in the area I might've missed.

We met at Molly's at the Market, "Seventy-two hours ago, I was approached by a frantic mother begging me to help locate her missing daughter. Have a look."

I held up the Polaroid.

"Twenty-four hours after assuring this poor mother that I'd do all I could, I discovered this poor girl's hand, with this very lime-green nail polish, severed and lying on the ground around the corner from where I shot the bastard trying to shove a knife into you."

Leda looked it over, then back to meet my eyes with a steely gaze.

I continued. "It was professionally severed, left lying on the ground like a forgotten condom. Palm down, thumb hoisted toward heaven, broken, with rigor. When you walked by it, you didn't see it?"

Leda's furrowed brows expressed genuine concern and bewilderment.

"Sorry—I did not, Fremeaux. I wasn't focusing at ground level. I was trying to avoid and forget the harassment back at the bar. Is there a possibility you imagined it?"

"I understand hallucinations can happen at three in the morning, but I'm confident it was real. Her name is Becca. Becca, from Arkansas. After ensuring your safety and placing you in the ambulance, I returned to investigate with Captain Barlow, and her hand was gone. Someone else must've been with us during the chaos. Hunting, maybe? I don't know. It hasn't been reported, so it was most likely a person who knows the whereabouts of Becca."

"So, you're sure it wasn't a Mardi Gras or Halloween prop?" she asked blankly.

"I pinched the damn thing. It squished; it was definitely the real thing. Look closely: you can see a distinct scar between the second knuckle and the nail on the ring finger. Like, she may have sliced herself pretty good in the recent past. Also, the pinkie nails are filed to a point. The hand I saw last night had this very scar, this pointed nail end. Someone took a life, and I now have no evidence to prove it ever happened. Shit, Leda, we have distraught mothers down here searching for lost daughters year-round." I took a drink of water. She looked at her watch.

"You have never been able to prove if those daughters shacked up with newfound lovers, or are truly dead and buried."

She stared at my badge, but then her sight slipped into the distance. I could feel her detaching from me and our conversation.

She drifted to some other place in her own time. She picked up her vodka, sipping it without seeming to sense the sting of the straight alcohol. Where had she drifted? The edge of her lips curled slightly. Could she be the good little student sitting at her desk at Leysin, cradled by the Swiss Alps, foreign languages, and her luxury?

I wanted to believe she was thinking of the first time she hired me to be her personal driver for her infamous night rides. Afterward, propping herself on the limousine door, she asked me why I didn't try to spoil her night with stares and inquiries, like other cops did. Then she thanked me with her eyes for being respectful.

She returned her elegant gaze to me.

"Who have you reported this to?" she asked, clearly not caring about my answer. Just moving me along. She had more to give—I was certain.

"I muddied the truth to Captain Barlow on the spot," I admitted. "I'm not ready to go public just yet. You know as well as I do that trust is a big issue in this city. Besides, I lost my proof."

I paused as I drifted farther into her dazzling hazelnut eyes.

"I'd like to know what you may have witnessed while smoking pot and nightdreaming through the streets. Did you see or hear anyone else lurking, or slinking from the scene? Can you recall anything that could give me a clue as to what my next move should be?"

Her eyes remain untelling. "Nothing caught my attention."

"Captain Barlow used a tone of voice that night that's stickin' on me, and I can't wipe it off. My gut tells me to protect myself at all costs with this one."

She pushed her back into the banquette cushion. She was the breed that would always tally reckonings, on her terms. Staring at my face with firmness, she reminded me to remain at bay until command. Her long, sinewy arm stretched out over the bench; her irresistible fingers tapped in rhythm across a white crocodile Birkin bag. Her skin, not quite tan, not quite white, or beige, or pinkish red. More of a darkened patina imported from ancient fairytales, keeping Benjamin Moore in a hot scramble for that perfect shade of bedroom luxury and lust.

A tone that sends me into visions of tasting caviar for the first time on a seashore far away somewhere. I imagine her warm lips pressed softly on my ear, whispering. I patiently wish her to want to touch me. She is a blaze of pure desire, which she keeps just beyond the world's reach.

She is making me wait still. The waiting is like stumbling upon an elephant in the night, chewing its cud. The weight looms before you, studying you for what you are. "What do I do about you?" It may ask. Or it may not hold the slightest bit of interest in you at all, but you'll never know that. You'll just sway in the awe.

I wonder if she has sensed I have fallen for her. I try hard to keep the telltale signs from exposing me. When I'm with her, it feels like reaching through a broken window on a back door, searching for the lock on the other side. Shards of glass threaten bloodshed as you hunt for a way in. If I possessed more clout and knowledge, I would gladly be her swan. Let her drain the power from my body...but unfortunately, I was not born to royalty.

I caught the edges of her face relax, her eyes wandered back. I noticed the bandage on her neck, behind the long, vibrant walnut-colored hair. It was almost invisible. I silently wonder how someone could come upon a bandage matching a skin tone such as hers so quickly. You had to strain to notice there was a long row of stitches hidden around the curve of her neck. She still had the poise to conceal the fact that a man had tried to slit her throat forty-eight hours ago. She finally broke.

"What about that asshole who attacked me Friday night? It was most likely a fool such as that?"

"That's the other thing. He had just made bail earlier that morning out in Bogalusa, but I had seen him plundering about the city for a couple of weeks or so. We may live in a city, but it's still a small town. I've witnessed the fucker lurk about our town, so when I shot him the other night, I knew the face. When we found his car out in Gretna, we discovered a crumpled piece of paper with your name and address, signed Gil. Gil is short for Galleach, the man who coordinates all the crime sprees for the Dixie Mafia from a seedy joint over on the Gulf Coast."

She didn't flinch a bit when I told her this. Wasn't tense in the least. I can't tell if anything is resonating at all. Not an ounce of concern. Just cool cucumbers on ice.

"And the U-Haul?" she asked.

"It had been reported stolen over on the coast. Leda, do you or any of your family have connections with this group in any way?"

She stared coolly at me again. "We would never stoop, Fremeaux."

"The man who attacked you went by Buck. His birth name is Arthur Bucknell, Junior. Does that ring a bell in any way?"

"It does not."

"I watched him follow you out of the Gold Mine. You two had some words, and I could see he was agitated. That's why I was there when he attacked from the shadows."

"Yes, this man did approach me a couple of times wanting my attention, but I let him know quite crudely that the merry-go-round would not be stopping for him. He wandered off, obviously holding his pursuit."

"As I can tell, he'd been in pursuit of you on the business of foul play for quite some time now. The possibility that he could include kidnapping and rape of a beautiful and powerful woman of society would have been on the bonus plan."

"I am grateful you were on duty. Because of your gallantry, I escaped with just a few stitches. However, things had just gotten started when you got to the scene. He would have caught a bigger fish than he could have been able to reel in all by himself."

I felt myself smile.

"This I know firsthand, Leda." I played along, "I am well aware I didn't save you from something you could not have handled yourself. I only shortened the duration and saved you the extra energy."

She smirked. "I must warn you." she said bluntly but with concern. "You must be careful to whom you speak in the future. All our neighbors have hidden worlds. You can never know which will be six degrees from the Saints or which holds hands with your demons. You could easily find your hide ripped from your body and your tendrils spread over a crawfish bed."

"Leda, I've never heard you speak with such malice before."

"As you've witnessed, I've seen many a thing and know very well the rancor men can impose on their fellow man, sweetie. There is a bounty of dirt that you just can't know about me."

"This I'm also aware of, and yes, I am working with rigid caution as most of this administration is just as corrupt as these dirty streets. Hell, this may lead all the way to City Hall for all I know."

"Fremeaux, you are most likely going to find yourself battling the world if you're not careful."

I pushed *my* back into the banquette to relieve pressure. I've become the mouse in the maze. If she has some cheese to give, I'll have to work for it. Those fire-bright eyes remained locked on my face as I noticed, over her shoulder, Xandi, a Quarter voodoo artist, enter the bar. She ordered a drink and winked at me as she crossed the threshold into the courtyard out back.

I returned my focus to Leda.

"What do you mean, 'by the world'?"

"Secrets, Fremeaux, secrets. The world has more hidden secrets than conscious realities. I'm certain you may open more underground doorways than you're ready for. And, for the record, Officer Fremeaux, I'm afraid I haven't anything to recall which could help you decode your lost little girl mystery in any way. I didn't see anything that night. I was stoned, mind you. But off the record, since you did intervene in my favor and you are my favorite defender, I will be glad to keep you abreast of the rumblings and report any evidence that could assist you in capturing a culprit of this nature. Nobody likes a beast wandering amongst us. Makes our paths home wistful without adventure."

She pulled her bag to the crook in her elbow and swayed her legs to the open end of the booth, as smooth and casual as a python gliding on her empire of power and ease. Strong, patient, and undisturbed, she stood, placing strands of hair behind her ear.

"Thank you for the beverage. I must be getting Mommy to afternoon tea, if you know what I mean."

She extended her long, tanned arm and grasped my fingers. A simple touch from her was all it took. My body shivered into some sort of mature comfort.

"Also, I will not divulge this conversation, and any further talks will be with you only. You have my word on that, Theodore. And just in case curiosity has you by the tail, I was wandering the Quarters alone because a girl sometimes just needs her space, to be completely free. And again, thank you for being there when I needed someone."

That was the first time she had informally addressed me using my first name. Was she letting her hair down? I'd been in her private security for five years. I'd witnessed her, in the rearview, commit almost every mortal sin and break commandments that would send good law-abiding citizens to jail for ten or more years, and she has never broken the hired hand barrier. Until now.

I wasn't hired to police her. I was hired to serve and protect her.

A sudden hot, wet touch pressed my shoulder like a sweaty New Orleans summer. I looked up into a smile from Xandi as she pushed an envelope under my badge.

"Put your hand over your heart, Officer Fremeaux."

I placed my hand on my badge, and my fingertips felt the crisp, cool paper. I pressed into my chest to hold it in place as she removed her warm hand.

"You're not alone, Fremeaux. This note is for your eyes only."

She winked and left me alone with something I wasn't expecting. What a town, I thought. Down here, everything is connected one way to another. Spirit and flesh, math and myth. God and Mr. Devil swim together in the same bowl, commingling in ways a mere man couldn't possibly understand.

I stood to leave, and as I walked to the door, I heard the bartender, Jim, yell back at Artie, the drunk sitting alone in the corner.

"You can never explain what your imagination can see and make you feel. That shit'll hypnotize ya, Artie?"

CHAPTER THREE

My thumb and forefinger softened the paper on the envelope Xandi just stashed on me as I moved through the decaying doorway. A sticky wind coming out of Chalmette stuck itself to my face. I swore I could smell the smoke from the cigarette dangling from Ms. Maylynn's lips as she dumped dirty rice, busted flounder, mirliton, and hot cabbage from the buffet table just upriver at Rocky and Carlo's.

On the corner to my right, the beer-cap tap-dancing boys from the ninth ward maliciously grinned and mimicked prayer as a young man from the corn fields, carrying the clods of the great and providing Mother Earth in the treads of his work boots, dragged a hand-scrawled sign stating,

Hell is hot and ready!

Jesus is discarding souls, strong and steady.

REPENT OR PERISH!

The fella was barging through their space, oblivious to other people.

I reckoned good news really did sleep till long after noon. I closed my eyes and bowed my head for a second. I guessed he was headed to plant the seeds of reason and truth into us sinners with the rest of the flock. The problem was, we were all here avoiding reason and truth. Everybody needed a break from that shit now and again. Across the street, the daytime chess players chose odds while debating *their* reasons why the world was going cock-eyed.

Hot, musty body odor, stale dog piss, and clove cigarettes emanated from the homeless encampment residing on this end of Decatur. I looked through the crowd of lost and ruined adolescents and found Nate slunk into a corner door jam, either going up or coming down. It was always one or the other with heroin addicts. These kids were the disillusioned products of disinfected wealthy parents, seeking charity without commitment. Lost, they drifted in bands from city to city, conning simpletons out of just enough money to not give a shit. It was an attractive life for young people trying to escape a harsh family.

Occasionally, a girl from a missing poster was found in the arms of one of these boys. They'd made a lovers run to another camp.

A half-dazed girl sitting at Nate's feet punched him to wake and lifted her finger towards the other side of the street. I followed her lead and caught Lieutenant Demortiers and Monsignor Moreno shaking hands and parting company a few blocks down. Demortiers walked away, aloof, with an envelope dangling carelessly between two fingers. *Fuck 'em all* was his philosophy.

The thing one noticed about Demortiers was the way his clothes seem to cling for dear life, waiting to jump off at the next stop. Too tight and too droopy in all the wrong places. The fabric sagged off the chest like a lady's blouse while clinging for dear life around the protruding belly. His ass and thighs were at a loss for contour, and stepping closer, I startled at the sight of the dark grey puffed circles under his eyes, thick as plump snails. A lonely man completely out of place, bloating with thin dreams. A truly base and shitty life on two feet. My distaste for crooked cops was reaching its maximum load.

Nate stood suddenly, wobbling till he caught up with his bearings, then quickly began a walk-jog toward Esplanade. Monsignor Moreno turned and strolled in the same direction on the other side of Decatur. This bonehead masquerade certainly piqued my interest—more so than the dirty cop dangling any kind of hush money. That kind of crap had been going down since mankind could deduce failure from fortune.

A damned hot draft of diesel exhaust from a city bus took some wind from me, but I kept my tail on the two of them. I hopped and zipped my legs through a maze of empty beer bottles and rotting to-go plates. Dirty hair splayed out on the sidewalk, like a hit-and-run victim, from a runaway girl who had decided she needed a ground nap.

I continued down Decatur to stand across the street from *Le Garage,* where the two were doing the secret exchange dance. Finally, the envelope was laid on a table of bric-a-brac jewelry and antique ceramics. A grungy little hand swiped it up, and Nate exiled himself behind a dressing curtain. At the same time, Monsignor casually exited like a young mother who had just whisked her child onto the school bus in some faraway Irish village. All she had to do for the rest of her glorious morning was to remind herself how lucky she was to have all she had gotten in this wild and wonderful life.

I walked across the street and scooted into the doorway of *The Abbey* to wait for Nate to make his stumble back into reality. I stood like a tourist, reading the rising crime statistics they posted daily on their street marquee, chiding the slow progress of my fellow law enforcement family, including me.

Nancy, the owner of the joint, slid herself through the open door next to me. She refused to ditch her punk rock get-ups at her age. Orange-yellow hair, safety pins in her ears, and everywhere else. She still looked like a ton of fun at any hour.

"Fremeaux, ya checkin' to see if them ACT scores gone up?"

"Ahh fuck Nancy baby, cut me some slack today. Could ya just look over my shoulder and nod when the homeless kid comes out from *Le Garage,* please?"

"He's about to walk out now. What gives, Fremeaux?"

"Tell ya later, sweetheart. Does he have anything in his hand?"

"Looks like he's cupping some cash."

"Just what I figured. Coming our way?"

"No. Headed for the Bywater. Ya boy's trottin' to Flop's for somma dat hey-ron."

"Yeah, Nancy, these kids'll be too blitzed to bother you in a few hours."

"Don't let 'em bother you none, Fremeaux," she said facetiously.

"I'll fry that fish later, sweetheart."

I dropped back into pursuit. I figure that with drugs in his possession would be a good time to apply a little pressure for answers.

The Italians used to call Bywater home, but as the Mafia's power dwindled, the drug dealers and street gamblers slowly took control of the streets, and nowadays it's a shit show. A den of street zombies taking a bite out of reality.

Nate turned onto Clouet Street, and I stepped into the entryway of a little cemetery to wait.

A shadow from a statue stretched across the sidewalk, forming the image of a hand holding a deck of cards—a winning hand of poker, perhaps? I followed it back to the source to find a concrete boy standing on a ball holding a dove with splayed wings. *Fuckin' reality*, I thought, as gambling in the form of craps had been introduced to America just a block over. There are thirty-two closed-curtain poker houses back in here now, and every week, a gunshot or knife blade halts somebody's winning streak. I smirk now at the sight of the joyous young boy forever holding up peace and freedom, but the ever-blinding sun darkens the sidewalk with artistic license. Gotta pay to play, baby. Freedom is either fought for or bought, and it's the cheat that always swipes it in the end.

Nate was a junior. His father, Nathaniel Sr., is the chancellor of Mississippi State. As with all the Nates I've ever come across in life, this one had also self-monikered himself Nate-Dawg. Added the W for a celebration of his family's educational institution, the Bulldawgs. It was tattooed on his forearm.

He fumbled his way past the thin cranny I'd wedged myself into, and I reached to grab the back of his skull, pulling him into the foyer of the cemetery with me. My fingers sank into some sort of head grease; I shuddered a little as I scrubbed my fingers against the brick wall.

Dark vacant clouds covered his eyes. A complete lack of yearning in his stare.

"Been to Flop's place, Nate?"

"No Fremeaux, just looking around for some free lunch."

"If I search you, kid, I keep what you got on you till you stop being stupid. Do you wanna be a big boy and talk to me?"

"Man, what's with all the harassment today? I ain't done nobody no wrong."

"I'll start easy. The missing girl in this photograph, have you seen her? Has she tried to hang out and score with y'all?"

"Not that one."

"Not that one, huh? Some have before?"

"Yeah, man. Some do find our joy, for sure, dude."

"What do you tell the mothers when they come asking?"

"We ain't seen shit. Tell 'em to fuck off, it's none of our business."

I paused and watched him squirm a little.

"What's with Monsignor giving you drug money?"

His eyes went vacant again. He no doubt wished me the death card as he speculated his best answer—knowing full well the hook was in his lip, and the truth was his best option to walk away with the money and drugs. If he didn't have something of value to lose, he could easily tell me something stupid. He knew this wasn't worth the paperwork.

"I help Monsignor save people from ending up where I am."

"In what manner of help are you to the monsignor?"

"When lost boys need guidance, I send 'em to him for salvation."

"So, he offers them shelter in God's mercy while handing you drug money as salvation? Sounds like a pot of horseshit to me."

"I'm telling you straight up, dude."

"It's not your story I'm calling bullshit on, kid."

"Can I go now?"

The melody of "Walking to New Orleans" tooted through the neighborhood from the Calliope of the Steamboat Natchez, working its way upriver.

"Keep this talk between us so I don't bust up your future dealings. Understood?"

He knew his father had bought strong connections down here in the form of free scholarships—that was why his sorry ass wasn't behind bars—but he still had to walk the tight line with us honest beat cops. We had the means to disrupt his drug flow, and an addict will do anything to stay fed. Alcohol choked back tears for the lonely. Heroin erased all responsibility, and unfortunately for some, responsibility is their poison.

"I got ya, Fremeaux. By the way, don't go fuckin' with the Pope man, they'll skin ya." He smiled devilishly.

I let him wander off freely. They'd be sky-high by the riverside in a couple of hours. The word of a score would spread quickly through the scavenging citizenry, causing the predators to surface, looking to poach free drugs. The chances of us fishing a dead body from the murky Mississippi waters in the early morning hours had just doubled.

I stared at the shadowed poker game painting the hot concrete again and thought of how holy money had forever supported a lot of this mess. It cut down on theft from local businesses, I supposed. Save a life, take a life? No other book understood this concept better than the Good Book.

I reach the edge of the Quarter again, and three attractive women wearing matching plaid tartan trench coats approached me. The shortest of the three asked me in a thick English accent, "Fancy Burberry, do ya?"

My face must've jumbled, as they giggled mirthfully, and in unison, snatched open their coats, giving me a full treat of nudes.

Six perky titties, three trimmed pussies, a visit from a voodoo priestess, and an ordained heroin deal, all before eleven a.m. Three hundred sixty-five days of conjured adventures occured within these seventy-eight blocks. A million nights of wonder and magic await you down here. Why live anywhere else?

I watched the ladies saunter off into a sinful holiday.

I passed another picture of Becca and three other missing girls as I moved toward the precinct. I found myself scrutinizing every person I see, even the Jesus freaks. Nobody could be that fucking perfect.

The paper envelope felt smooth between my fingers, and I slipped into the St. Louis Cathedral looking for an empty pew and open the note. Well, I thought it was a note, but as it turned out, it was a whole friggin' letter from none other than Don Lee Keats himself.

"Jesus," I said aloud. I looked around to make sure I *was* alone. Don Lee was our man of letters, our Bob Woodward down here. Hell, he won his Pulitzer for reporting a few years back. Celebrated for performing miracles with a just dab of writer's ink, he was not a man afraid to push the powers that be into the fray.

"A letter, huh?" I asked the statue of St. Louis perched just to my left. "Well, let's see what the old man has to say."

> *My dear good Sir, it is with great melancholy that I'm writing for your appurtenance. Surely, your grey matter must be stretched and washed in puzzlement, so I'll cut to the chase. I have what you are searching for. For I was quietly trailing you and Leda when that showdown in the streets commenced.*

I have a very good and solid reason for doing what I did, and I will be more than happy to clue you in to all of it. You must not interview another soul on the matter. You are, in a way, being forced to trust me in this, of which I take full account. And for this, I offer a satchel of gilded apologies.

I will provide explicit instructions regarding your next steps. In this new direction, you will meet more like-minded friends who share this cause. Know this, you now have eyes on you. Ours for sure, and depending on knowledge gained, others may be as well. You will come to discern the "us" from the "them" soon.

Although we have endured the shadows of the who's or what's they may be, uncovering those horrid figures hiding in those dark holes will be our main duty to these missing young women, now that we finally have hard evidence.

For twenty years, not a single thread of hair has been recovered. Not a single witness. Not one distress call has been recorded from our boys in blue. Only missing person posters and tears have collected in our streets. This weekend, as you are well aware, a mistake was made. It is now our time to untangle from the spider's web and undo these atrocious behaviors.

Your next day off is two days away, and this is what you must do exactly for us to meet. Please hold trust in your heart.

It will be an easy drive, but it will be three hours with one bathroom break. You take I-55 through Jackson, MS, up to the Natchez Trace Parkway. There, you will take the northbound exit for seven and a half miles. You will find signage directing you to Cheever's Watering Hole; it's an exit off the right-hand side; you can't miss it.

This will take you through four miles of narrow winding roadway, which will abruptly spill into the parking area for a small boat launch and my sister's waterfront lounge aptly named Cheever's Watering Hole. There will be a parking spot open and marked with an orange roadway cone at the back right corner of the building. If anyone has followed you, there will be no way for them to escape discovery, as their vehicle will spurt into the open lot like a newborn baby. All eyes on them sort of thing. If you have been followed, walk to the back door of the building and wait until a pretty lady opens the door to welcome you in. All this is staged, so be ready to act as though you belong there. She will be acting as your significant other, kissing you, and escorting you to a boat that will deliver you to your next location up the Pearl River. If you are not followed, then come through the front door like any other decent human being. Good luck and stay safe.

PS, pick up a copy of this week's Gambit. I have a full back-page declaration that I believe should delight you. See you soon, Don Lee.

Just like that, a blood-stained dirt road had appeared at my feet. The road never changed, but the people always did. Huey P. Long might have slapped some new blacktop on it for the poor and forgotten, but it had become laden with all the Willie Starks of the land, hell-bent on governing all the untamed lawmakers down here. All the while, meek souls accumulated in its ditches.

Plenty of God's good children had been taken and continued to disappear from this earth without a trace, and the baby Jesus on the cover of this pamphlet would do nothing about it. A call of duty rushed from my bones to my skin. I counted down with Becca in my head once more, chasing for a cure, again.

I looked closer at the picture of the Virgin Mary and her newborn child. I was feeling certain this scene may very well be the first occasion the simple edict was uttered, the one that all country grandparents love to spout when a chunk of life seems too big to carry.

"Well, baby, Gawd don't deliver us nuthin' we cain't handle arrselves now does he?"

I sure as hell hoped that was a true statement.

I felt a strong grip tighten on my shoulder. I looked up into the Monsignor's face.

Well, fuck me.

"You look perplexed, my son?"

"That could be said of where I intend to walk soon."

"As long as you stay focused on what the Lord requests of us, remain on the taut wire, my son, you will find yourself at the end of this long, dark journey before you know it. Millions of people love this land, and they depend on you and me to get the job done. When you finish this task that our Lord has set before you, your only memory will be of the stuff which redeems us in his eyes." He smiled.

He's got God's pocketbook all secured; I'll give him that.

A thick-boned man approached him from the other side, and he turned to the stranger. This saved me from saying something I'm sure I would have regretted.

"Good to see you, Monsignor. Would you have the time to take confession from an old warrior, sir?"

The fella was dressed in thick, dark grey pants—sturdy material for sailing treacherous and cold seas. Large, dense, good leather boots covered his feet. And polished to reflect light. A sight out of place down here. This is a fella that should be riding high on the cold decks of the *Pequod*, hell-bent for revenge.

A long, thin, deep rut of edging was missing from the left toe, like the talons of a harpy eagle had slid across it, dragging away chunks of leather and rubber.

Thickened fingers glued to monster-sized hands hung under the same dark grey colored sleeves as the trousers. Same quality material as a seaman would wear, but he wasn't a seaman any longer, I suspected. There was too much street in his eyes. I stood. He was a good six inches taller than me, probably six-six or so. He held a *Gambit* in his grip, which I asked if he was finished with. He said he was without taking his eyes off the Monsignor, and handed it to me without losing any of that blank expression. The two men went into a room in the back of the church. I sat and studied the paper in my hands.

I held up the *Gambit,* and there was the caricature of Don Lee Keats wearing a bard's cap. Captioned words instructed me to turn to the back cover. I did just that and read.

It's Nineteen-Eighty-Four and New Orleans is now, more than ever, an anything-can-happen town. Every single moment of every single day, dirty little minds open the doors to all things desired, and wishful hands slam them shut again. We're a conurbation welded together through unchecked human character and adversity, where bullshit stacks up like sandbags and irreverence drifts through the air like pollen.

"I know where ya got dem shoes" started as a simple street hustle and evolved into a philosophy for the whole Goddamned city. The idea of "gimmie' somethin' for nothin'" forged a community on the fringes and crammed us into the skin of a hooligan's city, but one thing is for certain: we stand united in this misfortune. The true difference between here and the rest of God's free country is that out there, everybody wants to tell you what you need. Down here in the city that care forgot, we simply give you what you need. We're a city brimming with sex, Jesus, straight shooters, and a wheelie bin full of squirrelly bastards all willing to give something for nothing, just to watch you unwind to unhinge. It's just that simple; all that is required of you is brevity, my dear children. Anything can happen at any time of the day, no questions asked. Our streets are littered with lurking, greasy gummatas eager to tickle your fancies and retire all those Christian inhibitions. Bring us your beleaguered souls, for we will be keen to reconstruct them for you. You just need to be durable enough to suffer our taint. Wander wisely through our bohemian circus, my friends. Life is nothing more than tumbling dice for some of us. Gambling with life is what we do best. Let this be a beacon of caution for all who come to visit with us.

And for those within our city boundaries, a warning is in order for you. We now have eyes that will expose those among us taking advantage of young innocence for personal gain.

Hear this, the notes from our magic flutes will soon float in with the fog and enchant all who are guilty toward early graves... Don Lee Keats.

I sit lost in thought, staring at a stained-glass image of Mary Magdalene and her urn at Golgotha. I must've gotten lost trying to attach to her mystery, as I felt distant eyes on me, breaking my reflections.

"Do you feel a confession, my son?"

I stood to leave.

"Not today, sir. I'm sure I'll be in need of redemption soon enough."

I moved between two empty pews, thinking how his hand on my shoulder held no effect. No reaction whatsoever. But the slightest brush of flesh from Leda sent shockwaves through my soul. Sins of the flesh.

All that was required is brevity, according to Don Lee's latest public rant.

CHAPTER FOUR

Earlier this morning, after punching the clock back in the city, a fella with grim eyes asked me for directions, and I could swear to God as he rounded the corner, I felt another soul slip into another dimension. Where the hell was the universe sending me? What god-awful twist of fate was wringing out my comfort?

Jackson, Mississippi, was a town I'd traveled to many nights in my youth. The drinking age over here had been overlooked forever, and we would make the drive to dance at a funky little neighborhood joint called *The Subway Lounge*. Beer was sold by an invisible person and delivered with parched hands from a darkened window in a civil-beaten, tin-roofed shack across the way. The price of the beer was lower for the pretty girls. Survival comes in all flavors.

Mississippi ground was where a man can sell his soul for wished talents. It was the birthplace of Don Lee Keats, a man born to tell a story without having had to trample out to the crossroads to make the deal too hard to refuse. He was a large hunk of flesh, and people meeting him for the first time rarely guessed he was gay. The man knew a little something about exclusion and secrets, banged his way to the top of his game with pomp *and* circumstance. New Orleans was a natural landing pad for folks keen to discover themselves with fearless dignity without giving up the decadence. That's why Tennessee Williams uprooted himself from here to there.

Still to this day, in the deep, dark depths of night in this rich, misunderstood land, one could feel deliverance back to the turbulent past. Dark souls still haunted time, and you couldn't help but get whiffs of those pains drifting in the air. Their work was permanent. It was the birthplace of the blues, and it was in that moan that a man can endure the adult secrets of a dark soul. One pant leg at a time. It all moved at one great, slow pace. Life could feel like an eternity in certain moments.

The sign for Cheever's Watering Hole suddenly revealed itself from behind a low-hanging oak branch. I hit the brakes and looked in the rear-view. There was no sign of another vehicle; there had been long periods when I couldn't remember being in control of the car, much less looking for a tail. I did remember checking the rearview a couple of times, unsure of what I was trying to avoid back there. I was convincing myself that life was prodding me with the spooks.

The thin, bumpy, twisting road I turned onto began to feel very much like a birth canal. I could smell the river's odor. Mud, tree life, frog shit, moss, and the dank, slow-flowing water. It was all there as I moved slowly along the dark, narrow tree-lined road. The quick curves only revealed more empty gravel ahead, and a looming forest hovered over my rearview. The curves were sharp and frequent, concealing any signs of being followed.

I suddenly busted out onto a paved parking lot that invoked the spirit of an early bayou landscape of George Rodrique. Dark black shadows loom with heavy green foliage lit from above the canopy with scattered skylight. A heavily shadowed river inlet meandered underneath the soft sway of the branches. The air was still but not mute. I looked back from where I had come, and sure enough, it looked like a small cut into the tree line. Anyone plopping through that would have no opportunity to turn back the clock for escape. Two trucks spilled out, both filled with beer-swigging fishermen towing boats. I parked in the place marked off for me and waited.

I looked around, and even the rivers in this part of Mississippi were different. The denseness of the air hovered above dark channels that seemed to swallow the past and shit out a future that weighed heavily in my chest. I could only pray I'd have the strength to swim safely through the under-currents if need be.

I couldn't see hanging around my car any longer, so I got out and walked through the front door as instructed. A woman resembling Maryanne from *Gilligan's Island,* except for the bouncing strawberry blond hair, came over and grabbed my arm.

"Hello, Fremeaux, it's nice to finally make your acquaintance. I'm Tippa, Don Lee's baby sister, and we're glad you made it safe. Are you alone, dear?" she asked with raised eyebrows.

"It's a pleasure to meet you, too, little lady. And as far as I can tell, I'm alone."

"Well, honey, you're better lookin' than Don Lee described." She grinned. "I do have my hands full here at the bar today, but I will have a drink with ya later at the house. Uncle Pap is gonna take you by boat to finally see my brother. Would you like a beer and BBQ sandwich for the ride?"

I told her both would be a good start, and she pointed out the restroom. I made my way, pondering the odds of stumbling upon the severed hand of a girl, with instructions to drive to Mississippi for answers. I was no psychiatrist, but I could understand the weight riding in the back of my skull like fungus on rotting squash.

Above the urinal was scribbled, *Billy Joe Shaver. I pissed here last week!* That was just like Shaver, if he wrote it, putting a timeless stamp on his trip. We would always be thinking about last week, no matter when we looked at it.

I washed my hands and catch a glimpse of myself in the mirror. *Good God,* I thought, at the sight of my beleaguered skin. I'd been mostly awake since seeing Becca's arm.

On the wall behind me was scrawled, *Beware of snakes.* Someone had taken the time to write it backward so it could warn from the mirror's view. Shitty philosophy for strangers.

"What a Goddamned thing to report to someone on foreign ground," I said to the claim of the invisible spirit. I dried my hands, pushed the old, creaky door open, and walked across the smoke-filled beer joint. Tippa walked me down to a river skiff where a man in his seventies, wearing a faded Mrs. Smith's Bakery T-shirt, had a wad of tobacco the size of a lacrosse ball bulged his cheek.

"This is Uncle Pap," she said. "Uncle Pap, this is Officer Fremeaux, the fella Don Lee is waiting for. Keep him safe, please."

There was still fire and youth in his eyes that seemed to say, *Bring whatever ya got, fella.* He spat a large brown liquid mass into the river.

"Sit back here, young man." So, I boarded, and we slowly backed into the dark greenish-brown water.

"I might look rough, but if you right by Don Lee, then you, my friend, good by me too. How's that sound?"

"I appreciate it," I said.

This river ride wasn't too far from reliving a river scene from *Apocalypse Now*, except I wouldn't find Charlie in this bush. This ride was filled with hungry gators, tree snakes, and river owls hooting at our arrival. Thick, dank brown mud everywhere. I kept telling myself I'd been summoned here for good reasons.

I watched a large cottonmouth curled at the base of a tree pull its mouth wide, exposing cotton-white skin and arched needle fangs upon hearing us mosey through its territory. Then it dawned on me that the person who wrote that warning on the bathroom wall had meant it literally. I could feel myself losing my cool. My ribs tightened. When I was a boy, my father would always tell me to never assume the negative. Never repeat negative assumptions aloud; that is the very root of becoming unpopular. Always assume the positive and let the negative prove itself.

Every so often, a school of fish would dance and paint at the water's surface with a precise rhythm. At other times, frantic bursts disturbed the water in frenzied warning. It was uncanny how the reasons for the flutter could be discerned. Almost like fish Morse code, warning of death stalking through their underworld. I felt my finger simulating trigger pulls as we floated through stooping shadows. I found myself adjusting to the concept of killing again.

After rounding a long bend in the river, the sky opened suddenly, showing a row of brick houses with private boat launches. We moored at the last of them, a red brick home with heavy green curtains edging the windows. As I lifted myself from the vessel, I could see Don Lee sitting in a lounge chair in the corner of the outside patio, drinking bourbon. I went to sit with him.

"Fremeaux, I'm very happy to have you with us."

Don Lee and I hadn't developed a close personal relationship just yet. We were Quarter acquaintances. We'd said our howdy-do's. Held cordial conversations. I'd made sure he'd stumble home safe on those late nights when he'd get too loose. He'd given me tips on when to be on the lookout, which made my job easier at times. But I thought all that was about to change. For the better, I hoped. I was acutely aware that crucial evidence had been stolen, and it didn't sit easily with me.

"Likewise, Don Lee. I'm here unofficially, but if you have taken what you say you have taken, it will become official. Just be aware, sir."

"Sit with me, Officer Fremeaux. Allow me to divulge why you're here. Mind you, you have been invited, and I do have much to divulge."

We sat.

"What you've done is illegal, Don Lee," I reminded him.

He nodded in agreement and disagreement at the same time. He continued in that genteel southern drawl that makes us all want more of the story.

"Twenty years ago, I lost my only niece, and my older sister lost her only daughter. She simply vanished from the streets of the French Quarter. She was entering her first spring break from education at Ole Miss and decided to visit with me for the duration. Her roommate, Kate, was to take a cruise ship from our ports on the Caribbean route with her family. They had driven down; she had dinner out with their family. The night turned late, and, apparently, vicious. She explained sweetly to them that she practically lived in the Quarter and would be fine walking to my place alone. She has never reappeared again, anywhere. Needless to say, my older sister has never, and will never, return to her former glorious self. Sadness looms heavy and forever. It is my brotherly duty to deliver the truth of what has taken our only daughter from us." He paused and took a drag from the crisp bourbon.

"You wanna get a little clearer than this? I've made a promise to a grieving mother. Why did you steal evidence, thereby hindering us from doing our jobs?"

"We understand your feelings and sense of duty, Fremeaux."

"You said we. What do you mean, we?"

"You will soon come to meet the rest of the group. Each of us holds a connection to a missing child, and each of us has made our own promises to one another. Young women were disappearing from our streets long before you put on a badge. We've waited for clues longer than you can imagine. A mistake has been made, and we now have solid evidence to show for all that waiting. I fully understand your place in the line of duty, but you're going to be subjected to our knowledge before you are allowed to form a decision. I'm sorry for the bluntness.

"I took the young lady's hand because I firmly believe people in your department are whitewashing evidence for these crimes. We can't prove it, but the department is willing to kill whoever tries to uncover the truth.

Truth is, son, they'll be all too happy to cover you in six feet of mud if you try to uncover the truth on your own terms. Yes, what I've done also provides you protection."

His words hit home.

"How did you get to the hand without a witness?"

"I was in and out. As soon as you pulled the trigger, I took my chances. Quick. I've been haunting the Quarter since the late fifties. I know when and how to make the proper moves."

"How did you know the hand was there?"

"I watched you inspect the area. Your demeanor became punched with unexpected determination, so to speak. I sensed you had discovered something special when you pulsed your flashlight, so I eased into that area just before you pulled your trigger, and I discovered what you had discovered. I also recognized the hand as that of the missing girl, for I had bought Linda, Becca's mother, lunch and consoled her that very afternoon. I was already made aware she had spoken with you."

"Why were you following me?"

"I wasn't following you per se. You see, I'd had a little romp with an old friend and was on my way home when, lo and behold, I caught sight of Leda smoking a joint and wandering alone. I was just about to bust in and join her party when I caught sight of the streetlamp glinting off your badge. I wasn't aware it was you for a minute until you walked past my darkened refuge. I became a voyeur at that point. No harm done. Can we end this interrogation? I assure you, we are trying to merge mutual motivations for a common cause. We are in a tick-tock situation, Officer Fremeaux."

I shifted again, remembering my haste with the warning on the bathroom wall back at Cheever's.

"Sorry, Don Lee, let's move on. Can I look at it?"

He stared into my eyes, smiling, and knocked on the window behind him.

"I knew your grandfather and became acquainted with your father before he was killed. Mother Earth lost an honest man that night," he said as the door opened. He knew that I knew that was bait. A lady walked out with a bundled towel.

"Your mother was a great teacher of literature," he continued.

"She's the reason I quote the classics and write proper police reports."

"Yes, I know this well," he said approvingly. "Before I pull back the curtain and begin this dreadful play, you must know that it wasn't a coincidence that my good friend Officer Gonzales paid a visit to your hometown precinct. We have had you in our thoughts for a long time."

"Officer Gonzalez is dead," I said flatly.

"This again, son, I know all too well. She was the only law officer I could trust. After her demise, we halted progress on our quest until now. Waiting till you and this God-awful new evidence were introduced."

He lifted the towel into the air, and there it was, cold and stark white. Like a sickened iguana trapped in your carport. You had to pick it up at some point to make something happen, but you just weren't ready for that foreign of a sensation.

Her wrist now had a bracelet made from some sort of animal hair. It surprised me that he would tamper our evidence. He picked her hand up, turning the palm upward, to reveal letters scrawled in black permanent ink. *MAG P.*

"Do these letters mean anything to you?" he asked.

I leaned forward. Nothing came to mind. He moved his fingers to underline the letters. I felt myself directing my trust to Don Lee's convictions.

"No."

"A space between the g and the p. We're unsure if the gap is purposeful or if the letters were written in stages. They're written in the same ink. Same penmanship. Looks like Sharpie. Our Becca looks to be shrewd. She may have stopped suddenly and picked up where she left off, avoiding discovery. Our Becca was trying to leave a message. We can't rule out the possibility of initials of some kind. Maybe short for Maggie or Margaret or something, last name beginning with p. We just can't be sure for now.

"We have one more clue. On top is an invisible ink stamp for The Blue Crystal on Decatur Street. When you hover a blue light over the top, it will glow. So, we now know that at some point she had gone dancing. Most likely bought an ecstasy pill and danced with everyone. As everyone will do. No harm in dancing."

I looked at him; my thoughts began to clod with the sudden planting of new information.

"What's with the animal hair? This thing wasn't on her the night I discovered it."

"Xandi wanted to perform a small ritual. She wanted to release any trapped spirits."

I thought about my visits from Becca. "This is something you approved? Are there more witnesses?"

"Xandi asked Maître Carrefour to allow Becca's spirit to pass through the crossroads and escape the passive limbo. Becca's spirit needed help reaching out to someone she could trust to find a final resting place. That's a ritual Xandi performs alone with the trapped spirit. A ritual that can leave an open wound in her psyche on occasion."

My humdrum life wasn't tempered for the heaviness of this new path of the occult. The hastily formed letters on her palm and her spectral apparitions left me deeply unresolved. Captain Barlow's inflection to me the night I lost her hand waves in my head. The absurdity of it now aligned with what Don Lee revealed about my coworkers.

"Who Is Maître Carrefour?"

"Carrefour is a what. A deity responsible for opening channels to the heavens or the underworld. Carrefour moves spirits into the spirit world. Xandi called on the god to release Becca."

"So, Becca chose me?"

"Seems so. Did you know her, Fremeaux?"

"We bumped into one another, and I promised to keep her safe on her visit."

"Well, son, you've been chosen. Now I don't subscribe to the world of voodoo like Xandi, but some things do make you wonder, don't they?"

"I'll scratch my head for a hot minute on this one," I confessed.

"Does Xandi know that Becca has found you?"

"I haven't confessed to anyone yet. I assumed I created her from a guilt trip."

"The universe is supernatural and mercurial; we silly humans will never unravel what we can't see and will forever chase what we think we feel."

"I'm supposed to be forever baffled?"

"The harsh truth? we all are. We take our stabs, kid."

What I already knew but wanted to ignore was that I had my own demons that needed releasing. But for now, they'd need to be put on a back burner, as an unknown number of my fellow officers were on the take and capable of murdering good people to hide themselves. Which ones?

Captain Barlow? I callously weighed it all out, all the way to where the pulse drummed out any pity.

"If you talk with Becca's mother about connections with a Maggie or Margaret, I'll stop by The Blue Crystal and show the picture to Teal while in my police uniform. That way, with the public, it'll look more official than suspicious. He was most likely the doorman that night and may remember her face," I said.

Don Lee's face softened. I'd given him the little bit of hope he'd been wanting to hear.

"You must remain on caution with Teal. His father is a riverboat captain, and his uncle, on his mother's side, is the police chief down in Ascension Parish. When you talk, they talk. Make sure you ask on Becca's mother's behalf, if you know where I'm coming from. After you shot Leda's assailant and went back to investigate the hand, didn't you take Barlow with you?" he asked.

"I did. Why?" I asked.

"Mind you, I made sure there were no eyes on me when I snuck in and out. There is most certainly an opposing task force assembling as we speak. How much does Leda know?"

"Just that I saw the hand, and it had vanished into thin air. She has promised to keep it between the two of us. I trust her. Is Captain Barlow compromised?"

"Almost every man who suits up is paid for by the elites. You'll soon learn this. As for Leda, she trusts you as well. She is by nature extremely skeptical of humans. Her family hides more secrets than the government can hide from its voters. Moral turpitude runs through the family DNA. She is on full guard the moment she rolls outta bed. Can you recall seeing or hearing anything out of the ordinary during your last couple of shifts?"

"Ruthie's ranting about the crows again. This time, she seemed in much more of a flurry about it. Monsignor gave an envelope of money to one of the homeless heroin addicts and a cop. Gobs of tourists in Panama Jack T-shirts puking up hurricanes. Nothing else too far out of the ordinary I could take note of."

"Ruthie's been ranting about evil-doing crows for as long as I can remember. I think Charlie the Crow must've assaulted her in some form or fashion back in the day; he won't admit to anything, and those damned

Catholics have always been up to some shit or another. Do you think anyone has been following you?"

"Anything's possible in the Quarter. Can't spot everything in the middle of everything."

"Some of our cohorts are combing the streets for anything looking like a kidnapping. We also tailed you over the last couple of days to ensure your safety. We didn't see anyone either, but I can't be too confident in such matters. We *have* been trying to spot some motherfucker for years, but to no avail." He trails off.

The bourbon is beginning to take hold of Don Lee; I sense a lack of sleep. Worry and frustration stoke his eyes. Sadness creeps with each sip.

High-dollar quality is what most folks perceive about Don Lee. His robust hands are entwined in a ball on the table. He has one of those *lived-in* faces. Makes me think of the plowman's version of Jackie Gleason. When his mind creeps off to one of those macabre places, where souls begin to fray, his fist tightens with malice. Fingertips turn white around the edges. My gaze follows the thick hairy wrist up the thick hairy forearm to the rough neck, then up to jaws grinding over that malice. He sips the brown gold and begins to talk again. Slowly, with thick, gentle, crawling words.

"The code in which we all abide was written long before humans could bus in the first hand job. The code that causes the eagle to soar and hunt. The con man to move outside his shadows. We can't have it altered to fit our democracy. We must live, breathe, and fight with it. Chew on it, but never swallow it in one great gulp. This code of fighting for survival was written in Mother Earth's winds."

He drew from the glass. I sat quietly on my cushion with no clue where he might be wandering. He continued slowly and cautiously.

"The fight for survival can become brutally immoral at times, but one mustn't wrestle and fight the code so hard that we believe we can conquer it. That kind of silliness will turn a man into Schrodinger's cat. You're in the box, sane and insane at the same time, googly-eyed, obsessed. People will forever unnecessarily kill and destroy to rise."

I cleared my throat, but he stayed on the subject.

"The cream rises from intent. Men rise through work and logic and love and distress. Only talking about rising causes man to forever stoop. Action and thought are needed. Compassion brings the tribe to stand tall.

Man must bend the code. Bend the code with compassion. When we fight for survival, we should be ready to help the ones we've conquered to stand again. If not, then we all fail. Babies deform from confusion, and society frays. We all will stoop to our knees, begging for answers."

The sunset brought shadows to darken our feet as a boat slowly pulled in to tie up. The pretty sister who greeted me at the landing is fiddling around in the boat, and Don Lee smiles again. Gaiety returns. I looked at a photograph on a table behind him and could sense it was of his lost niece. She wasn't beautiful, nor was she unattractive, but my eyes wanted to remain on her. A vision calling me to hold and caress the adult version of her. She quietly commanded attention.

Suddenly, the avocado-green telephone sitting behind Don Lee sounded off, making two birds perched at the pool's edge to take flight.

"Hello?" Don Lee answered, then let out a booze burp.

"No, but I'm certain I can find something out. Is this something you're sure of?" He paused and looked toward me. "I may find a lead on that very subject soon. Stay put. When you hear more, let me know. And dear, do me a favor, could you? Run by my place and see if any suspicious souls may be lurking at my windows, please. Thank you, love. I will be back in town in a few days. I shall stop in and have a burger, for we have a lot to talk about now. Love you right back, young lady."

He hung up and leaned forward.

"That was Mother. I'm sure you have been alerted to the fact that the fella who attacked our Leda was a hired gun through the Dixie Mafia?"

"Yeah, we found his car parked in Gretna."

"Did you relay this to Leda during your visit with her yesterday?"

"I did."

"Well, it's becoming known that Golda has her own security detail parked outside the man's hospital door. Her personal doctor has been placed in charge to ensure his breathing doesn't halt for any reason until she can acquire the fella's good knowledge."

"Golda? Leda's mother? How is this a possibility, Don Lee?"

"Golda is at the top of the food chain in this city, my friend. How do you think Leda can call ten minutes before you start your shift and suddenly, you're on *her* clock?"

"Taking a state prisoner into one's own personal possession is kidnapping."

"Well, kid, whatcha gonna do about it?"

"That's why I'm here with you, Don Lee. To find out what I can do about it. So, you reckon this asshole was a hire job?"

"Yes. This means someone quite possibly put a hit on her daughter. Someone holding just as much sway as her in their world. You just simply don't fuck with Golda. Shit may fly all over town soon, I'm afraid. Hell, I'd lay money down to the fact that Eastern European hitmen are boarding planes as we speak.

"Mother also informed me that Mr. Gilleach has suddenly taken leave and is looking to haul ass out of town. No matter, though, he'll be found within the week, and Golda will put the two men in a little house far, far away. Have 'em tortured till the proper yip is heard.

"Keep your ears open in your precinct. The only comments you should echo are the popular opinions of your penal peers. If you come to witness the corruption, parlay *their* sentiments. We don't want to censor ourselves from the bargaining table if we make it there."

"So, Mother is part of your gang?"

"Let's just call her a well-informed associate. My spider in the web, so to speak. She has managed to ensnare everyone from street performers to political suits at the governor's mansion. We cast a wide net for gathering pertinent information, if any is out there."

"Mother is a sixty-seven-year-old trans woman from Chile. Ex-stripper. Ex-call girl. Ex of an ex-pro football star, for God's sake. How on earth can she be involved?" I asked.

"She isn't. She is an ancient friend who knew me when my niece left us. My advocate. When she was young and gorgeous, no one knew her secret. Just a few of us. As age mounted, suspicions grew. She has danced at their parties; to them, she is a novelty, but she can still pick up a phone and force the grandsons of the old guard to pay her power bills if she desires. She is a social falcon.

"Mother knew at an early age her penis was not a comfort, and at nineteen, her father dictated his decision. She could surgically become herself, but would be forever exiled from the family. That machismo shit is for real. So, Mother plowed her way to America, without family, without money, and took it all down on her own terms. If you deliver yourself fearlessly without demands, people will take you as you think you are; you *will* soar like an eagle in this country."

A wad of fish began another frantic slapping spell out in the bayou. I almost tricked myself into believing an ancient spirit was beating the river with a thousand whips.

"A red tide will soon bloom down in the Gulf," Don Lee stated calmly.

"Is this some kind of warning?"

"According to river lore. The winter before red tide blooms, the fish up here go nuts. All the creatures that feed on them begin to move further inland, avoiding the drop in oxygen that happens when the fertilizers build up down there, over-blooming the fauna. Sucking the life from all the other creatures dependent on vital oxygen."

The telephone rang again. He turned to look at me and held up a finger to excuse himself from our conversation. I noticed the bossa nova music gently swaying through the undertone from speakers somewhere inside the house. I figured it would be Waylon, Willie. Billy Joe Shaver. The Stones, Diana Ross, Miles Davis, The BeeGees, but no, none of that. It was bossa nova. The groove that American and English music quietly ignored twenty years ago. I've never given it much thought till now.

I thought about the *code* thing again, I'll have to decide if it's worth buying into it or not. The door opened, and Don Lee slowly sat again in the fading light.

"Whatcha thinking about, Fremeaux?" he asked as he hung up the phone.

"Bossa nova, huh?"

He chuckled.

"If you've ever been lucky enough to catch a thrilling bout of fellatio while this intoxicating music is playing, you would never want to wear pants again. Never want to re-sheath the promised land. It's how I plan to go out. Quite possibly the perfect ending to a well-lived life."

"A beautiful dream to have, Don Lee," I jested.

"No, my boy, it's all been arranged. The person has already been paid. And paid well, I might add."

We sat alone with the music for a few minutes. Fellatio is a hard subject to continue, as it calls for a moment of private reflection. He pulled from the bourbon glass and looked out over the river's edge.

"You know, kid, I did know your mother well. Knew her before she met your father. I only met him once or twice at college functions. She became pregnant with you, and my life brought me to Louisiana. She worshiped your father and you. We would drink gin in those early days, talk poetry and Thomas Wolfe and such.

"She would tell me that your father wanted to listen to everything. That's what made a fine and fair small-town sheriff. He could read the needs and was strong enough to make the decisions that could make it all work out for everyone involved. He listened to her, letting her find the shy little soul behind the stone. He loved for her to read all the big thinkers of the time to him. She alone found the soft truth in his soul. According to him, she gave him *the sights...*" He trailed off.

That put some comfort inside me.

"Dad took me out at nine years old to teach me gun safety," I said. "He started me off with a three-foot-long .410. It seemed massive; the sight of it terrorized my small mind. He instructed me to never be afraid of the truth of the matter. It looks big, but it can be managed. The truth of the matter is always in the pudding, he would say over the few years I had with him.

"Get to know the thing for what it is. As you get comfortable with it, the fears begin to fall away, and you can achieve anything. All of it. When the fear drops for some folks, they demand control of it. Their fears only transform into something else, never fully disappearing. You, son, must handle it fully and craft it the way it needs to be. For us all.

"Put the butt of the gun against your cheek, let your eye seek the sight at the end of the barrel. Your right hand holds the grip, finger lightly touches the trigger. The left hand grips the underside of the barrel. Steady, not stiff. You need to be able to move and aim with accuracy. Pull the stock tight into your shoulder's saddle and keep the whole lot of it stable. When the puzzle is all together, pull the trigger."You will begin to learn what it really can be as you go. You will learn that you can come to understand anything. Even mystery is a thing. It can be mastered, and mystery is in everything we encounter. From learning how to properly shoot a gun to putting a man on the operating table, or the big screen, for that matter."

I had become so lost in those childhood memories that I hadn't even noticed the darkness gathering around us. Or that Tippa had lit candles all around and had been listening to me from another chair. The fire dance of the candle shadows flickered and swayed in sync with the cool flow of the music. I must've held a look of surprise as Tippa spoke to my last ramble.

"The depths of life expose themselves in slow moments. Remembrance demands time. I think this is why deeply layered southern stories are proper; we have plenty of time for the fine details. The proper amount of brush strokes. A nest of singing baby birds, we are."

Don Lee broke in again. Mimicking the mood of the bourbon. His voice lowered. Guttural punctuations.

"Has anyone found a clue on your side? Your father, I mean? For your mother's sake, I have tried to find the bastards who took him from y'all. I have been quietly poking and listening into old closets, but haven't stumbled across anything tangible as of yet."

"I haven't found the right door to knock down. A couple of years after Dad was gone, the cancer had a strong hold on Mom by then, the parish president at the time of Daddy's death retired. He suddenly found the good fortune to buy a house in the Caribbean and leave everything behind. I saw her love for Dad resurface in the form of desperation and anger. No one ever tried to help her discover the person responsible. If she had gotten to him as she was hoping, she was going to kill him before he escaped. She fervently believed he knew who did it."

"He's dead now. You aware?" he asked.

"I'm aware."

"Do you have details?"

"I know that it was too mild an ending. Natural causes, I hear."

Don Lee left it like that, open-ended but closed for the moment. We sat looking at each other for a while. Tippa was as silent as a child.

"I have to remind myself most days that I can't spend all my daylight trying to unmake the past," I quietly confessed.

"I need you to help us clean this thing. I need an inside strong arm willing to do whatever is necessary to stop this insanity. Will you be that for us?" he asked.

"I witnessed the pure fear in Becca's mother's eyes. I felt the sadness settling in her heart. Let me sleep on it. If I feel I need to take the legal route, I'll need to take the evidence back to the city."

He chewed on ice and spoke through the cold of it.

"Becca's hand, my friend, has taken a ride with my housekeeper. I can promise that if you break the case, I will suddenly discover its whereabouts and deliver it to court for us."

"That's mighty noble, Don Lee," I responded sarcastically.

"Man's gotta do what a man's gotta do, kid."

"I guess I'm being forced to help shoo the turkey to cross the street?"

"In case you awake in the correct spirits, everyone's point of contact in reaching me is Mr. David down at the Verdi Marte. If the heat turns up and we can't meet publicly, you buy sandwiches from him in the late afternoons. Cordial behavior, nothing personal. Howdy-do's and such. He will smile and ask the usual niceties. If all is good, he will slip a smiley face sticker in your bag. If communication is necessary, he will slip a smiley face with a bullet hole in the forehead. On the back will be a number. The number signifies a specific pay phone. On the outside of each phone booth will be the phrase *call a dickhead* over a phone number. That is the number you will dial from that specified phone. I have the maps for each phone booth and will give one to you when you head back to the city. You can also leave messages on my machines. Also, Ms. Juanita is always here at the camp house; she will generally know my whereabouts."

"Does it call for that much intricacy? At this point?" I asked.

"I set up this system for informants needing anonymity, so it's proven to work. They've killed before and will do so again without any fear of discovery. You will need that anonymity, my friend. No matter your decision."

"Got any names?"

"No. Gonzalez's suspicions were growing when she increased her inquiries."

"Then she got killed in the line of duty?" I asked.

"Yes, but we're convinced she was murdered. We suspect that the robbery was staged. Two of the fellas involved, the two killed in the action, were small-timers on the fringes of the Dixie Mafia. The getaway driver slowly drove past two officers monitoring the parking lot after the deadly shots were fired. This unidentified driver has never been heard from again.

"God rest her soul. The two hoodlums killed, I believe, were set up by the Dixie Mafia. I don't figure they were aware they were following Guy Fawkes into pre-dug graves. We estimate that the cops employed the Redneck Mafia to keep leaks from forming.

But, yes, to answer your next thoughts. I sent her to flirt and court you to come work that Mardi Gras years ago, to coax you down. She was looking for safe assistance on the inside."

I said, "Well, truthfully speaking, the timing of it couldn't have been better."

I started this confession with *truthfully speaking*, knowing full well I came down avoiding fallout from a shit decision. Criminal moment. I snapped; it happens. Vengeance is mine, sayeth the badge of honor. I mustered the pluck to continue the false narrative with a dry spot in the back of my throat.

"Small-town politics had been degrading with poverty, and I needed a reprieve from it. I would have needed to become soft to survive the apathy creeping in like ivy. Watching my fellow officers accept two-bit bribes from low-rent lawmakers and drug dealers and filch blow jobs in abandoned parking lots from desperate mothers trying to feed kids was beginning to scratch my nerves. Good mayors helplessly watch their communities collapse into ignorance; bad mayors open the back door to the drug trade. Obesity rises while enthusiasm plummets. I was on my way out as it had turned."

My thoughts tightly sealed the knowledge that a dead criminal is buried in a shallow grave just waiting for the wrong dog to sniff the wrong asshole. That's all it would take for me to be summoned to face my own justice.

Don Lee suspected the subject of the darkness that covered my eyes, but he lightened the conversation.

"Like my granddaddy used to say, son, you gotta keep yourself movin' else the ants'll come and bite ya. More of that code shit, I'm afraid," Don Lee said.

"I'm here now, Don Lee. Don't foresee becoming a casualty in my near future."

"Fremeaux, you're a young man, and in thirty years, the middle class will be confused, disjointed, undereducated, and angry at you and me or whoever else they can blame for their failures. The pollywog stew is going to boil over and singe every goddamned one of us. On that note, you two, it's one in the a.m., and I'm ready for sleep. Good night, sweet dreams, and see you two in a few hours."

Tippa and I sent our goodnights back. We settled back into our chairs, not ready to make a move.

"I'm sorry to hear of the loss of your niece. Don Lee told me the story, amongst other details," I said to her.

"Thank you, Fremeaux. She idolized him, and he adored her as if she were his only child. She would cook for him, and he would take his dear sweet time teaching her the world he had grown to love and hate. When together, the pair was inseparable. He has often said in a strained voice that the saddest part of it all is that his faith in anyone's sincerity is in decline."

We small-talked for another hour. As the moon listened to the water, our connection matured into a midnight attraction. Looking at me with trust, she stood, bringing her body closer. I grabbed her hands and pulled her to my face. Her lips were warm, soft, and wet. She slipped her tongue just far enough to break the seal on my closed lips. I pulled into such a state of comfort that I felt I might have just come home from a long war.

She pulled back and spoke.

"I hope you're ready for this. You were brought here for a reason."

She kissed me again. I sensed this may be yet another bribe. I can't pass up a good woman, no matter the reason.

"Come on, let's enjoy one another," I said.

Tippa bribed hard, and we fell into a deep, exhausted sleep, but

Becca's ghost followed me to Mississippi. I sprang awake just before the sun broke. All the windows were open, allowing the cool, musty river air to flow over my taut skin. The night creatures had finally exhausted themselves, too. It was quiet and peaceful. Nothing in the world beats waking up with a warm, soft, naked woman next to you, especially when your soul is haunted. She woke softly and pushed her hand to my chest.

"You sure know how to use your hands, Fremeaux. I can see how your high school football team allowed the fewest points scored back in your day. You're a big chunk of coal, my darling." Her country-time voice swayed.

She pulled herself to my mouth, and I lightly squeezed her breast. I thanked the cosmos for letting Fortuna's wheel spin for me.

The sound of fish slapping the river's surface pulled my eyes open to see the sunlight. Tippa kissed me good morning and went to cook eggs and boudin. I sat on the back porch watching the morning dew glisten along the riverbank, stretching all the way to God knows where.

Don Lee slunk into the chair next to me.

"Man's gotta take great care not to drown in his freedoms," he said as his dancing lips pulled from the hot coffee, continuing his morning ramble.

"After Gonzales passed, it was Leda who kept me pumped with party. She knows all too well that if a man says yes to Champagne, he says yes to life. She saved me then, and now you're here. I'm beginning to believe a higher power could be with us now."

"I haven't told anyone else about Becca visiting my sleep. I can't stop until we put an end to this horrific shit."

"Does that mean you're on the team?" he asked.

"I'll be arm and arm till the very end, Don Lee," I said.

"I'll cooperate with that. Remember, our knowledge through this is provisional. Every day will be a new day. It's imperative we communicate even the smallest details. Fremeaux, these people have retained invisibility. They have evaded me through the entirety of this unbearable duration. If they are watching you, then precautions are non-negotiable. I haven't kept my line in the water all these years just to let the story go to pot. No sir, we fully intend a catch and kill. You go back to the city. I will reach out and inquire into Becca's family and friend base for anything matching the letters on her hand."

A horrendous splatter echoed from the river's surface again; something wicked must be trolling the mud-smeared bottom. It disturbed me; I wasn't ready for my calm to be interrupted. I stuttered in my mind a little, and jittery words began to come out of my agitated lips.

"I didn't get the chance to finish about Mother last night. As her body weakened from disease, she began to read *The Little Prince* and Machiavelli to me. The thickness of life was blooming. I'm not sure if she was grooming me to be a good steward of life or an assassin."

"She wants you on top and safe. Out of reach of the things that found your father."

"You know, Don Lee, I still feel akin to the Jack Burdens of the world," I said.

"Living is like driving through the fog, kid. You're aware of where you want to go but..." He grinned deviously. "Somehow, when you get there, you always know."

"Hell, I reckon, Don Lee. As long as I don't find myself dancing with St. Vitas. Every time Becca floats in, I can feel a wrinkle form on my soul. Deformity hurts."

"Fremeaux, you're not a follower; someday you'll wake up and find you're just fine with the way the world works. Your father has loaded you with some grand skills. Take control of it. We are here to win the small battles. The small ones are pedestals that make the big ones look majestic."

Tippa brought us a plate of hot Boudin, crackers, pickles, and Creole mustard. She kissed us both on the cheek, leaving us to tend her bar.

"By the way, kid, the secretive phone call last night was with Xandi. She had become aware of a couple of fellas driving around your place last night. She went back with her dog to pretend she was walking through the neighborhood and found the pair parked down the street from your place. She stopped and asked if she could help them with anything. She said they had thick brown mustaches and newscaster hair, which smelled like Prell and cigarettes. Drove a beige Delta Eighty-Eight. An oilman's car. Does this ring a bell with you?"

"Not that I can recall. Dixie Mafia, maybe?"

"We can't be for sure. It could be related to retaliation for Leda, or, if the right person found you looking for the missing hand the other night, it could be our case. Someone protecting dead girls?"

We sank into the weight of it.

"Don Lee, I'd like for you to be the one who tells Xandi that I'm being visited by Becca, if you don't have a problem with it?"

"Why's this, kid?"

"I don't want to be a witness to too many hallucinations. Just let her do her stuff as she feels she needs. I'll handle the crazy shit as it comes."

"Can do, but she'll be asking you questions at some point."

"I'll go there when I'm there."

"Drive safe, Fremeaux."

CHAPTER FIVE

I finally made it back to my car and re-entered the gravel birth canal out of Cheever's parking lot. A pang of guilt hovered as the murder I committed back home had resurfaced from the altered confessions I made with Don Lee. I was reliving the look on Red Dertinger's face when I shoved a rusted machete through his throat. He murdered my cousin, Harte, from a paranoid delusion that he was going to confess he'd seen Red beat a kid to death over a payment. Harte was only driving through the woods looking for a place to plant a deer stand. He witnessed nothing, but just to be safe, an innocent boy and a limb of our family were destroyed. I don't carry the guilt of murder; I carry the anxiety of having to pay for something that was warranted. Red was married to the mayor's daughter, and Red wasn't going anywhere anytime soon. I dragged the bastard to a shallow grave and drove straight into the camouflage of NOLA, where big corruption feeds a bigger bloodline. A city filled with squirrelly bastards, as Don Lee wrote.

Don Lee confessed that I had been hand-picked and unwittingly solicited to work with his team. I feel like a history of me had existed in their minds. I had been included and excluded simultaneously. Becca had chosen me as well. What the hell kind of signal does my soul emanate?

Since I was this far north, I made a slight detour to visit my parents' graves. I guessed if I thought about it poetically, they were also here and there. The dead didn't really go away; we carry those building blocks with us. Becca didn't make her mother, so her mother would continue to live with a dreadful vacancy until her final breath. That shit was bothering me.

I keep asking myself the whos and whys, and what answers I might have filed away in my subconscious. I must've overheard or been a witness to something more that night. Hell, I had just learned Don Lee was out there with us that night. A clue had to be buried in me. Scour through everything, I told myself.

What was it Jack Burden said about knowledge? The end of man was knowledge. He couldn't know whether it would save him or kill him. He would be killed, alright, but he couldn't know whether he was killed because of the knowledge he had, or the knowledge he did not possess. And if he had it, could it save him?

Hell, I didn't know. I did know that I needed to know more. Right then, the question was, what did I know so far?

All I was able to muster was the image of the cute little puppy dog that meandered from one of the little cotton row houses on the square to visit me at Mother's grave site. Licking my fingers as I positioned the flowers. She was a storm-grey little thing except for the oval white spot the size of a quarter on her hind end. I don't know why my subconscious held it at the forefront of my thoughts. There she sat in front of my thoughts like a concrete block. Who the fuck knew why?

What the hell could I know? I asked the universe.

I knew Ruthie's been griping about evil crows roaming the Quarter again, with her ducks in tow, but her acumen is a bit of a disqualifier. Still, she and Charlie the Crow do roam the Quarter nearly twenty-four hours a day. Maybe Charlie witnessed something that could lead me to Becca's killer. He was too much of a drunk to harm anyone and too damned weak to kidnap.

And Ruthie. Lord, the first time I encountered Ruthie, she had grabbed my hand as I was pursuing a young man, whom I believed was about to commit a minor crime. It was Mardi Gras, and Bourbon Street was packed with wild hearts hunting for ecstasy. I was moving down the middle of the crowd toward Canal with no wiggle room when suddenly, a strong, roughened hand clamped onto mine. My shoulder snapped in the opposite direction as I was hauled, like a caught snapper, back into the depths of the Quarter.

Stumbling through the sea of arms and shoulders, I tried to get a bead on who had me in their possession. All I could see moving through the flesh trees was a large white and blue striped garden hat atop a short, squatty frame.

Detangling ourselves from the labyrinth of people, trying to reach a sidewalk oasis, we finally weaved our way to a small spot, and the hat turned. It was her. Her eyes had a frantic look. Confusion.

She inspected me, looking at my badge and name tag. I could tell she didn't have teeth by the way her tongue jutted around inside her cheeks, and her jowl clamp was much flatter than the average person's. I was beginning to believe she had wandered from a special home and needed to be taken back to safety.

"You don't belong here, you. Fucker," she growled at me.

It became clear she wasn't in any distress, but I was no less shocked as to what was standing in front of me. She pulled out a crooked and crinkled cigarette.

"Lost lighter," she grumbled.

"Are you asking for me to light your cigarette, ma'am?"

She looked beyond me and then at my name tag again. I asked the fella standing to my right shoulder if I could borrow his lighter and lit her cigarette.

"*Crows* are out tonight," she growled at me.

"Yeah, well, it is Mardi Gras, ma'am," I said back.

"Ya know how to catch a crow, Fremeux?" she asked, reading my nametag.

"No, ma'am."

"You grab that fucker by the tail. Stomp its goddamned head off. Make sure it's goddamned not breathing before you walk away. You'll know too, if you can stick it out," she barked in a rough and broken street voice.

She slunk back into the sea of revelers as I stood bewildered at what had just happened, asking myself if I had handled the situation correctly. New Orleans holds its own set of rules and rituals, I was coming to learn. That was my introduction to Ruthie and the city.

Why was that dog's ass still in my mind's eye? Why the hell was that white dot floating in my vision like a sunspot? It felt like a mental curse.

I stared off into the dark tree line for wildlife or anything that would erase the dog's rear end, but to no avail. The image haunted me like Becca's mirage. I entered the bridge over the Bonnet-Carre Spillway. Don Lee told me the poor who scavenge a life off the bayou floor down here call this bridge the widow's ride. Body parts were found stuck in the muck below from time to time.

Bad life decisions, the locals grumbled when questioned on why they don't report the foul play. *Hell, we don't know. Maybe God had a plan to feed the gators. Not our bidnizz.*

The narrow bridge rails, glimmering in the sunlight, captured my mind. In the cover of night, it was a perfect launch pad for purging guilty consciences of illegal souvenirs.

Hundreds of empty beer cans glinted in the sunlight under the heat of this Louisiana sky. A dried-out voodoo doll wasted away in a treetop at eye level, startling tired drivers on the heat-beaten asphalt. A fraying lost last wish calling for the spirits to alter the winds in favor of the downtrodden and brokenhearted, I suspected. Hell, Xandi could have thrown it there to remind me that I was on her time for now. The puppy made me think about my father's time again.

A few weeks before my father was shot dead on that dark, lonely dirt road back home, my mother could feel the stress emerging from him. He slowly distanced himself. She knew, but I wasn't at an age to comprehend that he had discovered something wrong in the world. Something that would eventually lead to his killing. She began to smoke in front of me from time to time. That was a pleasure she typically held as too vulgar for my witness. When I would ask, she said he never told her.

Would the Quarter nurture me or become my Pontius Pilate?

The spirit will provide, Xandi assures tourists regularly.

I traced the outline of the approaching city in the distance. A billboard perched high above Lake Pontchartrain: an Absolut bottle crowned with a sparkling white halo stating, *Absolut Perfection.*

The halo led me to think of the Monsignor the other day. My thoughts and visions teemed with sin and salvation. Death and deliverance, sprinkled with dog's ass by a gravestone. I had too much swirling to wrestle with. I needed a confession.

I could see the Monsignor wanting to give me courage that day, but a crook couldn't deliver valor. My mind's eye watched him turn to walk with the stranger. His biretta tilted forward with thick European hair bunched underneath. In hindsight, I saw a small white patch of hair interrupting the dark hair on the left side. It superimposed with the dog's ass as I daydreamed. The vision floated with the landscape, my psyche still trying to link the two patterns. *Why?*

Think Fremeaux. Think it out. Walk yourself through the Quarter again, I told myself.

I pictured Leda at the corner of Barracks and Chartres. It was dark, I shot, man down. Leda bleeding. House lights brightened the atmosphere on the balconies above me. People gathered to inspect damages. I pressed my shirt into Leda's wound. I handcuffed her assailant and assessed the wounds in his leg and abdomen. I scanned the area for any available help.

Ms. Lauderdale, who was gawking from her balcony, was dialing 911, squealing about what happened. My radio was all chatter. I held it to my mouth and responded. I looked down toward the dark end of Barracks Street. The dog's ass reappeared, and the Monsignor was walking away.

"Holy fuck, he was there," I yelled into the windshield. He was slinking down the sidewalk towards Rampart that night.

"Goddamnit," I yelled into the windshield again. "The motherfucker! Monsignor was leaving another crime scene. That sorry sack of shit was there!" I was spouting excessive foul language into the hot sky. Mother would be appalled, and I just visited her grave.

What was the Monsignor doing there at 4 a.m.? Was he looking to retrieve what Don Lee and I had already found?

I mentally scanned the interior of my house, wondering if I left my bulletproof vest there or in my work locker.

Dark allusions whittled my headspace as I steered myself into a city of bullshit, focused on the idea that one of the most powerful men in that bullshit city could be at the helm of Leda's attempted murder or Becca's disappearance.

First, Becca haunted, and next, a goddamned dog's ass hounded me. Somebody was slappin' me with some serious fuckin' gris-gris. I needed a drink and some answers.

CHAPTER SIX

Teal didn't seem to remember Becca's face when I showed him the Polaroid. But, as luck would have it, one of the pretty bartenders was outside smoking when I approached.

"Yeah, I remember her; she let a guy hang all over her that night. Trailer-park sexy with a Boone's Farm kind of grin. Yeah, he bought her drinks. They hunched on the dance floor and left around three, maybe four in the morning. They're probably naked in a trailer somewhere in Florida by now."

"Do you remember anything more permanent?" I asked.

"Oh yeah, he had a tattoo on the back of each fist. The left hand had a creepy black widow on it, and the other hand had the words 'shit happens.'"

"That's exactly what I needed. Thanks." I smiled and moved on.

Becca didn't quite make it to Florida, and I was having a hard time buying that a rambling kid with could dismember a body with precision. Much less have access to a place in the city that would provide the privacy necessary to pull it off. Now, I needed to find a set of shitty tattoos holding court with a cheap wine grin.

There were no closed borders to the French Quarter; any and all were welcome to attend the play. To triumph or to fail miserably. It had become painfully evident that humans could and will plunder every salvage yard, like hyenas, until all earthly pleasures were quashed.

I'd been patrolling the Quarter long enough that I could detect derelicts immediately, well-dressed or not. It was almost as if the hazy neon illuminated those traits like an X-ray machine exposed the very bones supporting our frail humanity. All the men out here were searching for pure ecstasy like a newborn baby would search for the sound of a mother's heartbeat.

If it didn't come by nature, it would be made by force. That was where I stepped in. That was when blood was usually shed because they had just enough booze to become an asshole. I must admit, on occasion, I felt a tickle of joy after ramming a chin into a three-hundred-year-old brick wall or plunging a head into a puddle of muck and piss and week-old booze that's been collecting in a break in the pavement.

That night, my patrol seemed slow. I watched and recorded eye movements. I wanted to find the people who might be watching young ladies in the wrong way.

In this cagey land, it was our songs that kept our hearts pumping, and I wanted this death metal hell music haunting my spirit to fade back to jazz before it sticks in my core. Mythology preached that death was required for new life; the problem was, I hadn't bought a ticket to that ceremony, and innocence shouldn't be the sacrifice.

Good people came down here to cut loose social constraints and be themselves, all the while, predators were wading among them. Generally, fear kept them at bay, but every so often, the emboldened strike. Smiles turned to tears as quickly as an eggshell fracture.

There was good energy tonight, though. The crowd was flowing with joy and fulfillment. The ladies were enjoying their men. When the conventions renting the rooms were from the professional set, debauchery had its limits on these special weekends. When the redneck college set is in town or lower-end business class, there was a lot more nudity, puking, and relationship disputes going public. I was constantly dampening social frictions, and sometimes I wish they would have just stayed home.

The night was a good one on the tracks. The comforting October fog rolled in and sat just above the rooftops, making the place feel like merry old London. The holidays were just around the corner, and the drinks made everyone feel warm and welcome. I could see Charlie the Crow standing outside the Touché Club, taking pictures for free drinks. All the street performers had been calm so far. None had come to report nasty tourist insults or threats of any kind. Money pots for the buskers had remained full all evening. So far, so good. I did see a young couple drunk and quarreling, but the boy was taking his butt chewing like a man, so I thought it would be alright in the end.

Under these conditions, it should've been easy to spot the sadistic body snatcher. Seemed he would've beed out of place mingling with this easy, happy crowd. More adults than young girls tonight, so the hunt would be more extensive; walk more ground. It wasn't easy to snatch if that was his mode.

I'd been trying to picture the fella. Dirty Reeboks and a Members Only jacket, sleeves pulled to the crook of the elbows, trying to look television? Or well-dressed sophistication, promising cocaine and weekend getaways? Hell, it might not have been a man at all. It could have been a woman like that couple in France, where the wife lured and drugged, and held the girl captive till her husband was ready to take her virginity and dump the lifeless carcasses in a hole deep in the lonely forest. I'd know it when I saw it.

I'm watching for you, asshole. Another photograph of another lost girl hangs on our poles and in our hearts.

Officer Olen Ray rounded St Ann onto Royal toward me. He was a good kid. Twenty-One came from a family of bodybuilders reared on Westbank. His modus operandi was to kick bad guy ass. Loved to tackle and fuck 'em up a little. Good to have around when the rednecks were in town and I was in no mood to wrangle dumb, incompetent drunks.

"What's up, ole man?" he asked.

"Not too much so far. Olen Ray, have you seen the latest mother searching for her daughter?"

"Yeah, I got a picture from her a couple of days back. Just before shift change. Hell, we can't ever seem to solve one of these cases. Don't anyone seem too worried about any of it?"

"Seems a little odd to me as well. Probably twelfth or thirteenth this year."

"That's just the ones attached to a loved one. No tellin' how many in total," Olen Ray added.

He was right. I hadn't thought beyond the mothers. Those were the faces I can see. The ones reported. The invisible, uncontested girls were a bonus for the bastards.

"Have you seen or heard anything on the street?" I asked.

"Can't say as I have. It's tough cookies out here. Don't talk to the cops if you don't have to, kinda thing. You know how it goes, Fremeaux."

Unfortunately, I did know how it went. According to the FBI's inside filings, the area from Canal to Bienville between Bourbon and Royal held the title of the highest crime rate area in the entire world. More crime was perpetrated there daily than in any other spot on Mother Earth. If, and when I patrolled at that end of the Quarter, I was chasing crackheads, pimps, and thieves all night. When a badge entered their scene, nobody knew nobody; it quickly became exhausting and futile. Crime wasn't real until it occured in plain sight. Just like voodoo.

I watched Charlie the Crow work his magic as Olen Ray flirted with a young medical student he went to high school with. I separated myself from Olen Ray and slowly walked toward Charlie. I wondered why I haven't seen Ruthie walking with her ducks yet. I noticed the new pictures of the new lost girl had been stapled to the poles and now covered the ones of Becca. Amongst all this merriment, terror and sadness remained stuffed deep down in hip pockets. Sometimes tears welled up and never seemed to find a proper place to dry.

Drinks and smiles were being exchanged, and I guessed Charlie mistook a pat on the shoulder from one of the ladies as a gesture of a sexual nature, because his hand pulled from the crow's gown and grabbed as much ass as he could get in that feeble-assed grip of his. That went over as well as a free pork sandwich at a bar mitzvah. Confusion, anger, and protective revenge swelled as the pretty lady's husband quickly punched Charlie squarely in the fabric beak. He hit the ground, and I immediately put distance between the two men. Olen Ray was already in hot pursuit and had the fella in a sleeper hold until I yelled, "Whoa, whoa, whoa! He's in the clear here."

Olen Ray released the man before he fell limp. I picked Charlie off the ground and walked him away by the shoulder, and we hobbled over to Decatur Street. I pulled him a stool to the outside window of Molly's at the Market and bought an Irish Coffee.

"You're feeling yourself tonight, Charlie."

"Bloody right on that one, mate." He smiled.

I looked down at his shoes while he fought the heat of the coffee to get at the Bailey's. He wore lace-up leather boots like the ones the man wore to confession that day, as I was reading Don Lee's letter in the cathedral. Except Charlie's were worn out. I was sure there was a hole in one of the soles. The tops were worn to a powdered grey hue at this point. The bottom of his costume wasn't as worn and dirty as I imagined it should be. I inspected it more closely. It was in pretty good shape for being out in these streets for twenty years or so.

"How long have you been wearing this costume, Charlie?"

"Too fuckin' long, mate."

"You've kept it up pretty well after all these years. You got someone helping with the upkeep?"

"Yeah, this nice Jewish lady over in Algiers. Her name is Janice. She pops around every year or so and checks it out for me. Why ya ask?"

"Just curious, Charlie."

"Nice lady and all. She calls me Tuna, after the television commercials, and I call her Jewness. I like her, she treats me with kindness, ya know."

"Charlie the Tuna, huh?"

"Yeah mate, that's it, Charlie, the tuna. I quite like it, ya know. Makes me feel welcome and all."

"How'd you come about meeting this particular lady?"

"I bumped into her during Mardi Gras a few years back. She makes costumes for the Zulu Krewe and helps mend the stuff for the Indians. She comes highly recommended. Does fantastic work for the common folk."

"So, she didn't initially create it for you?" I asked.

"No, it was provided to me back in the day."

"What do you mean provided? Were you in need of a costume for your idea and asked someone for help?"

"No, sir. I had just arrived here, and someone sent me to meet a gent, and he had the idea. He's the one who gave me the costume."

I watched his eyes droop and his jowls quiver.

"Are you hungry?"

"I could use a bite. Thanks, Fremeaux."

I went and ordered a gumbo from Coops next door and found Xandi sandwiched between two bodies across the crowded bar. We locked gazes and she winked—not the kind of wink that induces a flirt, but the kind with a slight nod of the head saying, *I got ya back, baby.*

Jesus, how on earth did she appear like that? I could feel a pair of eyes on me all evening, wherever I went. Scary but comforting. That was life in the Quarter, I reckoned. I brought the Gumbo back to Charlie; he had gulped the Irish coffee by then.

"Go on, Charlie, tell me your story. How did a fella from Australia come about wandering the Quarter for twenty years?"

"It's like this, mate. My journey here started on oil tankers."

I immediately thought of Prell and Cigarettes. They drove an oilman's car and parked outside my house.

"My uncle Holland got me a job riding oil tankers across the seas. I did that for a few years, and on my second trip here, I had caught some sort of sexual disease from one of the fuckin' prostitutes they employed for that trip."

"Hold up a second, Charlie. Prostitutes? Those people procure prostitutes to make the haul with y'all?"

"Well, yeah, Fremeaux. You got a hundred or more uncivilized blokes hemmed up on a boat with nowhere to go after work. Cuts down on the bloodshed, or even worse, murder. Some blokes go out their blazin' skulls just talking about sex."

"What happens to the women?"

"The strong ones make the journeys. The crazies get chopped up and fed to the sharks."

"Nobody ever speaks of this?"

"C'mon, man. The fellas in charge would just blame us. Shit, where we stood, they were in it for our well-being at the start. Getting rid of the crazy ensured our safety too, ya know?"
"Is there no one back home waiting for them?"

"Sure, there's been some legal troubles with it, but money and new cars will always lighten the burden on mothers and fathers in need. Besides, there isn't much of a bond if their daughters are shankin' workmen on haulers. If family love is supposed to be part of the equation. No Christmas presents for the lost."

"So, the women are just thrown out like trash?"

"Sure, mate. Nobody wants to deal with a lunatic out at sea. Besides, everything goes overboard when the lights are out. Even your Naval fleet does it. In the dark of night, when lights are out, millions of tons of trash are dumped into the seven seas. Boy, if those Greenpeace blokes could only get some footage of that. Every military, cargo, cruise, whatever ship is out there, they dump, mate. Plastic, metal cans, tampons, oil, gas, tires, undocumented people, you name it, it goes. Anything unnecessary and burdensome, poof. No ifs, ands, or buts. Almost like God formed the seas just so we couldn't get caught."

"Ok, I guess I can loosely grasp how that could become a thorn in the norm in this material society. So, you end up with a sexually transmitted problem, what next?"

"I go to the fleet hospital uptown and get it taken care of."

"Fleet hospital? What the hell is that? Is this thing owned by the tanking companies?"

"I reckon, maybe. They're not open to the public if that's what ya askin. No state or federal regulations. Nuthin' like that. Anyway, I told this doctor I didn't want to return to duty. I wanted to remain on American shores. I asked the man if he knew of a way I could be smuggled off. He looked up and commanded me to stay put. A few minutes later, he handed me a slip of paper with a name, address, time, and date. I went to One Shell Square and met an Englishman named Mr. Davenport. The rest is history, as we say."

"What about your permit to panhandle? Your green card? They take care of all that, too?"

"I haven't had to lift a finger, mate."

"Who's paying your permit fees?"

"No clue. It just shows up under my door every year."

"Where do you live?" I asked.

"Just by the spot you shot that fella last week."

"Barracks?"

"Yup, in the grey mansion."

My mouth went dry. That was where Becca's hand was lying.

"Who owns the building?"

"The archdiocese."

I'll be goddamned, I thought. "Do you see the Monsignor around the place?"

"Sure, they hold private ceremonies upstairs."

"What do you mean by ceremonies?"

"All sorts of things. Sometimes parties. Sometimes religious stuff. Sometimes costumes. I'm not invited, so I can't say for sure in detail what they're up to."

"Ever hear anything out of the ordinary?" I asked.

"Not sure what you're getting at."

"Girls, screaming. Yelling. Anything heated."

"No mate, I can't hear a thing on my end. Almost like it's been soundproofed."

"Which space do you occupy?"

"I have the end space, basement level on the Royal Street side."

"You've been there twenty years?"

"No, sir, not at all. About ten years. I previously lived in an attic apartment owned by the doctor I had visited. It was on Valence Street, uptown."

"So, the Archdiocese owns the building you live in now?" I asked.

"Yes. Only one way in and one way out."

"What do you mean?"

"The rest of the space downstairs is concealed parking. Only one stairwell leads to the second floor from there, as far as I know. I have no access to any other part of the building. Only my living quarters."

"What is the name of the doctor who put you on this path?"

"Dr. Fontenot was his last name. I have no other information other than that."

"Have you ever told anyone else your story?"

"Not really," he said. "Maybe Ruthie, but you know how she is. Nobody tries to comprehend her babble, and she can barely comprehend long concepts."

"Have you ever mistreated her in any way?"

"God sakes no, old man. Why would you ask such a thing?"

"She's always griping about evil crows roaming the quarter," I said flatly.

"She says the same thing to me as well. Don't know what it's all about myself."

"Have you ever witnessed other crow costumes out there?"

"I've seen other blokes dressed as blackbirds a time or two over the years, but that's about it."

"Are these blokes a regular thing?"

"Can't say for sure. Only spotted a couple of times or so. Dressed in very fine clothes, though. Thick fine wools and such. Something like military-grade materials, finely crafted, you see. Bespoke, maybe. The cape was heavy; it fell nicely about the shins. Beautiful jet-black leather boots. I kinda wanted one myself, ya know?"

His hands were shaking while eating gumbo. The poor fella was mostly worn—no, he's worn out.

"Do you have the wish to return home to Australia?"

"I got word some years back that my mother had passed on, so I don't feel any connection with my homeland. I'm rather okay with my lot in life here. It's been a good and easy life, you see."

"Do you know how and why some anonymous entity would want to support your lifestyle?" I asked.

"Been curious, but I'm not about to question the hand that has fed me this well."

"If you catch wind of these missing young ladies, come straight to me and no one else. I want to help these hurting mothers."

"Sure thing, Fremeaux."

I bought Charlie a boilermaker and moved back into my patrol. I took the route to make a pass by the grey house again, retracing my steps for the hundredth time. This time, with the knowledge that the Monsignor had been there that evening. Abstract clues were appearing, but they had no concrete connection. This muted building wanted to talk, but I wasn't sure how to listen yet. Nonetheless, I knew more now than I did when I found Becca's hand.

Time had a way of feeling halted in these dark, seductive streets on the backside of the Quarter. At this hour, all movement slowed to mimic the slow float of the fog overhead. Scattered lovers held onto one another and walked and talked and felt each other with more understanding than they ever would for the rest of their lives.

I moved quietly, peering deeply into the courtyard and grounds of the mysterious, dark grey building. The space Charlie occupied had no windows. Must've been dank inside.

The grounds were covered in darkness with dull splotches of light from the streetlamps highlighting the tops of the shrubbery and indented bricks leading to Charlie's side entrance. The garage must've been in the back, out of public view. The long second-floor balcony ceiling was sprayed with fern shadows, and the large louvers of the storm shudders were only slightly open, advertising a dampened yellow glow deep from inside the place. Barely visible—I had to stare for it. No sounds. Just stillness at this hour. I was hoping to see a moving shadow or something physical I could grasp that could expose a ritual. I could hear the vague routine of the workers three blocks down at Pap's cleaners beginning their workday.

I was hiding under the shadow of a balcony across the street. My thoughts bounced with the clippity-clop of the two police horses approaching. Officers Walton and Johnson were patrolling as they follow Bourbon back into the Quarter. Still no sign of movement.

As the clippity-clop of the hooves dulled, I heard a *psssst* and spied Xandi walking the opposite sidewalk toward the cleaners down on Burgundy. I took the cue and followed, taking caution not to be obvious. I approached the light spilling from a propped door at the cleaners and found Xandi sitting at an outside table at Cosimo's, wiping her nose with her index finger, indicating that I should look down Burgundy toward Esplanade. I did just that, and there stood Don Lee under a streetlamp, wobbling with a drink in hand. I approached, sensing some agitation. His bleakness has returned.

A darkened shadow figure had stopped to lean his back against a wall a couple of blocks down and light a cigarette. Don Lee began to speak in a somber and lowered voice.

"I have been physically removed from the Eagle's Nest this foul evening."

I could tell the devil in the bottle had whiplashed his tongue.

"I'm sorry to hear, Don Lee. Can I do anything for you?"

He chewed at the night air, grunting.

"Nobody quite knows which drink it is that takes them over the edge from being merely a hearty sociable gay partygoer into a morose, hungover creature with the creaks, the sweats, and the nightmares. It's always November in this state of mind, and three o'clock in the morning. There's nowhere to go, and you reach out for the cigarette. You smoke and think of all the horrible things you've done in these states of horror. And all the shames you've endured and the shames you've passed on to other people. All the wrongs that can't be made right. It is no laughing matter. All this crime and muck has been churning me into toad butter, and my barfly family has politely ejected me this hallowed evening."

And then he grinned. "Lordy, lordy, when Burton is on my tongue, the nerves must be stinging. No epitaphs, though, I *can* get on a stick from time to time."

"Shall I escort you home?" I asked.

"Nah, my legs know the way. Besides, I have my Xandi.

The trip up to Arkansas didn't provide us with any new pathways. There is a friend of Becca's family named Margaret, but her last name starts with the letter B. That straggling P could have been meant to be a B. The two had recently had a disagreement, so our Becca may have carried some guilt with her that night. Just have to see what shakes out."

I said, "I got a bag full of good information, but you're piss drunk, and I gotta make another round, then head back toward the precinct to make the reports. Shall we meet tomorrow when I start my beat?"

"That'll work. Come by the house just around sundown. People will be focused on shift changes and dinner schedules, so it should be easy to slip in."

He raised his eyebrows toward the dark figure leaning against the wall just out of earshot. "Turn your head toward Xandi and loudly command the lady to please come and escort her old gentleman home, for he has had too much revelry for one evening."

I understood completely.

I shouted to Xandi and waited till she took his arm and escorted him across the street. I waited till the dark figure walked up Esplanade and turned to enter the Quarter, the opposite direction from my friends, and meandered deeper into the Quarter's vein. The dark figure spawned the memory of my bartender friend shouting down to Artie the other day.

You can't ever explain what your imagination can see and make you feel. Especially at three-thirty a.m.

CHAPTER SEVEN

I parked my car by the University of New Orleans dormitory and considered taking the back-door journey to my house on foot, in case Prell and Cigarettes, or anyone else for that matter, were still hanging around my neighborhood. The fence line of my backyard had a small break just wide enough for a flexible person. It led to a four-block-long canal that wound its way to Elysian Fields; from there, it was a three-minute walk to where I sat. Some neighborhood kids had piled old, rusted, and broken bicycles at the bottom of the ravine, so there was a way to cross the water that would hold in the bottom after heavy rainfall without soaking your pants.

"Fuck that," I muttered in the rearview. If somebody wanted to visit me, now was as good a time as any.

So, I drove through the neighborhood and parked in my carport, scanning the area. Nothing else out of the ordinary caught my eye. I opened my kitchen door, and the smell of voodoo shop perked me from the long nights exhaustion.

I found parched white animal bones and drying innards hanging around my door frame. Stuff was burning, and some kind of powder had been poured all around the fence line and at the base of the wooden deck. Smoke danced around the room. *She doesn't have a key*, I reminded myself. She could've found this back way the other day. But recently, it seemed, Xandi was instantly *near* just when I thought I was alone.

Last year, a sober scientist, who refused to drink as his drunken newlywed daughter danced half-naked in the streets, held me captive with rants on how scientists were on the verge of mathematically proving that free will is non-existent.

He'd need a big fuckin' calculator to prove to me at that moment, when the quantum realm chose to use chicken bones and dried turtle nuts to conjure things that didn't exist into being. Hell, maybe he didn't have to prove anything. Maybe this woman who had floated into my house had been sent to me by another version of us on the other side of whatever this universe offered, scratching my own friggin' back, so to speak. Who the hell was to say, but here she stood,

"To expand your visions," she said in a low voice when she caught me inspecting the weirdness. I guessed Xandi was about forty-five or maybe forty-eight. Smooth, dark skin. Curly, deep chestnut hair. Dark eyes. Full lips made her thin, strong body seem okay with softness.

She said, "I want you to go inside and take a long, hot shower, and we'll get you ready for some proper rest." I did what she commanded.

When I came out wrapped in a towel, my bedroom was aglow. Some things were actively burning, and some just smoking around. Candles, incense, bundles of leaves, and a picture of somebody. She pulled a large metronome from her bag and made it tick. It was loud but comforting amid all this otherworldly stuff that had suddenly bloomed in my bedroom. She slipped my towel from my body, looked me over from foot to head, and smiled knowingly.

"Lie back, sir."

With her hands pushing and steering my chest backwards into my pillow, she lay me down where she wanted me. Her dress was dark green and plain. A button on each shoulder was all that kept it from falling to the floor. She reached and unhitched both, and it did fall to the floor. I didn't know if I would ever see anything so sensual again. A monstrous puffed scar curved up her rib cage like a shark bite. Looked like someone had tried cutting into her with the jagged lid from a rusted and ragged soup can. I ignored it. I didn't want to let it be known that it marked my imagination.

She put some sort of thick green liquid into her hands and rubbed them together, then covered my face. The metronome had found time with my heartbeat somehow. Her hands smelled floral and silky. One of them wrapped around my privates, and I swear, soft electricity buzzed me beyond my recent demonic visions.

Like an Amazonian mother, she carefully squeezed and tugged like she was pulling yucca root from the deep, nourishing earth for sustenance.

The universe was filling me with something; I could feel the healing. Her hands rocked and towed me into thinking that everything ever created was meant for me. She crawled on top of me; one of her breasts softly brushed my chest. Her warm, heavy breath washed over my mouth and nose. A passionate spell washed over my lips; her teeth lightly dug in. Full, warm lips followed by sensual sucking. She slipped me inside her, and I could no longer decipher the sound of the pull of the metronome from the push of my heart.

She was heated like the choo-choo chugging up into a mountain town. Strong and balanced. I envisioned myself wrapped in a velvet pendulum, pushed by my other self, the self far, far away nestled in the stars. No boundaries, no snags. Just this woman rocking me through time with the hammer and thunder of an ungovernable Mother Nature.

My body pushed and pulled like a wine bottle caught in the tidal gravity of the ocean's grasp. I eased one eye open, peeking through her fingers, and I'm certain the room was filled with fog, or smoke, or clouds. It moved above me like a sentinel. I couldn't see the ceiling through it. The light from the window was darkened by it. I quickly closed my eyes tight again. I wanted the mystery. Needed the mystery. She moved her teeth to my neck and pushed her voodoo into me. I could feel little pinches come and go all over my body. Not uncomfortable. Like the satisfaction of a good, strong scratch.

I was harder than I'd ever felt. Softer than I'd ever been. More pliable, like I was becoming our sweat. Dissolving into the smoke, fog, or cloud, whatever she was making with her fire. The rhythm of her push took my mind to its boundaries. What would I become when she is done? A dream opened its door. I could feel it building, swelling inside me.

The pinches. The rocking. *Poomf. Poomf. Poomf. Poomf. Poomf.* The teeth. The steady sound of harmonized flesh. The tick of time.

My heart felt like it was pushing sweat from its edges. The clock popped its spring, and all the energy I had been taking in gave way. Internal combustions were released throughout my body and my soul. I couldn't move another muscle, another millimeter. I hadn't done much, but I was exhausted. I melted into the bed frame.

We lay in soft silence until I was almost dreaming. She had placed Becca in time-out, it seemed. Her warm wetness pulled away from me. I turned to look into her eyes; her head was still covered in a cloud of something.

Her eyes glowed through the haze, a patina-golden red. Like lioness eyes caught in moonlight. Her wet breasts pushed into mine. Her hands grabbed and squeezed my temples. Holding me tight, she turned me to face the candles, whispering, "Sleep. Sleep deeply, dear, good man. Earth is your mother now."

I'm sorry, folks, but anyone who tried to dispel free will most certainly never received mind-boggling, water-parting oral sex. The universe served bad blow jobs all day and all night. When a woman deemed you the right man and crawls on top of you with her whole heart bursting with want, now that was a goddamn personal choice. That was free will, even if you were a devout Pentecostal. God didn't give a shit if you fucked well.

I wasn't conscious of it taking place, but she packed and left me like a spirit returning to Avalon. I was alone before I was ready to be.

I didn't know how long I slept. I didn't know what time she'd finished me. I did know I slept more deeply than any other time in my life. I thought I might have floated above *all* my demons.

I left my bed, spread some boudin on a cracker, and chewed while staring at the man in the mirror. I wondered if this was karma or prophecy. Possibly a satchel full of both.

"What the hell is happening?" I asked the dude in the mirror.

"Either you've been underestimating the power of women, or you've been shortchanging yourself, ole man. Two women in three days? Sheesh."

I splashed cold water on my face.

"The gods are bringing gifts, coaxing me to the arena," I mumble. There was a bright mark under my right nipple. Xandi was here.

I dressed and grabbed my keys and gun belt. I made my way back into the kitchen for another round of boudin and spotted the bank deposit key on a hook by the fridge. I had no recollection of putting it back there. The last thing I remembered was throwing it in the drawer by the bed. I couldn't remember seeing it there. On that hook. I wondered if the fact that it was in my possession plays a role in the new events taking over my life now.

The key came to be in my possession under bizarre circumstances. Looking at it now and recalling the sermon Golda had felt obliged to give me that day sent another wrinkle through my psyche. Especially since I was still finding confusion as to why Leda took the long way home the other night. That night, she stepped over Becca's hand. They say everything happens for a reason, and I had just received some kind of voodoo sex without asking. Maybe I'd gotten lost in the second circle of hell.

Leda had reserved my services. I was instructed to pick up her limo and park on the Baronne side of the Roosevelt. To be there no later than 9:30 in the p.m. I did just that.

A light mist filled the air, cool but not cold. It was the kind of dark and slightly wet evening that made French kissing more enjoyable somehow. I could see people sitting extra close to one another at the bar, smiling and grinning uncontrollably. An innate understanding of how great the coital prize would be sat in the back of everyone's mind.

Then I saw Leda wave from the hotel lobby, so I readied myself by cranking the car. I was about to pull up to her when she waved at me to stay put. I let my driver's window down.

"We will return in a few minutes, Fremeaux. Stay put. I will be the one to open the door for my guests. Make sure the partition is up and locked. I'll be right back," she yelled across the street to me.

She and two others walked my way. A finely tailored, refined fella, possibly a politician or high-dollar lawyer. And a well-dressed woman, but her walk wasn't as refined as the other two. I let my window down. Leda walked by me to get the door for them, then I got a good look at her as she passed my door. It was Wanda Ball, for Christ's sake. What in the hell was Leda up to?

Wanda was a lady of the evening. She had connections, obviously, but she was a go-to person for Officer Gonzales when she was alive. Wanda could find stuff. Raised in these streets, she knew its people intimately. I believed Don Lee used Wanda to bust the televangelist out on Airline Highway recently. The televangelist stated he had no idea she was a prostitute. Don Lee asked if he frequently had women crawl into his car in empty car lots? He did not, he declared. Don Lee wrote that God obviously loved the man more than his other children.

Wanda walked past my window, recognizing me as well. The two guests got into the back of the car. The rear passenger window lowered. A man's voice muttered a question. Leda replied.

"Not tonight, Branton, this one's all for you." She closed his door, walked around the limo, and opened the passenger door to where I was sitting up front. She closed the door to sit with me.

"Lock all the doors and windows, please," she commanded.

The partition was one-way; I tried not to watch them, totally removed from discovery. Over the years since being behind the wheel, Leda would sometimes pull away from the music and the decadence and look directly into the unknown, to where her mind figured the rearview to be, and catch my gaze. She would smile devilishly.

Right then, Wanda Ball was busy extracting a man's honor. Well, we'll just use the word *honor* simply because he was unaware of the fact that he was being set up. Leda must've caught my roving eye; she broke the silence.

"There are people in the know, and there are those who pretend to be in the know. In the art world, the person pretending is labeled a fraud. In everything else, they're a politician, palm reader, or preacher. The problem is that the less they know, the more dangerous they are. Sometimes it is wise to consider this and use these little shits for whatever serves necessity. Tonight, we're buying ourselves another senator."

"I'm a witness to this, Leda."

"Bend the code," she said sarcastically. "Just remember, you're not the monkey. He is."

"And you're the ringmaster?"

"In this case? *We* are."

Six months later, New Orleans was a very hot city. The season when beleaguered wives have been known to stab cheating husbands to death with butter knives. Painful and slow. Vengeful. Everyone was short-tempered in these long days.

I had just busted up a scuffle between two artists on the square. Silly turf shit. I heard Leda call me from her Upper Pontalba apartment balcony.

"Officer Fremeaux, can you come up, please? I need to file a report. It seems someone may have been trying to cut a hole in our courtyard gate last evening. I was just about to call downtown and have someone sent over." She threw a set of keys to her gallery entrance at me.

"Be right up, Ms. Leda."

I climbed the two-hundred-year-old cypress steps to her floor, sliding my hand on the cool brick moistened with sweat from a thousand brows. She opened her oversized door and smiled warmly. I walked into the foyer; a three-piece Kandinsky covered the immediate wall. She pointed to the small key lying on a tabletop in the doorway. Her energy was different that day.

Golda and Leda took great pains to make the least amount of connection with other people, even down to the act of passing off a simple key. But she was a little too off-kilter with me that afternoon. A little too aloof.

"This key is to a security deposit box down at Whitney Bank. Pick it up, please. It is now yours to keep. Keep it secret, keep it safe."

I did as she commanded and followed her into the living area. I recognized the impressionism, Monet, I think, maybe Pissarro. Lots of modern stuff I'm not up to speed on, sculptures everywhere. Floor-to-ceiling windows opened onto the terrace with eye-level views of Andrew Jackson and his faithful horse, Sam Patch.

The Pontalba was an enviable place to lay your head at night. We sat. She poured two Champagnes and handed one to me.

I tried my hand at an upper-class toast. "Here's to being on top."

"Being on top? Fremeaux? Are we toasting to rumors now?"

"Oh no. Never to rumors, Leda. Rumor spoils love and commerce. Rot sits at its core, planted from the deceitful mouths seated at the children's dinner table, squabbling for company. Isn't that how you explained rumor to your friends from Bosnia?" I played with her.

"Possibly. To being on top then." She raised her glass, looking at me cheekily.

"At the top, we can be embraced by the warm sunshine," she said and looked out the window.

I held the key she offered me and asked the obvious question with my eyes. She looked at me like she was searching empty pews for a missing earring but knowing where it lay all along.

"Embroil is a funny word, isn't it, Fremeaux?" She looked at the key and ran her fingers through that long, silken hair.

"An idea can take its hold, as slow as a snail, and build into greatness. Or just the opposite. It can corrupt and confuse as quickly as a cobra's strike. Coming in on the wrong side of embroil can have a fella digging ditches for Jim Jones. Mix lethal Kool-Aid."

"Are we embroiled in something?" I asked, confused.

"Sometimes we all can become embroiled in fantasy to some degree. Did you know that the man who created The Wizard of Oz had fervently advocated for the genocide of the indigenous people of this country? then turned right around and taught his generation that there is no place like home?"

"I didn't. This seems a little random for champagne, Leda. What's this all about?"

I suddenly had the feeling we weren't alone. Sensed another pair of eyes on me from somewhere.

I looked around the vast room. Art was placed at all four corners. A doorway was at the far end of the room; small oil paintings filled the exposed wall just past the break. An ornate gold-laden mirror hung just about hip level. *What an odd place for a mirror*, I thought.

A man's voice rose from the streets under the balcony outside. I believed it belonged to one of the men in the scuffle.

"Emotional bleakness was that motherfucker's inheritance," he yelled.

She raised her glass. "A toast to inheritance. Speaking of inheritance, Mother has a half-brother, Ferdinand—"

A sudden clearing of a throat halted her mid-sentence. I noticed a face move in that ill-placed mirror down the long doorway. Someone had been sitting in a chair behind the wall with a spy's view into this room. I stared and waited for the mysterious head to turn and make eye contact. A cigarette was lit, and a body stood just out of view. I stood. Leda watched me without looking around.

"Oh, Mother, have you awakened?"

Golda entered the scene and sat in a chair facing the sunshine in the open doorway. Brown liquor held captive in a crystal highball by her long talons. She slipped her grip to the side of the drink, locking her vision on me, studying for a moment. It was the first time I had ever been in her presence. Or shall I say, allowed to be in her presence? She certainly exudes the power and meaning necessary to make me feel the weight of it. She sipped.

"Money is energy, Fremeaux," she stated in an uncompromising Eastern European accent.

Those were the first words she spoke to me. *Money is energy*. I noticed she did not refer to me as *Officer* Fremeaux that afternoon. I'd pondered that statement hundreds of times since and had concluded that money was human dark energy. Moved us from disorder to order and back again. From minimum to maximum, exploiting through decadence.

I was amazed at her vibrancy that day. Beauty on hold. Leda with time in her pocket. Long, thin, strong, with the style of a handwritten poem. Backbone held a hurricane of a woman in place. It was obvious this was the mother of the woman that I knew I would have to learn to say no to.

"The contents of the safety deposit box hold career-damning evidence. There are three copies each of two separate senators engaged in sexual activity and drug use with one singular woman by the pseudonym of Michaela Farro. I believe you are acquainted with her local name, Wanda Ball, from what I understand.

"There are names, dates, and addresses. Explicit sex and drugs can be clearly seen and heard on a digitized video made on sophisticated equipment in Japan. There are still photographs as well. It is all in there. One senator represents New York and the other represents Rhode Island. A governor's reputation will soon be captured. Do you understand, officer?"

She used the word *officer* as a barrier.

I felt myself almost utter, *Yes, ma'am*, but I stopped. "I'm good on that," I said.

In circumstances like these, I thought it was best to say as little as possible. They had called me here on my behalf, I thought.

"I'm glad you are with us on this. The man in charge of handling the business at the bank is Arturo. If you want to verify what we've just explained, then you will need to ask for him specifically. He has been informed of your involvement."

I didn't like the word *involvement*. Had I just been purchased? Why in the hell had Golda pulled me into their world? Why the sudden appearance?

She sipped.

"Am I to help y'all change the world tomorrow?" I asked cautiously.

"Honey, I can only think of a few things that can change the world overnight. A man with the correct amount of nuclear weaponry at his disposal, an alien invasion, or the return of Christ himself. The rest of us who govern this garden of Eden plant our seeds at the right time in the right place and prune. *Prune* at the most opportune time." She sipped and continued.

"Our minds can mold and tolerate all things illogical and disagreeable, through necessity. Take abandonment and adoption, for instance, how does such a personality end up so far out on the social limb? Well, that seed was planted five or six generations back in time. Entropy is in everything, and the human mind can ignore that fact to no end, as long as there is a happy ending for somebody.

She paused, sipped, and stared at me.

"The average person simply doesn't have the capacity to evolve as quickly as the pace the world is evolving now. Most will succumb. The Great Society failed, and now they have overpopulated their social classes. Filled their beds with impoverished and exhausted spirits, begging for more toys. They'll turn on one another soon. Too dull to question. Too dependent to struggle. Just feed and entertain them, and they will gladly do the heavy lifting. Somebody must be at the helm when the wave swells. Many will be swallowed. This has been and always will be the human condition. If this is a concept you simply can't abide, then I suggest you remain childless. Seek a barren woman."

She sipped again, turning toward me without expression.

"Prune, son. Prune wisely."

I pulled the key from the hook and pushed it to the bottom of my pocket, wondering about my own survival. I had a to-do list. Good people still needed me, and this badge, on duty. For all the good people of this world, the real blues was no longer having a reason to hang the baby's jumper on the line. The very same jumper they had hung a hundred mornings. Death visited rain or shine.

CHAPTER EIGHT

Don Lee's eyes had puffed. Chest hair looked like a jar of honey had just been licked off him. In short, a mess. But still, I could see enough fortitude left in the man to wrestle a steer to the ground at a charity rodeo. Brows still held an attitude.

"All expansions and diversions of my vagrant imagination were cultivated in that most lecherous of muck and dirt in Mississippi. This mutation of myself, this pitiful vestibule of exaggeration you see before you, got nurtured and emboldened down in these here swampy-assed Louisiana boulevards."

"What the hell does that have to do with our case, Don Lee?"

"Hell, son, I don't know. I can't seem to *buy* a decent night's sleep. I've been mumbling mumbo jumbo shit like that for days now. Mental quilting, I suppose. Scrapping my identity back together, maybe."

Scanning his house, I found overflowing ashtrays lying about, Legal papers scattered everywhere, and newspapers, too. Half-empty glasses of every booze known to mankind sit on windowsills. It smelled like a coffee joint/barroom/red beans, and dark contemplation.

"I'm starting to feel like the old fool who would stop to give aid to the choking alligator," he mumbled again.

"It's two-thirty in the afternoon. Have more coffee. What the hell did you get into last night?"

"Before I saw you, I began the evening working under covers."

I gave him a wary look.

"Not in that manner. I was drinking pregnant canaries down at Nick's with off-duty officers, hoping the right crew would drop in to bait some conversations and see who'd slip something useful to nibble. But only the young bucks were out holding company, all they can offer for recital is their regimens. Then I got the tickle that needed an itch. I went out farther chasing the gleam of decadence, got grumpy, and showed my ass. Then I found you."

"Lil Alka Seltzer and red wine'll fix that. Last night, you said you didn't get anything substantial from Becca's friends and family?"

"They're good country folk, but couldn't gather anything useful. You stated you may have a sack full?" he returned.

"Maybe, are you aware that the archdiocese owns the building where you picked up Becca's hand?" I asked.

"I was not, but I was close to a decision on taking my realtor for a nice dinner. Do some plundering into that very subject. You have just saved The Picayune two hundred dollars on a dinner tab and an evening of bad intentions. For now, anyway." He chuckled.

"Charlie the Crow lives there, rent-free," I told him.

"Well, son, that sure is a bone to chew on. I believe I will have some red wine with Coke, on that one. Jostle my gizzards, so to speak. Can you grab them from the counter in the kitchen and a glass with ice, please?"

I mixed him an afternoon tonic. Then I reported the feeble facts to him about the boy with tattooed hands, and that Charlie's credentials are paid for by an anonymous source. Don Lee gulped the first one like a self-absorbed football star chugs for the cameras, so I made another. The tremble in his fingers slowed. His eyes lowered.

"There are still decent truths drifting with us. Just gotta yank back the draperies just at the right moment. But sometimes the draperies are heavy, kid. Heavy and hard to grasp. They'll snag if not pulled just right. Gotta wiggle and loosen and jerk hard at the precise moment to discover who is sneaking their way around the corner. Demands tenacity and perseverance," he said, rambling.

"Does it feel like the clues we need are going to be fed to us by someone behind curtains to you, too?" I asked.

"Some days I felt like a damn rodent traversing an enclosed maze, and the man with the cheese is some omnipotent pockmarked son of a bitch laughing at me."

"I've come to realize we can't look for support from anyone we would normally go to. I can't for the life of me choose my next steps. The search is shrouded in obscurity. I have asked a thousand pairs of eyes if they've seen a kid with those tattoos on his hands, and nothing. The kid seems to be fictional. Whatever comes our way is going to be a reward for not looking in the right places. How much do you know about Leda and her mother?" I asked. "You commented that moral turpitude runs in their veins."

"A few years back, Leda took one of my journalism classes out at U.N.O. Come to think of it, I never got her to confess why she took the class, but there she was. Anyway, she became a late-night buddy, and many mornings we awoke in other towns. As you know, she has a car, a driver, a plane, and a pilot. Her bloodline has been traced back to royalty. Golda's father is said to have stolen millions from the wealthy seeking freedom from Hitler. It's rumored that he promised safe travels from territories being invaded. Once the monies had been secured, he turned a blind banker's eye. It has also been rumored that he double-dipped from the Germans and revealed the secret locations of those unfortunate families in hiding.

"After retreating to Hungary with his fortune, the family name has ruled Eastern Europe from behind thick curtains ever since. As I have said, you don't fuck with Golda."

A phone rang somewhere in the back of the house, and he went to answer. I heard his voice rise and then drop. Up tempo, then slowed again. He hung up and quickly dialed two other people, holding two other conversations, then returned.

"Something funky's going down in the Bayou, kid. That was two old Cajun acquaintances. They have just shot and killed two men, dumping body parts into the Pearl River from their land. Feeding gators. Probably doesn't have anything to do with us, but they reported seeing a Delta Eighty-Eight hauling ass outta dodge. Leda has agreed to request your services for tonight, so you are now off duty. Big Dan George will be here directly, with Xandi in tow. We will be leaving immediately. Do you need me to gather anything for you?"

"I can't recall ever being this confused, Don Lee."

"That's the very definition of life, Officer Fremeaux."

"Are police on scene?" I asked.

"You will decide if other authorities will be needed."

"So, you're saying this may never have happened?"

"I got their uncle released from prison," he said. "Get my drift?"

"Who the hell is Big Dan George?"

"Bouncer for the area where Xandi lives. Kinda like her bodyguard. He's been known to bust skulls for Xandi." My eyebrows raised without effort as I gave a list of things

needed. "Gallon Ziplock bags, inkpad, blank paper, and a flashlight. It'll get dark while we're out there."

"You're in luck, I'm a newspaperman. I just happen to have all of those things here."

"We may be forced to take a life to have those curtains thrown aside. You ready for that?"

"To get Becca out of my head, I'm opposed to nothin'

CHAPTER NINE

I took the passenger seat in front of Xandi and caught sight of her reaching into a bag. She rubbed her fingers together and swiped something that felt like pig snot on the back of my neck.

"No, no, no, don't wipe it off, Fremeaux."

"What the hell is this all about, Xandi?"

"Keeping you safe is one of my duties as we trample through this together."

"Can you elaborate on that for him?" Don Lee asked.

"My job, Fremeaux. All I have now is a neurotic father, Don Lee, and Big Dan George here."

"What am I in all this suddenness? Jesus the Savior?" I asked.

"No, Mr. Man. You're a good man with a badge that's going to help us drive this thing to a close. I am going to do my part by keeping you from harm's way, as best I know how. And you will abide. You will not stand ignorant between me and my will, Fremeaux."

I looked over to Big Dan George. The man had a Macy Day Parade-sized noggin and hands as big as bobcats.

"Yes, ma'am," I answered, and we sped off to the swamps near Slidell.

We finally arrived in Indian Bayou and met a short Cajun fella named Lefort. We piled into a couple of backyard pirogues and shuttled the forty-five minutes through the darkening waters of the river basin to greet the Peychaud brothers, who were guarding the two dead bodies in the middle of absolute nowhere.

"Why didn't we just take the road as they did?" I asked.

"Parts of dis area are leased by small-time oilmen. Down that way, about half a mile, are two oil pumpers that have been in place since the late seventies. They have cameras monitoring the gravel roads that lead back in here. You don't need to be seen by them. On their land, they prosecute to the fullest. Nobody fiddle wid they oil."

"Good to know," I said

I stood over to inspect the dead bodies. One had been shot in the head. The other dead center through the heart. Both are wearing tan coveralls.

"Smell that?" Xandi asked.

"Swamp shit?" I asked

"Prell and cigarettes."

She leaned down and pulled open the coveralls to expose chest hair. Nothing else on the bodies but Prell and cigarettes. No wallets, watches, wedding rings, nothing. Just dead skin and body hair.

On the ground, two .38s and a duffel bag covered in blood stains lay next to the river's edge. Big Dan George dragged it to us and dumped severed hands and two blood-soaked heads out onto the ground, and there they lay, the hands of Mr. Shit Happens. I rubbed my face in disbelief and looked around the area. Darkness began to encroach.

"When we yell at da two of dem, da fucker done start shootin' to us. Hell, we had no choice but to shoot 'em dead. Den we hear a car peel gravel, haulin' ass outta here. We figured Don Lee could have some interest for himself, so we call him before gettin' rid of 'em," said one of the Peychaud brothers.

"Is this the way they came and left?" I asked.

"For sure." The same Cajun fella answered.

I walked down the middle of the two tire ruts. Smatterings of grassy spots dimmed under the dusk light, highlighting the two lines of crushed pea gravel. I doubted I would find anything connected. Mostly trying to catch all my thoughts from swirling from stumbling across Mr. Shit Happens severed body parts in the middle of a swamp.

I wandered to the back of a turn in the woods, about three hundred yards away. A small bunny jumped from a pile of leaves and scampered a little piece into the thicket, suddenly halting in silence. Just quick breaths, just beyond my sight, and my own breathing.

Some yellowing leaves had faded to resemble polka dots against the still, dark green ones as the sunlight dimmed more around me. I walked closer to the tree line and could hear one of the teapot oil pumps working the muddy hole in the earth half a mile from me. Peering through the foliage, a bright spotlight from Stennis Space Center, a few miles in the distance, lit the swamp water with a dazzling, dancing effect.

Just beyond my sight, I heard the thump and snatch of a small forest animal followed by a few high-pitched yips. Something caught the small bunny. Bound in a death grip. A snake, maybe? I could hear the wrestling through the dry, brown leaves. There wasn't any noise from another animal. Just the frantic yips and the thuds of the back feet punching into some sort of thick air-filled base. Like the sound of a country farmer after Thanksgiving turkey dinner. Gut filled with food and heated air, exposed, globe-like, from under his Sunday shirt. His grandson comes along riding a plastic tractor and thumps the protruding gut, forcing the all too familiar thick thud.

That's what I heard as the yips began to slow.

The trees, the leaves, the lights, and the water had all blurred into an impressionistic mass as I wondered if, in the last moments, near the final yip for help, and the last energies were being mustered, did the bunny seek out eternal wings? Or just say, Fuck it. This is fate.

Funny how heartbroken I was, rooting for the bunny as the struggle ensued, but as its time dwindled, I found myself admonishing it for not being diligent enough to avoid this fate. Fuck it for forcing me to care, kind of thing. Got what it deserved, for letting my hopes down.

When *our* fever dream breaks, will we extend beyond where all our religion and voodoo reside? Will we stretch for the light of eternity? If we don't make it, will our comrades feel defeated and curse our names as well? Is that the mystery at the root of us all?

If you don't dance. If you don't curse. If you don't steal. If you don't fornicate out of wedlock, or covet or kill, you too can be granted wings to forever land? And those of us branded unsuitable? Those of us who can't determine the value of the Lord's name, is this why we're taboo? Is this the reason they try hard to save us? If we fail, we fail in their hearts too. Game over, next soul, please. Is it that cut and dry? Well, thank God for Bourbon Street and forgiving women.

I could see two identical shadows far off in the trees, maybe owls, can't say for sure, they weren't moving, keeping a close eye on me, I'm sure. My sight blurred into the shadows, and I began to think how none of this would exist in a hundred years. It would all be new. New growth, new birth, new food, new death. Tonight, the foliage smells dank and old news, and our future is stacked against us. Whitling and blurring all plans.

Our present evolved to devolve. The future was forever constructing our daily life, our stage. Just as the hammer scarred the wood when it struck the nail, we were forever re-delivered slightly less in value. Something not completely right nor wrong, just different. Entropy, as Golda would state, is a matter of fact.

Seemingly forever, the future employed a gazillion god particles at a time to replace our jeans, footballs, tiaras, and even our souls every second of every moment. Reality was slightly altered each time we were reassembled, imperceptibly devalued until the fray begins, until we distrusted the very reliability we came to depend upon.

It was the same with social behavior; it becomes too grotesque to covet.

That was where these criminals were now. Encased in decay from the inside, fumbling and leaving deadly clues. Time was tearing them apart.

I figured that Prell and Cigarettes weren't going to give up any clues. Whoever is behind this was not going down like this poor little bunny did tonight. They would have had all their paths cleared for safe running, but the severed hands of the other two degenerates will have a story to tell. A past for consideration. You didn't end up in pieces being fed to gators for not buying the old lady flowers after pissing her off. I was certain Mr. Shit Happens would be in our database somewhere. He was probably just another moron, but morons can stumble onto important land from time to time. Hell, he'd found a partial burial on oil land tonight. That was worth a story or two.

I didn't find any physical evidence on the makeshift driveway, so I made my way back to the crowd.

"Did you go off and look into the future?" Xandi asked with a knowing smile. I smiled back in agreement, recollecting the mystery pig snot.

"What'cha reckon, Fremeaux?" Don Lee asked.

I looked at everyone's faces. The Cajun's eyes tightened, with head nods, telling me, *Whatever you need, young man.*

I looked back at Don Lee.

"We're going to remove the clothing and put all items in the trash bags. We need to cut Prell and Cigarettes' hands and heads off, too. I need them all for fingerprints. Put the heads back into the duffel. Don Lee, we will need to freeze all these heads and hands after I can get proper sets of fingerprints."

I looked back at the Cajuns, "Burn the clothing and feed everything else to the gators." They nodded in agreement.

Don Lee offered, "How about we get all the fingerprinting done with my friends in Mississippi? It will save time and be more inconspicuous for you. I want to keep these in my freezer in Jackson; we may need them for blackmail or prosecution."

I looked at Xandi. Xandi looked at Big Dan George.

"Georgie, can you do an all-nighter for us?"

He nodded yes, with a stretched, malicious-clown grin.

CHAPTER TEN

Don Lee and I got back to his place in the Quarter just as daylight was breaking. We opened his door and found Leda asleep on his couch.

"She has a key to your house?" I whispered.

"If you and she are on mutual ground, she is the greatest ally you could ever hope for."

He walked near her sleeping body.

"Leda, honey, I'm home," he said softly to her. She woke and sat up, looking almost ready to talk. Rubbing her eyes.

"Glad you two are safe. I just had an odd dream. Like a crazy arthouse film.

"I was riding a bicycle all around the Quarter. Up and down and all over. All the people I knew from all over the world were there. Right there in the streets with all the strange people. Kings, Queens, Popes, businessmen, and captains of industry. Hairdressers, stylists, photographers, chefs, you two, and everybody else. Waving and blowing kisses as I passed, every turn, every street. Everyone I passed was so happy to see me.

"I looked down at my feet and noticed my pedals weren't pedaling at all, just spinning. Effortlessly gliding through the joy. I rolled onto Bourbon; it was packed like Mardi Gras. All eyes and smiles for me. It was dark overhead, and the neon at the edges stretched on and on forever. Then, suddenly, the streets began to thin out of people, and I found another figure on another bicycle following me. The energy folded into bizarre anxiety. I couldn't forcibly make a turn for escape. We just rolled together, on and on.

"We entered a tunnel lit by the eyes of a thousand gargoyles. I tried to pedal harder and harder, to no avail; my speed remained the same, and the tunnel seemed to stretch into infinity as we moved forward into the darkness. After a while, a speck of light began to grow brighter and larger, and we suddenly dumped out onto a velodrome. Our speed increased as we circled the track. The other being was wearing a powdery silver-blue fencing uniform. Skin-tight. I could see forms on the chest, and I realized it was female. We pedaled for what seemed like all night, and she never gained or lost space between us. We remained fixed in time, directly opposite one another. I couldn't deduce whether she was chasing me or if I had gained pursuit. Round and round we chased and followed. I began a dream within a dream, until time itself meandered and folded reality back into itself. As if that makes any sense."

Leda wiped at her nose and looked at me.

"Then, I noticed a door labeled with the word *Ladies.* On the next pass, I came to a halt and tried to lay the bike down, but it wouldn't budge or fall. It remained upright. I looked at her, and she was in the same state as I was, directly across the track. I briskly walked around the track and then through the door as she continued her trek around the velodrome on foot, in my direction. The door closed behind me, and I went to the mirror. I had my mother's makeup on my face. The door sprang open, and suddenly in my hand was a matador's knife. My phantom stalker stepped into my space, and I thrust the cold steel through her heart. Blood spread through the shirt as she fell and stuck to the ground. I reached down to remove her headpiece. I flung it to the floor, gasping. It was me. I had found myself, my secret self. I had become my mother, stabbing and murdering my shadow. I felt as though I was skidding into frivolity. Then you woke me."

Don Lee lit a cigarette. "Goodness, little dear. How's your spirit now?"

"Just a silly dream, I'm with you now. Please, may we drink Champagne before Mother and I leave for family business in Europe?

"You're leaving us?" I asked, not ready to hear she'd be gone. There had been plenty of times when I wouldn't see her, but hearing it in advance left me feeling something I didn't know was in me. She looked at me, sensing my discomfort.

"I will be leaving later this afternoon and should be back before Mardi Gras, maybe sooner if all goes as planned. I'll return before you fully realize I've not been around," she said with comfort in her tone.

Don Lee fetched some bubbly; we toasted to honor and allegiance on Leda's suggestion. Her eyes tightened.

"How was it decided to give the bodies of the two criminals to the gators and not call in the authorities, Fremeaux?" she asked.

"It would not have been in our favor to involve any more corruption. As we sit now, the culprits think that only a couple of back-wood Cajuns are involved. They'll keep tabs on them for sure, so we need to have someone in the bushes out there. Spotting for them and us. If I were to have called it in, we would have gotten bogged down by the system for years. They would have had us chasing our own tails with tainted statutes. For now, we retain the power of surprise. We will decide when to alert them, on our terms. Don Lee can do that through the papers when we're ready to shake that snow globe."

She flinched eyes of agreement towards me.

"Would you mind walking me home in a bit, Fremeaux?" she asked with command in her voice. Like a housewife remembering unfulfilled chores. We finished the bottle and left Don Lee to himself so he could get some rest.

I'm not sure if the dream put her into a frail sense of vulnerability; if it did, then it's a vulnerability I haven't seen from her in the five years I've been in her employ, but she looped her hand to the underside of my arm as we turned to walk across Esplanade. As we sauntered past the fatigued homes, I felt my spine stretch. My spirit expanded.

I caught sight of the clodhopper dragging his cross into the Quarter down Bourbon out of the corner of my eye and secretly felt myself root for him and his mission for some odd reason. My mind conjured an image of the bank deposit key, and I asked her softly.

"Why me?"

Her grip tightened, and we walked in silence till we reached the old Ursuline Convent.

"Mother and I are in correspondence with a French professor out at Stanford. He has been developing a radical new theory on humanity, which he calls Memetic Desire. In the Bible, Jesus said he would reveal the truth hidden since the foundation of the world. Human culture was founded on collective murder. Culture begins when people unite against a single victim; each against one becomes a unity of all against one. The scapegoat mentality coagulates cyclically through all time."

"Leda, what could this have to do with me?" I asked.

She slowed our pace.

"It's the difference between boys and men, Fremeaux. In the frenetic swirl before a scapegoat is offered, societies foul themselves through imitation swelled with unbridled desire to covet, over and over, since the beginning. Greed causes men to believe they must keep their secrets close to their chests, so others do not steal their sacred treasures. They kill their brethren through fear of insignificance. Significance is embezzled from insignificance throughout time. But there are very few men who realize this is child's play. Very few men create their own paths, avoiding the trap. Creating their own peace, their own solidarity."

She stopped us at the corner.

"But the harder truth is that very few of these men are aware that those scared souls will often need to be killed to keep peace. The man who can do that killing is you, Fremeaux. Whether you are aware or not, you are that rare breed that will protect yourself without the drive of another man's treasure. You do not imitate. Your ideals are too cool for that." She smiled and looked forward again.

"So, that politician last year was a child imitating with Wanda Ball?"

"They're all children posing as the real deal. They destroy one another every day, all day. Wars will never cease, and that is the hidden truth. Jesus was not a martyr. Jesus knew he was a sacrifice for a temporary ceasefire. Hell, he probably thought he was protecting Mary Magdaline because nobody else would."

We stopped at the intersection of Ursuline and Royal and turned face-to-face. I could hear something scraping the concrete across the street behind me. She glanced at the noise accumulating over my shoulder. I turned and we watched Olivia Claire setting up milk crates for a makeshift stage. Ms. Claire wanders the Quarter from time to time wearing a cow suit the color of Mardi Gras, and I noticed her husband was absent. Maybe because her stage was just four milk crates, and she didn't need extra hands today. She stepped, stretching her head high toward the balcony above, and began to recite a poem.

Oh, Father, Must You Go

Funny, how you were thinking about it again

Unaware that you were even there- again

Or had you simply gotten yourself entangled in its murky visions?

Its eternal grasp?

You were alone.

Too tired for feasting

What were you seeking?

*You know now, as you did then, that you'd be alone when you final-
ly arrived*

With barren mind and burdened heart

Just you and God's breath

Filled with the last drops of its clear tenderness

And knowing another sun would come to warm your family

and your friends, to your children

green grasses to tickle their feet

But not you

Your boots are laced and ready.

Olivia lowered her head, and I asked which poet she was sharing with us today.

"Me. I wrote it for Poppa. This is where he was livin' when he passed on to the next show," she said in her thick Chalmation accent.

Leda pulled at my arm; she needed to be somewhere else soon.

We walked on to her gate, and I think that somehow the secret and real reason we can't be admitted into heaven will forever elude us. That bit of knowledge could never be revealed to our tired, overworked brains. Then, suddenly, without being conscious of producing the thought, I asked.

"Where is Arthur Bucknell and Mr. Gillieach?"

She shot a look of discontent. As if I had blundered into her powder room, unwittingly blurting discrimination, causing a pause in making herself ready for public view.

"In due time, my dear," she said coyly.

Maybe if I had led the question with, *do you know*, instead of being accusatory, my inquiry would have been received with more circumstance and less pomposity. Her perturbation put me off kilter.

"I'll keep my ideals on the right track while you're away, little lady."

"I know your bootstraps are laced and ready. The days of green grasses tickling your feet are far behind you now." She said with a smile. "That's why you are in my thoughts. And, when I took your arm to walk with you, you didn't feel the need to flex." She smiled. I ignored the feeling of that statement.

"Leda, why do you and your mother choose the most under-cared-for city in the country for residence?" She returned her gaze to me. It revealed she was pondering whether she should leave it for further discussion or not. She pursed her lips and, after careful consideration, she spoke.

"We will soon control all the wealth this river has to offer. We're acquiring the Gulf Coast, and someday our family will own the majority of the planet's coastlines. Every wall of every cell in your body is where the currency lies. Life or death depends on what passes. Control the entry point and the waterways, and you control life. Plus, Mother's true love is near. I need to go now, Fremeaux. I will see you soon."

She opened her gate to go home.

The gate swung closed. About mid-pull, it produced an awful, piercing squeal, much like a rhinoceros' scream as its spleen is being punctured by an elephant's tusk on the midnight plains. I remembered at some point her mother, Golda's family, reportedly had dealings of some sort with Stalin. That's the word I got from Don Lee anyway.

I then realized I wasn't going to see her for some months, and my emotions seemed to be hung up in yesterdays. A lonely whisper reminded me that entropy burrows into everything. I could feel the boots rubbing the skin on my feet.

CHAPTER ELEVEN

I turned back into the narrow, crowded streets, wondering who or what on God's green earth could be Golda's true love.

I caught sight of Tre Freeman heading into the parking garage of Place de Arms. I rushed over to catch him. Tre is a field agent for our local F.B.I. branch. He's about my level of authority, but in a bigger priority set. Doesn't quite hold a key to the office closets, but can get acquainted with the key rings and Rolodexes. You never know till you ask, so I called out for him to take some time.

"Officer Fremeaux, good to see ya, man. How've ya been? Seen anything interesting lately?

"Outside of sheer dumb crime, nothing but hints and allegations so far."

"Yeah, you and I get to scatter through chicken feed for now. What have you been looking for?" he asked.

I replied with another question. "What do y'all hold on the Monsignor?"

"Nothing. The separation of church and state benefits the church more than it does the state. Worldwide, the Catholics are stroked with velvet gloves as far as the American government is concerned. We aren't allowed to peek behind the curtains unless holy blood is shed and they invite us to come aboard. Them's the rules set from the bible, and they hold the money left over from the Roman Empire. Have you witnessed something?"

"Couple suspected payoffs in envelopes. What about the disappearance of all the young women over these years? Do y'all keep any files from us, or for us?" I asked.

"Now that's a subject known in the department as the transfer case."

"What the hell does that mean?"

"Well, if you're wishing to get the hell out of this godforsaken swamp, all you have to do is press into the subject, and you'll get your transfer, alright. It's happened before."

"Good ole human compassion takes the back seat as usual."

"Now, wait a minute now. You and I are in the good fight together, so don't go giving up on us that easily. I'll see what I can help you with; I just gotta remain invisible."

"If what you say is true, then heads of state are keeping electricity in the chair for the good fighters, too. You and I could be forced to take a seat. Learn the hard way."

"That's likely the case, but we can still climb the trash pile and peek over at the rats, can't we?" he returned.

I looked in his eyes and darkened the mood of our talk.

"I may have a lead on a kid last seen with one of our missing girls. I should have fingerprints soon. Can I get you to run a background at the federal level?"

"You have heard hints and allegations, haven't you? Keep me posted, Fremeaux. I'll help in any way I can. I do still have higher people to answer to remember."

"Yeah. I don't expect you to create harm for yourself. I just may need a push getting this thing home."

"I got ya, man. By the way, Tressy was askin' about ya yesterday. She hasn't seen you patrolling her side of the Quarter in a few days."

"I guess I should swing over and show some support for my old friend Tressy Tingle. Thanks, Freeman. Any little thing could help."

So, I moved toward Fahy's over on Burgundy to check in with my favorite bartender at my favorite Irish joint.

"Howdy, Tressy," I said to her backside as she popped out onto the street with a watering can in hand for the plants sitting at the doorstep's edge.

She turned and gave me a strong hug like I was a long-lost brother. I had noticed through the doorway that Ruthie was having a beer at the bar. Her two ducks stood at her feet, eating crumbles of po-boy bread from her fingers.

Two out-of-towners sat with their backs to the open door. They were dressed in nouveau southern riche. The man's wore tasseled leather shoes and no socks. Her hair could have altered the strut of a repenting peacock.

"How've you been, Fremeaux? You look tired."

"A lot on the books all of a sudden."

"Yeah, Xandi passed by and had coffee this morning. She looked exhausted. Glad to hear y'all are working together. She and Don Lee need to put an end to this stir in their souls."

"We got some solid evidence, but none of it sticks or connects with anything at this point. Something big and terrible will have to happen to bust a hole in the stuff, I'm afraid."

"You're not on duty, are you? Isn't it a little early for you to be around? You should be getting some sleep."

"I got a ghost in my dreams, baby. Sleep's not on the prescription pad."

"You work tonight?"

"Yeah. I'll be checking the clock at five."

"You wanna crash on my couch for a bit? Fremeaux, you look like shit."

"I'm good, thanks. I'm headed to see if I can't run down Ms. Koozie. She should be hitting her mid-morning break in a little bit, so I'm making my way over to the wine shop. Just wanted to stop and say howdy."

"Glad you did. It's comforting to know that if I need an asshole removed, you're around. We got two farm-town colleges playing the dome tomorrow night, and those rednecks always come through this side of the Quarter fucking with us."

I had forgotten. On occasion, they scheduled a highlighted Thursday nighter once a season. It turned into a long four-day drunk asshole fest.

"I didn't realize it was this week," I said with some dread. "I guess that explains those two sitting at your bar wandering past the poverty line."

"Yeah, they plopped down with disdain from the start. I wish I had gotten out of town like everyone else," she confessed.

She was right. I mentally revisited all the homes down Burgundy that had been closed and quieted. The Quarter would be swimming in childish mayhem that weekend.

The two outsiders inside the bar voiced criticism of Ruthie's appearance and behavior in what they believed to be "concealed talk."

Tressy rolled her eyes and was about to march to the rescue, but we heard Ruthie slip from her stool and shuffle to their side. In her broken, gravelly speak, she asked.

"Mistah, how much you pay for 'dem drinks?"

The wife scooted her chair closer to the wall. The man nervously stared at his drink, hoping for rescue. His wife refused engagement.

Ruthie stood her ground, puffing on her cigarette and licking around the inside of her loose cheeks. She moved a little more into his space. He wasn't about to provoke a woman who pushed dirty fear into his safe little world.

He finally answered, "Six bucks."

"Well, asshole, I didn't hafta pay shit. So, who's stupid now?" And she stepped through the door where we stood outside.

"Fremeaux!" She spoke gruffly and defiantly. "Kindness sometimes got enemies too." She walked off. Her two feathered buddies waddled carefully down the steps in tow. The largest of the two craned its neck to one side, almost looking completely to the rear toward us, and honked harshly as if putting the final stamp on Ruthie's declarations. If the thing had lips, I'm sure foul language would have been awarded, too. The three amigos gallantly walked into their blissful future, fully aware of where they had been and always aware of what lay ahead. Ruthie burst into singsong.

"If ever I cease to love.

If ever I cease to love.

May fish heads grow on apple trees,

May da moon be turns to green cream cheese,

If ever I cease to love."

Tressy looked at me with small delight. "I hope Ruthie doesn't think it's time for Mardi Gras."

"Tressy, I think Ruthie knows exactly what time it is. We're the ones always guessing for Mardi Gras Day."

I got to the Veaux Carre wine shop on Chartres and pushed the tight door to stumble into Ms. Koozie, looking up from the flimsy card table, smiling as if she knew I was on my way to her.

"I knew you'd be coming round some point, Fremeaux. I have been wanting to thank you for getting Uncle Jacque out the tank the other week."

"No problem, lady. He'd been in there long enough. How ya livin' baby?"

"Keepin' the food rolling, you know me. You ain't been through in a while what ya got goin that's keepin' ya out the bounds?"

"A lot."

'You here inquirin'?"

"You could say that."

Ms. Koozie sat me across from her at the little card table. Probably the most important table in all the French Quarter. Heads of state had sat here. Pirates, lovers, cheaters, strippers, chefs, and priests all gave their versions of truth and graded other people's lies. It was here our newly elected governor, Harold Heralds, touted to our favorite local news anchor, Roda Lotchbee, *The only way I'll lose this election is if I'm found in bed with a live boy or a dead girl.*

The man was right, of course, and Louisiana had found itself being led from the nostrils by yet another wild-eyed, loose-lipped commander.

Ms. Koozie's hands were soft, warm, and comforting. She squeezed mine until my body wilted into ease. Her plump, round face was dotted with dark, rich freckles that were born on the Caribbean shorelines. Not the ones that have a certain shine and seem bright. No, hers were opposite the sunspot kind. Powerful, like the dark side of the moon, manifested from deep within. Swaying and hypnotizing your inner thoughts as you try to count them. Hauling the questions you'd been mulling all day to the sticky edges of your lips. Forcing you to form them just the way she needs them asked. Mutual, for her and you to understand together.

She called herself Ms. Koozie because she swore she invented the koozie by using a sock to keep her granddaddy's beers cold on the hot beaches of Haiti back in the fifties.

"What be you needin' from ole Momma Koozie today, Fremeaux? You have more worry and confusion in your body than I've ever seen."

"I got myself stirring two different gumbos, baby. On the one hand, I've been working with Don Lee and his missing girls. The other is Leda barely escaping a hired Dixie Mafia hit. I need something that may be lying in the streets that'll help steer me, so I don't stay twisted in my head."

"Down here, most shit is connected somehow, Fremeaux. Everybody gets dirty together. The missing girls are a place too far for me to venture. Now Ms. Leda's little issue will eventually lead somewhere too far for you to dream."

"What the hell does that mean?"

"That's a secret hallway I can't say too much on. Golda and Leda are shadows in my little world. Do you know of the Impastata twins?"

"I don't."

"Well, you haven't a reason to. I'm not telling you this, but you will need to seek out Wanda Ball."

"Wanda Ball?"

"I'm not saying anymore on the subject. They's people out there, Momma Koozie, don't get near, if ya hear me, baby. You can get what you need if you can get Wanda to trust you."

"Okay," I said with confusion in my tone.

"You're going to find yourself coming face to face with strange voodoo."

"What do you know about the Monsignor?" I asked.

"Fremeaux, if you knock on that man's castle, you'd better be ready to fight or play ring and run, those folks'll burn you to ashes."

"You know what they say? The longer you look, the more the suspicion grows." I said.

"That's the scientific view, Fremeaux. I say, the longer you look, the more interesting it's gonna get. You're not in Mason City any longer, Fremeaux. Human rituals devolve when social limits are loosened, and comfort zones are busted."

"Wanda Ball, huh? This should get interesting."

She smiled and let loose of my hands. "So good to see you, Fremeaux. But I can't share what may come back to bite me in my ass. I got family too."

"I won't let Wanda on that you sent me to her."

"It's not Wanda that will come back. The Impastata twins are another matter, if ya hear what I'm telling. They connected."

"Gotcha, baby. Is this information for Leda's altercation or something leading to the missing girls?"

"It's a starting place on the Leda playground. Just trudge the mud and be ready for the haunted voices."

"I've already invited those in, sweetheart."

"Fremeaux, the world is violent, and it wants to take you with it. Violence is the path of least resistance. It's easier to let a man drown than to save him. To save him is an effort of love. Love is work; violence is excess leisure. I do like the way you swim, young man."

She smiled and left me to stir her own pots.

Sal, the owner of the wine joint, walked over after she was gone.

"Fremeaux, the monsignor said he's seen more of you lately. Says you could be stalking him a little, maybe? If you was born with good sense, you'll opt out."

"My job is to watch and keep folks safe. The wrong person could come and do him harm, maybe. What objections could the Monsignor have on that?"

"Just so it ain't the other side of the coin."

"If it's the other side, then the monsignor needs to know he can't part the Mississippi."

Sal looked at me with street warning in his eyes as I stood to leave.

"Take it easy, Sal, it's all good, Paw Paw," I said and left him chewing on his cigar.

When my toes reached the curb's edge, Xandi flitted around the corner of Conti Street, passing out little baggies of voodoo paraphernalia to tourists.

"A couple of boys in blue hanging around corners keeping peepers on you." She said it in a quick, low voice and went to a group of tourists to spread her speech about black magic remedies.

Across Chartres, a street performer named Ms. Jou Jou stood at the top of the steps of the federal court building with a look of surprise and confusion, like she had just stumbled upon two mentally challenged teenagers in the middle of a motel pool fucking.

With her fiddle resting on her hip and using her bow to point at a drunken woman with a houndstooth-patterned skirt hiked above the waistline. The drunk lady was bent and pissing into Ms. Jou Jou's tip cup, and Ms. Jou Jou seemed to be asking with her eyes, *Is this shit even possible?*

The sight of the congealed skin on the hindquarter of the soiled wench gave me an idea to keep my unwelcome stalkers, and myself, occupied through the weekend's bullshit that's certainly on our horizon. I would spend the next four days filling drunk tanks with these *Southern Babbitts*. Paperwork alone could waste hours and keep the spies at bay.

The streets would be littered with visitors in Panama Jack T-shirts, pleather loafers, sans the socks, and Walkman headphones hugging clammy necks. If I'd seen one, I'd seen a thousand this time of year. Snotty, entitled parents *and* their offspring had everything they need to avoid civic duty. Let the masses deal with that kind of shit.

This would be easy pickings. They would get too drunk to dance and trample the toes of good and decent people, and I would just lock 'em up for the weekend. Scare the shit out of them down at the Parish prison.

Tressy had called it. It was gonna be a long, shitty weekend. The fringed-out Lucky-Dog vendors would, no doubt, be pissing in the bloated wiener baths, avenging themselves for the lousy social torment they'll endure.

Hopefully, the hard, steady work would mark some kind of parameter that my sanity can cling to. Then, I would see just what the hell happened after that.

CHAPTER TWELVE

"Everybody's in love with somethin', mister. Looks like you're in love with abuse, man," said the last redneck I cuffed, on the last hour of my last shift of the too goddamned long weekend. I watched blood stream down his chin from a gash on the side of his eye and busted lips, still feeling the throb in my fingers from the blows, as the doctor escorted him through the steel doors for X-rays and stitches.

"Slick, I'm sure that'll be the last time you try to shove your fingers up a lady's ass without permission. You weasel motherfucker." I looked at the doctor. "Make sure he understands it wouldn't be a good idea to return to my city anytime soon."

My nerves are shot to hell, but my paperwork is done. It feels like these last few nights have stretched through the other three hundred sixty-two days of a full fuckin' year, and I forgot to celebrate my holidays. I could feel my own people's eyes on me, waiting for me to make a move on their level. They'd love to pin something on one of their own. Crooked cops, is there anything more harmful?

"Help me, Gonzales, baby," I said to the heavens.

Halloween's among us, and all social fairies will fill our streets. This is our weekend. All locals spring alive for the macabre joy, smiles and reverie will return to the roost.

I wished to hell I could open my back door and Xandi could be there, naked and wanting. But I gotta catch up with Don Lee. Get back in the saddle. So, I drag my wilting ass towards Verdi Marte, with all I got left to give, for one of their overstuffed Andouille-egg and cheese biscuits, and any helpful information I can summon, using the least amount of brain cells.

I stepped into the loathsome teeth of an unusually bitter cold north wind. I shivered with a creeping delusion of reality, not too different from dozing off just as your subconscious delivers a latent near-death memory. Or maybe it wasn't a freak chill in the air. No one else seemed to be as affected. Xandi's gris gris must be fading. I don't feel her safety blanket right now.

I peek into the storefront window of Solano's Botanica, scanning the shelves of the black magic market as I walk by. In handwritten oversized red letters, a sign above the entrance reads.

Death is not finite like a period. It merges and verges through the dimensions of heaven and earth, timed with commas. Order and disorder are where the soul and the body dwell.

A pair of flat black eyes lingered on me from a dark, Mediterranean-looking dude sitting under dim fluorescent lights. He had an almost dead smile under a trimmed mustache that looked as though it had been glued in place. I could feel the dark stare of the Nzumbi follow me till I walked beyond view, and I created the eerie belief that I would never be free of that gaze, forever under mystic suspicion.

I remembered Xandi saying that voodoo gods were not dissimilar from catholic saints. Both desire the manipulation of the disorder in man. Voodoo says man is sacred and fluid here on earth as well as the great beyond. The dead are not dead. Spirits without bodies exist in heaven, hell, and earth at the same time. Constant energy flow carries us through all time.

The monsignor says God's voice created everything, and it is the only thing that commands forever. Marie Laveau says *you* command forever.

I feel the meaning of these obtrusive words every weekend through the streets of the Quarter. When the hive mind springs from higher, more polished energies, the women seem to smile more broadly. Especially when the collective is similar. Less chaos, I could assume. But men revel in chaos. Men grin like devils when a little turbulence is in the air. That's when the breasts heave and the bacchanal swells into a wild disbelief. Disbelief that sin could ever feel this good, and it's this kind of sin; the being allowed this kind of never-ending sin, that keeps our streets full. They're not in Kansas anymore.

I'm enjoying my momentary peaceful walk, so I cross the street to Tulane Avenue and continue toward the Quarter on foot, leaving the cruiser to rest in its concrete bay. This area of the city looks like the raunchy streets of New York from the camera lens of the seventies. Paper trash is blowing and floating in desolation. Dingy grey covers the canvas everywhere the eye wanders. Cracks seem to show off through the concrete and the aging storefronts. Telephone poles need vitamin shots. Electric wires droop from their cross ties as though a nation of vultures perch through the midnight hours, waiting for the decay to peel up.

This isn't a parade route, so it doesn't need vanity. Its source of value is in prisoner transport to and from Charity Hospital, and the easy access to interstates when someone needs hauling to Angola.

I step into Nick's Bar for an early morning shot of tequila to round out my edges; to put some wiggle back in my stride, so to speak. Ms. Dora is wiping down the bar and making coffee for the night workers who are about to punch the clock in search of an alcoholic's breakfast, just like me.

I take my tequila down as a commotion catches my eye through the front bay window. Four motorcycle cops pulled out into the middle of Tulane Avenue with lights flashing to halt traffic from both directions. A long black limo pulled onto the bleak, empty street from the back lot of the seedy motel across the street and quickly peeled in the direction of Broad, leading to the on-ramp for I-10 bound for Baton Rouge.

The windows were bulletproofed and blacked out. The black paint had recently been polished to government standards, making it look like a street torpedo determined to rewrite the time stamp, so it all adds up to the fake receipts hiding in a secret register somewhere. Nobody ever beats the clock; I guess they haven't figured that one out yet.

"Looks like something illicit took place over there last night," I stated flatly.

"The guv's son was in here thanking you boys in blue last night. You missed out. You musta been on duty, huh?" she said.

"Yeah, I worked it all weekend. I forgot about the big party. Or just got here a little late, I guess," I lied. I wasn't given the news of the stuff.

"Yeah, they had four of them streetwalkers in the bathrooms all night givin' out special awards, if ya hear what I'm sayin'. You shoulda come down and got yours, too, sweetie. All y'all deserve some special treatment for what y'all gotta see every day."

Well, I'll just be damned, I thought. The *guv* brings prostitutes into a cop's bar and everybody gets greased up for the coming holidays.

Two years ago, I met the governor—well, he hadn't been voted governor then. He had just hatched the idea of running and was kicking off his announcement. Leda had brought me on board for the security detail that night. They were fundraising. I had only worked on three or four projects for her and didn't know too much about her social prowess back then.

Fifty or so of the city's elite gathered on the posh rooftop condo of the Royal Orleans Hotel. It has its own private rooftop pool and patio the size of my house. I was all alone on this detail.

I escorted the guests from the street to the roof. The incumbent, Harold Heralds, arrived last with his then-wife, Tiff. She looked like she was a quarter his age. French doors opened onto the outdoor scene on the cool marble floors as he held up a bottle of champagne, using a sailor's rendition of a Shakespearean war chant to stir the pot.

"Crack the bottle, shall we not partake?

Stroke us well, shall we not ejaculate?

So, let us slit the dogs of merriment. Nudity shall be our coats of armor tonight."

As the ladies began to undo the top buttons, Senator Halby, from my district up in Mason City, raised his glass for a toast.

"Here's to our future king. Do you folks know why he tours hospitals when he is out politicking? He likes scullin' the infant wards looking for his next wife." Laughs lifted spirits as Leda escorted me to stand outside the front door.

"Fremeaux, this is where you will earn your money tonight. No one is to enter. Not even the police chief."

The only sound I heard after that was a crazed fella failing his shot at cunnilingus just on the other side of the door I was guarding.

Five hours later, Leda opened the door and asked me to leave. The last thing these folks wanted to peer at was an image of upright behavior. So, I nodded and left, asking myself what's her part in all this. More soul purchasing? She didn't look coked out, and her clothes seemed to have remained on her body through the debauchery. But then again, she can be a great actress.

It was none of my business, but the sighting of an official black limo leaving a seedy motel had certainly piqued my interest. Whoever took pleasure in these toilets last night is the very ones clutching me by the collar, directing me to the blind side of the law.

"Cheap blow jobs," I muttered.

"Did Don Lee stop in last night by chance?" I asked Mrs. Dora, hoping for eyewitnesses.

"No, babe, he didn't. He was in one night last week sometime. Drinkin'nem pregnant canaries and cuttin' up wit da boys, ya know."

I knew. I could see it all too well.

"Can I get one more tequila before I go to sleep for two days?"

"Yeah babe. These are on the house for missin' out last night. I'll put em' on the governor's tab." She poured a triple.

"You *look* like you need a rest up, kid."

I pulled the tequila down and spotted the thick fella that had come through the church the other day looking to confess something. He lurked from behind the same wall where the limo had just made its getaway, wearing the same dark grey clothes as the first time I had laid eyes on him. I set my empty glass down, thanked Ms. Dora, and hustled out the door just in time to catch him hopping a cab. There goes my pregnant canary, I thought.

I continued across the street into the parking lot of the motel to have a look. All I found were empty whiskey pints, used condoms, and the feeling that more than a handful of dreams had fallen off track back here. I retraced, setting back on track for Verdi Marte.

Turning the corner at Marti's restaurant, I headed into the Quarter. I walk towards Chicken Man, another voodoo dispeller, prescribing mystic brews to a short, balding fella for getting his lost girlfriend to rediscover him sexually.

"You gotta get ya-self' one a dem red candles for fixin' broke hearts. Fetch a pair a her panties and tie 'em together with a pair a your underwear, and wrap 'em around that candle. You take a clipping of her hair and some of yo hair and burn it right in the flame. Let that candle burn all night with them underwears, and within the week you'll be ready to knock on her door again."

"Where do I get a pair of her panties from? She won't let me near her."

"That's your problem, I can't help with that, but if you get caught stealin' em, the spell ain't gone work no matter what you do."

Chicken Man used to work the nightclub circuit performing a black magic act, portraying a man dancing with the spirits and biting the heads off live chickens. Once the PETA folks got wind of the cruelty to poultry, he lost his performance privileges, so he now walks with a large tree limb cane, selling spirit dolls and spooky advice. Sometimes a man can simply swerve a little too far, clashing with the other half.

I turned and headed to the corner for the Verdi Marte. The heroin kids had all piled together in a doorway across the street, scamming cash from tourists. I could hear irritability in their voices. Must've been getting desperate for a high. They were dirty and smelled of rotten feet. Not even Martha Gellhorn could feel pity for these self-made assholes.

I see a new girl hanging with them. Her clothes are clean and not time-torn just yet. I'll keep her face in my memory just in case her photograph appears on our poles. Half of Nate's face is swollen and bruised. I could feel a death stare. Something's got the nest hostile.

David looked me in the eye and winked. Put my sandwich and a sticker in a bag.

"Stay safe out there, my baby," he said to me. Keeping the talk generic, as two strangers had walked in behind me and stood at the beer cooler.

"I intend to."

When I got back to the sidewalk, Nate was in the middle of a come apart as a couple of tourists crossed the street to avoid any interaction with the street moles. He looked over at me and seemed to be fueled by the sight of me. Not sure if my questioning about the monsignor business cut his money flow, but the little shitbag had obviously formed a grudge.

He strutted over to the community board next to the entrance of The Verdi Marte, where posters of the lost loved ones hung, and spit the slimiest, nastiest snot-filled loogie on the image of Becca and the others.

"Fuck a bunch of stupid bitches." He scowled and threw a cup of soda at me.

Can't say if it was the tequila, lack of sleep, dormant anger and anxiety, probably a stew of it all, but the blood of a thousand billy goats rushed to my head. I could feel heat radiate inside me. My sight blurred, and the disdain of it all overtook me. I let loose of my sandwich, grabbed the boy's head—I say *boy*, but he's big enough to play middle linebacker for his dad—and dragged him to the ground. Before I could regain any awareness, my thumb was deep in his eye socket. I caught sight of a twisted pupil and spurting blood.

Spittle flew from my face as I felt powerful hands dragging me backward to the ground. I investigated the faces of two officers and then looked across at Nate. He didn't look too good. I must've gotten a couple of good, hard punches in before taking him to the ground, and blood was leaking from an ear as well as the eye socket. I felt shame for a second; then I recalled what I suspected was his involvement in the disappearances. I watched him wriggle in pain, thinking about Becca losing her body parts.

I sat in a slight daze for a few minutes, not listening to anyone. I'm sure there was screaming somewhere at some point, but all I heard was my mother's voice telling me to get ready for bed. Officers Walton and Johnson walked to the other side of the block and let me know the captain was on his way. I wasn't to leave the scene.

I walked across the street and picked up my sandwich that had landed against the wall of Verdi Marte. I opened the bag, and the smiley face had the bullet between the eyes. The ambulance came and whisked Nate off to Charity Hospital and Captain Barlow finally arrived. We took a walk.

"Fremeaux, what seems to have happened here?"

"Lost my temper, I guess."

"Word around is you had some interaction with the kid last week? A conference of sorts, in the streets?"

"I had some questions about a drug buy."

"How does that involve the Monsignor?" he asked bluntly.

"I don't know. I thought I saw the Monsignor and the kid having some time on the street, just wanted to cross my T's, I guess."

"Cross your T's? What exactly does that mean?"

"Just that. I wasn't sure why the two would be talking, and Nate went immediately to buy drugs."

"Maybe the monsignor's lecture caused the boy more insecurities. Maybe Nate can't handle the pressures of responsibility. Afraid to accept the social constraints his father places on him. You know the Monsignor cares about these lost young men."

"Could be, Captain. I didn't think of it that way." I made sure to leave out the fact that I had witnessed the exchange of money.

"Sounds like you're still looking for phantom hands. Due to the level of violent retaliation in a non-crime-related act, not to mention the booze on your breath, I'm gonna hafta ask for your badge and gun. You're on a week's suspension until an investigation can be conducted. You know the kid's dad has some inside pull on this, don't ya?"

"I remember."

The kid's dad ain't got that kind of pull. Captain Barlow is pulling low-hanging fruit to conceal the real faces behind my demise. I'd sure as hell like to have my Catholic rights just about now.

"Besides, you look as though you could use some time off. What's got you so worked up anyway, Fremeaux?" he asked wryly. As if he were hoping to lead me to some kind of confession.

"Just this Leda attack. The asshole who did it was discharged from the hospital and is MIA. Could come back around and try again," I stated. Making sure I kept my responses from leading into Becca's case. The last thing I need are dirty cops suspecting I'm on the hunt for what they may be covering up.

"Leda's out of the country right now, so I think you could have relaxed. The Monsignor doesn't have anything to do with Leda's attack, so I think it's wise to leave him be."

The captain gave me a hard, inquisitive stare. I could see he believed I was concealing something.

I gave him my badge and gun and raised my head toward heaven, "I didn't need *this* kind of help, Gonzales."

I walked to my precinct, changed into civilian clothes, locked my locker, and pointed my Hush Puppies toward the Alibi for more tequila. The overnight strippers would be coming in after the long night shifts, giving me cheek kisses and hugs, and I could use a spiritual boost. I provided escorts for them to and from work when the Quarter spirits become dark. Or when they asked, I'd make sure I was there for them. In turn, as I need a good picking up, I'm not ashamed to stop in for overdue adoration and free drinks.

I got to the bar, and a lady with glistening skin gave me the soft eye and smiled, but her man was not far away, so I averted my eyes and ordered a full glass of tequila. The girls slowly trickled in as my high sprouted wings.

The dice had been rolled, but the dark eyes of the strange man at the mojo market must have glued my fate to the bottom side of the coin.

"I'm gonna hold on tight and let them good times roll," I told Casper, the bartender. He smiled and poured another.

CHAPTER THIRTEEN

I sprang awake to the tinny-tink of cheap metal tapping into thin, brittle ceramic tile. I raised a sore head up and over toward the closed, battered door of what I figured to be a dingy bathroom in a dingy motel. I rubbed my eyes hard and wondered how I got myself to this mystery hole.

My clothes were neatly hanging on the back of a chair in front of a small desk with two thin drawers for whatever street nomads needed storing. The smell of a freshly lit cigarette stifled the air inside the brown room, and I hurt from head to toe, from spirit to skin. I could not immediately recall much of what may have taken place after the Alibi; time will have to unfold on this one. I did remember walking out and looking into the faces multiplying on Bourbon Street. I turned the other way and scampered toward The Bombay Club. That's where my recollection breaks.

"Shit, Fremeaux, you can't run from demons this fuckin' hard," I scolded myself.

I wondered who or what is tidying up in the dingy bathroom with me right this minute. I could only pray for Xandi to walk out, but she didn't smoke cigarettes. The occasional cigar or joint, maybe, but never a cigarette, and apparently, she didn't waste time on protecting me from embarrassment.

I'm stumped and anxious. Possibly a stripper, but I'm pretty sure I walked out of the Alibi alone. A hand roughly grabbed at the loose door-knob, and out walked a thick Black woman with curves and folds and a little girl's mirth.

"Well, ya ass finally up, huh?"

"If you wanna call it that. I'm up from the count."

"I thought you was gonna wake up alone and not get to meet me. I was about to leave ya ass up in here all guessin and shit."

"Did we have fun?"

"We didn't do shit. You had too much booze trampin' through ya. We slapped. We tickled and sucked to no use. Hell, you even tried jumpin' on the bed. Yo, snake just wasn't gonna strike for nothin'. Hell, he was on strike." She laughed.

"Where'd we meet? Where did I acquire your services?" I asked.

"Services, hell, you needed *something* before you got locked up. Your butt was on fire, and yes, cops can get arrested too. The sun had just gone down, and you was already floatin', big boy. Ms. Dora asked me to get you out of Nick's before you pissed somebody off. She handed me a bottle and your hand. The younger cops acquired my services for you. I brought ya lil white butt over here."

"You telling me that Nick's bar is just across the street?"

"Just right over there, baby."

"I was just in this parking lot. I watched some shady shit go down here this morning."

"Yesterday morning," she reminded me. "I'm gonna need you to get dressed. You gonna get me a cab so I can go catch my kids."

"What's your name?" I asked.

"Nunya business. Now it's time to go."

I looked at her. Plump cheeks propped up eyes that were saying, *C'mon, fuck with me, mister*. Her business was being laid down. Playtime was over.

"Sure thing, Missie," I replied and started a wonky-wobbled dressing routine.

"Did any of those cops last night approach you to solicit whatever information I may have spewed?"

"There were just a couple of cops left. They had all walked out by the time you were getting riled up. Ms. Dora said some other people would be coming later and didn't think they'd want to hear your shit."

"What the hell does that mean?"

"Fuck, Paw Paw, I don't know. Sounds like somebody on the force might just have it in for your ass."

"Did I say anything incriminating?" I asked.

"No, you just yakked about some girl named Becca and wished your dad were here to help you figure some things out. Said he left your mother sad."

"That's all?"

"Lotta rambling about freeloaders, hit men, missing women, and shit. Mostly nonsense. You just got suspended for kickin' some punk's ass, and we could see you was pissed. Can we go now? I gotta get responsible again."

"Yeah, let's get outta here," I said, opening the thin metal door. We stepped out onto the wobbly balcony and into the hot sunshine.

"Oh shit," she said, looking over the balcony and hiding her face. I looked down into the parking lot just in time to see the picture snap.

"Fuck me," I said.

I reached down and grabbed a small clay pot being used as an ashtray and gave it my best heave in my condition. I pinged the fella and we heard the heavy thud as it whacked the ankle bone. He yelped and hobbled around the corner out of sight.

"Looks like you got yaself a fan club, Fremeaux."

"Someone's trying to taint my reputation."

"If that's all you got to worry about in this town, Paw Paw, you doin' better'n most. Reputations be like sands through the hourglass, honey, you can always flip and restart."

I heard the car door slam on the other side of the motel as the mystery man peeled off, gone before I reached the stairwell of the upper balcony.

I put Nunya Business in a cab, finished dressing, and walked across the North Broad Street bridge to the specified payphone in the back of Buddy's po-boy joint, and dialed Don Lee in Mississippi. The accent of his Hispanic housekeeper answered.

"Sorry, you miss him, but Don Lee leave earlier this morning. He say he wants you to meet him in Slidell this afternoon. He will be at a place called the Chicken Drop by four today. It's in The Rigolets. He also giggled at your situation this earlier this morning. He say you finally got your pants down."

It was unsettling to know Don Lee had gotten word of my morning unease so quickly, but I would surmise the fucker worked for the Picayune and got tipped by one of my teammates. I was glad to know I gave him a chuckle, but it didn't offer any ease from the debacle. I began to wonder if I should take up smoking too.

"Did he say anything else?"

"If you need escaping, you can go to Calamari Upholsteries on South Carrolton and ask for Mrs. Henry. The Frogman has informed her to take you anywhere you need to go."

"I can make that happen," I told her, and walked outside to catch a cab to find Wanda Ball. It was early enough that she was either in the middle of a Sunday morning come-down or readying for a brunch somewhere. Either way, I figured I'd be able to catch her in the process of something. She'd still be puttering around her place, and I knew where that place is. She was Officer Gonzalez's landlady. I know, I know. A cop paying rent to a woman of ill repute. Can't make the shit up.

Her double camelback sits in the middle of a row of six on Hillary Street down in the Black Pearl neighborhood, a stone's throw from the river *and* the railroad tracks. Periwinkle blue with red shutters.

Not far from her sits a small cottage where Mahalia Jackson had been reared. Back when the poor folks wasted their health on homemade corn liquor and penetrating gospels. Down where the yellowed, hot-wet weather settles in the bend of the river and pulls at the paint jobs like itchy, heat-rash skin. A place tucked just out of the way that law-unabiding crews could catch some refuge from time to time. Lore has it that a one-legged hit man slept in most of the beds down there through the sixties and seventies before disappearing forever, leaving behind only an imaginary shadow stuck in the corners of idle minds.

Wanda Ball's eyes were a shade of green I've never wandered into. Out at the very edges of emerald, metallic shimmers mesmerized you, almost as if she carefully inlayed flecks of gold and silver just before applying eye shadow. The glimmer could spark unexpected delights.

"I hear it all the time, Fremeaux. Mostly when someone is handing me a wad of cash, and I'm certain you didn't come here to tell me my eyes are pretty. Wha'tcha ya looking for, Slick?"

"Need help, baby."

She looked amused. "We all do. Spit it out, kid."

I felt I should start the conversation with a sense of honor.

"If I tread on a subject that infringes on your safety in any way, it's your right to send me on my way." I watched her eyes as she stood in front of me, comfortably but still ready to call bullshit. "I need help finding who may be stealing young women from our streets."

"Okay." Her expression merged into a mix of concern and mystery.

"Without confessing a point of reference, I've been sent to ask about the Impastata Brothers. What can you tell me about them, and how could they possibly lead me anywhere?"

"Come on in."

We went to her kitchen, sat at the table. She ran her fingers through that tangly hair, vexed.

"When we were kids, the twins lived down here in the skid marks with me. They work the bar down at Magine's now. Both are deaf and mute, so they work off handwritten notes and sign language. They don't have anything to tell on those missing girls, Fremeaux. What else?"

I could see the boys meant a lot to her. If I hadn't connected with Officer Gonzales, I wouldn't get anywhere with this conversation. She put her trust in Gonzales and I hope she'll soften with me.

"Grew up together, did ya?

"Brothers I never knew I needed."

"Stay in touch?"

"We gather as often as we can grab the time. They work hard to keep the prestige at the joint. Know how to play *give and take* with the jet setters. So, not much free time for them. Hell, you know my schedule, I can hang anywhere, anytime."

I could feel she was stretching out feeble news, hoping I don't ask hard questions.

"Why would someone send me to inquire on them? Seems harmless?"

"They're in the know to what certain people are up to."

"Are they connected?" I asked.

"It is fairly known under the table that they're illegitimate children from an affair Marcello had back in the day. Mr. Impastata adopted them when Marcello gave him the restaurant. Be aware that whoever develops a problem with the ordered system is encouraged not to return, if you know what I mean. You smell like you've been up all night, Fremeaux. Looks like you could use some food?"

She went to the fridge, grabbed us some hog cheese, mustard, and pickles, and turned the oven on to toast the French bread.

"I've never been inside Magine's. I've heard it's on the swanky side?" I said.

"It's not stuffy, but it does feel like old money. Penny tile floors and mahogany. Well-dressed energy. Folks I don't hang with, beyond closed doors and cash transfers."

"This is good hog head cheese. Where'd ya get it?"

"Dorignac's. A man makes it down in LaRose and brings it up twice a week."

I nodded in appreciation to the Cajun palette.

"Ya know, Leda was almost killed recently?" I told her.

"What? What happened?"

"Somebody put a job on her. Fella from the Dixie Mafia drove over and tried to take her out. I happened to be trailing her home, and the fucker attacked in a dark corner of the Quarter."

"Holy crap, who'd pull such nonsense?"

"Don't know just yet. Golda has the shooter and old man Gilleach stuffed in somewhere."

"How is Leda?"

"Still walking like the clouds are her shoes. I know she and Golda frequent Magine's. Do you think there is any kind of connection there? I can't for the life of me figure who could be so bold and stupid as to go after them."

"Ms. Golda has been good to me, Fremeaux. When I do a job for them, they reward extremely well. I have clients who have been treated well, too. Lives resting in the cradle of the gods. While others are left to dangle like drying meat, drooling like unforgiving hyenas. She's made herself a few enemies, too."

"Yeah, but these folks know the consequences. Wanda, you of all people know that. There's gotta be something else. Something bigger I can't see. I miss Gonzales, I sure as hell could use her right now."

Wanda reached and took my hand. I felt something loosen with her.

"There *is* always something bigger at work. Hell, that's the whole fucking basis of the banking system. And hell, Theosophy for that matter too. Bigger, invisible truths stir the big pot of life, baby."

She went to the cupboard a pulled down a bottle of tequila. Took two shots.

"The word is that Golda's family is making some kind of shift and looking to rearrange her power and standing. Their trip abroad has to do with putting an end to or beginning something beyond my scope of knowledge. That's all I know. It may or may not be true, but dat's the rumor."

"How could two deaf bartenders walk off with such inside information on Golda?"

We sat in silence and sunlight for a couple of long minutes.

"Is there something I'm missing here, Wanda?"

"Fremeaux, there are only about five or six of us who know the twins' secrets."

We sat again. She tapped the floor with her foot. I shifted.

"You know you want me to know what I need to know. It will never leave this table. You're trying to figure out how to say it. Just put it out there. I can put it in my pipe and smoke it," I said.

"The boys made a mistake one evening, and Golda and Leda noticed the fail immediately. It was early. Golda and Leda were alone at the bar, talking amongst themselves, and Leda mentioned to her mother she was in the mood for a French 75. Without making a written order, and only her face was in their view. In that very moment of preoccupation, a French 75 was placed on a napkin in front of Leda. At first, they continued talking, and the boys looked at one another, knowing they'd just fucked up. A moment passed, and relieved thoughts of the defective move possibly going unnoticed began to take root when suddenly, Leda took her second sip and looked at Golda. The boys knew instantly. Golda, without voice, miming with her lips, *You two can read lips, can't you?* They'd been caught.

"What's the big deal? Lots of people can read lips."

"Only five or six of us know this. Golda seized the opportunity and bought full rights. Within the week, she bought a house and two cars. The boys live rent-free out in Algiers. She has them stashed way out across the bridge. Away from the hullabaloo so no one else can approach after hours."

"What does that mean, bought the rights?"

"The boys record every important conversation that takes place in the joint. Nothing gets past them. They are constantly jotting it all down throughout the night, unbeknownst to the power set. Golda is privy to who is doing what at any given time. And the boys transfer the gossip and rumors that their compatriots create about them. She has edged herself to the top of the cream pot. Golda will cut a man's throat to keep her boys a secret, ya hear?"

"I gotcha, sweetheart. Where do these writings go?"

"Leda picks them up Sunday nights."

"Do they tell her everything?" I asked.

"Any and everything that places her at an advantage. If the government or a tycoon is going to remove one of its own, she isn't interested unless this person has valuable property. Stuff like that."

"A fuckin' information highway."

"Yes, a fuckin' pipeline on their rivals, Fremeaux. Now you are in on it," she said.

"Have you been involved?"

"I've used it from time to time. The boys tell me who to make a loan from, knowing it won't need to be paid back."

"That's accessory after the fact, Wanda."

"Live by the sword, die by the sword, Fremeaux. If you kick the hornet's nest, that's your business. I'm not gonna go tell every bully's mama her baby boy's about to get in over his head. That's her business."

"Have you ever heard anything on the subject of kidnapping and sex trafficking? One of the boys last seen with one of the missing girls was running cash deposits for the Dixie Mafia. I'm still trying to tie all this shit together."

"No," she said. "That's subject matter that is most likely spread in warehouses."

"Can you keep your ears open for anything that could help me?"

"I can. I'm happy to help catch whatever could cause harm to Leda. If I hear any Dixie Mafia news I'll be glad to share. But, you know as well as I do, they're tight-lipped."

"I know, babe, but ya never know who may be pissed about their situation. You should also be aware, Wanda, that in the next day or so, a photograph of me leaving a hotel with a part-time hooker will appear in the Picayune, so don't be alarmed. I'm being made the face of police misdoings."

"What the hell is this all about, Fremeaux?"

"I got suspended for kicking some white trash ass because someone doesn't want me looking into these missing girls. Tarnishing my image may put the muzzle on me, or so they hope. Guilt is flowing through the department, and it belongs there."

"Set up with a cheap street whore, huh? You fuckin' asshole. Why didn't you just call me? I would have treated you much better than that."

"I'll keep you at the top of the list for next time."

She scrubbed the top of my scalp with her nails. I looked up into her face for a minute.

"So, tell me, how *does* a one-legged fella become a successful hit man?" I asked.

"Good balance, I'd guess."

"So, he's real?"

"Babysat me a few times back in the day. He's very patient. Good friend to me. Mama and I miss him."

"Teach you how to use a gun?" I asked.

"I can pull the trigger when the devil puts me on that spot."

"Is he still around?"

"Can't say. He doesn't touch little girls, so he's of no concern for you today."

"He may have the inside scoop on the guy going after Leda."

"He's retired somewhere now, but if I can reach him, I'll ask," she said, protecting an old friend whom she suspected was innocent in this matter.

"The memory of a good friend never dies," I said.

"Yes, and tears of lost love linger till death, too." She smiled, and I did the same. We fell into a contented silence, eating hog's head cheese together.

"Crooked cops are pushing *my* buttons now. My affiliation with Gonzalez has them scrutinizing me with snapper eyes," I said.

"You're also in cahoots with Don Lee. Don Lee hasn't held his tongue on their lack of interest in helping him find his culprit or culprits. Honey, right now you're caught up in swirling water headed for the drain. But for some odd reason, you have Golda and Leda in your corner."

"I can't seem to figure that myself."

"Golda is her own gatekeeper, so she obviously has an idea of your value to her. Trust me, she has some kind of plan in motion out there."

"Leda mentioned a while back that Golda's true love was here. What the hell does that mean?" I asked.

"I don't know anything on that, but if Golda wants to pet you like a kitty, then buddy, it will behoove you to learn how to purr."

"I gotta meet Don Lee in Slidell at three," I said. "Are you in a spot where you can drive me?"

"Sure, I'd like to catch up with Don Lee. It's been a minute since we've had time together. You ready to go now?"

"Hell, I'm suspended till I get a new clue."

"You just found one: the twins and me."

"You know Wanda? You dig deep. Deep down through this Louisiana sludge. Down to where the clean water runs and runs clear. You soon realize we got the only water in the whole world that's loaded with the cholesterol."

"We gotta drink the water all the same. Let's take a ride, buddy, and see what we see," she said, grabbing some things. Wanda Ball was always ready for a new adventure.

CHAPTER FOURTEEN

The Chicken Drop's a hell of a sight. A shit hole on the lake. Crab traps everywhere. Chickens in pens, for what I assume is for baiting gators and poor women.

High on a wall above the decrepit bar hung a very large framed black and white photograph of a thick group of men squeezed tightly around a square table. They appeared to be shouting at one of these contorted chickens. Fists full of cash surrounded the pestered bird. One of the faces I recognized was ex-governor Uncle Earl K. Long. After inquiry, I learned that the table supporting the flapping chicken had a square grid drawn upon its top. The bartender drew his finger from the photo above to the very table, as it stood twelve feet from where we sat at the bar.

"You buy as many squares as you want, and the hope is the chicken shits on *your* square. If she does, you get the bounty for that round," the chubby barman explained.

"So that's what that picture tells me. Grown men terrifying a fuckin' chicken until it craps? I'll just be goddamned." I said in disbelief. I looked around. "So that's what I smell. Decaying fish and chicken shit."

"Gotta make it through this old life somehow, Paw Paw. Why not have a little fun makin' it?" He chuckled.

"How do ya know when they gotta shit?" Wanda asked.

"We overfeed 'em an hour or so before the crowd shows."

"You've got 'em figured, do ya?"

"Look closely at the picture up there. It was taken back in—oh, I'd say forty-eight. We've been scarin' the shit outta chickens for ova forty years. Uncle Earl's brother used to come and poly-tik with us. Governor Long spoke better from the top of a crab crate than behind the podium, any day. Huey had nuthin' to hide. Hell, even an old bull crawfish would walk out the bayou and vote for the man knowing all along he would be the night's dinner."

We sifted through the faces in the black-and-white shadows, wading through lost time and lost secrets.

Up there in frozen time, the empty old tabletop I was just introduced to is filled with life and a chicken forever captured in mid-squawk. On closer look, it captured number two in mid-fall, and all eyes were in search of its landing.

The barstool I was sitting on was built to anchor down trailer park dreams, and by the looks of it, the joint hadn't been through any evolutionary phases, but surprisingly, everyone in the picture was dressed like they were at the Ritz ballroom. Suits and ties. Silken dresses, polished leather shoes, and handbags. Coiffed hair. Uncle Earl is the only one in a J.C. Penney suit and tie. Wearing an aged and crumpled fedora. Head down in the foreground. Cigarette held loosely in his lips. Wrinkled eyes searching for chicken shit, clearly, the prime subject for the photographer.

"What gives?" I asked Wanda.

"Whatcha mean, what gives?"

I explained what I saw. She caught on to the class difference between the here and now and the high class around the table of chickenshit.

"Oh, look how the ladies are all so pretty. And the men are just looking *so suave.* The nightlife was polished back then. Taken in with lots of care. And respect."

Then I saw her up there. I see her time-stamped face just this side of the doorway, in the far background, and I could see her from my barstool. She was looking into the face of a man whose face couldn't be seen. Just the back of his head and body. It's Leda. *Leda?* I questioned my sanity.

"Do you see what I see?" I asked Wanda.

"What do you see?" Wanda answers my question with a question.

"I see Leda."

"What? You've got it worse than I thought." She smirked.

"Look, she's standing just on this side of that doorway. In the far background." I point to the door we just came through and then to its doppelganger in the photograph.

"Oh my God. That's Ms. Golda. Look how beautiful she is up there. My goodness, she *does* look just like Leda. Holy shit, Fremeaux. This means Golda arrived in New Orleans much earlier than thought. Her thick accent has led me to believe she's maybe been in the country just a few years. I can't get over how utterly beautiful she is up there. And still is at her age. Hell, man, I'm attracted to her," Wanda said.

I can't help but stare. I'm a little shocked at this little discovery.

"Is that allegiance and maybe something else in her eyes? Have you ever seen her freely give her allegiance to anybody? Is she capable of it outside her agenda?" I ask, knowing an answer will not come.

"I have never seen her smile like that. She is smitten with whoever that fella is."

"Look, who's the older gentleman talking to him and her? I've seen that face before. Who is that?"

The scruffy bartender pointed at the scene.

"That's Mr. Marcello before he was a Mister. When he was just Carlos, in charge of the streets. His Uncle Frank would pass just a few days after this picture was taken. Making Mr. Marcello the Boss."

Wanda and I looked at one another. We raised our eyebrows at the implications.

"Golda was present at the founding of the Boss. In the inner circle, Fremeaux?" she chimed.

The bartender interjected, "Oh, shit. You Fremeaux? Hell, I shoulda put da two and two together. Sometimes it takes me some hints to figure stuff. You sposed to be waitin' for Don Lee, right?"

"Yeah, we're here to meet him. Why?"

"He was here but got a call from his foreign lady in Mississippi. Somebody had tried to commit suicide somewheres; it shook him. He left a note for you and this manila folder."

"How long ago did he leave?"

"Hour or so."

"Is he a regular out here?" Wanda asked.

"He knows my father. Dad would take Don Lee to meet and interview folks out in the bayou before Dad moved out to Vegas to run nightclubs for the Italians with Mr. Segrato. So, to answer your question, ole Don Lee does stop in to give regards now and then. He usually drinks too much and passes out in the family trailer just down the bay."

I opened and read the note.

> *First, my apologies once again, sir. I wish I didn't feel bad about standing you up like this, but you see, Becca's mother has tried taking her own life. She may or may not make it through the night, and I'm certain I must make a house call. This has shaken me deeply.*
>
> *You were right about the two gentlemen: no trace of identity in the system. The hoodlum was just as you presumed. Criminal records in Florida and Alabama. His name, brace yourself, is Bobby Dale Vice, and he is attached to a trailer and a wife in Vernon, Florida. A town just north of Pensacola. Her name and address are inside this envelope with other documents.*
>
> *The story about you will run in two days, so be ready. I will be writing the story, and I have a plan. I am going to call you at 11 in the morning at Leda's, so be there to answer. I have a doozy of a plan of attack, I'll explain then. We will be turning this rotten egg into a golden goose, I pray. Also, I pulled an I owe you from Leda, and inside the envelope is my key to her Pontalba apartment. She more than agreed that you're going to need a safe house. If you can, try and go into your house and escape out the back. Lead people to believe you are holding up in your house through the shit storm.*
>
> PS *Get ready, we're about to go for a bumpy ride. You have my best, talk tomorrow. Don Lee.*

"You ever been to Vernon, Florida?" I asked Wanda.

"Don't cross state lines too often."

I sighed and looked up at the picture again. "Do you think that could be Leda's father?" I mumbled, not expecting a reply.

"Never can tell. Her eyes do tell a story, though. No one has ever mentioned who could have fathered Leda. But there are whispers as to where that person may be. Possible he's six feet under."

"Jesus," I said.

"Amen, brother."

I turned to Wanda. Despite her rugged street façade—her slightly pocked face and thick tangled hair—she really was quite cute if a fella took the time to look for it.

"So, she put her hooks in the Impastata boys, huh?"

"She's nobody's fool, Fremeaux. She reads the moment and knows when to unsnap the pocketbook or unsnap the holster, for that matter."

The bartender finally meandered out of earshot, and Wanda took the slot to inquire.

"Since you have come to me for offshoot knowledge, I'm guessing the puzzle lacks detail. Do you have a smoking gun at least?"

She knew how to phrase. Watching me closely, she wanted to know if I would betray the case or lie to her confidence. Wanda is as streetwise as anything I have ever seen. I stared into those jeweled pupils and made a long pause.

"Yes," I admitted. "But it isn't anything that I am ready to expose to anyone else as of yet. I don't want to look foolish too soon."

She looked back coolly. I didn't let her down, but I didn't include her fully. She became okay with my decision.

"Did Gonzalez confide anything with you?" I asked.

"Not too deep. She said she didn't want to endanger me either. She confessed that whatever was creeping around was hiding in a deep, dark tunnel of legitimacy. She also felt that Golda and Leda are a much larger presence than most know."

"So, Gonzalez wasn't in the same position as me?" I asked.

"Not at all. You have found yourself in a place where very few find themselves. The cops wanted her gone, like you now, but Leda kept Gonzales at arm's length, even though she and Don Lee were working closely together. Seems like you're being groomed for something, mister man."

The word *groom* wiggled around my mind. I hadn't considered that; I guess it was due to Don Lee being in the equation.

"Remember," she continued. "Gonzales was removed for what you're looking for, and you're still walking the streets."

"Well, my badge has just been removed, and the cops have no idea I'm still searching for the culprit of the missing girls. They mostly think I'm interested in busting the Monsignor and homeless drug abuse, and yes, I am aware that most of them are crooked. I'm not gonna overspend my trust."

"I know you know your limits. You must keep it that way." She paused and looked closer at me. Almost inspecting my principal.

"Do you have access to or a copy of that video of me seducing that politician in the back of Leda's limo?"

"Safe deposit box downtown."

"Jesus."

"Amen, sister."

"You gonna let *me* have access if I need it someday?" she asked with a bully's tone.

"Just ask, and I'll be there with it, sister girl."

"I appreciate that. I will get you to the boys soon. I'll see what they may know and send you in."

"Thanks, lady. You wanna drive me to Pensacola? Just to put a bead on a lead?" I asked.

"No, sir buddy. You need sleep. Your eyes look near dead, and you'll fuck up your inquiry. Your exhaustion could scare a nurse right now. Halloween is coming, and if there are children involved in this marriage in Florida, the mother will be preoccupied, and you'll end up on a dead-end street with her. Besides, my mother needs my help with her business."

"What's her business?"

"Cat house, of course."

"Jesus," I said.

"Amen, brother. C'mon, I'll take you wherever you want to go in the city. I have something that will knock your ass out. You're going to need all the energy you can muster when that picture of you goes public. Also, I think your little lady over in Florida will be more likely to talk with another female, alone. I'd be willing to help you with that, if you want."

"Do you have something in mind?"

"I figure she doesn't know her deadbeat husband is no longer among the living or even missing for that matter. I'll approach as though my husband is missing, too. That our husbands were acquaintances, and we owed the kid some money. Make her feel I'm obligated to give the money to her. Make her think I believe they're both dead. Push the idea that I'm concerned with her getting by as well. That we're sisters of misfortune kind of shit. A wad of cash and a bucket of sympathy ought to get a name or two."

Wanda agreed to run me by my house to grab a few things and slip out the back like Don Lee suggested, which I thought was a solid strategy. We had the windows down while driving Esplanade, and the fall winds coming off the Pontchartrain smelled fresh and salty like the inside of an oyster shell. The slight chill in the wind carried me back to running the country roads in high school again. I caught myself reaching for the imaginary bottle of beer that was supposed to be between my legs. I looked at Wanda's profile and for a moment felt we were about to park down by the water and screw like heathens. I snapped back to reality at the sight of the six live oaks standing guard at the head of my street. We took the right into my neighborhood, then the fast, sharp left around the curve, doing a quick California roll through the stop sign. Out of nowhere, the blue lights were in my side mirror.

"Looks like we caught an asshole. I wonder where they were hiding?" She said.

"Don't stop here. Go ahead and pull into my driveway."

She looked over at me, "I can do that? Just keep driving?"

"Yeah, it's the third stop sign down, and besides, he needs to be fucked with a little. When we stop, meet him at the back of your car, I want to hear if he mentions my name without seeing me."

"You know every cop in this city knows me and what I do, right?" she said.

"I'm aware. Let's see what their motivation is: a traffic ticket or surveillance."

I rolled down my window as she closed her door.

"Well, I'll be damned. Ms. Golden Crotch herself. Wanda, whatcha doin' cruisin' in this neighborhood? Dropping off a john or an ex-cop that might like it dirty?"

That motherfucker, I thought.

"Officer Clintern, if you're giving me a ticket for rolling through a stop sign, then let's get it done. You know as well as I do what's in my car is none of your business."

"Sure thing, honey." I heard him taking steps toward me. "Fremeaux, Fremeaux, Fremeaux, I see you're not wearing a seatbelt."

I heard him smirk as he walked the long way around the front of the car to my window.

"I'm sittin' in my own driveway. I unattached it when she put it in park, Paw Paw."

"Sure, you did. I'm sure you did just that. Boys downtown tells us you kickin' the church pots around the quarters. Might be itchin' to spread your no good out here in our jurisdiction. Sposed'ta keep an eye out for anything out of the ordinary."

"I don't give a shit what you do with yourself. I'm going to bed. I'm tired of all the bullshit for now."

He wrote Wanda a ticket and made sure my address was used as the spot of violation. She got back in the car.

"Just let me know anything I can do for you," Wanda said. "These motherfuckers piss me off. They do whatever the fuck they want, whenever the fuck they want, with no consequences."

"Drive over to the dorms at U.N.O. I'll meet ya there in about twenty minutes."

I went into my house and grabbed the right clothes, another gun, a hunting knife, running shoes, and mud boots. All the things I could think of that I could use in a jam. I looked at the hook in the kitchen and remembered the deposit box key was in my uniform pocket in my locker in the Quarter. I eased out the back door, leaving some lights on, and snuck out to meet Wanda. I was happy to see my escape route still sacred. We drove the long way around the lakeshore. Becca floated into my daydream again. *Ten, nine, eight, seven, six...*

"Fuck me," I muttered at the full moon.

Wanda popped up onto the curb at the edge of Jackson Square and went to unlock the gate, pulling it just wide enough for us. She then grabbed a blanket from her trunk and opened my door.

"Step into this. You'll be covered."

She got me inside the gate and closed it.

"Go up, I'll bring your stuff to you."

I opened the door, and the abstractions on the walls welcomed me again. The darkened statues of African women against the stark white paint seemed to say, *We've been waiting for you, young man.*

The Francis Bacon, head and torso twisted and blurred in spurts of exposed red meat. Disfigured mouth and tongue flailing around chaotic teeth. Even with all that distorted flesh, I still felt a sense of comfort. Maybe, just simply because of the charity I've been offered, but all the same, I felt I could finally sleep.

Wanda laid my crap in the hall just inside the doorway, put a pill in my hand, looking at me hard and soft at the same time.

"You're in good hands, so get yourself rested. I would like to see Don Lee become his old self again. If that's still a possibility. Gonzales's death needs validating, and they all need closure, so you need to be back in action, lucid and ready."

She put her arms around my back and hugged me.

"You going to be alright?"

"I'm fine. Thanks, Wanda."

"Then it's all good, Paw Paw." She smiled and left me to my own devices and her knock-out pills.

CHAPTER FIFTEEN

Darkness surrounded me like the comfort of my favorite old blanket as I slipped into a half-conscious fantasy, ready for the pill to overtake me. I drifted past Becca, and somewhere in the world, a pair of rich, red lips parted to lick an envelope's edge. Contoured fingers, the palette of what most people could imagine as the color of Cleopatra, sealed the envelope and gently placed it on a cocobolo wood table, under soft, golden lamplight.

The long legs of this lovely woman moved toward a softly lit bedroom to file a nail. Those tempting red lips sipped champagne. She stood to fill a small purse with cash, ecstasy, marijuana, and lipstick, pulling the thin, oiled leather strap of her party purse over her shoulder. She slipped into a plush driver's seat intending to take in some night air, to feel the breath of life. She would most likely find herself dancing the night away with friends and strangers in the throbbing glint of disco lights.

The aged version of that finely chiseled hand reached for the envelope with fingers that had now ripened into long, sharp, gilded talons. The word *Mother* centered on the envelope. A sturdy nail ripped the edge. Contents were read.

Fremeaux is marching again.

She refolded the message, slipped it back into the envelope, and placed it back on the silver tray to rest. She moved to stare out at the lit cityscape through her darkened balcony window. Her blurred reflection, with coiffed hair and cast-iron face, colored the inside of the pitch-dark glass as her lips savored the brown liquor, chewing on the crushed ice.

Three thousand miles away, I could feel my numbing lips move in unison with hers as my wasting mind pulled into her cadence. A guttural voice crawled around in my guts.

"Order! Order from chaos." I felt myself mime with her mirage.

"Time to strike is always now." Together, we peered into imagined twinkling lights.

"Evil is the side cost of doing good deeds. If little boys are in need of train sets, then trees must fall. Coal must be unearthed. Eight million little boys on this planet now." I began to slip further and further into a comfortable slumber.

"Someone must force men to dig. Dig like it's their goddamned dominant fetish." I hammered with her mirage as the night air carried me off into a distant dreamland.

The phone jarred me awake. A shiver ran through me. I had left the balcony door ajar, letting the cool October night wander in. I searched the room for the phone and realized it must be on the table in the entryway. I trotted over and grabbed it on the seventh ring. The room was sunlit and golden again. The early morning sighting of the distorted Francis Bacon on the far wall made me reach up and squeeze my lymph nodes, pushing pressure into my cold brain. I was expecting to hear Don Lee's gruff country tone.

"Hello."

"Good morning, Sleeping Beauty. How do you like being in my place?" The soft voice excited me just enough. I felt my muscles relax.

"Hell of a nice place you've got here. And thank you for doing this. I know you and your privacy."

"I'm in support of you and Don Lee. Both of you have been there for me in times of need. Besides, it's the least I feel I could do. How are you holding up, Fremeaux?"

"Pretty well now that I got a full night's sleep. I gotta figure my next move."

"So, you found yourself a fine piece of meat?"

"It's not what it sounds like, Leda."

"I hear there is a picture coming soon. I'll be the judge then."

"I got drunk, and my so-called partners set me up," I said.

"I'm sure, sweetie. Make sure you get yourself checked out. My family operates a maritime clinic that heals the mariners when they come into the harbor with those types of maladies."

"What malady, and what clinic?"

"STDs. It's Uptown near the Fly. This side of the Zoo on Tchoupitoulas."

"There are doctors there?" I ask curiously, but knowing something odd is in the air.

"Yes, private doctors. All those foreigners just can't pop into a local hospital. My mother's siblings provide health care for the ship workers from all over the world."

I immediately recalled my conversation with Charlie the Crow. He was treated there. And prostitutes and their fates. The Catholic Church owns his place of residence. Restlessness molded my thoughts.

"Are you Catholic?" I heard myself blurt without process.

"No, we're gentiles from ancient times. Our ancestors were expelled. My family landed in Eastern Europe. Scattering even more after the big war. Why?"

"I don't know, impulse question. No meaning to it."

"Mother and I don't practice forgiveness. She came to New Orleans and fell in love with freedom and opportunity. Incognito, she likes to say."

"How about your dad?"

She avoided the question without skipping a beat. "I'm having something brought to you today."

I'm guessing her father is a subject best avoided.

"What?" I asked, ignoring the transition. And relieved to learn there's no way in hell she could be a Catholic.

"Unlock the gate downstairs. After three o'clock today, a package will be placed inside the stairwell. It's for the holiday weekend coming up. A Halloween treat."

"Okay? Thanks, I guess."

"Fremeaux, you need to relax a little. Don Lee tells me you're on the brink of tight-assed exhaustion. You can roam the crowds and keep your anonymity. It's a costume to conceal your identity."

"Oh, well, in that case, I think that's a fine idea. Leda. Does Don Lee know what you are sending?

"We haven't discussed it yet. I got the idea after he and I spoke."

"For now, I'd like to keep it that way. Keep it between us. How's your trip?" I asked.

"Busy. I have a lot of loose ends to tie up over here. Solve some old-world family issues. Playing catch-up with old school buddies, kind of stuff. I'm serious, if you develop odd sensations, let Don Lee know immediately. He knows how to contact me."

"Leda, I was way too drunk to do anything. I'm clean, don't worry."

"If you were too drunk to do anything, you were probably too drunk to remember. I'm being summoned now, so I *must* let you go. Goodbye for now and do be careful."

The dial tone was the next sound I heard. I went downstairs to unlock the entry gate and went back to search for coffee, and wait for Don Lee's call. I found myself mulling the facts that there's a connection with Leda, Golda, and the Catholic Church via Charlie the Crow via a mysterious medical clinic. I kept chewing on the pieces of this puzzle, hoping to spit out a complete image. Or, at least, form an image.

Maybe Ms. Koozie had the clearest vision after all. Somehow, all this could be connected, and right now, the Dixie Mafia looked to be central. Could they be kidnapping young girls? What was their motivation? Increasing the odds of leaving evidence for just a sex romp doesn't sound like motivation. Or could these girls bring in cash? That would call for finesse; low-brow rednecks weren't known for finesse. Could there be a pipeline filling backwoods strip clubs? NOPD hates the Dixie Mafia boys from the Corso murder, so this didn't figure up. The local cops might have been corrupt as hell, but they wouldn't hide or ignore evidence to cover up killing Frank Corso for a bunch of rednecks even if there was a payoff. Fuck, I was still just as clueless as the night I found her hand in the gutter.

The phone rang again.

I picked up. "This you, Don Lee?"

"It is, sir. How are you holding up, young man?"

"I'm rested, feeling stronger, but I got a knot in my gut with all this crap hovering over my head."

"I hear you loud and clear."

"I had a new thought. Do y'all have the cops on the list of suspects?" I asked.

"We're not excluding them, but we've carefully tried to keep watch who's being arrested to match with the missing faces on the posters. So far, we haven't made a match. Gonzales felt it was someone from the public. There may be compensation for evidence concealment."

"What's happening with the publication of my downfall, Don Lee?"

"As far as the public is concerned, you're the biggest turd with a badge they've never seen. I haven't seen the photograph yet, but I'm told it's quite the doozy. I have already spoken with the mayor and confessed I've seen you pull some pretty shady stunts while on duty, and I think you have the potential to be a disgrace to the city uniform."

"And, you are going to trash me, why? I'll be removed from the force."

"Don't worry about that. I have everyone pulling together a cash pile for your bills and survival. We'll then follow that version with your side. In this second story, you will be recanting the department as corrupt, and now that you're out on your own you will privately investigate the disappearance of the girls with insinuations that the force is covering up or is directly involved somehow. *You* have been gathering evidence from secret sources that will corroborate you being set up.

"Well fuck, Don Lee, you're ready to kick the lion in the balls, just like that, huh?"

"Someone dropped a smoking gun in our lap, so somewhere their seams are fraying. Besides, I'm well beyond ready to force their hand. If the cops are covering for someone out there, maybe, just maybe, they'll be willing to sacrifice someone. You did well by losing your cool with that street kid."

"Yeah, you right. How's Becca's mom?"

"The lady pulled through in the last hour. She lost a lot of blood and went into a twenty-four-hour coma. She's restored the ability to hear and understand words this morning. I'm going to tell her to stay strong; we're close to catching the suspect."

"I need to get in touch with Xandi," I said. "We need all eyes in the Quarter. It's Halloween weekend. We need a snapshot of as many women in costume as possible. Since Halloween falls on Sunday this year, the revelers will be in the same costume for three days starting Friday morning. If any girl goes missing, I'm certain the photographs brought and hung on the community boards and poles will have the missing girls in costume side by side with what they actually look like. A 'this is what she was last seen wearing' kind of thing. Maybe we can place the costume with a person in their crowd or vicinity. Anything we can get will help."

"Fine idea, Fremeaux. I'll spread the word and get as many people as possible roaming the Quarter this weekend. They can retreat and sleep at my place. I'll turn my home into a Howard Johnson's. I'm certain I can borrow walkie-talkies from an old acquaintance. I'm in contact with every festival photographer who'll be out there capturing images for publications, so we will have access to archives. We can try and retrace the footsteps of the girls who may go missing."

"Good deal. When will we meet again?" I asked.

"I'll write the story and let you have a go with it before running."

"Don't worry about that. Just run what you think will wash their nests out. Let's get this shit rolling."

"Yeah, you right. Bye for now, Fremeaux, and get rested. You may have to scuffle with some big fella after this story hits. And remember, it's going to be a full moon for Halloween this year. It may get extra hairy out there this weekend."

"I can feel anticipation building in the streets already. People are shopping for wigs as we speak. Drive safe, Don Lee. Look forward to reading your trash talk. By the way, it looks as though I'll be making a trip to Florida tomorrow to gather information on Mr. Shit Happens."

"Good luck, kid, and be safe out there."

We hung up. I peeked through the balcony doors and returned to the couch, listening to the crowd chatter bound about below me.

"Happy voices conceal troubled souls," I mumbled out loud to the hot air.

CHAPTER SIXTEEN

Vernon, FL, looked like any other ragged-out small town desperate for a cash influx. The only thing looking healthy out here was the tropical sweat of the plant life. The number of missing appendages on the townspeople was starkly noticeable. According to Life Insurance Consensus, there had been a high rate of claims processed for lost and/or irreparable limbs that lived under suspicious considerations. It was evident from the look of angst on the faces wandering about.

I pulled into a gas station to get directions to Double Gobble Road and a couple of beers. Wanda had recently purchased herself a tiny-ass coffee-colored 280Z, and I'd been crammed behind the wheel of this thing. I thought I was in dire need of a chiropractor. My knees had been jammed into the dashboard for four hours, my hips had locked up, allowing the grooves in the interstate to continuously budge a seat spring up my ass. It was Miller time as far as I'm concerned.

"You okay with Miller?" I asked.

"Get an eight-pack of ponies and a pack of L&Ms, please. I don't like my beer to get too warm before I finish it."

"Regular or menthol on the L&M's?"

"Regular."

I asked a short fella with a thick, misshapen, brown mustache standing behind the cash register where I could find our girl's trailer.

"That little bitch has done gone and run up a big fuckin' line of credit with me. Hell, I can't seem to run her ass down myself."

"How much?" I asked begrudgingly.

He grinned. "Eleven hundred."

I paid for the beer and cigarettes. "I'll be right back."

I pulled the amount for the debt from the stash we were using as bait and bought directions to Double Gobble Road from the fella who resembled a cross between Danny Devito and Mr. Whipple. I crammed myself back into the tin can of a car, and we whizzed down a rough two-lane country road looking for my turn-off. I sucked down two pony bottles fairly quickly and spotted the beech tree that stooped in a thick growth of briars. A hundred years ago, the local Indian tribes had trussed it up to create a trail marker, and this one had grown the trunk to form the capital letter E. Three medium-sized trees grew from the humped-over trunk, and that's what I had been informed to look out for. I hung a quick left onto the gravel road that was just on the other side of this oddity. I followed Mr. Whipple's direction without certainty he was being truthful. Wanda threw a cigarette butt from the window and uttered the words "creepy" and "depressing" in a sentence I didn't fully catch.

"I'm certain you're staying in the car while I approach. I need to ensure she doesn't freeze up on us, right?" she questioned me with a demand.

I looked at her with a grin. "You're on the lead with this one, lady."

She was all good as the gravel pathway stretched off into thick, narrow, browning brush. A fickle tree line guided us into a yard covered in tall grass and adagio plants that were beginning to bow with the coming winter. There wasn't a designated path, so the grass rubbed the sides of the car and curled over the hood of the low-slung Datsun. Tan, dried-out seed pods danced across the coffee-colored hood like shooting stars as the car slowly pushed through.

We rolled farther into a front yard dotted with trash, broken toys, twisted bikes, rusting vehicle shells, and a trailer home, of which the last rivet was put in its final resting place thirty years ago. A small dip down in the holler held another trailer home completely sunken in from rot. The cheap insulation was soaked in mold, exposed from the busted rooftop that had caved down like a fallen dinosaur rib cage; it resembled dirty diapers soaking in the rain.

I drove beyond the living quarters and parked under a live oak whose branches were trying to hide the sunken home from public viewing, but were failing in their task, and parked. No outside dwelling animals ran out to scare or greet us at any point. I was slightly relieved but still wondered if we were spotted driving through the tall grasses.

"Inspect everything while you're in the trailer. Canvas everything, countertops, signs of pets, and photographs for anything and everything. Drug paraphernalia, weapons, and get an idea of age from every person or image you see," I commanded.

"Fremeaux, I was raised around criminals. I know what to do, honey. I'll be good in there. You just stay put till I signal. Okay?"

We opened two beers, toasted one another, and shot 'em down. She held up the seed money.

"Keep the cash in your hand until you get all the answers you want. It's your dangling carrot. Let her know that we paid her tab at the gas station as well."

Wanda rolled her eyes. "Let's just hope she's desperate enough to talk honestly. Wish me luck, big boy."

I nodded as she sashayed around a tall patch of grass up to the front door and knocked. A stout girl with shockingly bright red hair greeted her with concern. They talked and nodded for a minute, and then Wanda went through the front door, and it closed shut. My internal timer started.

The rotting aluminum, the browning oak leaves, and the grass seed covering the windshield can coax a mind to feel the need to lash out at nature's callousness. Dead center, the lip of the dark-brown, sloping hood stood a single seed pod, defiant, and daring me to move forward, even an inch. It had the shape of the planter's peanut mascot, plump on top and bottom, with dusty, crusty follicles. I looked at it for a bit and named it Poppy. I asked Poppy if she had seen anything lately, and, by God to hell, a small breeze brushed her to shudder a little, then with dignity, she stood perfectly still again in the noon sun, seemingly saying, *Take a guess, slick.* The sight of her shape and defiance conjured the image of the painting hanging in Leda's guest bathroom, where I shaved this morning.

Three bright white bags of curved peanuts sat atop a black, wrought iron table perched on a patio high above a lush green valley, seemingly floating in the open air. One bag in the forefront with a red banner, embossed with the words Roasty-Toasty Peanuts in yellow cursive. The other two bags were tucked behind, with one having been ripped at the top, spilling nuts around the black iron tabletop. The loose peanuts lay around as blind and listless as forgotten children, periodically claiming the center of attention. The patio and the stark white bags were seemingly floating into a lovely cloudless blue sky.

Beyond the tables and peanuts, a plush green tree line stood off in the distance, flanking a large white colonial home with a manicured lawn and lovely brick patio.

The peanuts had been painted with a perfect roast to the hull, and could make your mouth water if you took the time to look closely. Just as you, the viewer began to ask what it was all about, the eye pulled to an image of skin at the very top right corner. Like a bird of prey, the very bottom of a hand hovered in an invisible zephyr. You scan further and begin to understand, as art can be sometimes, that those peanuts were meant for other people; they weren't for you. Sparking wars of the heart. Inspecting the base of the tree line and the manicured lawn down below, the eye caught a secret lady voyeur standing behind an oversized attic window, camouflaged by drooping tree limbs, spying on you and the unknowable hand that was forever hovering above your shoulder, through a pair of binoculars.

"Who's that?" you asked yourself. "Did she stumble on the scene just as you have, and both of us are out of fashion? She could be spying on a thief's hand just above your shoulder. Wanting to give you a warning."

Then you realized that you badly want to eat a Goddamned peanut. Did she want to be offered one, too? Or did she seek revenge for not being invited?

Suddenly, a small cadre of buzzards flung themselves from the ground behind the rotting shell of a trailer and perched in the tops of the trees, pensively skulking at the form that had interrupted their dinner. I spied the hot black creatures above and began to smell the decay.

"Something's dead over there," I mumbled to Poppy. I dropped another empty pony bottle in the cardboard slot and looked at the newspaper I've been avoiding. I wasn't ready to read Don Lee's slander just yet. I wanted to wait until this escapade was a done deal. I slowly opened the door and dragged my stiffness out, sniffing the air. The decay smelled as though it had been lying on the ground for some time. The bile had probably mixed with the drying blood and dirt by now. Maggots had surely come and gone.

I walked through the grass and kicked some dead tree limbs out of my way rounding the back end of the hump of rotting metal and spotted the carcasses of three Doberman Pinschers. I couldn't find a definitive cause of death, but this homestead didn't look like a place that could afford to house three Doberman Pinschers of this size. A Pekingese or Basset mix, possibly, but these folks could barely provide food and clothing for themselves. Keeping three one-hundred-pound dogs fed properly into adulthood was out of the question.

I was wrong about one thing, though; there was still a mound of maggots mulching around inside the sunken carcass, finishing up the bounty. Lost flesh exposed the drying, yellowed fangs.

About a hundred yards deeper into the woods, I spotted the shape of a car under cloth.

"Are we hiding more remains, gentlemen?" I ask the invisible men.

I tore through the thick weeds, stepped onto the tire trail, and maneuvered my way over, then lifted the cover over the hood. I discovered a brand-new paint job hiding under there. I yanked the whole covering to the ground and discovered a Porsche 911 without a license plate had been hiding out here in the middle of nowhere. Someone had been up to no good. I wrote down the VIN and returned the cover, so as not to give evidence of discovery.

The thick thud of the trailer door slammed behind me about fifty yards away. I turned and found a young boy of about eleven or twelve, with furrowed brows, pouncing around the back of the trailer home. The area was filled with trash, rusted-out appliances, whiskey bottles, and mud-matted stuffed animals strewn all over. The boy kicked at them with fury and threw rocks at the backside of the trailer to induce anger in the people inside.

The door opened, and a voice commanded him to cut the shit, slamming shut again. He spun on a rusted television antenna that was warped and almost detached from the trailer itself. He shook it with rage, and it finally gave way as the very top broke loose and nearly took his ear off. I could see blood form at the edge of his jawline. He didn't flinch or seem to care. Bending for the aluminum pole at his feet and the frustration gave him a reason to strike all the appliances with zeal. He paced the area like Napoleon in the heat of his blistering exile, taking stabs and waging war on the very human behaviors that had enslaved him there alone with no sign of reprieve. A trickle of blood dropped to his chin and then off onto his little shirt.

Boredom and necessity nested in his eyes as he looked down at the red stain on his shirt. He gritted his teeth and swung the pole with full might into a whiskey bottle, and a shard of glass nicked his top lip. He grabbed for the wound, formed balled fists of rage, and began punching into a rusty washing machine.

My foot slipped off a small soft root and rattled the leaves, and he caught me witnessing him amongst his ruins. He stood as still as a panther staring into the tree limbs that camouflaged my identity. His eyes were as black as the hate in his heart. I could foresee his life being taken at the wrong time and the wrong place someday.

The line of duty was formed to combat empty hearts like his. Abandoned and alone, I could feel the boy dare me to expose myself. He swiped at the blood on his face, broke his stance, and moved into the tall grass on the other end of the trailer home.

I returned to Wanda's driver's seat as I scanned the thin Florida forest for any other sets of eyes that may have been following me. I crossed my heart as I sank back into the bucket seat and cracked open the last beer. I wondered again if I should start smoking, as it seemed to settle other people's nerves.

Wanda returned and closed her door.

"This Billy Dale kid was just a low-level criminal learning the ropes and surviving," she explained.

I chose to keep quiet about the disturbed boy's yard dance.

I backed the car out of the field of dreams and drove us back to the main road. I watched Double Gobble Road, and the beech tree that grew the letter E slowly disappear from my rearview. According to Mr. Danny Whipple, the term Double Gobble is the holy grail of turkey calls. Men have avoided going to the bathroom and even turned down sex to discover its source. To hunt and kill is serious business over here.

"What had our boy Bobby Dale Vice been up to?" I inquired a little further.

"He had been employed to pick up money from Western Unions all over the area, from East Texas to the Panhandle. He was instructed to take these collections to Mr. Gilleach."

"Somehow everything backs up to the Dixie Mafia," I mumbled. "Did you see any pictures of large Doberman Pinschers inside by chance?"

"No, there was a picture of a Yorkie from some years past when the kids were infants." She lit a cigarette, inhaling with gusto.

"How many kids?"

"Six."

"Eight people crammed into a trailer. Hungry," I mumbled again.

"Well, seven. I don't think our boy Bobby Dale hung around too often. I'm sensing he had another family somewhere else. Just a hunch from talking to this poor woman. Not everyone can succeed."

I wondered if the truth in that statement was predetermined. Did the underpinnings of our reality map out just which network of neurons was to fulfill prophecies? Scientists thought so; they just can't prove it. Entropy was in everything, I had been told. Even information.

She looked at me.

"So, are you ready to learn how your image is being shared with the city?" She grinned as I thought about the three dead dogs, the disturbed child, and the stolen Porsche out of place, all of it without a plausible excuse.

"Why the hell not? Another road. Another chase."

She reached and unfolded the *Picayune*. There I was, crowned in Louisiana glory. Shirtless with a hooker on the balcony of a cheap motel. Liquor in my blood, confusion in my soul, and pain in my ass. The headline simply read, *CAUGHT*. My name was captioned under the photograph. Wanda read some of the article aloud.

> *"It's just gross negligence on our part. We uphold ourselves and our citizens' best interests in the highest regard, so when bad cops are allowed to roam the system and the streets, then our duties fail. Fail us all. This tainted officer has been removed from his duties and will be fully reprimanded as any other law-breaking citizen of this city. It is with a sad heart that we have allowed such behavior to fester and will be launching a full investigation to remove any and all officers who may be using the shield to protect their dishonesty."* Commissioner Farragut stated in the opening paragraph.

She lowered the paper. "Looks like you're no longer employed."

"Well, we're off and running the course now," I said.

As far as the public was concerned, I could soon see the inside of a jail cell if the allegations could stick with evidence, etc., etc.

"We're driving back to Halloween weekend," Wanda said insightfully.

"There could be kidnappers dressed as angels out in the streets." "I'll be out waiting for their strike."

"Cops will be dressed as cops, protecting those angels, and looking for you, Mr. Man. Stop and get another eight-pack. I feel like catching a buzz," she demanded.

"I'm tired of hiding," I told her, exiting from the main highway. "My health needs the spirits put to rest. It's like being in a Kafka world, with the universe dangling ghost solutions. I didn't choose any of this. All this started from someone else's crimes. So far, my life has been directed by other people's crimes."

"Lifeguards exist because other people drown, buddy," she said.

"Recently, I've felt like I'm saving myself from the quicksand by pulling myself out with my own hair. What kind of lifeguard is that?"

"Be patient, Fremeaux, you'll find the hair of an asshole standing on safe ground soon. It'll come. The universe says you gotta keep pushing that boulder, brother."

CHAPTER SEVENTEEN

Becca visited because she demands to be saved or avenged. Red Dertinger sat in a lounge chair at the back of my mind, just waiting. Waiting and grinning. Fuck me, sleep was becoming intolerable. Was the universe sending them, or was I keeping them handy for my own death march? The next time I killed, it would be recorded for innocence. Nobody escapes time's merciless truth.

Mirth-filled voices leap up through the balcony window. Halloween is here, and it's the biggest, grandest, kinkiest backyard party in the country. I could feel my guts pull to the action, but I had to exercise patience. I had to wait till I was undercover. I stared at a large black and white photograph of Leda dressed as a falconer on a mountaintop somewhere. A magnificent bird of prey was strapped to her forearm, sitting in wait. Head strapped with a leather cover. Leda's stare shoots straight to the soul of whoever is standing in front of her.

I opened the box Leda had sent and found inside a Venetian Volto. I slipped the three-cornered hood over my head and strapped it snugly under my chin, snug as a football helmet. There I stood, polished white face, menacing. The mask had been outfitted with New Orleans modernity. The bottom lip pressed down to fit a drinking straw, and a speaker box had been inlayed to amplify my voice.

Oh, the silly shit money can create, I thought. I could hear my breathing inside this thing, creating deeper contact with myself. Camus's absurdity?

I stepped out to the balcony to leer over Jackson Square, and caught Olivia Clare in mid poem again,

"Open a pathway through the slow, sad sail.

Throw wide to the wind the wings of this wandering boat.

That my voyage may begin to the end of my wound."

I could hear my father's voice telling me to stay cool. *Your wounds can be mended.*

I must've looked ominous up here, ready to haunt and hunt.

Over in the mezzanine in front of the river, a colorful dance troupe had built a crowd with break-dancing acrobatics to the "Double Dutch Bus." At the doorsteps of the Cathedral, a bunch of kids gathered with a couple of boom boxes of their own, listening to a repetitive song. It was "Captain Sensible:" Everyone was swinging and swaying, lost in a groove.

My eyes found Charlie the Crow, coddiwompling through the crowd in front of the Cathedral. This just happened to be the weekend when his costume was of no value. No one was stopping for a picture, so money wasn't to be made this weekend. He meandered under the balcony, probably headed to Harry's Corner Bar to start his night. Closely following him was a passel of Pulcinella's in tell-tell white. Seven extended white noses sniffing out the sins of the streets. Nosing for big desires and sweaty passions. Funny, I thought to myself, looking at the sight of Charlie and the band of mischievous squats, a small herd of manufactured confusion, led by a man of no opinion.

Chicken George lurched around the corner behind the white splotch of Pulcinella's, adorned with dried chicken bones and Bocio dolls, walking stodgily like he had been cursed into Clairvius Narcisse. Maybe he was already too drunk to dispel. No one seemed to catch sight of the dead and bleeding pigeon swinging from two fingers at his hip as he meandered to the place where hands of voodoo swipe through the hot air, mixing birth and rebirth.

The air did fill me with a bizarre sensation that an answer was lurking out there—something I could put in a bottle and place on an evidence shelf.

Under the cape, I was dressed out. I had my gun, knife, and handcuffs. It was time to plunder this Bacchanalia for a grim collision with these bastards, wherever they may be. I could feel them. The universe knew where they are. All knowledge was built into time itself. Xandi told me, time was all dimensions, too. Information was infinite. She informed us that we held the ability to communicate in all these dimensions at once. No one hid forever, not even me.

I contemplated my options if I were identified by the wrong set of eyes. Fuck it, I'll pull that chord when it happens, I told myself.

I entered the Quarter ready for anything and everything. I had previously checked the hotel status, and the capacity is a fifty percent occupancy, so there are plenty of out-of-towners for a kidnapping. It appeared the kidnappers had avoided taking local girls all these years, so that reminded me, we were most likely looking for someone who lived among us, someone who knew the difference between local girls and tourists. I was also looking for Xandi and the crew to see if I could pass the big test of secrecy.

I wandered through the painted faces, acid-lifted grins, and marijuana-fueled giggles: the champagne and the fearlessness.

Fearless, as if everyone became aware that the Lord got his ass kicked the first time around. We still got his back, but if he decided to show again, there won't be any sins held over our heads, stuff—no dangling of eternity at our noses. Don't come slumming on our part; we've got our own mercies to dole out.

I brought myself to stand in line at Kaldi's for an espresso to go. While waiting for something big to happen, I figured I could sit across from the homeless encampment and spy on the vagrants for a bit.

Near me, the Chess champions were hard at head-scratching again. They might have looked like homeless shelter material to the street novice, but these ragged-looking fellas held doctorates. They were intently staring at the chessboard, silent as church mice. It almost made me believe a pigeon would be taking a shit from way up at the edge of heaven somewhere, and the masterminds were waiting to settle the bets. Without uttering a word, the pack of Einsteins shuffled pawns and rooks while I stoked around for kings of destruction.

I spotted a new balloon animal clown in town. Dirty, disheveled. He wasn't local. Had a predator's demeanor. Getting a little too close to kids while their parents grinned a weary smile of discontent. I wondered if he was just passing through, or was he here for our mild winter weather? The Devil was forever walking. He'd made my list of people to watch out for. I suddenly realized I hadn't seen Ruthie in a while.

A voice from the chess table made me turn.

"I got one for ya, fellas. Maybe this concept can move the idea to the corner." The others around the table pulled into the thought.

"Supposing you were a slave rower on the Viking's ship, or any other for that matter, pulling all that weight through the blaring, wild sea waters of the North Atlantic. You and a hundred or so strong men sweating for other people, but *you* have a bit of a lazy streak."

I caught sight of a kid I thought I recognized as another street urchin, dipping into an adult sex toy shop down at the far end of Decatur. I kept my attention on the doorway and the conversation at the chess table.

"You and the fella next to you have been sharing the long oar. The two of you have been pulling and stroking for half a day now. But you have that lazy bone and are calculating when you could abandon your post. Go through the motions, it's in your nature, mind you. Throwing caution to the wind, you succumb to that inner temptation without the thought of getting yourself trapped in delinquency. You are unaware that self-absorbed behavior is readable to the tribe, so you ignore the timeline of being noticed by your fellow unfortunate, or the man with the whips and chains. But there you are, going through the motions of rowing with your partner.

"The tribe is fully aware of your character, but you think your deception is invisible. That's the curse of being self-absorbed. Your bench mate, looking to get better favors with his captors and rid the tribe of a parasite, makes eye motions to alert the man in charge. Your time is up. You've been held accountable, and therefore, you're snatched, chained, and whipped until blood leaks from your skin. After being advertised as to what you caused for yourself, you are taken to the bow and thrown, bloody and broken, to the sharks. How does that work for true social justice?"

A familiar voice of a city worker unexpectedly chimed in from the trash cans.

"The sad part of that story is if there was a cruise ship of do-gooder assholes passing by at the very moment your man was fed to the sharks, they'd immediately pass false judgment on the ship's captain. Being completely unaware the dickhead had set his own fate; they'd demand justice for they own damn hearts. Just like them half-wit folks tied to watching The Donahue Show, instigating audiences to condemn poor folks with half-truths."

The table turned toward the city worker, nodding in agreement. The voice continued.

"And me? I'm happily emptying trash down here in New Orleans, where we don't impound our lunatics; life sho is a damn unfathomable mystery... That's why we voted Harold Heralds back in the governor's mansion; he may be wrong, but he shows right on most occasions."

The chess boys chuckled, "yeah, you right."

"You up for some finger-Fehler with us when you clock out, Ernst?" One of the scholars asked him.

Ernst popped a trash bag open and pushed it to the bottom of the can, "Not today, fellas. I got to go down to my boy's school after work."

That's when the kid caught my eye again. The greasy kid whose address was somewhere over in Mobile. He usually crept through the Quarter during daylight hours, probably the reason I rarely spotted him since he was generally gone before I hit the clock. His shirt was what caught my eye. The Peaches record store logo. It was the same shirt he wore the day Don Lee pinned him to the ground until Deputy Fleetwood ran down and cuffed the kid. Fleetwood proceeded to kick him in the head a couple of times and purposefully dragged him down the asphalt, telling him that Captain Dowd needed to talk with him, in a tone loud enough for public inclusion. Fleetwood ripped a hole in the back of the shirt that day.

Same grease-string blond hair, and a natty upper lip, but his biggest giveaway was the fat, dark brown, wire-haired, bark-like mole just above his left eyebrow. He was clutching a dark brown Naugahyde briefcase. A thin, shiny gold thread down the middle of a braid around the outer edges. Looked like something a science fiction freak would use to carry video tapes. He stopped to lean on a pole in front of the homeless encampment, bending to harshly scrub one of the homeless dogs. He stood again to scan the costumes in an odd, twitchy manner. Almost like a little boy scanning the horizon for Treasure Island and spotting a shark instead. As he panned toward me, I averted my mask straight into the open door of Kaldi's. The drawback to this costume I was wearing is that once you've seen it, you can't unsee it. So far, I was the only one who loomed.

He stood in place for a few more minutes, then, casually, he pulled something from his pocket and sets it atop the phone company box, then hustles off. A stoned girl from the pile of putrid bodies rises to remove the item and quickly carries it under a blanket tent with the others. I guess they've landed yet another heroin trade.

I became his tail as he trucked it down Decatur toward Canal. He made a slow right onto Toulouse and bumpily walked to the corner of Bourbon, and he set the briefcase on a yellow bucket sitting upside down under a small white dingy door next to the hallway entrance to The Dungeon. The door didn't have any concrete steps to center it to the earth, so it hovered awkwardly above the sidewalk in empty space. Oddly, the sight of such an eccentric door hasn't caught my attention before today, or the universe was saving it for me.

He scanned the area for unwanted eyes and ordered a hot dog. I curved off and skirted further down onto the crowd on Bourbon, hopping in step behind a Han Solo walking shoulder to shoulder with a Richard Simmons doppelgänger. I trailed closely behind the pair, trolling slowly toward the kid. He took his hot dog and sat on a handrail on the other side of the street, opposite the dingy white door with another brown case next to his feet. Han and Richard stepped into the middle of Toulouse near him as I crowd-surfed myself between them and the kid.

Slowly, I shuffled myself back into the crowd at the intersection of Bourbon. I glanced at the Lucky Dog cart, and there stood the ugly mug from the Cathedral, and the motel parking lot, wearing the same thick grey outfit. I quickly looked at the kid and scrutinized the new briefcase. It was exactly like the other one, except the braiding was missing. A switch had been made. I snapped my head over to the bucket where he had set the other one, but the cart and the hot dog maker blocked my view.

I spun back forward and found myself smack-dab in the middle of a wall of people dancing and shouting. A second line was escorting a wedding party down Bourbon, and the entire procession, dressed in skeleton suits, was waving large white umbrellas carrying cocktails with tiny pink umbrellas in their free hands. I got caught in it and needed to get on the other side so I could get my eyes back on the scene without giving away any intentions.

I hopped and wiggled and pushed around the front of the procession just in front of the Grand Marshall, brushing my way to the sidewalk, and returning my gaze, I found that I had lost them. Neither of them was in their place, but I did spot the kid turning left onto Chartres a block down and heading back toward the Marigny. I took the same direction going down Bourbon, trying to play catch-up. I wanted to know what was in this new briefcase. I wondered if it was payoff for protection, heroin, or girls. There was always some sneaky shit taking place in the world, and it seemed all at once some days.

I dodged myself down to St Peter and ran quickly up to Chartres to try and spot this dirty little asshole.

I didn't see him. I searched in every direction. He probably ducked onto another street, so I decided he must be headed to Esplanade in hopes he could use it as his exit route. I ran like hell the next eight blocks, dodging the crowds like I held the game-winning interception. As I crossed and spied down Barracks Street, I ran right by Big Dan George sitting on a stoop across the street from the house where Charlie the Crow calls home, eating a Po-boy. I figured Xandi had posted him on the lookout.

I landed at the corner of Esplanade, and a large crowd gathered at the mouth of Port of Call waiting to drink Red Turtles and eat cheeseburgers. I scanned the avenue and wait to see if I could catch a glimpse of the dingy Peaches T-shirt.

I glanced into the blue sky over the river. It was clear and calm as the sun bleaches the back of my head. Not a cloud to be seen, but a quick, sudden bright neon-pink lightning streak left a vivid sliver in the blue skin of heaven's edge: no thunderclap or anything to give way that it was ever there. If I hadn't been looking up, I'd never have known it to happen.

Was Zeus breaking passage? Slipping in to mingle and seduce? Or a getaway from a fresh conquer? Anything was possible, I thought. I waited for half an hour, pondering just how the hell did we all get here? And just what the hell else had been eluding our sights? I felt I had lost the kid in the chase.

With the barrage of corruption corroding my brain, I began my walk back to Barracks Street to get another look at the house where Charley lives. I found Big Dan still pacing the area, dressed as an Indian Chief. Xandi rounded a corner, dressed as Joan of Arc in Nike shoes, walking to greet him. I took this as my chance to test my secret identity. I was hoping to remain as anonymous as possible for now. When my cover does blow, someone will inevitably ask me to help somewhere, and I'm happy being alone for the time being. So, I slowly walked past them and felt my cape brush them both. They stopped talking as I approached and said nothing more until I was out of earshot, keeping their eyes on me. I could feel them. My name wasn't called, so I thought I was in for the long haul anonymously. I did notice the walkie-talkies, though. Don Lee came through, and I was sure I would pass him at some point. Looked like the Quarter was under surveillance; now we waited for the other players to set their stage.

Golda had my only available sources for answers, tied in a house, out of touch. Access not allowed. The two fuckers were most likely able to give me insights on Billy Dale Vice. Why was Golda acting as the puppeteer? Patience, son; that was what my father would tell me right now.

Charlie's dwelling still looked as docile and innocent as ever, but there was unblessed blood somewhere on that hallowed ground. I could smell it. Big Dan was still staked out around the corner. Xandi had to be asking where the fuck I was at. I'd expose myself later that night. Get back on board with the crew, but for now, I could put a bad eye on some *good* cops, see where that got me. They killed my friend Gonzales. What if I were to return the favor?

CHAPTER EIGHTEEN

Taking a dirty cop's life *was* a form of justice. The hive mind frowned upon it, but the church mind remained shut when the innocence of children is destroyed. Some folks could cocoon themselves into self-prescribed altruism, but when the shit hits the fan, it all became white noise to me. Yeah, I'll take a dirty cop out, but I won't be bought.

How can murder be of lesser value than a bribe? They'll pretend to ask. I wasn't tied to someone else's dirty philosophy if I executed the bastard with the dirty philosophy. If I took his money, then I had to exchange my beliefs for theirs, and it would be a cold day in hell before I demote for a payoff. I might not have been the straightest arrow, but I didn't torch value.

I watched Olen Ray turn and walk toward the river; he was a good, solid young man. He was in my boat, but the shit bag walking with him, Officer Demortiers, now that was another story. He was part of the detail that ended Gonzales's life. It looked like I'd found my Thanksgiving turkey. Mother Jones preached, "Whatever the fight, don't be ladylike," so I followed, hiding behind Halloween.

The two ended their stroll in a small wad of blue uniforms in the curve of Jackson Square and parked themselves in a self-absorbed huddle, planning out the evening's posts.

I looked over the thousand or so motley-colored bodies gathering and wandering and saw the lavender and pink outdoor umbrella with the advertisement *Hubris the Magnificent* written on its down flaps. Don Lee was right; he's back. Back for the haunt, and I wondered if his tarot and crystal ball informed him that he was in my sight. That my costumed alter ego would be disrupting his aura. I felt it was time for some prophecy.

Avoiding detection as I spied on my fellow officers, I sat in Hubri's trap, a metal folding chair.

It was hard for me not to picture Hubris's naked and bloated lardass; that was how I saw the bastard for the first time. Naked, sweaty, and drunk, pinning another naked man to the floor and trying to rip his ear off with his teeth. Patrolling Burgundy Street, a frantic commotion spilled through the door of Rawhide Bar, pushing a wad of highly excited men toward me. I found Hubris in just the state I described on the floor in the back hallway of the bar. Hubris, in some sort of trance, and the poor man's ear was ready to detach. I tried to yank him off the poor sucker, but his teeth were almost through the soft tissue and weren't about to loosen. I stood and went back to the front bar and found Jony Creaux, a well-known drug lover who could produce anything the nearest pharmacy could dispense.

"I need you to bring me anything that I can use to knock his fat ass out," I commanded.

"I don't know what that has to do with me, Fremeaux?"

"Jony, I'm not asking. A man is about to lose an ear, and another will go to jail, all over a lover's dispute. If you were on your back right now, you'd be begging me to do something too."

"I'll be right back," he said, rolling his eyes.

He returned quickly with a syringe and liquid inside. "This is a horse tranquilizer. I haven't used it for anything, so I don't know what it will do to a human being."

"It's in my hands now, not your problem." I injected a little over half of the liquid, and Hubris succumbed not too long afterwards.

The poor kid on the losing end of the argument wanted to press charges, so I had no choice but to haul Hubris to central lock-up. The fat bastard woke up wrapped in a dirty blanket with nothing but a headache and the taste of blood on his lips. Since then, he'd taken it upon himself to harass me in the streets when he was in the mood.

"My road to hell's been paved by your good fuckin' intentions, Fremeaux." That's what he would tell me. That's Hubris for ya.

I was looming over him, this time behind this white plastic face, wondering if the universe knew about this motherfucker too.

"Would ya like a readin'?" he said, slightly flippant. But then again, everything he did was slightly flippant.

I nodded. "Yes." He pointed to the empty chair.

"You got familiar energy. You from the area?"

I shook my head no.

"Where ya from?"

I point my finger indicating up north.

"You don't talk?"

I nodded; no again.

"You'll need to ask ya question for me to begin anything on ya," he said.

I motioned for a pen and paper. He dug through a dirty knapsack and handed me a pen and notepad filled with pornographic drawings. I scribbled, "I'm a lost lamb and don't know where to go. Can you help?"

"Did someone put you up to this?" he demanded.

I shook my head again and tapped my hand over my heart. He shuffled.

"Let me see those palms," he said.

I held them up. He pulled them across the table, spreading my fingers to flatten the palm.

"Skin's too white to be mafia. Ya prolly a dirty fuckin' cop."

I wondered if he talked to all customers like this. The other soothsayers dress like witches or cosmic hippies, but not Hubris. He's wearing his usual thin, dirty, way-too-tight pink T-shirt. Man-boobs jiggle above the mass of the gut and brush the tabletop. Even though he didn't look like the textbook spook, he kept a long line of dreamers; somebody was talking about him. Maybe lost souls are attracted to hubris.

"Humph. These ain't da hands of a little lost lamb." He sneered.

I patted my heart again.

He shuffled a thick stack of cards; one fell to the ground, and he returned it face down on the table. I was instructed to pull four cards from the deck and place them face up in the middle of the table. I did as I was asked, I was a good boy. He put the extra cards in a box on the ground. Sitting back in his chair, he looked directly into the eyeholes of my mask.

"You brought'ny harm to anybody lately?" he asked.

I shook my head. His movements and inflections have strong effeminate overtones, but the night I met him, he was in full combat mode. Seek and destroy kind of shit. Still blaming me for the house arrest. He would shit himself if my headdress fell to expose my identity. He would immediately go for an ear, I'm sure.

"Tarot ain't for predictin' ya future. What I'm makin' is a tool for usin' ya intuitions more keenly. To cleanse the soul, find nat shadow self. See what the path the universe is keepin' from ya. No more lost lamb. Nod if ya understand me or not."

I nodded.

"You did draw that fool card, so you are on new ground. Your energy doesn't exude blind innocence, so I don't know what you have gotten yaself into. Ya challenges comin' up are gonna be many and may be overwhelmin' at times, but the white dog at ya feet says there's somebody out gonna guide ya. Find 'em. Use 'em. The feather in the hat means there's truth to what you do. Stay with dat truth. Remember this: the soul will provide, but you gotta be careful not to get all impulsive. You also drew The Tower, The Ace of Swords, and The Two of Cups. There is a relationship on the horizon, but before that, your life will go through some kinna turmoil. Something is coming apart, making ya feel lost. Let's see what this other card that fell could be. This is a bonus card since the ghosts of Jackson Square tossed it out before we started."

His voice had the same pitch as Truman Capote's, but with a more disturbed, effeminate St. Bernard Parish drag. Hubris turned the concealed over.

"King Of Cups. Well, like that white dog, you got somebody coming to give ya some guidance. This is a person you respect; you ain't alone. The tower card tells that ya soul's gone dark. Ya universe is in falter as something has you descending, but ya inner self has ascended somewhere spiritually, and that is something that you can prevail.

"The Ace of Swords says that truth will be delivered. If something in the universe is hiding, it will be uncovered in this journey you're on. Stay calm and let ya ego rest while ya soul deciphers the messages. Bottom line, it seems my initial read on you was false. You *are* lost, but hands are reaching for ya. The people who are, or have recently entered your life, are there to dissolve the bad faiths you've constructed. Hold those hands tight, and when it's ova, the sun will shine again. And, by da way, that mask is too fucking much."

I noticed a well-dressed short fella enter the huddle of blue and give small instructions, then he and Demortiers, Walton, and Johnson broke out and walk to the other side of the square, stopping under Leda's balcony.

The fella quieted as the three men leaned in closely to take in the new information.

Hubris had sat back again, annoyed that I had sent my attention elsewhere just as he was wrapping up. This lump in front of me just told me mostly what I was already aware of, but love, who the hell had time for love? And with all those fuckin' cards, he couldn't decode my identity? But the bastard did keenly read my predicament, and with empathy to boot. The tub softened my opinion of him. There was kindness in his skepticism. Someone who wanted to do his best, not just the snotty bitch who would bite an ear off if he didn't get his way. All coins have two sides.

I held the thumbs up and handed him a fifty-dollar bill, demanding that he keep it all. He warmed up, and I went to stand under the arch of the doorway to the cathedral to keep a close eye on the new direction this bunch of cops is taking. The four men walked back to the original huddle, and two others retraced the steps back to the other side with the stranger. I noticed Olen Ray was excluded from these private chats. Directly, Demortiers walked down Charters and was quickly driven away in a black Mercedes. My Thanksgiving turkey had escaped my intentions for now, but not my judgment. I would see him again soon.

The tickle that a bigger truth was still somewhere near sat in my gut. Olen Ray broke out in the direction of the station house, and a fella dressed out as the Pope stopped to mimic the sign of the cross toward me.

"Holy shit, what timing?" I said to the passing impersonation. The swiping hand from the fake Pope triggered a realization in me. The church and the local assholes pulling the strings weren't about to share stolen pussy with the Dixie Mafia. The Bobby Dale Vice trail was just a bed of ragweed, but that stolen Porsche had some value to my story. Dr. Fontenot bought something too big to fuck, at some point. And so had Bobby Dale.

Bobby Dale might have some kind of connection, but it was just small shit. He and Becca must have stumbled into a bed of snakes that weekend, and both paid the ultimate price. We found his ass, but where was Becca's body? The real big shits were right here under my nose somewhere. I needed a tequila.

As I walked toward Napoleon House, it dawned on me that I still hadn't come across Ruthie and her fowl protectors. The shot was pushed into my hand, and I could now take the time to mark every face that passed through. It was a damn good spot to map the girls that could become prey.

I waited for the moon to float again before I made off into the crowd to hunt.

CHAPTER NINETEEN

People populated the stoops along Burgundy. One of the daytime street bands had been hired to play for the locals tonight; it was a six-block neighborhood party, and the energy along Burgundy was infectious.

I looked through the door at Frahy's, and Tressy was slinging drinks. The street party's boundary ended at Orleans Ave, and I found myself standing in a moment of quiet and darkness. I heard the squawk of waterfowl and looked to find Ruthie waddling in my direction from Canal, which placed a sense of relief on my tired mind for some reason. I waited and watched them walk out of the dark with one another. I heard her scold one of her feathered buddies about not drinking beer from strangers' cups. And she slowly waddled closer, smoking and cussing in her broken, scraggly words. She stopped just in front of me, wobbling and blowing smoke. She looked up into my white mask and scowled harshly, as though she disapproved. We stood and stared at one another. Neither of us dared to move out of each other's path. Her ducks stood guard, then she suddenly barked.

"Fremeaux?"

I stiffened in wonder. How on earth could a, pardon my tone, a half-wit be keen to my identity? Know that it was me standing before her, hidden. I remained still and silent.

"Fremeaux, that fuckin crow is out again." She barked in her mangled attempt at speech, standing on her ground. Eyes fixed, she wasn't going to move or let me escape without a response. I relaxed, trying to figure out what that response should be.

"Fremeaux! No bullshit," she held a finger toward Bourbon, two blocks down. Dauphine was dark as well; the only thing visible was floating costumes in the neon river, and that damned Lucky Dog Weiner cart.

"You not see?" she asked.

I just shook my head, no. That was how I confessed that it *was* me under here, silently. She grabbed my cape, pulling me deeper into the dark patch, moving closer to Bourbon. She stopped us just before we reached the corner and the patch of streetlamp exposing the edge. She pointed again. Looking directly into my eye holes, she chewed her cheeks with defiance. I followed her finger and scanned the crowd. Mostly getting peeks of half-naked women in laughter. Ribs exposed and breast bouncing. I looked at the hot-dog handler, and he just looked like someone I may have arrested a time or two. He was squirting bright yellow mustard on a red wiener, handing it to a fella dressed as Mr. T. I looked back down at her.

She jolted her elbow to make her forefinger pull and push forcefully. She got annoyed and held a finger for her ducks to stay put; they did just that as she began to waddle off and around the backside of the Luck Dog cart. I followed her with my eyes as she abruptly halted, staring straight at me. The largest and most powerful of her ducks sounded a loud honk, cocking her head into a kind of crossbow pull and whacked the shit out of my kneecap. I bent down in pain to swipe the damn thing away from my leg, and as I returned my gaze to her wrinkled and agitated face, I saw it. Just in the shadow. A crow costume.

"Well, fuck me," I mumbled. "Another crow."

Ruthie could see that I had finally witnessed what she had been trying to tell the world for quite some time now. But I still don't know why this person has been so worrisome to her. She returned to me, and I shrugged my shoulders.

"Is this the guy?" I asked through the voice box.

She nodded. "Now-go bus his shit straight back to hell."

Of all the people who couldn't call me out from behind this mask. This woman right here distinctly knew. How? Could Ruthie be the universe? Were we all in her magic show, and she calls in the players as needed?

"Okay, sweetheart," I said with not much enthusiasm. I had no reason to believe he was more than some guy who fucked with her and her ducks, but just so she would leave me alone and not bust my cover, I figured I'd just talk with the guy, so I moved that way.

But there he stood, like every other partygoer out tonight. About five-five, covered in fine quality materials. Long black cape-gown-looking thing. All black hood with a dark golden-yellow beak drooping straight down the neck, made of silk, or rayon, or something. Hands covered with white gloves at the edges of this cape thing. Fine white silk stitching was woven around the edges of the draped black wool. The man looked tight and right. A small white rectangle hung on a thin wire thread around the neck and sat just above the stomach, about the lower chest. In childish hand-scrawled letters, the small signboard read, *Bad advice for $1.* He looked up at me. I chuckled for show.

"Just a dollar?" I asked.

"That's all it takes these days."

I looked just beyond his right ear and spotted the yellow lone bucket, on which a certain brown suitcase had been placed earlier in the day. Just beyond that, a darkened silhouette of a large man stood leaning his back against the wall, concealed in a dark shadow. Wearing a copycat costume to the little fella, the pants and shirt of which I recognize.

"Hmmm," I said to myself.

The entry door to The Dungeon was slightly ajar, sending a bright, thin ray of light just across the lower leg and foot of the stranger. If the door were to open wider, I imagined the exposed light would make a person feel the cold distance of a Hopper painting. A tormented and lonely soul staring at the ground for an answer. To what question, I had no idea. I looked back down upon the little fella. I could see bright blue eyes and a thin sliver of white wrinkled skin around the eye holes in the face of his costume.

"Nice costume. Most folks wouldn't go through the trouble of making their own Crow outfit this high quality?"

"I'm a Magpie. Think Heckle and Jeckle from *Dumbo*."

Holy fuck, I thought. I spelled it out in my head. M-A-G-P...I-E. MAGPIE. MAG-P, the same letters that marked Becca's hand. My gut rumbled, and my throat choked for moisture. The murdering motherfucker was standing right in front of me. I felt my jaw tighten, my chest heave, but I held composure. Goddamn, it was on. The needle had touched vinyl.

Ruthie had been right all along, just no one would take her seriously. Not even Charlie.

"You talk local. Do you know where the loose women are drinking tonight?" I asked with forced mirth.

"Son, just look around. They're everywhere. Like sittin' ducks. All ya gotta do is show 'em a good time and next thing ya know, ya got one or two in the bag."

"You don't say." I laughed along with him. "So, what do you do by day?"

"I practice the law."

"No shit? I reckon you go and charge the high rollers big money for sound advice and come down here and give shitty advice to us poor folk for a little ole buck?"

That put him at ease with me. I watched the stranger in the dark begin to pay more attention to us.

"Aw, it's all just advice. Depends on how ya look at it," he said.

"I don't have any cash on me, or I'd buy some bad advice."

"Next time, young man. Next time."

You bet. *Next time,* I told myself. Damn right next time. I looked at the dog vendor again to get a good ID. I'd track him down for some questions later. I scanned the name plate on the front of the cart and saw that the name written on it says Dud Foil on duty. I knew these fellas were rarely in the same place twice in a week and usually remain in employment for only a month or so before they move on to another life with a pocket full of new cash. I wouldn't get any kind of long-term information, but maybe he would remember something I could use. Maybe Lady Luck would drop a magpie turd on my square tonight.

I stepped past the magpie man to walk just beyond the stranger and study the illuminated leg. I followed the dark trouser leg to a polished pair of seaman's boots. A thick cut from the top passed over the toe to a missing gap in the edge. I knew that boot. Confession, my ass.

You can get one or two in the bag, that sack of shit said without hesitation. I guessed Zeus had slipped in after all, in the form of a five-foot-five magpie. *Fuck me,* I would have figured him to be a little bit bigger than this. Broader in the shoulders, maybe, but I guessed the bulky sidekick was the one in need of broad shoulders.

I crossed, hustling through the Bourbon crowd and back down Toulouse to where Ruthie stood in the dark. As I got closer to her, I saw Walton patrolling one side of Bourbon and Johnson on the other. Vidrine was farther up Toulouse. It dawned on me that certain police officers were occasionally assigned to patrol this area. Now I understood. They were there to keep me and others away from the game. Well fuck me. I felt dumb that I'd never questioned it before.

"Ruthie, go find Xandi. Find her quickly and send her to me, please." She nodded and told her ducks to remain where they were.

I stood guard with the hoodlums in sight. I moved a little closer, remaining in the dark. Unseen. I watched girls approach this magpie bastard, laugh a little, then move on. This went on for a good while, when a couple of young girls in store-bought matching Wonder Woman costumes came close. I sensed they weren't local. He grabbed their attention, and I watched as he did all the talking. The girls occasionally looked at one another and nodded in some kind of agreement. They listened for a bit, and what looked to me to be two small business cards were handed to each of the girls as they walked away smiling.

I needed to know what was on those cards, so I made a move toward them. I waited till we were all out of his sight and made an approach.

"Excuse me, ladies." I could tell the voice box, and the imposing mask startled them. "Could you let me see those cards the gentleman in the crow suit handed you?"

"Go get your own card, man. These are ours."

"I just want to see what is written on them."

"They're just free drink cards, you creep."

"Where to?"

"None of your fucking business. Now, could you leave us alone, sir?"

"I'll give each of you a hundred-dollar bill for your card. That'll buy you twenty drinks each."

They looked at each other. I pulled out two one-hundred-dollar bills and held them up. They handed me the cards, took the cash, and giggled.

One free drink was written on one side. On the other was the letter R with an address and phone number underneath. It was a card representing the R Bar. I'd gotten a haircut and a shot on a Monday night here before.

Shadows twitched and danced on the underside of the fog that has blanketed the rooftops, as I stood guard. The streetlights tried their best to give relief through the insincere neon flashes. Now and then, an unlikely hot guttural vapor wisps around street level, like hell herself had opened tiny holes and spewed a little extra audacity into our world.

It was a fact that night kisses were far superior to kisses stolen in the daylight. It was far more pleasurable to uncover hidden pleasures under the veil of darkness than to try getting lost in the sunshine. The mind chased those dark passions like they were the keys to life. The crowd was in love tonight, and it was a damn good feeling. As we all celebrated our pagan roots, greed gave us the idea that we might have the chance to grab and stop the hands of time. To trample this wonderland forever.

I stood motionless in the swirl of this great social petri dish. This garden of never-ending order and chaos, mercilessly watching the magpie lure girls into his ritualistic sphere. Ritual is where silly, confused souls will manufacture beleaguered truth.

After a couple of hours on this stakeout, a warm hand finally rested on my shoulder. I sensed Xandi. Ruthie appeared in front of me with a look of *I told ya so* on her face. Even without teeth and that collapsed, wrinkled face, she could still convey a declaration. I looked down at her as she curtly kicked my shinbone and went back to her ducks that were still waiting patiently for her return.

"Why didn't you let me in on this costume business? You passed by us earlier today and didn't stop?" Xandi asked.

I didn't answer her. I watched her inspect my eyehole like I had done with the magpie man earlier. I held my arm up and pointed beyond the Lucky Dog cart. She followed with her eyes.

"Repeat these letters," I said into her confused look.

"M-A-G-*P*-I-E." She understood when her lips pursed out the letter P. She stood silently, glaring.

"That's what we're going to kill. Have they been using Charlie the Crow as a public smoke screen? Let him be the crow talked about by society, all the while lurking in the shadows. Have you ever seen this jack-off?" she asked.

"I've patrolled this place for four years, and I've never laid eyes on them. There is another character standing guard just behind that one. You must remain cautious, we're in a Garden of Gods now, baby."

"Where are you headed?" she asked, knowing I was putting her on task.

"He gave these two cards to two girls earlier. I'm going to sit at the R-Bar and wait. Probably for the rest of the night. Find what you can here, and we'll bust these motherfuckers soon as we can."

"Don Lee has a walkie-talkie for you. I'll let him know where you are. Check in with me when you have it."

She squeezed my hand and nodded. I could feel vengeance dripping through her blood.

"Shit's about to get real. Tie those laces, big boy," she said as I was turning away.

I walked into the crowd feeling the frenzied, wild energies bumble around. It was in this thickened soup of chaos that crime hides in plain sight. Back home in Mason City, the criminals took shelter because they stuck out like sore thumbs. But not here. Amongst all this rumble, they could mingle their cult of doom and steal warm bodies right out of thin air. Murderous intentions developed long before the written word. Murder haunted us with dark, dank shivers. The black and white of death lurked with us through images of lifelessness that visit our imaginations more often than we wished to admit.

I grabbed the spot on the short leg of the L-shaped bar. My back was to the corner wall, where I could monitor the comings and goings. It was all coming through, either stopping in to dance or grabbing drinks to go. Every costume you couldn't think of. Bowling pins, dick-taters, abortions, Lestats, ghosts, Oscar the Grouch, and then there were the lonely dressed in shabby messes thrown together at the last minute, all by themselves, somehow wishing they were Quasimodo, hoping to rescue a fair maiden.

A big, burly bastard, looking like an ancient back lot bard from the dark ages, bellied up to the corner and held his hand high in the air for service.

"Man, what is it with us human assholes?" He looked at me, and I nodded in agreement. "What controls us? I mean, I'm the same person I was thirty years ago, maybe a little different. Wrong in every way, some days. I had some babies back then. They were my world, all-consuming, ya know."

He threw back two thick shots of vodka and rumpled his lips around like a horse does sometimes when the bit is first shoved into its teeth.

"They love me, I love them. The very thought of losing them to some horrific accident, never holding them in my arms again, could petrify me on the spot. I make mistakes, you make mistakes. They haven't contacted me for several years; I now wish for numbness to the pain of loss. Go figure, man, go figure. I've lost their hearts, but they're still breathing, probably out there right now dressed as angels."

He toasted his beer into the air.

"Here's to learning to live with the what-ifs and the could haves." I

nodded to him in approval once again. Then the burly man stumbled back out into the revelry from whence he came.

I'm figuring this ancient-looking white mask must conjure confessional desires as he was the fourth-twentieth-century human to shrink to some kind of weird *guilt-and-confess* self-crisis. Hell, I wanted to confess too, but it was impossible when I was vetted in secrecy. There was an all-girl band clad in bikinis calling themselves The Artificial Twats playing rockabilly on the corner stage. A man's suffrage could quickly be eased in such sights.

I hadn't witnessed any out-of-town young ladies handing over free drink cards since sitting there. Everyone so far had been thirty and above. It just dawned on me that in haste, I forgot to ask the girls an all too important question.

"Did he give you any extra instructions?"

I could be sitting here on the wrong night. Fucking rookie mistake, and I knew better. For a few hours, I felt I was the guy who knew the secrets, but now there was a ripple in that confidence. I'd run into the girls again at some point. When I was on nightly duty, I could see the same faces over and over throughout the weekend. I'd have a chance for at least one more inquiry. If something doesn't happen tonight. They're around somewhere.

We had the fish on the hook. Xandi and the crew would be put on stakeout. We still held the element of surprise. The release of the next article from Don Lee could cause a knee-jerk reaction, pushing them to try and hide or change the course of evidence. We could very well catch them in a desperate act.

I stared off into the faces and feel the thump of bass. Took me back to Mom and Dad dancing and fooling around the kitchen to Fats Domino.

Sometimes I could still feel myself sitting in my father's old truck an hour before sunrise, waiting for the last of the morning drizzle to end and the squirrels to awaken and leave their nests for food. I would listen to the gasp and thump of the old windshield wipers, too heavy for the tiny little motors that carried them to and fro. These new Japanese ones today were too quiet for nostalgia. They couldn't keep time with daydreams. Allowing us to count the beats of new ideas and visions.

Out there in that country night air, we kept the windows open, and the loudness of the insects could pull my imagination far up into the dark trees, and I naively believed I would very soon unravel the mystery and truth of living.

Here, immersed in these city nights, nature is a different animal. Us.

Don Lee appeared in the doorway, looking around the room, dressed in a Friar's brown robe and white rope belt. I was caught lingering on the hoax. He came and sat next to me, smiling. The bartender immediately placed a Rusty Nail on a cocktail napkin in front of him. He sipped and began another one of his tales.

"Shortly after I moved and called the city my new home, I attended a lovely garden party of an old friend of my grandmother's. I was sitting alone on a garden sofa when I first encountered my dear old friend Tennessee. He plopped his ole self next to me, obviously had made inquiries into my character, for he laid his palm on my knee.

"Young man, you have finally made your way into this Gordian Knot of bewildering, beguiling, slippery souls to live with us, I hear?"

He squeezed my knee tighter for effect and grinned with lips moist with alcohol.

"You'll fit right in even with that sopping wet Mississippi mud on the soles of those atrocious boots. You're one of us now, kid," he told me.

"After I covered the story of the crazed sniper shooting into traffic from the Holiday Inn out by I-10, Tennessee asked to see me one day. We met at one of the bohemian joints, and that's when he expressed that it was a marvelous piece of journalistic expression. Even though it was a tragedy, the story had read to his ears like the comfortable nibble from an old, trusted family Labrador. Let's see what we can do about that he told me. Lo and behold, in the first quarter of the new year, I received word that I was being awarded a Pulitzer for outstanding journalistic endeavors. Those of us who do our best in life bond and support, as do the criminals. They, on the other hand, will eat one another when the heat turns. Soon, these fellas we're chasing will follow suit and fulfill the prophecy of greed. We will soon attain our justice."

"So, I take it you've been filled in? You've found me here," I said.

"I just left Xandi and got a good look at our suspects. I can't believe I have never caught sight of them. They use the shadows well."

"Ruthie *has* been trying to tell us. I've never seen you drink a rusty nail?"

"It's my drink of choice at this joint. Here's your walkie-talkie." He laid it in front of me on the bar. "That's one hell of an imposing costume you got yourself. Where'd you get that doozy of a get-up?"

"Leda sent it to me."

"Fashionable idea. You won't be able to follow people too long in that thing; it's unforgettable. Especially since you're a full head taller than most. You certainly do impose, sir."

"You got anything more suitable?"

"I'll make a call in a while. By the way, we have spotters and photographers where Xandi sits. In front of the church, in front of Charlie the Crow's building. Are we missing anything more?" Don Lee asked.

"My place, I guess."

"Leda's got that covered."

I ordered myself a rusty nail, surprised by what I had just been told. "How's that?"

"You'll need to take that up with her. What did you discover about the kid with the tattooed hands?" he asked.

"Your intuition was correct. Hustling for the Dixie boys. Abandoned wife and kids. I guess half abandoned, he still hides illegal stuff on the property."

"Like what?"

"Dead dogs. New Porsche 911."

"You get numbers?"

"Yeah, it's registered to a doctor here in town, but unlocatable at the moment."

"I'll be damned. Probably someone employed over at that maritime health clinic, I'd bet. We do have peas in our pea patch."

He looked off past the other end of the bar. Harry Dean Stanton sat across from us with an attractive, dirty-blonde with California cleavage. He wasn't ready to give up his Repo Man outfit just yet, and she was a tainted fairy that weekend.

"There's evidence floating about that Kirksey Nix is running scams, trying to raise money to get himself ejected from Angola," he continued. "Our Mr. Gilleach is reportedly holding those funds. The problem is that my friends over at the Sun Herald can't find anyone willing to talk. I'm sure if we can track down Gilleach's lawyer, we could put a tail on him. There could be a fish there."

An effeminate cowboy rested himself against the bar. His makeshift sombrero had pink pompons circling the underside of the rounded brim. He ordered six different shots and waited. He turned to Don Lee and nodded. The shots arrived in a procession of two at a time, and he did the first two quickly, espousing his distaste for the government looking to place more controls on his American rights, as he saw it. Looking at Don Lee.

"Honey, did you read that fucking Nancy Reagan has gone and said no to drugs? She and Grampa got their fill and now want me to say no, too? Gag me with a fuckin' spoon, man. Mark my words, Don Lee, America is headed for a future just as dull and listless as them two. Social lobotomy is what we're in for. Lurd, Lurd, Lurd, it never ceases to amaze me as to what humans can and will do to one another."

He looked me up and down.

"I don't know what you look like under that pearly white mask, mister, but I'd do ya," he said, looking directly into the eyeholes.

"I'd bless that." Don Lee returned cheerfully, shaking my elbow.

The young man did his last four shots and danced back into the streets like the roads had been placed layer by layer just for him tonight.

Xandi's voice came over the walkie-talkie.

"The Magpie went through the white door behind the Lucky Dog cart."

"Copy that," Don Lee returned. I picked up the talkie Don Lee gave me.

"Did you notice if the Lucky Dog vendor's changed shift?"

"They did that about two hours ago."

"Good deal. Get the new guy's name," I said.

The clock above the bar read three-fifteen in the morning. The two girls I bought the drink tickets from stumbled in with two yuppies wearing matching white sweaters with blue piping. Gold-stitched emblems sat just above their nipples on the heart side of their chests.

"Thanks, Xandi. What's next?" I asked.

"Big Dan is going to remain on site for another hour or so. Where you two at?"

"R-Bar still. C'mon over, we need to find a person who can quietly pop the lock on that white door."

"I know someone, but he's tending bar uptown right now. He'll probably get off around five a.m.," she said.

"Where's he bartending?" I asked.

"Benny's Uptown."

"You talkin' about Booker Lott?"

"The one and only."

"Ok. Let's take a ride when you get here."

"Can do," Xandi said.

I turned to Don Lee and pointed at the girls and the two yuppies. "That's the two I got the tickets from. I forgot to inquire as to what else may have been discussed. If you'll excuse me a moment, I'm going over."

He grabbed my shoulder. "Let me. I'm trained in the art of unintrusive interview operations, plus you look like a goddamned executioner from medieval days. Don't want to make the boys feel threatened in any way. Just wave to them when they see us, I think that should be a sufficient introduction."

I raised my thumb. They turned and looked. We both smiled and held our drinks in the air. Don Lee made his move and bought them a round of drinks. They laughed together as I watched him lean in for the prize.

"Seems our bad advice benefactor asked the girls if they were open to dancing topless for some wealthy men for fifteen hundred dollars. They declined, so they said, and were given the tickets in case they changed their minds."

"What about the yuppies?"

"Hampden-Sydney. A couple of highbrows looking for love under the covers. Got the cash and charisma to pull it off."

"Makes one wonder what happens to the girls that say yes to the fifteen hundred."

"I think I got an idea. But remember, our little Mary Catherine was snatched after a family dinner, and my Mary Catherine would never have fallen for such nonsense. I'm certain of that."

"That was quite a few years ago. These folks have most likely multiplied their techniques."

"Sounds par," he agreed

Xandi squeezed in to stand between us.

"Fellas," she said with confirmation. A confirmation laced with feelings that she was ready to kill. Don Lee looked at me.

"What about the second article? When do you want to write it?" I asked.

"It's already done, dear boy. I must apologize for my haste, but I didn't want to stop a rolling ball."

"Hell, I ain't bothered at all. That's your department."

"Fremeaux, you should still *make an appearance* at my house around ten this morning. No costume. The article will be on stands first thing this morning, probably being loaded on trucks now. Nonetheless, we still need to be seen together in public. They need to think I've been interviewing you. This way, we can wander freely out of costume as we must be seen together."

"Gist still the same?" I inquired.

"Yes. You have uncovered a connection between certain crimes, possibly missing girls, characters in the Quarter, and possible protection from the force. You are being scapegoated."

The bartender brought two shots of tequila for Xandi. She tanked 'em. "You ready?" she asked.

"Yeah, I'm gonna need a bag to put this outfit in."

She yelled to the bartender. "Clyde, you got a Schwegmann's grocery bag back there?"

He reached for a brown paper sack and handed it to her.

"I'll pick up the tab; you two get out there and get us something we can use. See you in a few hours," Don Lee commanded.

"You gonna be, ok? Sure, you don't wanna roll too?"

"Not tonight, sweetie. I want to run by Nick's just to see what's hanging out. Maybe slip a little gossip into the ears of the younger boys in blue. Make 'em question their anonymity."

CHAPTER TWENTY

We stopped at a red light on the corner of Canal and Carrollton, and I watched a drunk couple outside the Popeye's make out while refusing to lose grip on two chicken legs. The entire parking lot and inside the restaurant were filled with young, sweaty bodies taking a break from a dance floor somewhere. Through my passenger window, a harsh screech from an angry male voice passed to me.

"You, fuckin' cunt! I'm taking your ass out for that shit."

I looked over at a two-story, nondescript all-white house behind a brick wall that had also been painted white. I couldn't see the people, but could hear a tremendous struggle for life in progress.

"Fuck, does life ever take a break?" I asked.

Then I heard the female's voice. "Get off me, motherfucker."

Then the male voice screeched in pain.

"You little cunt. You can't get away from me."

I knew the female voice. I'd just returned from a road trip to Vernon, Florida, with that voice. I opened the door, sprinted hard to the wall, and scaled it. A big fella in a business suit with blood pouring from an eye wound was walking toward Wanda. She held what looked like a pair of pliers in one hand.

I rushed from the shadows and put an elbow into his other eye, and we both fell to the ground. He twisted us as I fell on my back, whacking the base of my skull on the sidewalk's edge. I almost went out as I blocked a fist coming at me. I pulled his body to the side and elbowed him hard in the liver. He winced in pain as his head was suddenly pulled away in the opposite direction. Wanda held a wad of hair and was pulling as hard as she could. I put a hand around his throat and pushed his head to the wet ground. I felt Wanda move behind me. The man screamed like a city bus had just rolled onto him as he doubled over like a baby boy.

I stood straight to investigate. Just then, a side door opened, and twenty women came out to drag the screaming man into a small, dark room just inside the hallway.

I followed and found a handful of confused, shirtless men looking down hallways and around corners. Wanda locked the doors, turned, and pointed to the closed door where the man lay squealing and wailing, "Oh my God, help me."

She pulled at stray hairs that had become stuck between her lips and held composure.

"Gentlemen, this is why it's safe for you to come be with us. We take care of bad business ourselves, but rest assured, we take care of ourselves first. Keep your cocks and chickens in their pens. I don't tolerate being publicly flogged, as you can see. Go back to your rooms and forget you ever saw this. We're all safe now."

She turned to me. "You're gonna need to leave. Now." She then turned to her girls.

"See this face, he is one of us. He can be trusted."

One of the girls spoke up.

"Isn't he a beat cop in the Quarter? I've seen him in a uniform down there."

Wanda answered, "Trust me, ladies, you can trust this fella." She opened the door again and escorted me to the side porch. "This is my mother's place. Big politicians keep us shielded from law enforcement in return for favors, and you will never speak of it again."

I looked at her strong face and wild hair. "Can I ask one thing?"

"What, Fremeaux?"

"What did you put on that motherfucker's dick to stop him like that?"

"We call it the showstopper. An old acquaintance makes them for me. Would you like one? They come in handy and never fail."

I thought about the big guy protecting the Magpie Man.

"Yes, baby, I would."

Wanda went back inside the house and quickly returned with two pairs of vise grips that had been modified to have three sets of clamping teeth with a row of pins in between the clamps. She held up one set.

"Shove them in place. Don't need to be precise, as they are designed to never miss their target. They will never miss a nut or any part of the penis. Clamp till you feel the lock. Then, this thin little bar on the end here will lock them in place. So, the only way to release this lock is to squeeze 'em tighter to break this little hook-in. No man can figure that he needs to squeeze his nuts harder to escape the pain. Cardiac arrest usually happens within a few minutes. Once you lock them onto your victim, it's a done deal, baby. Then you take 'em to the river."

I looked at her. I had no words. I thought I might be overqualified to be a cop from there on out.

"There's a small gate in the corner of the wall on the back side of the house. You can follow the sidewalk back to where you came." She stated flatly. "And thanks, by the way, Fremeaux, you helped me."

I shrugged and walked away.

Turning the corner to the location where Xandi's car was when I ran off, I found it parked with the driver's seat empty. I heard a thump and watched Xandi walk away from the brick wall she had just scaled.

"You ok, Fremeaux?"

"All good, lady! You ready? We need to leave immediately."

"Sure." She looked at me with a question on her lips, but she cranked and drove forward in silence. "Are you in any trouble?"

"Not tonight," I said as we sped off.

We walked into the dark and funky Benny's Uptown Bar; it was packed with drunks wobbling about. Coco Robichaux was high, playing some sort of acid zydeco. I felt everyone in the joint may have ingested acid or shrooms or something. The knot on the back of my skull and the throb in my head made the laughter sound erratic. The energy was uncontainable. Like a pickle bucket with a hole in the bottom, something heavy swirled and condensed somewhere in the middle of my chest and flowed through me with a concentrated rush.

She found Booker at the other end of the bar, and I followed her down. They talked for a minute, then she turned to me.

"He can't come with us now, but tomorrow morning, around a quarter of five is good. Do you want a beer?"

I looked around. "Just take me home. I need some quiet."

"Okay." She said and waved to Booker, affirming a meeting tomorrow morning.

As we drove down Elysian Fields, I thought about the smoke and magic that appeared the last time she was in my house. We turned right onto Oriole Street into my neighborhood and then the quick left onto Lark. She parked on the street in front of my house, and I looked in all directions to ensure I didn't miss someone on another stakeout.

"I didn't see any either," she affirmed. "Besides, if someone really wanted you harmed, you'd be harmed. The universe has put the big eye on you."

"I'm just tired from the fight right now."

"How about a good fuck and a power nap?" she suggested.

"Burn me, baby. You seem to know exactly what I need when I need it."

"You're lucky you know a woman who carries loaded dice."

CHAPTER TWENTY-ONE

I woke again to the slow drift of burning voodoo as new smoke floated through the thick humidity of the bedroom. Fresh animal heads lay about. Silence is all I heard—no shuffling about. I called out, but no one answered. I was alone again. My body felt as though it had been tied down to the mattress. I lay back on the pillow, rubbing my eyes closed again. A dream resurfaced. One that must have been working itself out just before my awakening.

An image of a human body draped in white cloth, strapped to an army cot, dangled and twisted through dark space. It slipped through the folds of my perception when I realized it was conjured—a dream taking hold of my consciousness. The cot was a long distance away, so it seemed small and insignificant, but I slowly recognized it was my worn, useless body folded inside the flying bed. Illuminated and floating like an electric fish at the farthest depths of the seabed, it spun uncontrollably. I could feel my head dizzy; I was trapped in the spinning cot, sinking like a pebble in hot tar.

I became aware that I was looking down at a white medical blanket covering my body, spinning against the darkness. My pestered spirit heaved as though it was a loosening bandana clinging to a thief's face.

A peevish yellow beak, attached to pitch-black feathers, pecked at the skin on my toes. I could feel the claws clenching into my flesh. Blood oozing and flinging out into the nevermore. Phantom pains throbbed, and I couldn't wish the bird away. Trapped in agony, my temperament squirmed for an end to this misery. The wretched creature and my nightmare body whirled like an asteroid, down and down, as a bleached-white decaying human hand swooped and dipped above my skull, it would halo the creature, clasping my feet.

Chaotic and dizzy, my consciousness perceived it was powerless in the back seat of this hallucination, as the skeletal hand began to rise higher and higher until I could barely perceive its existence. Then, like a pair of paranormal scissors, the fingers clipped an imaginary string, causing my fall. The sudden drop through this murkiness caused the winged beast to rip more flesh from me as it caught a nonexistent wind and began to encircle me as I plunged. Swooping toward an eyeball, it wanted more of me for its own sustenance. I just kept flinging my head from side to side until a bright white light penetrated my eyelids.

I landed on something soft and looked about the room. I was in bed in a room in an unfamiliar place. A nun's habit then approached with a glass of water. She bent and tied her apostolnik around my bleeding toes. A female face I recognized but couldn't place stood behind the godly apparition, soon turning from the doorway and exiting, leaving me there to my own devices. The nun placed a warm hand on my forehead and whispered.

"Open your eyes, Fremeaux. Open your eyes. There's a new world to see."

I pushed and pulled my feet under the covers voraciously. I felt a strong grip on my ankle and opened my eyes to find you standing over me.

"Xandi, you weren't here, so I dreamt a little longer. It got a little weird this time."

"That green smoke over there is to help you with visions."

"That's good to know. In the dream, someone was watching to make sure I was alright. I couldn't make her identity."

"There are a lot of people making sure you are alright, Fremeaux. You were born under good omens, but you still have a long fight ahead."

"I didn't figure I could sleep that shit away. What's in the bag?"

"Everything in your fridge is expired, so I went out and got us a couple of hot sausage po-boys. Dressed and ready. Something funny is out there. I stopped at two stores and two newsstands, and the *Picayune* didn't make it. You find that odd?"

I got up, slipped on a robe, and looked over at a pile of chicken feet, bewildered. I answered. "Yeah something's up. Hopefully it ain't sabotage." I followed her into the kitchen. "Did you call Don Lee?"

"I tried, but he's probably still passed out."

"Did you ask the store clerk?"

"He said it's happened before. Once the printer's jammed, and once some fool's ass lost a set of keys. Whatever the fuck that's supposed to mean."

"Something should turn up in the Quarter. When we get close, we'll call on the radio."

We took a couple of bites of our sandwiches, and I got bored with hearing my teeth tear through food.

"You wanna talk about that scar on your ribcage?"

She looked me over with an *I don't like to dwell on this* look, and drew a deep breath. Drank some of her root beer. Rubbed her eyes with her thumbs.

"Okay."

She went to her purse and took a pill.

"What was that?" I asked.

"Ecstasy."

She planted herself in the chair again, resting the points of her elbows on my table.

"It had rained earlier that day. Before we had gotten to town. Mandeville was to hold a festival that weekend, and down the road, Franklinton was readying itself for its annual county fair. My people and a couple of other tribes moved in to sell jewelry and other wares. The ground was all muddied out, but we found a couple of small, raised mounds that were dry enough to pitch for the night.

"The sun set early, and the streetlights began to sprinkle their light through the bare tree limbs along the roadway. We could see the lights of the causeway stretch far off into a point leading to the city's edge. Dinner was almost ready when one of the girls whispered that there were people up near the trees." Xandi pulled tequila from a purse and swigged. Wiped her lips and began again, disjointed.

"I focused on the smell of beans burning on a hot plate as men held me down in the back of my father's little pick-up and raped me. My father was tied to the front bumper. The men remained eerily quiet as they raped me, I reckoned they were intent on hearing the pleasure I was supposed to be feeling. My mother held the box of money in her tent, and her friend Juacinta had all the good jewelry in hers. I remember hearing my mother say the words, *No, please no,* before I heard the thud of heavy metal push through bone and flesh.

"One was on top of me as two more held my feet. A rag had been pushed deep into my mouth. I'll never forget the choking as the torn metal lid from the opened can of beans sliced deeper and deeper into me as they hunched. As the metal tore my skin searching for my ribs, I drifted into a reptile's existence, lying still to survive. I could no longer feel the men on me. They somehow became insignificant. The metal finally reached bone, and I fell unconscious.

"I awoke bloody, stung, and bound in a small room somewhere. I had been abducted without knowing where the hell my family was. Whether my mother and father survived or not. I was a captive and a concubine.

"A little time later, a greasy horse trainer came to stitch the wound, and there I sat, a wounded whore for the taking." She paused.

"Can you identify any of these people?" I asked.

"They were identified and killed, Fremeaux. All except for one, and he is incarcerated in Angola. You've heard the name Kirksey Nix before."

"Does every shitty two-bit crime trace back to the Dixie Mafia?"

"Most likely. They have been on a rampage for the last twenty-five years. But, due to redneck greed, they began to kill one another off for their bounty. There are a few stragglers still taking the occasional hit job or small-time theft in the streets."

"I've heard you speak of your mother in the past tense," I said. "She didn't make it that night?"

"No. I found out after I had escaped that she had died instantly. My father lived a few more years, but depression finally chewed his soul down. My sister moved in with a clan down in South Louisiana, but she was taken from the French Quarter a few years ago.

There is an empty grave in Meridian, Mississippi, waiting for my sister's soul to join our mother and father. Horrendous people must be killed when they're found out. Period."

"Why Meridian?"

That's where our parents are laid to rest. My great-grandparents were considered the last king and queen of the American Gypsies, and it's where their fates ended."

"How did you survive? Were you rescued?"

"I was dumped and left for dead in a small body of water.

"A day came when I heard them talking through the walls about a large heist being planned, and they weren't sure when they'd return. If they were caught, the last thing that needed discovery was a girl stolen from a previous crime scene. One of them calmly blindfolded and gagged me. They tied my hands and feet and put me in the trunk of a car. We drove around for several hours, stopping periodically. We'd park. They'd leave and come back. Sometimes ten, maybe twenty minutes, sometimes an hour or so. After I felt the trunk space cool, I realized it had gotten dark, and we parked. I could hear crickets, so I knew we were in the country somewhere.

"The house I was held captive in was far out in the country. I could hear night owls and the usual critter symphony late into the night.

"Finally, they opened the trunk, and one of them was surprised to find me alive. They figured the excessive summer heat and lack of sufficient airflow should have been enough to turn me stiff. I was curtly escorted to the middle of a bridge. I could sense an open range and a cool draft from below, and the smell of tepid water hit me. Bullfrogs began their warning croaks as I listened to a large pair of wings beat the air in escape.

"They turned my body toward the openness, and the blow came quickly, followed by another to the back of my head. I buckled and pretended to be unconscious, relaxing every muscle. As they shuffled my limp body upward, trying to toss me, I peeked through the bottom of the blindfold that had wiggled its way loose to see where I might land. It was water, alright. Black as infinity. Dead leaves dotted the surface like dull eyes; it looked sinister and unforgiving. I felt as though I was about to enter hell.

"They threw me over, and the ice-cold plunge sprang me fully awake. I quickly sank into a squishy, mud-laden pond bottom. Thick, cold, congealed mud sucked onto my skin. I knew the surface had ripples, and I knew I had to endure the long wait until they subsided. I didn't move a muscle.

"I waited. Slippery things brushed my skin, probing the alien that had just landed in their kitchen. Fish mouths nibbled my skin. Worms found my fingernails. I'm certain a water snake wiggled and sliced through my thighs to settle into the mud under my weight. Still, I waited.

"I could feel the breath from my clan reaching for me through the thick void. Their chants pulsing to my heart. I couldn't open my eyes to search;

it was too dark, and I knew floating sand, slime, and algae would settle behind my eyelids if I did.

"Life itself extradited its needs from some forgotten place and brought it to me. I lay listening to the voices of my people, that alluring gypsy cadence feeding me their knowledge. Life would persevere, and calm would be my nurse.

"I realized the water was my mother goddess at that moment. Like a baby in a womb, I waited. I communicated with her by doing nothing. I let Mother Water hold me. I let her create, that's what she does best. My lungs smuggled the fresh breath that lived in the patient depths somewhere inside my blood. She created an atmosphere for survival.

"What seemed to be hours were only minutes as my time was coming to an end. I knew all I had to do was stand, and my head would reach the outside world, and I could breathe the night air again. I just hoped the two men would be gone.

"Just when my muscles began to sting and burn, I knew it was time. A thick, soft voice commanded me from somewhere. *Go, child,* it commanded. I felt the snake wiggle free, and I burst through the surface to see nothing but dark trees bending in a strong wind. The bleak air caused my body to shiver harshly."

Xandi looked at me again. "They were gone, and I made it out alive."

"How long were you held captive?"

"Almost a year."

"How did you find safety that night? Who found you?"

"I slowly hopped my way to the road's edge and stood there, tied and freezing, until a farmer came through. He had been on the other side of the state selling goats earlier that day, and he took me to the police station in a small town over in Mississippi named Kokomo. It wasn't too far of a drive. Some good country people took care of me and drove me back to the city a few days later. I wandered around the Quarter until Officer Gonzalez recognized me from descriptions and took me to Charity Hospital."

Xandi looked at me sternly. "That's it for now, Fremeaux. I get moody talking about the kidnappers, their fates, and what else happened to me."

I stared off for a couple of minutes. She spoke again.

"Go take a shower. I gotta relieve Big Dan, and you need to be seen with Don Lee. It seems a government limo exited the house on Barracks around five a.m. this morning."

I did as I was told and went to shower off all the shit that had stuck to my skin the last couple of days. I dried and walked to the bedroom. Xandi walked to me and pushed my fingers under her shirt and over the deep scar on the back of her ribs.

"This is not as important as finding the other people. Everything else is in the past, and I'm ok with it all. The people involved with my sister's disappearance are my future."

I nodded in agreement, and we left for the Quarter. Nearing Canal and Rampart, Xandi held up her radio.

"Anyone read the paper this morning?"

After a block and a half of silence, a voice I didn't recognize finally broke in.

"Yes, I did. Almost didn't find a copy, but a stack was on the ground outside Café Brazil. Just read the article on Fremeaux. Tell him if ya see him to be careful, they gonna be looking at him funny."

Oh boy, I thought.

Don Lee's front door had been left cracked, so I pushed and let myself in. I could smell a cigar. He was in mid-conversation. The extra-long avocado-green telephone cord stretched through the doorway, motioning for me to come in and make myself at home, so I poured myself an early gin and tonic and sat on the couch listening to one side of journalistic banter. With whom, I have no foggy idea.

"Ya reckon he's the real deal or a plant by Bush's leftover CIA regime? Kept around to further instill fear in our national security, maybe? *And* distract from the crap Reagan slips under our noses?"

He paused. I could tell he was listening intently. I watched the curled cord twist tight and then unwind. The pitter-patter of bare feet on old wood. Smoke filled the doorway.

"The real deal, huh? Now the fuckers have us sending ballistics to Afghanistan, fearing the Russians will inherit something special."

I sat in silence for a second or two, then his voice returned.

"You said it, brother. America will inherit a stench-filled wind on this one. We'll suffer the consequences of this *minor* infraction for a hundred years or more. Hell, my sister's great-grandchildren will lose limbs from fighting the recoil of such a premature knee-jerk." He paused, then spoke again.

"That narrow-minded Middle Eastern crap must be considered an irritating fire-ant hill. You have two solid choices: either annihilate everything or completely ignore them and leave them to their child-laden tantrums. There is no salvation in a world that eats its own."

Another pause and a re-twisting of the cord. I listened to a marching band outside moseying through the Marigny. I could see brightly clad people through the thin slits in the blinds; most were dancing, most were drinking, but all were smiling. What a day for them to be alive and well.

"I've heard a quiet rumor that Reagan is doing some shit down in Nicaragua to fund some of this shit?"

The cord stretched at least sixty feet as Don Lee walked to the bar next to me, poured himself a drink, winked, and returned to the other side of the wall.

"Yeah, Carter was the last of the good guys, but you can't be a good man in a house full of abusive fathers."

He laughed.

"Ahh hell, those fucks would pilfer the hair off our asses if they could posture a way to get their hands down the backs of our britches without a picture peggin 'em to the scene. As far as those backstabbing buffoons are concerned, poverty *is* the standard, wealth is for the lucky thieves."

I stood and opened the blinds a little more to peek at the roaming crowds. Some fella had gone to great lengths to look like Ziggy Stardust. Don Lee laughed heartily again in the background.

"That's some truth. Money feels great in the hand; power feels best when shoved up someone's ass."

I listened to a Bic lighter spark over and over.

"It's our solemn duty to slap the shit out of the self-absorbed."

I poured myself another drink and secretly wished for an ecstasy pill. The sun is out, and I wanted to be as well.

I drifted away from Don Lee's voice, thinking about the ecstasy Xandi took and the fact that I've been itching for a rerun. I drifted off to the last night I enjoyed a roll-on ecstasy. Spring break twelve years ago. Drove over to the French Quarter with Deborah D'Iberville and two other friends. Blue

Crystal had just opened and was the hot new joint for an MDMA revival. Tucked into a dark corner off the dance floor was a small closet with a thick, solid oak door. A small square hole had been hacked out in frenzy, about eye level. It had no doorknobs. It was a haven to hide and have sex while watching everyone else love each other. Everybody fucked in that closet at one time or another. I'd seen judges, doctors, lawyers, teachers, mechanics, mafia, and upstanding mothers. White collar, blue collar, and brown collar. I'd watched it all go in clean and come out painted.

At three or four a.m., we giggled our way down Causeway Boulevard and got sidetracked in a Burger King parking lot. Deborah decided we should have an orgy in the big plastic burger playhouse. And so, we spent the last leg of our journey in an almost unconscious fit of passion and glory. Finally exhausted and sticky, we passed out cold. In the middle of our little catnap, a thunderous vibration pounded us awake. A lady in her sixties stood holding a scrub brush, cleaning rags, and a Virginia Slim 100 dangled from the corner of her mouth.

"I'll be opening this family establishment for breakfast in thirty minutes. You, kids, have fifteen of those minutes to get your clothes on and clean this thing out before any children are brought in here to play. You got me?"

I looked down at the name, Ms. Peggy, who knew a thing or two about keeping quiet. We were fully aware of our position in life, so we fumbled through underwear, traded socks, and did what was politely commanded. It's almost impossible to want to live anywhere else. Outside of Louisiana, some overly moral zealot would have had us arrested and publicly humiliated for fully flaunting the pride of our youth. Also, it was obvious she had made this speech a few times, and she probably had a husband to raise somewhere in the city.

I had Xandi on the brain, so I picked up the walkie-talkie to inquire how everyone was doing out on their stakeouts. She checked back.

"I'm sitting across from the lucky dog cart. There's a fella on a balcony down on the corner with a camera and a lens as long as a pool cue. So far, no sign of them, but I'm sure those two won't fly outdoors again until nightfall."

"Anyone else have anything out of the ordinary?" I asked.

"Big Dan reminded us that a long black limo had exited the house on barracks around five a.m., and nothing has moved since. Nothing to speak of over at the cathedral either."

I tapped at my thigh with the antenna of the walkie-talkie and peeked out at the world again as I caught sight of her long, dark hair taking the corner to Esplanade. "What the hell?" I asked the window.

A sense of loss slugged through my heart as I wondered why she wouldn't have wanted me to know she was back in town. I threw the walkie-talkie on the couch and set the drink on the table by the door as I ran like hell through it.

Remembering the feel of her grip on my arm, the last day we talked together, eroded any thoughts of how much energy I was using to get to the corner from where I lost sight of her. My heart pounded as I searched the heads in the crowds looking for that walnut brown hair. My hands were hot.

She stepped to the right from a small wad of bodies back into view as I yelled her name, but she couldn't hear. I watched her enter Buffa's Lounge, unaware of my wanting. I sprang toward her and knocked over a couple of vampires carting a wagon of bloody heads with pupilless eyes, opaque and glowing. I apologized after resetting the wagon of death onto its wheels. I was off again at high speed, careful not to barrel into other people again.

I bolted through the tavern-like door and scanned the room. I couldn't find her. I rushed through the crowded bar, hoping to end this feeling in my chest. I pushed through a doorway, headed to check the restroom line, and caught sight of the back of her head using a payphone at the end of the long, dimly lit hallway.

I raced down to grab her elbow, frantically asking, "You're back?"

I was greeted with a scream and deep brown chocolate-chip eyes. My heart jumped with anxiety as I realized I had lied to myself. It wasn't Leda.

I calmed the girl and headed back toward Don Lee, perplexed. How could I have fooled myself like that? Leda doesn't dress low-rent bohemian, even if it is Halloween. What had I been hoping for? Deep down, I knew I wanted her to be here. My steps were heavy, like I was forcing my way through the headwinds of an oncoming hurricane of ghosts. I struggled through confusion. My thoughts skidded when I saw the golden Rolls-Royce parked around the bend from Don Lee's. An odd bastard's nostalgia washed over me for some ungodly reason, like the comfort of a warm bath, but realizing a stranger had just dirtied the water just before you jumped in.

It was a rare sight to stumble upon; Golda's chariot wasn't usually roaming this side of town. I slowed my steps and inspected her driver standing across the street from Don Lee's front door, scrutinizing the flow of partygoers.

I caught the slits of the blinds snap back into flatness from the very same window I spotted my imposter. I wondered what those reflected lips were whispering behind the glass now.

I crossed the street in view as I pretended not to have noticed, conscious of my stiffening steps. As I passed the wrought iron gate, I heard the front door break seal and slowly open. Her eyes found me immediately as she stood, with a glass of brown liquor in her grasp, waiting for me to come closer. Her gravity is inescapable. Lightning wrapped in velvet. Coiled barbed wire. We stood toe to toe.

"Good afternoon, Ms. Golda. It's good to see you again." I wondered why she had decided to bring me to her once more. She had the two men tied away somewhere, gathering all she needed for her daughters' protection.

A wrought iron backbone held her beauty high and lofty. She stood eye to eye with me, and that level of refinement instantly drew sweat to my palms. Even though she was entering the fall season of life, she was still fresh, with the polish of a spring flower. She sipped, letting the waves of energy unsettle me. Unyielding, she let the flavors swim around her mouth before she swallowed God's sweet gift.

"Off the force for a bit, I hear. Knowledge is power, they say. With that power comes burden. Everything crumbles eventually. Yeats does remind us that things fall apart; centers do not always hold.

"You can't tell me that not one of those men standing three feet from Hitler didn't reimagine his future? Didn't secretly conspire to murder a madman? I'm sure some did, but chose to remain ignorant. Who the hell would want to martyr when the rabid pack can't smell the rot? We allow things to fall apart, and that is our burden. I, myself, hold what needs to be braced. I rip what must be torn asunder, so now you know. All will be righted for you someday, Fremeaux. Keep your faith intact."

She pulled the last of the bourbon into her mouth and put the cool glass into my wet grip. I could sense this lady would readily saddle up and drive hungry lions down to the killing floor if it was necessary to ensure Leda remained safe and sound on her pedestal.

I wonder what kind of man could make her bend, who or what could be her one true love? She glided past me toward the gate, and her driver walked to open it. I felt the wild courage to ask if there was a question.

I called out, "Ms. Golda," and she pivoted to look.

"Any chance I might have a chance at asking Leda's attacker a few questions?"

"I have my own plans, Officer Fremeaux. And, by the way, Fremeaux, to make things par, it's Golda. You can drop the formality."

The door was pushed closed as she sat straightening her dress collar. Her driver spun secretly, giving me a short affirmative nod of the head. I had no idea what it truly meant. Was he reaching out that he and I were blue-collar colleagues, or did he hold an inside piece of her ideas, and I was on the right path? Or maybe something more sinister, like sending me down the wrong trail to protect his stake in the game?

Hell, who can I trust? Suspension from my post. Prostitute, dingy motel. Mental state in disorder. Fuck, I tried to maim a kid for just being an asshole.

My life seemed to have turned into a bucket of coal dust. I heard Don Lee's voice coming from inside. I watched the golden Rolls-Royce turn the corner, and something seemed to whisper, *Trust the process,* as I turned back towards Don Lee's front door.

The avocado green cord stretched through to the refrigerator. I could tell by the tone in his voice that it was a different person he was talking to now. He waved and began to walk toward me. His face carried faded grandeur into the room.

"Mother Nature plants the reason to kill. It starts as a tickle in the tummy, expanding into dinner plans. Some of us stick to a belly full, while most other fuckers plunder about the psychopath's pantry wanting it all for themselves. Deceitful bitches. It's all about dominance, my good man. Pure dominance. On that note, my ace in the hole is sitting on my couch, and I'm afraid I must say goodbye for now. I'll call you back soon."

He was trying to end the call, but the fella wanted to add something more. Don Lee gulped his drink, miming to me if I was ready to go. I nodded.

"Frank, I gotta go, man, I have an interview scheduled; gotta beat feet. Glad to hear from you. We'll talk next week. Bye for now."

He went to the other room and put the phone back on the hook, and returned with a look of, *Let's get the fuck outta here.*

"C'mon, kid, walk with me down to the Monteleone. I'm scheduled to interview Jim Henson for *Mississippi Magazine,* so we can kill two birds with one walk."

We both watched off-duty cops wander out of our sight, heading down Royal, not really saying too much about it. Street clothes, not even trying to dress for the festivities. What stood out the most was the absence of uniformed patrollers. I did see Olen Ray in uniform walking over to Decatur when we first entered the Quarter.

"What was Golda doing earlier? I thought she was to be in Europe till Mardi Gras?"

"Not sure why she's in town, but she had read our article in the paper and was wondering what we were planning. I explained our plan, and she nodded with approval."

"Nodded? That was her response."

"Just a nod of the head. Leda is doing stuff for the family over there, and Golda has urgent business here for some reason. She asked if I'd be willing to write and post some articles for her, too."

"Who does she need to bamboozle in the press?"

"That I wasn't told. Just forming a long-term plan, I guess."

We stopped at the corner of St. Ann, allowing for traffic. Don Lee stooped at the *USA Today* box and read the headline aloud.

"Emanuela Orlandi's whereabouts are still unknown. You're gonna tell me a daughter born in Vatican City goes missing, and the fucking Pope can't pull the right strings to find her? Shit, kid, this tells me he's pulling the strings to keep her from being found. These fuckers can get away with whatever in the fucking hell they want, Fremeaux."

"It's here too. Like an octopus, the empire, with all her riches, folded itself into the church, then she slowly extended her tentacles all over god's green earth." I added.

"They confiscated a religion from the poor and are still stealing resources from all around the globe. Robes are the new army uniform," he said.

"Jesus saved our souls, but we'll pay the interest on that debt for eternity. We may not need to cry for our sins, but we'll sure as hell do all the crying for his. How's that for a gift that keeps on giving?" I said flatly.

We moved on into a crowd dressed for ritual.

"Love is only one habit away from freedom," he said as he bid me adieu and headed to the Carousel bar. I took a left at Bienville, thinking about the fate of Emanuela Orlandi. I talked to the walkie-talkie again, and the walkie-talkie reassured me that all was status quo for the moment.

Ruthie popped out onto the sidewalk from the door of Peligro Gallery, pinching a fresh cigarette and a fresh cocktail given to her from the girls inside. She came over to me, taking my hand. Looking up, she smiled and slowly walked me down to Jackson Square, her ducks chaperoning us the whole way.

She parked us on a bench under the live oak that butted up against Decatur, and we sat in silence in the voodoo that every one of us squeezes through every day of our lives. She moved her hand to my leg, and I put my arm around her as she sank herself into the concave of my ribs. We graciously monitored life for half an hour as her ducks took in the warm sunshine, without making a sound. I listened to her lips smack onto one another ever so often. Waiters and bartenders would occasionally stop and wave to her as the costumed dancers danced around our quiet moment. I'd steal a side peek occasionally. The sunken cheeks made a meaty pile that stretched wide around her collapsed and heavily wrinkled face.

A duck squawked to move forward and turned back to face me. I could see beauty in Ruthie's eyes. Folks didn't often get this close to her, and I hadn't felt this much appreciation and love since before my mother passed. Like Obi-Wan Kenobi, Ruthie was a simple woman holding treasures that could save lives and bust holes in souls.

"Is there more you know that I should know?" I asked.

She nodded. "Governors and preachers' men," she said in that graveled voice of hers.

A tiny grey cloud floated overhead from the river, bringing a sprinkling of rain. She stood, held her hands up like that statue down in Rio de Janeiro, and turned to me.

"Water, Fremeaux, water's our creator. Our quiet, loving Goddess, you drink her and respect her. We're poisoning her, and soon she's gonna return favor." She waddled off again.

That was the second time today I was informed that water was our goddess. Our creator. Was there something I've been left out of? Had the collective changed its mind?

I sat alone for a few minutes, watching raindrops slip down the grass blades further down into the black earth. While insects crawled up to the surface edge, drinking in the wetness, I recalled a conversation around the chessboard about information.

Information transfer might have spurned the beginning of this universe, and all evolution, for that matter. Information must have a carrier. A host for it to travel through empty space. Space comprises most of our universe. In between cell walls, there is nothing but empty space. Particles carrying information pass through our bodies and the earth, in constant motion, a never-ending force. Even this daydream I'm having is powered and carried by something unknown.

I wondered if some of that information transferred at the quantum level could be false. Intentionally false? Does the universe deceive itself with bad choices? Does it alter its own path of reality from time to time? From what could it be hiding such details?

Rain washes everything away. Clean slates. Everything but information, according to the Chess players. If you don't believe it, just drive slowly through a ghost town, where all the human souls have escaped something. You'll feel "nothing" scratch at your bones pretty fucking quick.

As I pondered the idea of false information, the Christians arrived on the scene once again, lugging a rubber raft filled with stuffed animals through the square. The spray-painted signage commands us to *Follow them to safe ground.*

The good people carrying the rubber contraption are dressed as Noah's family, triumphantly pouncing through this pagan ritual.

How about that for a misconception? Ten thousand years ago, the Sumerians told a tale of their Gods flooding the region, calling upon a mere mortal to save all the wildlife. A few thousand years later, a fella called Noah builds an ark.

I reckon God secretly commanded to all the beasts aboard that there would be no eating, shitting, pissing, or fucking for forty days. *And* nights. No belly aching on that boat; humanity depended on it.

I don't know if you've ever searched for the forbidden toilet on Mardi Gras day, but those last few seconds before standing in front of a toilet could be the most painful thirty seconds of your life. I was pretty certain desert turtles wouldn't be able to piss overboard and not fall away into extinction. I also couldn't imagine having access to a piece of ass and marking the wooden wall with days missed. That might've been the biggest *bummer, dude* ever recorded. Maybe that's where copulation without love burrowed into the minds of the modern-day believers. Created by the very ones who disavow it. How was that for questionable information that's been floating around for a few thousand years?

A squirrel hopped near my feet, unaware that its biological imperative had been hocked from the throes of oblivion by the bravery of that Biblical-scruffy, courageous, superhuman family. The squirrel stood fully erect before I heard the sirens.

In unison, I stood with the squirrel and immediately halted as we sprang our eyes up to the passel of sirens quickly screaming toward us from somewhere out in the concrete and wind. Mayhem has just erupted somewhere.

I happened to glance at the cathedral to find Don Lee, Jim Henson, his wife, and Big Bird halt in front of the cathedral entrance and turn to investigate the goings-on. Big Bird mimed wiping a tear as the others turned to enter with the Monsignor. I felt like a man who had just won a battle as I watched the Hensons walk through the cathedral's door.

I didn't know much about other people's lists of greatness, but I believed I had just caught sight of Mississippi's greatest gift to the entire world.

Folks up in the Delta and over in Tupelo would vehemently argue for the blues, cotton, and Elvis. But cotton only covers the ass and knees. The blues and rock and roll only highlighted the scars of a man's soul and the occasional leg wiggle. What Mr. Henson offered the world was pure magic for every human on earth. A recipe for rejuvenation of the soul. Imagination plus joy will pull any stubborn mule from the mud bog. Acceptance of other people is our greatest struggle, and Kermit holds all hands with an abiding heart. And that, my friends, is something a man can hang his hat on. Could that be the universe's honest wish, to live and die together in harmony?

The blaring sirens pulled my focus back to the marked and unmarked cop cars speeding past us on Decatur. Red-blue, red-blue caused the undersides of the leaves of the oak trees to glow purple-brown. Something huge was going down. The drivers of those raging vehicles all glanced at me in the park as they screamed by. I saw Olen Ray running at full trot in front of the cathedral toward a waiting squad car. I shouted for him to fill me in.

"Not sure for now, Fremeaux, I'll find you later."

I spotted a leggy woman walking arm in arm with what looked to be an insurance man from Nebraska. As they got closer, I saw it was Mother, making me realize she had been out of pocket since I heard her voice on the phone out at Don Lee's River getaway. They walked a little and kissed a little. I bet myself the fella had no idea he was engaging in adultery with a former member of his sex, but that's neither here nor there as far as I should be concerned. I guess my mind was still on the false information track.

As she got closer, I saw she was wearing only panties, a T-shirt, and flip-flops. The T-shirt just barely covered the panties. For a sixty-eight-year-old woman, she still had nice legs. If a dirty limerick had grown two long brown legs, I'm certain that's exactly what I was witnessing at just this very moment.

Her T-shirt stated the four commandments for living in NOLA, with the letter O in NOLA containing a smiley face.

1. Don't kill or maim anybody.

2. Mind your own business.

3. Don't piss on your neighbor!

4. Have fun & love well.

That adds up to five, but who's counting at this point? I stood to wave and catch their attention.

"I've missed you in the streets recently. How ya livin', sweet lady?"

"Oh, fine, my darling Fremeaux. We're lovely. This kind gentleman flew me to Barbados for some R&R. How are you? Did you hear the awful news about Charlie? He has been shot dead," she explained in her broken English. She's resided in this country for forty years, and she still insists upon communicating as though she hopped off a ship three days ago.

"I hadn't heard. So, was that all the commotion? You got any details?"

"I do not. We were just passing the station on Royal Street and Chief Barlow fill me in. Say it look as though he try to kidnap a girl, and an off-duty officer heard her screams and intervened. He said Charley tried to fight back and resist. Say he pull his gun on the police officer, that's all I was told."

"Well, that's interesting since Charlie was barely strong enough to squash a mosquito," I said.

"Sounds fishy to me, too. This lovely man here has to leave for New Jork later tonight, so I'll catch up and check in with Don Lee and the gang soon, okay?"

"Thanks, Mother."

"Love you, baby." She dramatically kissed up into the air in my direction as she and her harmless beau meandered off arm and arm through the costumes and merriment, smiling like thieves.

Funny thing about naïve men, when they dance with what they see as a beautiful woman. Many personalities swirl around inside them, or all of us, for that matter.

The purple coward in us peeps through fearful cracks for safety. The mirthful green dog sniffs for the pat on the head. The blistered rose-colored pig in us snorts about for ease of opportunity, but ultimately, we become the reckless king looking to control their emotions. On occasion, the ladies will wait cautiously as we dance through each character. Sometimes that patience wears thin if we waver too long. What they truly want is for us just to be okay with ourselves.

As Mother and her lover wandered off, I began to feel numb. I wouldn't watch Charlie wander any longer. *Charlie the Crow was just shot to death.* If a man ever seemed to be born in the ropes, it was certainly him. If Catastrophe had a lap, then poor ole Charlie had just spent a lifetime climbing into it. But he's just another victim on a long list of victims that's gonna grow even longer as we move toward capture. I pulled the walkie-talkie to my mouth.

"A reliable source has just informed me that Charlie the Crow has just been shot dead by the cops. Our mission has just been kicked into overdrive."

"What the fuck?" Xandi exclaimed.

"They *have* retaliated," Don Lee added.

"Yeah, they're gonna try and pin this shit on me. Say, Charlie and me were cohorts," I answered.

"You need to get back into costume," Don Lee said.

"I'm in the park. In front of the Cathedral. Someone needs to get me; I can't walk into Leda's like this. I could give away the safehouse."

"We'll come get you," Xandi answered.

"Big Dan George! Pick me up from the parking lot at the dingy motel across from Nick's bar," I demanded.

"The one where you were photographed?"

"Yes. I'm going to catch a cab from here. I'll dodge anyone who may be of concern. Is your car near?" I asked Xandi.

"Yes, the Marigny. Big Dan is only five minutes from it. He can have you picked in fifteen minutes," she said.

"Gimmie thirty."

"Gotcha, Fremeaux," Big Dan answered in that thick husk-rattled voice of his. I must say, I took comfort in that sound.

I took a cab up to Zaras on Prytania. I gave the driver a hundred bucks and told him to sit for thirty minutes and then leave. I went in the front door and walked straight to the restroom, and through a door in the back. I hustled through the Uptown neighborhood and back over to Napoleon to hop another cab back to the shitty motel. I crawled into Xandi's backseat, and Big Dan's head shadow covered most of the backseat. I slid down into the shade and told him to take me to Calamari's upholstery shop on Claiborne.

We pulled up, and I told him to go inside and ask for Helen Henry. Told him to let her know Don Lee has a stowaway outside needing a lift. After a few minutes, he got back in the car.

"She said, drive around back."

I switched back seats, and she drove me to U.N.O. I left the Schwegman's bag with the costume in my kitchen this morning. I would need it, after all. I had informed Big Dan to let our folks know I'd be back undercover soon and would reach out when I did.

I got into the house and peeked through all the street-facing blinds. I found a couple of oilman cars down two different streets and wondered if Leda's security knew about them or if they were her security. I realize I don't know what the hell is going on and just who the hell is directing who at this point. I ain't in Mason City anymore.

I grabbed the bags and guns and got my ass back to Ms. Helen. I changed clothes as she took me to the curve at The Pontalba.

"Son, you'd better be safe out there. I don't know what kind of crap you got yaself into, but keep them eyes open till ole Don Lee can grab ya."

"Thanks, Helen. Hope I won't be needing you anymore after this."

"Don't bother yourself, son, we take care of our own out here. You need me, come see me."

"Thank ya, baby. Tell Frogman howdy for me, please."

I promptly got back into the safety of Leda's and took out the walkie-talkie.

"I'm back. What have I missed?"

"Where y'at?" Don Lee's voice answered.

"You know where. Just a walk away."

"Stay put. I'll come to you. I've got something for you."

"Gates open, doors unlocked," I informed him.

Big Dan's voice broke in.

"White panel van just went round the back of this building."

"I'll be right over, Big Dan," Xandi answered.

The same voice informing us about Don Lee's article came over the air. "Monsignor walked across the square and made a call on the pay phone outside Maspero's. Hung up and answered another one. He's talking now."

"Keep an eye on him. Report if he does anything out of the ordinary. If he meets or even waves to someone." I told her. Then I asked the crowd if the photographers were all in place. I found that all our spots were covered.

Shit was shaking out quicker than I could have imagined. Don Lee didn't fuck around. A sudden ring of the phone startled me. I wasn't expecting it. I had forgotten there was one even near. I looked at the Francis Bacon again and reminded myself that life can be a murderous blur.

"Hello?"

"You've been busy, I hear," Leda answered.

"Busy at what, I couldn't tell ya. I feel I've been moving somebody else's checker pieces around a faded board. Stacks of captured checkers keep stacking up for the Dixie Mafia and the Goddamned Catholics, and I can't seem to see the jumps. Hell, I've jumped over myself. I'm walking around in a batshit crazy costume trying to find a fucking clue as to why."

"Well, Mr. Man, sounds like you've got a bucket full of the blues."

"That's a no-shitter."

"Don't forget, if you need some extra pull, you've got yourself a senator in the bank."

"Speaking of pull, a little bird told me you have my place on safeguard?"

"I had a friend roll by and make sure my favorite driver still had his legs. I did. But that's not important. What's important is that you remain out of the cop's sight till you and Don Lee solve your mystery. Can I do anything for you two?"

"The two criminals your mother has tied away somewhere. I'd like to talk with them."

"Their safety is my safety, Fremeaux."

"I just need to know about some kids connected with their crime ring that may have had contact or made connections to crimes leading to the kidnappings. We found a stolen Porsche on the land of the kid last seen with Becca. The car was registered to an address at One Shell Square, to a Dr. Fonteneaux. No one seems to know the whereabouts of this doctor. One Shell Square is where Charlie the Crow was sent to defect from working on the tankers. It was a doctor from the Maritime clinic that your family runs. Do you know anything about this, Dr. Fonteneaux?"

We sat in silence.

"I don't keep up to date with the comings and goings of the clinic. It's just a service my extended family provides for the workers. I'm coming back through New Orleans earlier than planned, and that's why I called. You've been good to me, and I wanted to reciprocate by taking you to dinner. How bout I investigate the clinic and we can talk more then?"

"I just need to be patient, I guess. I'd love to have dinner with you, Leda."

"Good, I've missed you. You make me feel safe, and I could use that feeling again."

I was taken aback by that statement.

"If I'm not tied in the trunk of a car somewhere still trying to figure what the hell is going on, then I'll always be here for ya."

"Don't forget what you told me one night in the limo. We gotta pull our big boy pants up and live and work with the least amount of fear we can muster, remember?" she asked.

I looked up to the woman with the bird of prey tied to her arm. "Yes, lady, I remember."

"Do you remember what I told you that night?"

"You told me that when you were eleven, you met your mother's father for the first time. It was in the shifting lines of his face you felt that birth itself could be the true crime of the universe. You calmly walked to him by candlelight and kicked him in his shin with all your might. In that moment, you learned that all little girls must learn how to be impolite."

The phone line sat silent as I waited to hear if I had remembered correctly. Then her voice came to me with a slight choke.

"I'll be home soon, with surprises."

"I'm here, lady."

I hung up the phone and looked back at the bird of prey strapped to her arm in the oversized photograph. "I know, buddy. I know."

I suddenly realized that Becca hadn't hounded me in a few days. I must be on the right track.

Don Lee comes in with another Schwegman's bag and throws it at my feet.

"Your street partner, Olen Ray, dropped this off with me. Said he snuck it from the back of one of the cruisers, and you should have it."

I reached into the bag and pulled out Charlie's crow costume. I looked up to Don Lee. Both of us were at a loss but delighted to be at a loss.

"Can you smell the ghost of Charlie?" I asked.

"They're out there looking for your ghost as we speak. With both of you dead and blamed for all the gossip? They'll be trolling for you. Without worry," he added.

"They're unaware we've laid eyes on their magpie. Xandi and I will soon pick the lock on that white door and see just how far we can get."

"We need to get into that fortress on Barracks, too," he said.

"I may have an idea on that. I need to find my old FBI contact and get some information. I'm probably gonna need you and Wanda Ball to take a trip to Florida and steal that stolen Porsche."

"Sounds like it could be hare-brained, but I could get behind it. I've sensed that this crime ring was starting to unravel after all these years. Some kind of rot has set. I just want the opportunity to kill the person responsible for Mary Catherine. If that person is still breathing."

"Can you find Olen Ray and bring him back to your place?" I asked.

He held up his walkie-talkie, "If anyone sees Officer Olen Ray patrolling, put the grab on him and let us know, please. I'll come to him."

"Ten-four, Don Lee," a voice responded over the airwaves.

"Fuckin' magpie," I mumble.

"I'm gonna head back to my place, Fremeaux, to wait. Do you need anything before I go?"

"I'm good, Don Lee."

I looked out over the sea of folks in full bloom, rambling through Jackson Square. They've left all those high-brow philosophies and religions in the drawer next to the tampons and Tylenol, just below the hairdryer. You don't need unwarranted guidance when society grants you full reign over your life.

Hubris's umbrella folded down, pulling my attention toward that corner of the church. I watched Monsignor cross the way to a payphone. A few minutes later, Officer Desmortiers approached and waited for the reverend to end his call. In all this pleasure, this bastard in blue was the sore thumb. The only fucker walking stridently, twitchy. Rumor has it his wife vanished. He said she packed up and left. Most folks I'd talked with said otherwise.

I was ready to stroll. Do some hunting. I had the pistol in my left pocket, a knife in my boot, and the showstopper in my right pocket.

I lifted the talk box and asked Xandi if we were still on track for picking locks later tonight. She confirmed. I told the team to keep an eye out for Officer Desmortiers. I wanted to put my eyes on him tonight, and he'd be out of sight by the time I reached the square. Hubris had told me to stay the course. I turned out the lights one by one. I said goodnight to the lady with binoculars perched beyond the bags of peanuts and locked the door behind me. Feelings can sometimes come true, so I'd be walking for Charlie tonight.

CHAPTER TWENTY-TWO

I stepped into the jubilation with malicious contempt for the party poopers dressed in their tried-and-true blue garb, fooling themselves and us. I continue to fill with murderous contempt.

"Sacks of shit," my mother could be caught saying over the telephone. She could also be heard saying, "Some assholes can stink up a bathroom just by thinking about it. Stay away from fuckers like that."

I held up the walkie-talkie and asked a one-word question, "Showstopper?"

"Purse," was the one-word answer.

I moved forward with spirited winds brushing at my cape, trailing for the man with the Habsburg lower lip, Officer Desmortiers. An eye for an eye, as I see it.

I crossed the square and moved down Chartres, where I had last seen him disappear into the costumes and shadows. I walked in squares for an hour when I was beckoned through the talk box to make my way to Don Lee's. Olen Ray had been located, and we would meet up there, so my journey made a two right turns as I walked straight down Royal towards the Marigny.

A passion of red light spilled out of a doorway, stretching across the concrete sidewalk just ahead of me. Shadowed figures moved vigorously within the redness. I walked past the open doorway and through the red light I caught sight of intense fellatio. Intense enough to turn a man green with envy. Nothing I hadn't seen before, but the sheer lust of it made me think about Pasiphae and her uncontrollable desire to mate with her husband's prized bull. Lust is a powerful thing.

If it had been Golda in that Greek tragedy, she would have slit the throat of the beast herself, dining on steak and wine all the while daring the gods to intervene. *Deal with it. My pussy, my terms,* she'd mime while chewing fresh kill.

Olen Ray was there waiting when Don Lee opened the door.

"Fremeaux, you got a little war on ya hands, huh?" Olen Ray amused himself.

"Hell, I reckon. What's the talk on the inside?"

"I don't know if it's for peace of heart or ill fortune, but we've all been placed on the lookout for you. Looks like you've been amongst us the whole time in that crazy assed get-up you got on. I saw you last night and had no idea it was you."

"How'd ya get a hold of Charlie's outfit?"

"I found it stuffed in the backseat of Dowd's squad car and thought it was a little out of place. Know what I'm sayin'?"

"What's the story they're peddling?" Don Lee asked.

"A girl at the scene says Charlie told her he would drive her out to Metairie, but he needed to stop and get something first. He pulled a gun and told her to get inside, and as they reached the door, she saw a man up the sidewalk, and she screamed out. And lo and behold, that man was an off-duty officer from Chalmette. Charlie was shot and killed on the spot."

"What do you mean by drive her? Charlie doesn't have a car."

"Hell, I haven't been on the force too long, but I ain't ever seen Charlie in any frame of mind to drive, even sober. I was just as shocked as you when I saw an old, rusted car registered to him sitting with all the doors open on the street." Olen Ray said.

I looked over to Don Lee, and we nodded in agreement that their plan had been well thought out over the years.

"Where's the girl now?" I asked.

"Not sure, they whisked her away pretty soon after I got there."

"Did you get a good look at her?"

"Yeah, young, pretty. I got the sense she was streetwise by the way she smoked her cigarette, rough like. Not in the jr. college dainty way. She wasn't afraid of the smoke getting in her eyes. She walked like a gal from the wrong side of the tracks, but somebody took the time to put her in nice, preppy, mall clothes. Kind of like glamor shots done at a low-rent beauty parlor somewhere."

"This sounds silly, but do you think you could describe her without the makeup to a sketch artist?" I asked.

"I'm certain I could."

"Don Lee, what ya got?" I asked.

"I can get my man over at the *Picayune*. Have him here tomorrow. Maybe Wanda could peg an ID?"

"You got time tomorrow, Officer Olen Ray?"

"Sure. Any time before four. I've still got to punch a clock."

"I can make that happen," Don Lee said.

"Has anybody on the force spoken about me possibly hiding under this crazy Venetian costume?" I asked.

"No, they just think you'll come around at some point. They're trying to reach out to reinstate you. That's the word being passed out at roll call? I don't trust 'em, though. Somethin's fuckin' around behind those doors."

"That's our gut feeling, too. I think they want to zip this bag up tight and let history erase our names like Gonzales. I need two things tonight, Olen Ray. First, I saw Desmortiers earlier. I need to know where he's stationed and what time he gets off. And could you run down Agent Freeman for me? I need to get inside information on that greasy-headed kid with the fuzzy mole on his forehead."

"Otto?" he asked.

"Is that his name?"

"Yeah, that's all I know. I've heard him called to before. What about him?"

"I want to know where he lives. I have a half-assed plan and need to track him down. I do know he lives over in Mobile somewhere."

"Ok, I can do that. When I find out where Officer Desmortiers is, what do I do then?"

"Xandi will be sitting on a stoop across from the Lucky Dog cart on the corner of Bourbon and Toulouse Street."

"Ok, Fremeaux, let ya know as soon as I do. What does this Xandi look like?"

"You know Olen Ray, the hot little voodoo queen in the Quarter. You see her every damn day."

"Oh, that girl? I never knew her name; I've just called her sexy. That's what all the fellas in the street bark at her when she talks with em. Okay, okay, let her know I should be around to see her in an hour or so. Anything else?"

"Don Lee, ya got anything?" I asked.

"I'm good for now, kid."

I pulled up the talkie and told Xandi to expect Olen Ray soon. She affirmed.

"Talk at ya soon, Olen?"

"Is all this about those missing girls?" Olen Ray asked.

"Yes, son, it has a little something to do with the girls," Don Lee answered.

"Look, fellas, I'm on your side. If there's more I can do?" He raised his eyebrows, letting us know that we shouldn't hesitate, and he turned back to the streets. I stopped him suddenly.

"Olen Ray, there is one other thing. It could be risky for you."

"What is it, Fremeaux?"

"Xandi and I will be doing a breaking and entering this coming morning, around the time you're headed back to do paperwork. If it's doable, we could use some distraction on the opposite side of the Quarter."

"Where ya'll gonna to be doing this?"

"The white door behind the Lucky Dog cart. You'll see when you stop by and talk with Xandi later."

"See what I can pull for ya'll."

"Much appreciated, Kiddo. Ya know Olen Ray, you can call over the radio that you've just seen me in street clothes headed into the Treme after we break in. That'll mislead 'em and give 'em confidence you're on their team."

"Sounds good, old man. It'll be the nuts." He smiled, shook our hands, and left us.

"Don Lee, didn't you tell me you picked up Gonzales's stuff from the precinct for her parents back in the day?" I asked.

"I did. What are you looking for?"

"You still got anything of hers around here?"

"I got one of her badges. She left one over here so I could flash around town when I needed assistance. Why?"

"I want to use it later. It may be a while before we get it back, though," I said.

"If it'll flip the kitty, it's all yours, bud."

"Oh yeah, it's gonna flip a kitty."

He left the room and returned with her badge.

"Have you talked with Becca's mom lately?" I asked.

"This morning, we talk often. I also put her in touch with some of the other grieving mothers. Therapeutic, ya know?"

"It'll be a relief to know the truth, but it's gonna kill her when we are finally able to give her final news," I said.

"Yeah, Fremeaux, it bums me, too. I'll do it in person if you're up for a trip?"

"I'll be there with ya, old man," I told him.

I investigated his haggard and crazed Mississippi eyes. I could envision thin walls behind 'em, windows with half-closed shades, and long hallways leading to a spiral staircase that seems to crawl down forever. A cold draft leaked up through the slats of his ribs. If a man were to brave those rickety stairs and eventually find the bottom rung, he might discover a sign tacked to those thin walls reading, *Demon est Deus inversus*. I was standing here looking into aged blue eyes caked with the devilish grin of southern nobility.

I left and walked around the corner to stand inside the R-bar for an hour or so listening to Marcia Ball, no relation to Wanda that I'm aware of, for over an hour, hoping to catch a young, pretty girl with a free drink card. My gut said they'd lie low for a period, but one can never tell around here. Olen Ray's voice came over my radio; he must have found Xandi, I thought. "Repeat," I said.

"Desmortiers is on private detail over at The Bombay Club. I remember hearing some politicos are in town, and Dr. John was hired to put on a good show. Sposed'ta punch the clock around three this morning."

"Good deal, Olen Ray. Make sure you're nowhere near the back side of the Quarter tonight. Stay near Decatur and Rampart."

"Gotcha, Fremeaux. Can I ask what ya got on the guy?"

"He was on-site at Officer Gonzales's murder. He's on the naughty list. Speaking of lists, I gotta get all the names that were there that day."

The voice changed to Xandi. "I've got the list. Everyone on the scene, plus the mafia getaway driver."

"Good news, baby. Any luck tonight at the stand?"

"Nope. Nothin' so far."

"My gut says this thing is going to break up for a time, folks may go into hiding until I'm discovered or caged. Fill Olen Ray in on the well-dressed love birds we're looking for, would ya?"

I could feel her look Olen Ray up and down. It was silent for a second or two.

"You sure about this, Fremeaux? Could put you in a bigger hot seat?"

"I trust Olen Ray. Good family. Use whatever tone of voice you feel."

"Okay, big boy."

"I'll be around in a while. You and I have a task." I told her.

"Ohh, sounds gritty," she returned.

"Oh, it's gonna get gritty. Gristle and blood kind of shit."

"I'm ready."

"I'll be around shortly."

I took the long, dark walk down Burgundy and hung a left on Iberville. I slowly walked past the garage that hid the front doorway of The Bombay Club in the back of the concrete cavern. I saw Desmortiers standing guard at a brown podium with two ferns on either side. I stood in a shadow across the street and watched him bounce from toe to heel. He looked at his watch, yawned, then swung his arms about. His bottom lip protruded like a pouting kid's. This'll be easy, I thought. I'd been looking for a chance to get to know the showstopper a little better. I moved on toward Xandi.

"You ready to take a man's life again?" I asked her.

"It's been a while."

"Does that mean you're ready?"

"Who and why?" she asked.

"Officer Desmortiers. Send a message and avenge Gonzales."

"The one with the droopy lip?"

"The one with the droopy lip," I confirmed.

"When and where?

"Three-thirty. I was thinking of Cabrini Playground. When he walks out to the street, I'll put a gun to his ribs and walk him down. You follow close behind, and we can slap the showstopper on him. What 'cha think?"

"Showstopper could get a little too loud. Alert the girls working at Pap's. You know they'll be getting those steam machines cranked up about that time of the morning," she said.

"Yeah, you right. Got anything better?"

She bit her cheek and looked out into the costumes dancing around.

"How 'bout I lure him with the thought of a little woo woo. We'll walk him down; you can be just a little behind us. When we enter the park, you slip around the edge of the park and wait behind the park bench nestled under the old oak tree in the back corner. When I've got his pants below his knees and his dick in my hand, you'll have all the freedom in the world to tiptoe right over and slit his rotten little throat. No worries, no noise. A simple and quiet little murder in the park."

"Hell, I'd follow you to Slidell for a little after-work woo woo."

"This I know, Fremeaux."

I looked at my watch. "It's ten o'clock now, how you wanna do this?"

"I need to put some gear in the car, grab some potions, check on Big Dan, then I'll head on down to begin the flirt. What do you need to get done?" she asked.

"I'm gonna swing over and grab the bag with Charlie's crow outfit and wait for ya across Burgundy on the Rampart side. When we're done, we'll go pick up Booker and pick a lock?"

"I like the way you think, big boy. I'll be there. I'll have the sorry bastard so friggin' horny he'll be close to shooting off at every stop sign we pass."

"Jesus, lady. You can be a little spooky when you want."

"It's the only way I know how to be. Sometimes a lady's got to get a little scratchy to change her situation."

"You got a gun?" I asked.

"Purse. You got a sharp knife?"

"Strapped to my leg. I'll be down there by two-thirty at the latest. You get him hopped up. It'll be quieting down about that time anyway," I said.

"I won't be looking around for you, so don't stand me up."

I smiled and walked across the street to inspect the floating white door before we returned to break in later. I held the radio to my mouth, pressing the permission to talk button, and looked over my shoulder at Xandi.

"I really wanted to use the showstopper tonight?"

"Kid with a new toy. Never been a bigger gospel truth," she preached.

I snorted and had a pep talk with myself, knowing I'm on a path to take another man's life. Denial or discount? I don't know which.

I got to the garage early and took the back stairs up a few flights, changed into Charlie's crow costume, and snuck back down a set of stairs that led out to Burgundy Street. I parked myself behind a pole in the shadows and waited. This was the side of the Quarter where there were hardly any people, even on Halloween. I double-checked my gun and knife. Pulled the costume straight, it smelled like Charlie-spilled booze, ashtray, and Ferdi po-boy drippings.

They appeared at the corner; she was rubbing his lips with her index finger, fake giggling. He rubbed her entire body like a goddamn car wash. Hopefully, he could wait till the park. I didn't want to spring into action on the street. I wasn't about to carry a bloated, dead bastard's body farther than it could fall, and besides, I wanted this dead body to sit and rot on the bench for a while before discovery.

His stride closely matched Red Dertinger's, loppy. The swell I carried that night had reset in my chest. A wrong of this magnitude automatically conjured harsh judgment. Tough old grandmothers raised hardened fists at such people, demanding somebody do something. Well, I did, and I was about to again. People like this didn't need an extra day stealing our air.

Red's eyes seemed to fully comprehend when the blood lurched from his throat. As the muscles holding his cheeks full lost their will, his eyes knew. The light dimmed as I swear, he gave me a knowing grin, the lips pursed quickly, carrying acceptance, or he was signaling to me that it was I he was leaving behind to endure the atrocities of a life's journey. Almost like people like him develop a criminal's behavior because they're too chickenshit to pull off a suicide. He forced another man to end his agony. Whatever the reason, I was still in the fight, and I was certain Demortiers was hiding behind a badge for longevity. The motherfucker certainly wasn't lookin' for an out. I'd soon be his judge and executioner, just because.

Xandi teased him all the way down to the bench, like a pro. He plopped. She made him stand again to unbuckle his pants, pulling them to his knees. I watched as she pushed his chest till his fleshy ass plopped on the cold steel again. This time, he yelped a little, and I hoped like hell the girls' smoking cigarettes outside Pap's Cleaners didn't hear him. I looked through the bushes, but no one seemed to be aware we were out here.

I could hear her churning dead butter between his thighs. I took that as my time to shine. I stepped slowly up to the back of his head, crooking my knees and locking them in place. I pushed my chest closer to him to steady myself. I timed my rhythm to the sway of his head. Raising my hand just above his forehead, I readied the knife just to the side of his neck. Xandi slowly moved away from us, watched my face.

And, like I was going to hug a telephone pole, I grabbed the top of his head in the crook of my arm, pulling the dome into my chest as my killing hand slid the knife across his neck, deep into the fat, slicing a clean slit. I felt the blade of the knife scrape spinal bone, and just like that, he was gone. Couldn't make a call for rescue. His neck was cut before his thoughts could break away from his dick rub. None of it pulled guilt into my heart. I did what we needed.

He choked and flopped like a magician's hand was shoved up his ass, but we held his arms too high and wide for him to move in any direction. He choked and gasped, then slowly deflated. He slumped down like he needed a nap and slowly began to bleed out. I watched the grey seal of death paste over his eyelids. His stare powered down far away into the unknown. I looked around the park and smelled the cigarette smoke of the ladies taking a break outside the launderette.

I scanned the gate to make sure no one was entering the park with us. I caught the reflection of three sets of cat eyes glowing atop one of the art installations from a streetlamp's glare. It startled me a little. I wasn't ready for judgment or an audience of peers just now. I remembered long ago a voice from my past explaining how one of the Pope Gregory's from centuries ago believed the cat was some kind of Devil's accessory and decreed it a ritual to kill as many as possible. I wondered what he was caught doing in the dead of night, just like me. Had he been witnessed by the sly, glowing feline eyes in an illicit act, too?

We heard two sudden fowl honks and looked up Barracks Street to catch three shadows scampering up the street. One short human and two crooked necks with pointed beaks. We looked at one another in disbelief, then dropped the dead man's arms.

I took out Gonzales's badge and closed it in his fists for discovery. Xandi pulled a soiled pair of panties from her purse and threw them under the bench near his feet.

"Stole 'em from a laundromat on Elysian Fields, that should make 'em scratch their heads for a couple of days. One down, one to go for the night," She remarked.

"This'll surely send a message. Where you parked?" I asked.

"Up Barracks on the opposite corner of Decatur."

"Ok, split at the gate. I want the girls over there to get a good look at this crow costume. I want them to report what they saw in the area. With all this crazy evidence, Dowd and the boys won't know where the hell to point a finger. Go ahead and run uptown by yourself, I need to locate Officer Olen Ray and give him further instructions," I whispered.

She looked at me oddly. "Sure you don't want me to stay with you?"

"I'm sure, meet ya at the white door. Talk to me when you hit Canal. Be safe, lil lady."

She left, and I walked up Barracks and did a U-turn, making my way through a small passel of workers going about their business at the laundromat. They followed me with inquisitive stares. I took a quick right and disappeared into some shadows, slipping behind a live oak out in the neutral ground. I could hear last-minute bar hoppers up toward the river. Or it could have been a homeless encampment. I stood still to make sure the voices weren't coming closer. I quickly stripped OFF Charlie's costume and returned it to the grocery bag. I threw my Venetian rig over my body, strapping on my headpiece. I hurried down Rampart to the St. Claude exchange to a dilapidated newspaper box Don Lee uses for secret drop-offs. I hid the costume inside, reattached the wire holding the door in place, and casually strolled back toward the Quarter. I could hear the rhythmical drum of a voodoo dance somewhere off in Treme. The faint sound of a tortured chicken pricked at my skin.

I investigated all directions, but so far all I'd seen are stray cabs and winos. No cops or zombies out prowling.

I asked the walkie-talkie for Don Lee's whereabouts.

"I'm sitting at a table at the window at Harry's Corner. I saw Xandi speed out of the Quarter without you, where y'at?"

"Pap's, headed into the Quarter. If I haven't come to you at Harry's, I'll see you and Xandi later at the white door. I need to talk to Olen Ray, so if you come across him, send him in my direction."

"Will do. I'm going to pay and go on the lookout as well. What are you wearing now?" he asked.

"I'm Italian again."

"Be safe. I'm on the lookout." he said.

Gunshots rang out in the dark back toward Chalmette somewhere, then the sudden sound of sirens cranked up. I slipped back into the arms of the Quarter and decided to head toward Bourbon and Toulouse and post up for Xandi's return with Booker.

I eased past Fahy's and watched Tressy wipe down her bar around a small group of animated drinkers. She didn't look up, so I kept moving along. The streets seemed like long, dark hallways with a river of light flowing across the ends. Small stragglers stumbled their way through the muck, looking for strange arms to fall into. I crossed through the slow current of wilting flesh to the other side and kept stride up to Bourbon, passing the spot where the Lucky Dog cart usually sat.

"Where y'at, Don Lee?"

"Over here, grabbing Big Dan. Where you at?"

"I'm here patrolling the area, making sure there are no uniforms near."

"Well, it's close to shift change, as you know, so hopefully it won't be too dangerous for us. I'm grabbing Big Dan, then heading by the cathedral to grab a friend. Marcel is headed your way from the Blue Crystal, so when Xandi and Booker arrive, we'll be in place. Oh, I saw Officer Olen Ray over here near Big Dan. He's coming down Bourbon toward you now."

"Good deal," I said. I passed two young ladies outside a bar; one was holding the hair of the other as she puked in the gutter. I stepped around funky debris. I could see the blue uniform three blocks down. I approached my ex-street partner.

"Hey buddy, I can't have you use my name as a diversion, you will come to understand later. I may need you to do something that could put you in danger, though."

"What's that?"

"We're about to bust in over here. You wanna hang tight with your radio and keep us posted on the whereabouts of the other officers?"

"Sure, Fremeaux."

"Let's go, then. Hang around the Bourbon side over there and report anything that you hear on your radio. We'll do the rest." He walked farther down Toulouse, and I watched him stop to talk into his radio. I turned back to the door and saw Don Lee and Big Dan turn onto my side of Toulouse. A wad of bodies was coming down from Decatur, and I felt uneasy. If they stayed in view, they could hold us up. The radio broke in with Xandi's voice.

"We're crossing Canal. Gonna park on Decatur and walk down. See you in about twelve minutes."

Don Lee got closer as did the wad of bodies. We stood together as I alerted him of the crowd with a roll of my eyes. He turned and grinned.

"They're with us, amigo. We're posturing an impromptu street party."

I grunted through relief.

"I told ya, kid, there's a lot of aching hearts in the shadows, and they're all willing to do what we need. Stay up all night? Hell yeah. Chase an asshole into the bayous? Hell yes."

The wad of stragglers lollied up with a cooler of booze, a boombox, and a reason to live. I looked at all the faces, and it felt like a multicultural party at Epcot. Booker parted the crowd with his locksmith's tools, and everybody moved into place. They created two small bunches around the door at the street edge. One small bunch at the corner of Royal and another in the cross street of Bourbon as Xandi and Booker went to work.

I stood as though I was with old college buddies at the edge of the street, and without any sound, the door was soon unlatched, as Booker raised his arm to give a silent thumbs up. The crowd quieted and became as still as hunters in the plains. I slowly eased to Xandi and Booker, as did Don Lee. Three flashlights were raised in offering. I pulled Booker by the shoulder to move him toward the crowd as I stooped and slowly pushed the door, trying not to make a sound, aware that these old hinges could creak in the night. I signaled to turn up the street sounds as I slowly nudged the door.

The door cracked to about six inches, and I quickly popped the flashlight on and back off again. I saw it was a tight hallway about thirteen feet long. Church-white with art clinging to the walls. I slowly pushed the door farther slipping in and pushing it back into place behind me. I stood still and silent, letting my vision render itself to the new environment, but to no avail. It was pitch black. No light from anywhere. I cupped the front of the flashlight to keep my light source from blaring and pushed the on button. My fingers glowed as I saw the hallway come into vision. Whatever this room was, I felt I was alone, so I quietly moved forward. I could feel Xandi slip in behind me and push the door back.

I turned to her, and she nodded. "All good, let's move on."

I placed the light in front of us as we crept forward into the lonely hall. We followed it to a bend, as there was a door at the end of this second walkway. We walked past oil portraits of men—we had no idea of their value to anyone—and I reached for the second knob. It was locked, too. I motioned for her to bring Booker. She turned on her light and went around the corner as I stood looking up into the painted eyes of a man, whom I felt I should recognize. I tiptoed back into the tight hallway painted pure white from floor to ceiling. Crown molding. Granite statues of naked women lined the walkway. Not a speck of dust or dirt or trash anywhere. The space was immaculate. It wasn't what I expected behind a dingy-assed door leading into cheap debauchery.

Booker had unlocked the door before I knew it, but it was jammed on something. I didn't want to push and have something scratch across the floor, waking someone, so I held tight. I quietly walked back to the first door, trying to figure out my next move. That was when my light washed over a thick white brace-board leaning in one corner and a shillelagh next to it. I looked around further and found two braces on either side of the door frame. In haste, someone fucked up. Someone didn't lay the board back across the inside braces on the door we just opened.

We had just gotten ourselves another lucky break. We shouldn't have been as far as we were. The second door was barred as planned. This hallway was supposed to be impenetrable from the outside. This meant that over on Bourbon was another door that lead into here from the barred side of the second door. Two ways out and one way in. Whispering, I asked Booker how long it would take to make me a key to this outside white door.

"Fifteen minutes," he said.

"Get to it, please. Asap," I said.

I picked up the brace board and saw on the back side a small splattering of blood.

That's why they keep it immaculate in here, I thought.

Don Lee walked through with a journalist's eye. Flashed his light about, made some notes, and quietly stepped back out.

Our deeds were done, and we disbanded as quickly as possible. We had a lot to consider, and I made my way toward Olen Ray to see if he was still around. He wasn't in sight, so I decided it was the right time to head over to Verte Marte for a breakfast plate and then back to Leda's. I needed food and sleep. It had been a long fuckin' day. And night.

CHAPTER TWENTY-THREE

The sun was coming up, and I was going down quickly. My legs had grown weak, and my arms were turning into noodles. I'd contracted jelly brain. I opened the front door, made a glass of ice water, and walked to sit on the deck to eat and listen to the crack of dawn. Quiet was a rarity in this part of the world. It only happened between three-thirty and five a.m. on Sundays, Mondays, and Tuesdays on hot summer mornings. I listened to the voices of a couple of street hustlers passing under the balcony, headed to set themselves in place for the first round of tourists.

"You gone get Uncle Leon anything for his birthday this year?"

"I'm ahead of that muthafuckin' game. For once, I had some cash on stash. I got him one of those nice rayon shirts with all the colors he likes and done prepaid for some pussy."

"Fuck me, Paw Paw! He cain't complain about none of that. Ain't no complainin' bout shit like dat."

"Yeah, but he'll find somethin' to complain about. He always do."

"What the hell could he possibly have to complain about? New shirt, free pussy!"

"Knowing that mutha, he gone call my ass up and have the gall to tell me both the damn thangs was too fuckin' big."

A much-needed chuckle jiggled through me, something I had forgotten I needed. I finished my pancakes thinking about things being too fuckin' big.

There were painted bags of roasted peanuts lying on a wrought iron table in a still life on a wall in this apartment that everybody wants but no one is allowed to taste. Was it that the rayon shirt and pussy were too big, or that the grasp of life was just too fucking big, or was everything out there just a gigantic letdown?

I reclined in the lounge chair, taking in this October coolness, listening to the folks mingle in the early morning day of the Dead. I'd never had the time to meditate, but I thought I was drifting into a French Quarter meditative state as I contemplated the idea that I was now twice a murderer. Murderer for a cause, that is. No guilt, just wonder what's next. And still no Becca. I was feeling a little Becca lonely. I thought about the lady with the binoculars and briefly wondered if she'd been talking to Becca.

"Fremeaux? You okay this morning?" Xandi's voice asked through the radio.

"All good, baby. I can see *your* mental scars more clearly now."

"All tracks lead to the same place, my dear."

"Xandi?"

"Yes, Fremeaux?"

"I'm going to need Big Dan and some Romani muscle."

"I can get that."

"As soon as I get the information I'm waiting for, we're headed to Mobile. Gonna do a little kidnappin' ourselves."

Don Lees's hoarse and scratchy twenty-four-hour voice chimed in. "I may know a hundred games of solitaire, but my wrinkled ass is still at the poker table. You can't leave your ringleader out."

"Don Lee, we need you to get with Wanda Ball asap. We need that Porsche stashed over here. I have a full-of-bullshit plan to throw a monkey wrench into their fan."

"Gotcha, dear boy. When do we need the Porsche?"

"Get it as soon as you can. Do you have a place where it can be stashed?"

"706 Dumaine. Private parking garage. I have access anytime I need," he said.

"Good deal. I'm sure the keys to it are somewhere near or inside with the young widow. I'm sure it is in an easy-access position for when Dixie Mafia wants to grab it when necessary."

"I'll run down Wanda, buy a battery, grab a can of gas, and we'll hit out as soon as we can. Look, kid, I have no problem ramming that thing straight into police headquarters if need be."

"How bout we shove it up the ass of one of those limos leaving the scene at three a.m., driven by one of their own bastards?"

"Ohhhh, Big Daddy likes," Don Lee said,

"I'll get some family muscle rounded up. Get some rest, we've got a lot of shit to pull. Talk more tonight," Xandi said.

"Are all the doors covered?" I asked Xandi.

"Yes, I have a spotter on the white door and have put another set of eyes over on Bourbon on the front of the building. There is a narrow green door on that side that could be a private throughway. If anyone opens and closes either door, we'll know immediately," she answered. Then the radios fell silent.

I looked up into the clouds and felt a small sense of comfort.

"Thanks, Xandi. Goodnight, folks. Talk soon."

It felt odd saying goodnight with the sun doing its thing. I could hear the voices grow in number below me. Boom boxes across the square play the new electronic energy. I could feel the art of living simultaneously. The universe didn't make mistakes; it created the phenomenon. *It is what it is*—just another way of saying anything and everything goes, deal with it.

I got the sense that the universe had put its knowledge inside us, but we couldn't access it; if we did, we would dismantle our reality. Television told us life was an illusion, money was God, and God's word was forever. You couldn't make any kind of deal with any of that—just take your stab at life when you can. Grab all the knowledge that puts you closer in touch with your soul. Be decent, for God's sake. If you couldn't, then you had to be ready to suffer the consequences like a man.

Familiar voices from below broke through my thoughts.

"Have you seen Fremeaux lately?" the cop's voice asked.

"No, I haven't," Hubris's voice answered. "What's going on, guys? I hear Fremeaux is throwing shit on a lot of people?"

"He's causing unnecessary problems for himself. If you see him, tell him the Chief wants to reinstate him. I know you don't like the sound of that, Hubris, but could you just play along and notify us when you lay eyes on him?"

"Be glad to, officer."

The comfort I just got from Xandi has now grown little spurs and is catching in my gullet. My belly is a mound of fire ants. I wonder if those fuckers' names are on the Gonzales list. If not, they're on mine. Sometimes you just had to shit on other people to clear a path for the safety of the masses. Don Lee told me sometimes you gotta slit throats before the fist gets shoved up your ass. The elites call you white trash until they start a war, and then they call you buddy. Fuck, now I'm pissed again.

I got up and made another drink. In my head, I'd opened the door, cranked the car, and loaded the gun. I'd strapped my boots and prayed for the souls I'd be taking. *Mother was right; I am an assassin. I am a peacemaker. I'm not an innocent bystander any longer.*

I made a second drink and a gambled by dialing the number Wanda wrote down for me. She picked up on the sixth and last ring as I was about to drop the phone again.

"How can I be of service?" her voice answered.

"How do you know, Wanda?" That was all my mind and mouth could spit out.

"Fremeaux? Is this you?"

"Yes."

"How do I know what?"

"When to love, when not to love. When to kick nuts, and when to walk away?"

"You sound tired, Fremeaux."

"Yeah, my brain is fumbling through non-essentials."

"Oh. I see," she said. "Hell, I don't know for sure. I can tell by the look in a man's eyes what he's there for. I mean, they're all there for one thing, the peripheral is what I'm talkin' bout. It's what they think *we* want."

"Are we all fucked?"

"No, not all of you. You got the ones with big dicks but no direction, they're just big dicks. Some think they have big dicks and bang away like obsessed bunny rabbits until the world becomes bored with them, then they develop lifelong anger issues. Then there are the ones who don't give a shit about what God gave 'em; they're there to get the job done. What we really want is a man who'll tend his garden."

"Hell, I'm tiring, baby."

"Yeah, we know Fremeaux, but the world is changing fast nowadays. With this new trickle-down government, these anti-trust changes in policy are pushing people around all flotsam-jetsam like. The girls come down from up north to work for me and say the executives nowadays can afford more trips to the parlor. They now run in and rush out to grab bags of fast food for the kids and ignore their ole ladies in pursuit of a big reward. The family sits in the back seat while adults meander into self-fulfillment. Soon, a mass of kids will mature into self-absorbed dumbasses too ignorant to catch a joke."

"You sayin' my job is quickly becoming the rodeo clown?"

"Yup, sounds like our little gris-gris is gonna get washed downstream."

"Fuck, Wanda, I've already done things I wasn't ready to do," I said. "I'm running with the devil, now."

"We all runnin' with the devil, Fremeaux. Speakin' of, have you seen the *Sunday Times* this morning?" she asked.

"No, I was out roaming all night and was about to get some shut-eye, till I got myself all riled up. Why?"

"There's a picture in the business section from across the pond in London. Reagan, Thatcher, Friedman, and a bunch of other suits have been negotiating the deregulation of the markets over there. Trying to "unslump" their economy."

"And? What's that got to do with my conscience?"

"There is a small crowd behind the powers that be, and buried in that crowd is Ms. Golda."

"Oh, I see. Our Mrs. Golda is everywhere the world needs her to be, huh?"

"Seems," she said. "You know it's Halloween Sunday and Magine's is closed. The boys and I are getting dressed to cruise the Quarter later. You around? You want to meet them?"

"You know I do."

"It's gonna be a few hours before we make it that far. Are you hiding out in the Pontalba still?"

"Yes," I said.

"You know I left another pill in that little blue bowl by the entrance, don't you? If you need sleep, take it. I'll wake you when we get down there."

"I'll unlatch the gate. The front door will be unlocked. If I'm not on my feet, nudge me."

"Will do, Paw Paw."

I searched for the pill, took it down with the last of the gold Tequila, and poured one more. I turned on the radio and listened to the Sunday morning Fais do-do on WWOZ as I closed my eyes.

Billions of stars zoomed in from the background of black space as faces morphed from recognizable friends to old Hollywood stars. Xandi turned into Princess Diana turned into Ruthie turned into Lana Turner turned into Michelle Pfiefer turned into Lucinda Williams turned into Hank Williams turned into Don Lee turned into Golda turned into my mother who bent down to kiss me on the cheek, my heart sank into warm water. Her face pulled back above me; Leda was smiling. My libido held salutations while the black cape of unconsciousness unfolded over me.

CHAPTER TWENTY-FOUR

My big toe suddenly shook vigorously. I opened my eyes to find a punk mocker grinning over me. A lime-green T-shirt with an orange globe on it, around the top read, *Eat the Rich,* and hugging the bottom of the world, *Fuck the Poor.*

That was enough to jump-start consciousness. I sat up straight, rubbing my eyes. From behind, I heard Wanda. His brother had donned the ever-popular AINT'S paper bag and aT-shirt stating, *I'm Purdy, I promise.* Wanda looked like a country Tinkerbell. Purple tutu and green leather cowgirl boots.

"Don Lee called right after you did. I guess I'll be travelin' back to Double Gobble Road?" she confessed.

That husky, Suzanne Pleshette voice made my insides wiggle. It was the kind of sexy that makes all men want to take a ride to Double Gobble Road.

"Seems I've got a stupid idea up my ass," I said.

"Get yourself killed, kind of stupid?" she asked.

"No, just some gasoline on fire kind of shit. Can you do it?"

"Yeah, we're going over on Tuesday, Don Lee says."

"You gonna introduce me to your friends, Wanda?"

She smirked. "Sorry, Paw Paw. Didn't mean to be rude. This is Val and Leo."

I stood and shook their hands, made a respectful nod, and looked back at Wanda.

"Make drinks if y'all want."

"Can you sign a question I have about the murder attempt?"

"They can read lips, Fremeaux. Don't be afraid. It'll feel weird at first, but you'll get used to it."

I mimed the question, exaggerating my lip movement. They shook their heads in jest.

"Just talk normal. they can follow. If not, I can sign," she said in words that stretched awkwardly like a drunk fella trying to explain an enigma, being cute.

"Are y'all aware of the attempt on Leda's life?" I asked.

They signed to Wanda and she translated. "Yes, it is still a hot topic among our guests."

"Have you come across any one of those highbrows talking about hiring the Dixie Mafia?"

They looked at one another and chuckled.

"We get the sense you care, but you're just a cop. Well, you were a cop, but believe us when we tell you, Ms. Golda will take care of it all," she translated.

"You're telling me Ms. Golda can do more than law enforcement?"

I could feel them stonewalling. Wanda sat next to me on the couch.

"As I've alluded to, Fremeaux, Magine's is the refuge of the elite. From mob bosses to the Governor, they talk business with one another only; they facilitate their needs, if you will. The boys can't venture out with you on any of this, as it could mean life or death for them if it came to light," she explained.

"I figured. Just wanted to see what I could uncover."

Val placed his hand on Wanda's knee and looked at me.

"We will say this. There is something dark developing with their family over in Europe. Ms. Golda has been growing very angry recently. She has made comments that could mean a demise in their fortune. The best way for you to be of service is to perform whatever task is asked of you, no questions asked."

"That's all I've been doing since meeting Leda. The problem is that every piece of pie I turn to eat has a Dixie Mafia finger in it already. I may be the one who needs assistance."

"Well then, ask them."

"I have."

"Well then, wait for it." They signed.

Wanda added, "You know, Fremeaux, the other day I was listening to the Writer's Almanac and Garrison Keillor read another writer's take on the word soliloquy. He described a soliloquy as when you've been digging through the haystack searching for a needle, and you discover the farmer's daughter. Patience and diligence are where you are, and it's what you gotta keep doing. The farmer's daughter is gonna pop up at some point."

"Oh boy," I said. "Dig for turnips, find a fucking Krugerrand."

"That sounds like a damn Talking Heads song," Wanda said.

"Indeed," one of the brothers mimed.

I heard the walkie-talkie click up. It was Don Lee's voice.

"A discovery was made in Cabrini Playground just now. Stay on your toes, this will be getting fah-ugly soon. Fremeaux, I've retrieved the package you left in my secret box the other night. Stay in touch with any details, folks."

Chattered "Will Do's" came in quick procession.

"Fremeaux, we're ready to get out and about. You coming with?" Wanda asked.

"I've got too much to figure out. Don't wanna be a stone in your flip-flop. Thanks, though. Boys, it was nice to meet you both. I hope y'all have a great night out there. I'll stop by and have you make me cocktails."

They smiled.

"We'll probably ring in midnight dancing at Oz if you have a change in mood," Wanda said.

I kissed her on the cheek and bid the boys farewell. The paper bag on his head gave me a new idea for a new look. After bidding them adieu, I searched through the drawers in the laundry room and found what I needed to make my own Aint's bag. Behind a door on a shelf was a pair of painter's coveralls. I was set again. New look, new direction. I'd crossed a line and can't go back. Happens every day. It all began with the first family in the Bible.

I threw myself back into chaos. Rubbing shoulders with the happy ones. I found myself taking notice of all the other Aint's bags, like when you buy a new car and mentally tally all the other cars just like yours on the road. I saw Satyrs, fairies, and Supermen galore. And half-naked, everything you could want to see. Caligula's dream.

Some moments made me wish my boat hadn't sailed these waters of responsibility, as I wanted to ride tonight with ecstasy in my gut, but anger and guilt had nested and were digging at the worms in my brain.

Standing here now, looking at Hubris's pudge veiled in that thin, dirty lavender T-shirt, I'm reminded that I'm also on a mission. I raise the walkie-talkie.

"Xandi, where y'at?"

"Lucky Dog cart."

"Have you seen Olen Ray?"

Don Lee's voice interrupted.

"I'm headed toward Canal on the hunt for him now. Where you at Fremeaux?"

"Headed into Pirates' alley."

"Head toward Canal. Let's meet in front of Werlein's. At some point, we should run into Olen Ray."

"Think Aint's bag and white painter's coveralls," I said.

"I'm still a Friar."

"Xandi, stay in place. When I get our info, we need a plan to go get our boy."

Big Dan's bull moose of a voice made the speaker in my hand vibrate with gusto.

"Y'all need to get over here now. I was just removed from my place and told to move up to Decatur. The entire backside of the Quarter has been blocked off, and every cop car from Destrehan to Slidell is down here. Lights twirlin', faces scowlin', cops huddled up like lions in a pride. I think I even see the F.B.I. on the scene. Crazy shit's going down hard. Get over here, quick."

Even under the hot burn of sunlight, the blue and red lights lit the walls and rooftops like a high-dollar titty bar on the Vegas strip. We stood in the T where Decatur and Barracks converged. The action was four blocks down on the other end. I couldn't make out faces and badges, so I grabbed Xandi by the elbow and told Don Lee and Big Dan to stay on this side to witness stragglers of any value to us.

"Xandi, we need to be closer to the scene of the crime."

We made our way down Esplanade toward Rampart to get more acquainted with the shreds of evidence presented to the authorities. As we walked through thick patches of spectators, I could still feel the blade of the knife scrape against the bone in my mind from last night's malice. Phantom pains of guilt, I guessed in jest. I became suddenly aware of all the leering witches, hot spirits, and reddened eyes of the characters inhabiting the Quarter.

Like a hive of busy bees, blue uniforms darted from place to place gathering evidence, but unlike bees, these fellas were as quiet as church mice, whispering and covering lips. The radios were silent, furrowed brows outlined faces troubled with omens.

The hollow bucketed thud of a voodoo drum from out in the Aether scratched at the scene with ominous rhythm. I looked at the slumped wad of dead meat drooping on the park bench and facetiously remembered an ad for Coco Chanel in The Picayune some years back.

They had gotten an R. Crumb type to illustrate a comic strip of a hippie woman mindlessly walking off the roof of a skyscraper under construction. Her body fell through the concrete sidewalk, leaving a dark, shadowed hole. In the last framed square of the strip, her ghost reemerged on an escalator headed to the skies. Her ghost was immaculately redressed with a Chanel pantsuit, coiffed hair, and topped off with dark-rimmed, Jackie O sunglasses. She had been transformed into a style goddess. The caption offered was to let Chanel rebirth you, ready for heaven. *Who's gonna ready this motherfucker for his escalator ride to hell*? I wondered.

I remembered the smell of rot he fumed when I stepped closer to run the knife blade across his larynx last night. The clues to a man's soul are always available if your attention is sharp.

"We kicked 'em pretty good, Fremeaux," Xandi said with a smile. She crossed her arms and looked at the paper bag covering my head.

"Ya killin' me with that bag on ya head," she jests.

I smiled an invisible smile. She pointed across the playground toward the bench holding a dead cop's body. Desmortiers looked like a forgotten Halloween pumpkin, slumped and folded into itself. Deformed and useless.

"Oh, lookie lookie, Fremeaux. Officer Dowd. He's top of the list on Gonzales's scene that day. I'm of the understanding that he's the mastermind of her end, too."

I studied the face under the graying hair. Dowd had recently left the NOPD and taken employment in a special division of the State Police. A project that reported to the Governor's office. I suddenly felt a presence behind us. Xandi turned to look, and I heard Agent Tre Freeman softly speak to us.

"I have what Officer Olen Ray asked me for. Ms. Legbra, could you slowly exit and meet me on the other side of Buffa's, please? Your friend will need to stay put. He can meet you afterward."

I could tell by the energy and tone that he knew whose face hid behind this paper bag. Xandi raised her walkie and shook it slightly at me as she slowly disappeared into the crowd and on down to cross Esplanade.

I made myself scarce for when our radios called for us to meet her. I didn't want other ears to become privy to our clandestine communication, so I wandered back up Esplanade to rejoin Don Lee and Big Dan. To fill them in without alerting the airways.

"Fellas, we're getting the information I've been waiting for. Soon we're gonna throw a big bag of crap in their air ducts," I said.

After a while, Xandi's voice reached out to us.

"Don Lee, come home and bring the boys."

"All right, big boy, we're on," Don Lee said.

"What do you want me to do?" Big Dan asked.

"Stay put and keep your eyes on the house you've been watching. If anyone is allowed access, let us know."

As Don Lee and I walked toward his house, I tallied all the shit I'd witnessed since this crap began, and I realized I hadn't seen the two girls since the night they were given the free drink tickets. I wondered if they'd left for home early or if something more sinister had happened. Would another set of parents be coming to town with photographs and hope? I also hadn't crossed paths with the grey man since we discovered the Magpie roosting behind the Lucky Dog cart.

I felt the sense of slithering just out of view. Somewhere in the shadows, a Loup Garou polished its claws. Were we descendants of beasts and brutes, or a dishonest universe? We'd probably never know.

I'm fully aware that the universe's sole purpose is to birth and reclaim, but fear of death can be spiritual gravity. It's up to us to search for the joy in survival, but I can't help feeling as stable as a stick caught in the river's current. I'm rambling again. With a bag over my head, for Christ's sake.

That was when a quick, pronounced chuckle interrupted my thoughts, and the weight of a hand on my shoulder pressed down.

Don Lee spoke. "Don't get yourself lost in guilt, my son."

"Was I rambling out loud?" I asked.

"Yes, kid, you were. You gotta remain our fullback, not become the referee. You've been caught with wonder because you have taken a life for just cause and not self-defense, as you have been taught. Remember, if someone had done so in your own life, it's quite possible your father could still be with you. It may not be the letter of the law, but I'm not saying anything. What's good for the goose is good for the gander. What's good for the criminal is good for the crooked cop."

I looked down the street to find Xandi holding a large brown envelope at Don Lee's front door. "I'm still with you, Don Lee," I answered him.

"Your mother instilled in you the keys to surviving the world of bullshit, and that's just what you're doing. All this may lead us to your father's killer eventually. Unfurl that back, young man, you can't wander off now."

CHAPTER TWENTY-FIVE

"Whatcha find out, Xandi?"

"These people fuckin' suck."

"Well, this sounds juicy," Don Lee said as he mixed three rusty nails.

"The mom is the ringleader. The dad is a Hell's Angel, imprisoned for double murder, kidnapping, and drug running. You name it, it's on his record. The kid, Otto, named after the founder of the gang, is the feet of the family ring. He runs whatever goods need delivering and brings the money, or people, back to Mama," she continued.

"This is the first aspect of this ordeal that doesn't connect with the Dixie Mafia. The Hells Angels and Dixie Mafia mix like oil and water. Got an address?" I asked

"Yes."

"We need them both," I told her.

"The question is, are these people connected with NOLA cops or the church, or both?" Don Lee pondered.

"The cops for sure. I don't give a shit about the other, I'm gonna use them for our needs," I said.

"I have Romani Calvery headed our way now. We'll scout the area and devise a way to have them duct-taped, gagged, and stashed as soon as possible."

Don Lee looked over the rim of his glass at me with shrewdness. I felt my back tightening and straightening. He pulled his drink away and winked. He had painted his face to look chalk white. In his friar's frock, he resembled a cowled and possessed monk headed to a sacrifice.

"All this converges on Halloween, no doubt. Hell's a-poppin', sounds like a lady you'd want to make love to after a decadent, midnight dinner." He smirked.

"If only you could make love to me, Don Lee," Xandi said.

"But, if we all really do live in Yeats's gyre, we never truly know what could be on the next ride, do we? But, don't tell that one to the scientist. Science is just another word for something else to prove. It's good to be a dreamer," he said back to her.

"Truth's the same as impossible." She frowned.

"Impossible as it may be, the word possible is still in the word, baby." Don Lee winked.

"But you gotta remove the I and M, which, if one can imagine, is another way of saying the self, or Homo Erectus, dear sir," Xandi returned his wink.

"You sneaky little bitch, you. I can't separate my id from my super ego. You trusted the snake and bit the apple first," Don Lee joked.

"Truth is tough to swallow, big boy."

"Touche, my dear. Touche."

I felt the inevitable silence after the banter open, so I asked, "Are we all aware of our tasks at hand?"

"Yes, we were just playing a little. They don't do this kind of shit in New York, too cerebral. I'll have the Porsche in the garage on Dumaine by Tuesday eve," he answered.

"We should have two shitbags under wraps by then as well," she added.

"We're not planning on killing anyone else before then, are we?" Don Lee asked.

"I think we're in a sit-and-stare period for now. Keep a close eye on the two places where we've witnessed criminals in action. Until something happens, we wait," I said.

"The cops aren't the kidnappers; they're around to prevent our snooping. So, the kidnappers may keep their plans in action," Don Lee said.

"Yes, but they sacrificed Charlie, so they will need their plan B. When they move, we move," Xandi reminded us. "I'll execute my half as soon as we possibly can."

We agreed. We drank more, and I asked Xandi for some ecstasy pills. I could feel my current stride was tightening from too much malice. I'd give anything to have all this behind us. Lay on a deserted beach somewhere with a lone pelican trying his damndest to tell me about the fish he let get away earlier that morning.

We all finished our drinks.

"I'm gonna get another look at the commotion in the park. Swing over to their secret place to watch the doors," I told them.

"Ok. When the family lets me know when it's time, I'm headed to Mobile to extract rotten teeth," Xandi said.

"I think I'll go drink some Pregnant Canaries over at Nick's. See what kind of buzz is in the air over there. Hopefully, I don't wake up next door with a naked prostitute," Don Lee jested.

I felt the joke and slipped the bag back over my head.

"You fuckin' redneck. Stick with me, old man, I'll keep you at the typewriter."

Xandi and I strolled out the front door like the world had given us all we needed. I suddenly had an aimless feeling. The waiting is the hardest part.

The cops had slowed their scrambling and had formed huddles throughout the area. Some were waiting for instructions, some were passing information, and the top dogs deciphered and pointed fingers. I listened to their radios for some kind of clue, but they were still silent. Facial expressions told me they had no direction, just as I hadn't myself. The crowds had broken up and returned to ritual, so I did the same and headed down to put eyes on Big Dan.

His monstrous hands gripped the top rail on the barricade as he watched the other end, where all the commotion took place. I looked that way and could see the grey house of interest to us.

"Anything?" I asked.

He slightly nodded that lunkhead to the negative with his big circus grin.

"You need a break?"

He made the same gesture. Sometimes words just aren't necessary.

"Have you seen Ruthie today?" I asked.

He raised a hand and pointed.

"She broke the barrier on their end and talked with one of the cops for a few minutes."

"When was this?"

"Couple of hours ago."

We stood quietly. I figured he had it under control.

"Big Dan, I'm headed down to put a looksee on the doors of where the magpies roost. Ok?"

"All good, Fremeaux. If you need me, you know what to do?"

"Gotcha, thanks." I moseyed toward the Blue Crystal with my intended goal in mind. As I reached the curb at the corner, I heard Big Dan call out to me.

"Hey, Bagman?"

"Yes?" I turned.

He stood motionless. Rolled his lips over themselves. I could see the courage reach for his lips.

"Love is essential." He blurted this with stumbling excitement in his voice. I raised my arms with a thumbs-up. The suddenness of the exclamation coming from the mouth of a man you'd hire as a bouncer at a monster truck rally gave me amusement. I returned to my journey. He was right, though. Love was essential.

I pass the front door of The Blue Crystal and watch Teal hand ecstasy pills to a couple as I look through the bodies rubbing on themselves inside the bar.

I spot the homeless encampment just this side of Coop's place and see Nate-Dog wasn't mingling with the gaggle of homeless. The sidewalk window at Molly's was filled with the local off-duty news anchors dressed up as characters from *M.A.S.H.* I return focus to the task at hand.

Some days, walking through these ancient, dingy corridors felt like moving through the bowels of a goddess. Deep inside, you cursed the rest of the world and yourself for being so damned insolent.

I took the right down to Toulouse and stood under a rickety, weather-beaten balcony to spy our lookout lady. I nodded, and she nodded back. A fella with a camera near her did the same. All points on this side of the Quarter were covered, I noted.

The dingy white door was vacant. I walked down to the Lucky Dog cart and asked if anyone had exited or entered through it. The answer was no one had been around all morning, which I figured was going to be the case. So, I went around to the Bourbon side of this den to inspect the doors there. I saw the lady on our team on a bench across the street.

"Anything?" I asked.

"Nothing so far."

Two green doors and one white door were the three ways leading through the bars on the ground floor. Those hallways could lead in either direction, I told myself. Which door was the right door? It was anybody's guess at this point. The bigger questions hung in my mind: who the fuck was hiding behind the Magpie outfit, and where the hell was his bodyguard? I fingered the ecstasy in my pocket and dreamed of relief, but I wasn't not quite ready for it just yet. Too much responsibility on the brain.

Costumes passed, signaling childhood regalia, but my heart just couldn't find the reason to deploy jubilation. Where to now? I asked myself. Just sit and regroup, was my answer, so I joined the watch lady on the bench.

"Please do, sir," was the answer after asking permission to join.

We sat in silence; a hot sun burned down on us. I couldn't cover my eyes with sunglasses with this dadgum bag hiding my head, so the world seemed a little too bright for the confusion I was feeling.

My thoughts conjured the image of the boy on Double Gobble Road trapped in a hellish nightmare, and I could relate. I wanted to kick a beer can through the streets and make some racket myself.

Sweaty laughter filled my ears, but my brain didn't feel like dancing with the culture, so I jerked myself from the concrete steps and saw the man with a camera on the opposite corner. I looked toward the back end of the Quarter, mentally scrutinizing an image of Desmortier's dead, swelling body.

I wondered if I could get around to the back of the house where Charlie lived without disturbance. Could I get a peek into a window? Discover another body part? A toe, maybe? A bloody saw blade? Nah—I doubted I'd find anything without busting down a door.

My internal burning was coming to terms with the idea that people sworn to protect fed off innocents seeking refuge from the daunting pressure of the suburban thumb. Take, take, take, every waking moment someone is taking. Taxes, tithes, traffic tickets, nosy neighbors, everybody's in somebody's business. The solace from abysmal adulthood was what they sought out here in our streets of desire.

When I threw Hubris's fat, naked ass in the back of the squad car that night, he scolded me.

"My road to hell is paved with your good intentions, Fremeaux. You'll rue this day, fucking asswipe."

I laughed. "If you'd been bleeding from the ear, you'd have been crying for me to rescue you too, slick."

"I know how to survive, Slick," he fired back.

Smug motherfucker. *I know how to survive.*

What takes that kind of mindset to the next level? To deploy destruction on those who may not have that level of resolve? I couldn't answer that, but I could sure as hell pave another fucking road with good intentions.

An unexpected figure popped out from the front door of the 504 Club. Well-pressed business attire, five-foot-five. Polished shoes and gelled gray hair cut to perfection. Black clothing from head to toe, but these shoes were not the ones the Magpie had worn, but then again, the sunlight hours weren't where you'd find a ten-fingered Magpie anyways. His face was turned away from me, looking across Bourbon. I motioned to the photographer to get the shots. His body size did ring a little too familiar.

I could see a blacked-out town car parked down on the corner of Toulouse and Dumaine. I followed twenty feet behind as he headed to it. Passing by the photographer, I whispered for shots of the vehicle in question. I stepped between a beer truck and a taxi to peer at the license plate. The plastic *Tag Applied For* is set in place with three blue asterisks in the lower right corner. I had never seen one in person since being on the force down here, but the unspoken word is that these vehicles are immune to inspection. Just another private car with the magic pass, its passenger just exited a juke joint on Bourbon in the middle of Halloween, dressed for passing judgments. I held the walkie up just as they sped out of sight.

"Big Dan, are you there?"

"I'm still here, Fremeaux."

"Blacked-out, two-door private car just left my sight. Keep a lookout."

"Will do."

"The last one that entered the premises over there was it a two-door?" I asked.

"No, four-door. More of a party limo."

"Ten-four. I'm headed your way anyway."

"Go Arch," someone yelled at my bag as I brush by the cheerful folk. I've got a friggin' paper bag with eye holes over my head, and it's not for the holiday. It's for protection, I remind myself. The right set of eyes finding me could spell a bloody fight for survival. I realized I'm my own Halloween scavenger. *Trick, or treat, baby.*

Or could I be the universe's fucking lab rat all of a sudden? *Keep him in the fight just a little longer. Let's see just how much more shit we can put him through. Dangle a damsel in distress in front of him, and he'll do whatever the hell for my pleasure. The universe spins.* Heidinger said we're just tumbling dice all, Caymus said it's all absurd, Sartre demanded a person must remain faithful to self-honor, Schopenhauer said it was all a bucket of shit, and Robin Williams said, just drop another fuckin' tab, dude.

None of that shit helped when murder is involved. Nine lives was the main idea that bounced around the noggin in situations like these. I hope I got 'em, which sounds absurd. Mortal man could rip worlds apart, and Mother Nature would quietly come behind us with a reorder for the next crew.

They'd shrunk the security around the park. Six or eight packs of blue shirts were wadded around the outside of the park, which was still taped off. Traffic wasn't allowed on the corner yet; the cops would continue surveillance for a few more days, I was sure.

Big Dan was leaning on the aluminum barricade, his head bobbing toward the earth, eyes stretched upward. Looked like a man ready for the next big thing. I had a good reflection of my torso, topped off with this square brown bag. I looked like a modern-day Frankenstein; it wasn't the typical crime-fighter garb.

"Nothing?" I ask him.

"Not yet."

I fondled the Ecstasy pills in my pocket. I secretly wanted to hop a space ride through a different part of another world.

The black car stopped at the red octagon on the four-way at Decatur. Blinker said it was coming our way. We stood and moved back a little more off the corner, less visible. It turned and slowly drove to the front of the driveway and stopped in the street. We waited for the gate to open so it could turn. It sat. Nothing happened. We stood still, and it sat still. Two minutes passed, and another car, a little green junker filled with partyers, waited behind it. Nothing moved. They honked to no avail. When exasperation began to expand, the limo rolled forward and turned the corner onto Esplanade and was soon gone.

"We need to bust into one of these cars," Big Don said.

"Working on it. So, the other day, the white van came and went six times?" I asked.

"Well, there was three different vans. They each came and went over to the church twice apiece," he answered.

"Three different vans?"

"Yessir. One had a red WWOZ bumper sticker, and one had a yellow WWOZ bumper sticker. The third had a bullet hole over the driver's front fender."

"One at a time? How long did they stay?"

"Yup, one at a time and about fifteen minutes. One would drive out, and another would slip in behind the same open gate. It was timed somehow."

"Xandi says that about the same time frame was on the other end, at the back of the Cathedral. Yes, we're gonna need to get inside both soon," he said. Then he confessed something else.

"I hopped the fence about 2 a.m. before the cop was killed down there. Ruthie took a look out for me. Only one way in on the back, and that's a tight garage. Whatever they do in there is a solid secret. Now, the balcony up there is gonna be tricky because there is razor wire all at the base of the tree line. I'm quite sure that if you did get to the top, you'd be hard-pressed to know how to get through on the first try, and I doubt there would be a second chance if the first was a no-go," he said.

"Has a photographer been hangin' around this area with you?"

"He would come and go. But a new guy and Xandi are up in a room there." He pointed at the B&B across from us. "She got the room on the third floor where the side window faces the house over there," he finished.

"She got her radio?" I asked.

"She do," he said.

"Xandi, I'm outside."

"Meet me at the desk inside the lobby," she commanded.

"Gotcha," I answered.

The window was covered with a thin white curtain. A camera and two extra lenses were on the table next to it. A veiled view of the house and the portico could be seen through it.

The windows across the way told no secrets. I looked into her eyes as what looked to me as storm-induced dishevelment entered from the kitchen. The stranger heartily introduced himself as Cochran, and by the butter-churning handshake he delved out, I sensed he would be more than happy to voice his opinion on the sins of meretricious souvenirs with gusto.

"Nice to meet you, too, Cochran," I said, questionably. I gave Xandi a *what the hell is this*? eye roll. She smiled.

"Cochran, you think you got it?" she asked.

"Goddamned right, little lady. I got this. For my dear baby girl, I got this by the balls."

"Holy fuck," I whispered into thin air.

She grabbed my arm to lead me out the door.

"I guess you can figure why you haven't met Cochran before?"

"Behind closed doors is the perfect place for this fella. Is he safe by himself?"

"This will work for him if he doesn't get too excited and forget to turn out the lights before pulling the camera into the window. I did inform him that it would be best if he just sat in the dark and watched."

"We can always pray," I said

"He's been hounding to be part of the team, and I figured this is the perfect location. We both benefit without too much sacrifice."

"I notice he doesn't have a radio. That's a good call," I said.

"He will later, as I'm giving Big Dan some time off tonight. By the way, the Romani, as you like to call us, have scoped out ya boy's place."

"Already. What the fuck, can you people teleport?" I jested.

"When money is involved, big boy. When money is involved." That was all she said, twisting her neck and sucking her bottom lip inward.

"What can I expect?"

"Ready to kill on Wednesday. Same as Don Lee and the car."

"I got two days to get ready," I said as I looked off into those two days.

"What do you think you're gonna do?" she asked.

"We gotta get a look inside one of those vehicles. Don Lee will have the car stored on Dumaine in a garage. A car goes in, a call goes out. I think we can put the kid behind the wheel and Big Dan in the passenger seat. The kid will ram the front wheel of the limo as we're on the scene. We can then open the doors, making sure all is safe. You got the drift?"

"How are you going to get the kid to do this?"

"To save his Momma's life. If he doesn't, she dies. Just that simple."

"Can we promise him an escape route? He's just not going to pull this kinda stunt and expect a death sentence from us."

"Yes, she'll be tied in the backseat of a car next to the Porsche in the garage. He's going to think that the two will escape with a payoff. A bigger payoff than they've ever seen. Money and a house near San Quinton, where his father is housed."

"What really happens?"

"When the crash happens, Big Dan snaps his neck, we place the knife we used the other night and the bloody crow costume in the back seat. Big Dan casually wanders off, and we save the scene. Or bust the scene, whatever comes next."

"This sounds nuts, Fremeaux."

"Fuck, Xandi, it's all I got that'll put us face to face with someone in this crime organization. Besides, the kid has connections to the police covering for this in some way."

"Neville would never die of ennui down here," she muttered.

"What? What does that mean?"

"Just a character from a children's book my mother used to read to us. Doesn't have anything to do with our jug of jelly, just being silly in my head for a moment."

"Did this Neville die of ennui somewhere?" I asked.

"According to the artist, he did."

"Are you ok if Neville dies with a popped vertebra?" I asked.

"Neville needs to die, and that shit-ass mother of his."

"How often do you think about your mother and sister?" I asked.

She stopped us, for the first time since knowing her, I felt her soft spot. "Every fucking time I look into the mirror."

I had nothing more to say; I felt dumb.

"Have you been back to the Pontalba?" she asked. I thought it an odd question. A question without relevance.

But I answered anyway, without satire. "No, I haven't?"

She stared at me. "Have you taken your ecstasy yet?"

"I haven't."

"Do you have all your ducks in a row?"

"I don't have any ducks to put in a row, I'm unemployed."

"When we get the kid, you'll be ready?"

"It's mostly you and Don Lee delivering the goods. Everything else is waiting on a black car or a white van."

"How's your self-esteem holding up through unemployment?"

"I'm still on a mission. I have a job to do, and I'm doing it."

"Good." She held her palm up, giving me a look of anticipated adventure. I dug down for the pills and placed the ecstasy in her hand. She reached into a bag around her neck with the fingers of her other hand and rubbed a black powder behind my ears and the back of my neck.

"Is my soul safe?" I jested.

"No, but your butt is." She pushed a pill into each of our mouths. "I hope you don't need sleep tonight," she added slyly.

"I don't know what that feels like anymore."

She grabbed a wad of my white coveralls and pulled us toward Decatur.

Curveballs, I thought. Life is an endless procession of fuckin' curveballs. Starting with the murder of my dad. Was it just my life, or was this how it blows for everyone? Some curve less, and some spin completely out of control.

The wad of religious clodhoppers prescribes God's word. Their heavenly father has thrown a hell of a lot of curveballs in his eternity, then hangs his son on a cross to make us feel better through the confusion. Pray and swerve, pray and swerve. Well, I didn't feel like praying, and I sure as hell wasn't gonna swerve.

"Where ya dragging me, I ask?"

"New religions." She smiled.

Humpf. I stared at her bouncing hair, thinking about the hair bracelet on Becca's wrist. Was she planning a purge? New fuckin' religions! Gimmie a break.

I looked up at the sign of the place she dragged me to. "Blue Crystal, huh?"

"It's time we put some jingle back into your jangle, Fremeaux."

We walked to the bar. Two tequilas were at the edge, sitting in front of a huge balsam wood carving of a Billiken. I say two, but there was enough booze in each glass for four drinks. I tore the mouth hole in my bag face wider. We stepped in front of the Billiken, rubbing its belly as we raised our glasses.

"Everything's possible, and anything goes," I toasted as we took the Tequila down and returned the glasses. I took note that neither of us had ordered the drinks that were waiting for our arrival, causing me to wonder if I was part of yet another plan. I would've liked to think that Xandi had a standing order upon entry. She did move in mysterious ways.

I looked at the tips of the ears on the statue. "They point up."

"Never let the truth of life stomp your heart flat," she said, smiling, and wandered off toward the dance floor in the back. I followed. The Cocteau Twins were dreamily swaying a small club of bodies under the mirrored ball and the dim blinking. Outside was where time stretches back forever, but inside it was here and now. Nineteen-eighty-four, and the electric spinner was on high. People on the new groove and the new drugs filled with big kaleidoscope wishes. It's a time for new love.

She hopped on a high-top stool in a dark corner, and we waited till the energy rose with the body count. We waited till the stuff Nancy Reagan hated kicks in.

Light and time began to swirl, and my muscles and skin melted a little. The eternal smile landed inside of me. I think about what Don Lee told me: no matter how rough and tough things get, there is always a fresh, new blade of green grass to admire.

Even though Nancy didn't understand and wanted to end this feeling among the people, I still loved her for trying to care. In her own disconnected way, she wanted what's best, but for God's sake, couldn't she listen? The problem with the conservative mind is that it lacked the imagination to make the changes that count, and the fucking liberals lacked the balls to hold the lazy and self-absorbed accountable for their refusal to be productive. So, I moved through life murdering and protecting with a bag over my head. *Never let the truth of life stomp your heart flat*, she said. Truth is impossible.

The arrival of another tequila brought me back to the flotsam-jetsam of human bodies. Music pulsed through us while the universe opens itself up. Smiles grew from corner to corner, and I'm feeling electro-magnetized as Switchblade Symphony sends dark energy through the swaying souls on the dance floor.

My hand was grabbed, and Xandi was ready for some wine and swindling. Our bodies moved like waves over the sand, exchanging and stealing from one another. Sweat, heat, energy, the music pushed us around like seashells. Colors and light flitted just above our heads, and all of us out there felt the same thing. Another world existed, not forever but just long enough to capture the ugly and push it into the back of the closet.

Bends and dips. Swirls and juiced-up energy. Breaks from reality, spirits lifting. . .how did she know exactly what I needed when I needed it?

Loose and free, I let myself hang out, fully flaunting pride, and doing quaint deeds. Life was for the bold and ready.

The Cult pushed vibrant energy through us, and not a frown nor a fear to be witnessed. Mohawks and shaved heads. Black eyeshadow and Barbie makeup, it was all here. Time slipped even further. My consciousness stretched as my heart swelled with good fortune.

Xandi looked like an Egyptian goddess sending her song to Jupiter; it just couldn't get better. Dead men couldn't enter here; their souls sat at the windowsills wishing for us to take a break.

She pulled a vial from her pocket and rubbed something that smells like nothing I have ever encountered onto my lips and neck. Something I could only imagine to be goat breath.

I soon felt eternity slipping in. That was the only way to describe this, my soul or whatever falling through black time. Everything around me looks like it's at the end of a tunnel.

Where was I going? We moved through the crowd, and people pressed into my body, and it felt great. I wanted more. I saw the Billiken's smile as I floated to the front door and out into the street. I could hear Xandi asking someone to give us some room, but I couldn't seem to find her with my eyes. Suddenly, she was there laughing as she told me something. I felt like a balloon floating through dimming streetlights and fading voices. We were walking somewhere; hollowed buckets drumming voodoo, and chanting voices fade in. I'm a captured soul.

Life doesn't show up for the fearful, I told myself as I peered through a break in a shabby, wooden fence. Sweating bodies convulsed in a backyard, as if invisible ghouls were twitching their limbs like marionette dolls. Hypnotic eyes fixed on phantoms no more than four inches from their faraway gazes.

Those pulsing sounds burrowed deep into my psyche, something otherworldly tugged at the heart inside my chest. Bare-breasted women caused my toes to dig into the bottoms of my boots, searching for firm ground. I watched her hand reach out to unlock the gate, and we entered. I felt the bag lift away from my head, and the freedom to be myself kicked up a notch. I must be on safe ground.

All sound intensified when my tunnel vision saw it. The scratch of a goat's hoof across the rocks and broken concrete brought my skin to a pucker. A live goat hiding in the back corner of the yard bellowed thunder through me. Squawks and chants came from the tall, shirtless man as he danced, holding four chickens by the feet. Feathers flew in all directions, and blood dripped onto his shoes.

Metallic noise came from the ground around my feet. I looked down to find bottle caps strewn all over the concrete, and I was convulsing in rhythm with the drums and the chanting without will. I found I was shirtless somehow and moving in the cacophony with zombie-like attention.

I was suddenly surrounded by sweaty bodies as we danced farther and farther into the yard near the goat. I realized the goat was tied and wondering, like me, just what the hell we'd fallen into? I'd slip in and out of awareness. Dreams and images from another darkness came and went from my visions. When I remembered where I was, I searched for Xandi. I sensed her presence, but I couldn't lay eyes on her anywhere.

Half-naked bodies bounced all around, and the wind seemed to be heated, thick like syrup. Sweat danced on my skin as my scalp stung with sunburn, absent the sunlight. Large, dark birds sat along the top of the fence row under the raw glow of a full moon.

Female screeches echoed from somewhere as Mother Earth pulled my body to the ground. I lay on my back watching, limber bodies, faces, and stars swirling all around the darkness. I heard a thud and a quick bark above my torso. I looked and found the goat being raised into the air by three men, its blood draining from the fresh slit in its throat into a thin, rusting tin tub.

A plump, round face lowered from the parade of faces from just past my focus. A smile as big as a church door welcomed me. Ms. Koozie bent down to me, her freckles now twinkling like the stars, mapping the world in my eyes.

"I knew you'd come be with us, Fremeaux," she whispered and kissed me softly on my forehead. I softened.

A gorgeous female body appeared from nowhere, her face painted a deep, wine-blood red. When the light lay on it just right, it shimmered like liquid. There was great definition in the jawline, sharp, slanted, and strong. I searched for recognition. Her skin, deep, dark, and enchanting.

A billion tentacles seemed to climb up through the dirt beneath me and attach to my skin. I felt the sting of imprisonment as I tried to lift my head a little higher to inspect my space. The topless girl returned with bleeding chickens flopping at her sides. I searched her ribcage for the soup can scar but found nothing. This girl was smooth, smooth like granite. I tried hard to focus on my recognition, but starlight seemed to stretch all the way from space to cloud my vision.

She twirled and swayed, blood drips down her stomach and onto me as I lie in bewilderment. She straddled me, plucking at the white, bloody feathers. I watched them float down and pile on my torso. I could've sworn I knew her. Another person danced around my head, and a puff of white powder made a cloud over my face, slowly disintegrating and drifting into my eyes and nostrils, drying my mouth.

The red face of this princess swung above me as her body pressed into my groin, and I couldn't tell if my pants were on or off. I felt deep heat and liquid. She pushed harder. She raised a dried chicken foot high into the air and began a long chant in a foreign language. She trailed off into gibberish as she swung the chicken claw across my abdomen, and again, I couldn't tell if I'd been scratched, cut open, or if it was all phantom pains. She sat above me, rubbing herself onto my chest. A goblet of the goat's blood was delivered to her.

The tentacles seemed to draw blood from my back as she raised herself erect; her chest was covered in blood, and I wondered if I needed to be taken to a hospital. I was suddenly surrounded by what seemed to be an entire village. They knelt in unison as a thousand fingers grabbed and held my body. The clan began to chant low. I felt tingling from head to toe. Faintness built as I was going weak. The chants grew louder as my mind wanted to shut off. The sound was almost unbearable, and the pain of being held was maddening.

She slipped into a deep trance and took drink of the goat's blood. The hands holding me shifted, and my head was covered with wet fingers. She was convulsing on top of me. I was sweating profusely, or at least, I thought I was. Just as I thought I was going to recognize her, starlight seemed to wrap itself around her face. I tried to reach my hand to her face, but I'd become paralyzed.

A dark man in a loincloth suddenly appeared with large bones in one hand and something billowing smoke in the other. Every piercing in his body was filled with small bones; his face was painted white with orange zigzags.

In unison, all the fingers tightened on me, and my jaws were pulled wide. She gulped more goat blood and began to let it flow from her mouth into mine, clogging my throat. I gasped for air, but I was forced to swallow blood to find breath. She repeated the process as I fought with the hands, but just as I wrangled free of a few of them, the bone man bent to my face, and I saw rotating universes in his pupils as he blew a huge puff of smoke into my face. My muscles convulsed, the hands set me free, but I was in suspended animation. I was powerless as I felt my mind flittering away. I closed my eyes and watched my body walk into the darkness. I was gone.

CHAPTER TWENTY-SIX

My legs threw a sudden fit and kicked themselves toward the end of the bed, waking me from a dream or nightmare, I just couldn't say which. I looked around the room. I was back in bed at the Pontalba. How I got here, I couldn't say. I lifted the sheets and found myself naked, with no dirty clothing on the floor or anywhere in the room, for that matter. I ached from head to toe; my muscles didn't want to cooperate. I was mostly clean, but I saw a streak of dried blood through my pubic hair, and some specks of red in the creases of my fingernails. Whatever I thought I had dreamed wasn't a dream. I'd been somewhere and back. I heard something move out in the apartment and hopped onto my feet. Pain from sore bones shot through me. I stood still, quietly waiting for what, I don't fucking know.

"Theodore?"

It was her voice, soft and strong. Soothing again.

"Leda?"

"You're gonna make it out alive after all." She pushed the door slightly open, keenly aware of my privacy.

"You're back early. When did you get home?" I asked.

"Just in time, I'd say. You need a shower; we can catch up in a bit. I'll have Libertine place your clothes on your bed; she'll also change the sheets while you clean yourself."

"Leda, how long have I been asleep?"

"Couple of days."

"What day is it?"

"Wednesday."

"Shit. Leda, I have to be somewhere."

"I have your radio, Theodore. You have plenty of time. When you're clean and awake, Don Lee will be ready for you to reach out."

She closed the door, and I heard the outer door close as well. I let the sheet I was holding slip to the ground and went to the bathroom to turn on the hot water in the shower. I spun around to let the two days of fluids run free. I looked at the painting again and swore the bitch with the binoculars had a smile underneath those black-rimmed lenses.

"What in the fuck are you smiling at?" I ask her. "Were you smiling the other day? I can't remember seeing lips the last time I saw you."

The peanuts still look freshly roasted. I jumped under the hot water, harshly scrubbing off whatever coated my skin. Images from the night emerge and disappear along with matching emotions. I tried siphoning some kind of reality from dreams, but it was still too muddy. The soreness of my muscles told me I took a beating, and my soul took the back road back to this bed. I could remember half-naked bodies, bleeding birds, my body bound to drumbeats, but that was about as far as memory stretches. Drying off, I wondered what the facts are and what would fit in a fiction story.

My bed had been made clean, and clothes folded on top of it. I dressed and sat to put my boots on. I want to decipher the mysteries in my head, but I'm a little consumed by the idea of Leda being home so early and why I'm still here, just as much as how I got here. I took a deep breath and opened the door to her. She stood with the phone to her ear. I looked across the room to inspect the mirror of convenience between the doorway, no sign of secret spying eyes this time. Still, no confirmation that Golda isn't over there somewhere waiting to pull out.

"Is that what you want to do?" She asked on the phone. "Okay, I'll be ready."

The call felt staged to me. She turned to look at me. An ankle-length silk dress, the color of an oyster shell, hugged her naked body. The only thing between her and eternity is the dress; I saw her nudity through it. I could burn through a millennium just thinking about her.

"Well, partner, what did you do? Get yourself kidnapped?" she asked wryly.

"I can't rightly recall the facts of the case just yet. I do know I started with some dancing."

"You've been a busy boy."

"Busy, but I lack settlement."

"Mother is quite amused with your results so far. She's rooting for you."

"I'm happy to be passing the first rounds of exams. How about the two criminals you have in your custody? I feel they may have something that could lead to a connection here with the missing girls. Every rock I overturn seems to be uncovering old campfires left by the Dixie boys."

"We're aware. We have gathered what we needed, and the boys are en route to you. Do as you please."

The phone rang again, she stood to answer, and the dress clung to curves that could start another war.

"Yes, that's fine." Her back was to me.

"Hour and a half?" she answered again, glancing at me with trepidation.

She placed the phone back in its cradle. She looked at me differently; her energy and tone opened another door. I felt a different kind of acceptance. Her face was striking; she was nearly nude. I felt something pulling me from within.

The curtain had lifted, and we were all alone on the front porch swing, dimly lit by the dull porch light. Full moon, crickets, the stars just beyond. No one was around, parents were gone, and won't be back till morning. Just us, our rules. Our needs and wants.

The image of a painted red face swept my mind's eye. I felt a drumbeat somewhere inside. Was it a drumbeat or a charge in our rhythm? Something had changed, moving, crawling through the flesh. Her skin against the white and grey silk glistened. She wanted it to glisten for me. Was I lying to myself? Was I in another fable?

I stood, looking into her eyes. All the water in all the lakes, rivers, and oceans of this everlasting planet must've been calm this very minute as the possessed water in my blood pumped ungoverned, from a pulse from way out there somewhere. The keen ones must've been staring at their glass-surfaced lakes, mesmerized by the power of Mother Nature, while disillusioned revolutionaries steered into paranoia, fearing their world was being hijacked. Love and death began in the blood.

Her eyes locked with mine, and much like the falcon attached to her wrist in the photograph behind me, I would soon be released to fly my own hunt with her. Slowly, we closed the gap between us and held each other in the power, silence, and myth of something I wished to know more about.

Our fingers lightly grazed to test the connection, and I could almost unravel the mystery. Drumbeats pulled my chest to its very boundaries. We were together in a tender fight, a rough mingle of passion and hoodoo. Two souls meshed, pulling at the edge of our wishes; her lips were there, and I took them. I sucked her tongue. Rolled her hot skin on mine. She danced with my tongue, her teeth scraping the edges. She pulled her mouth from me, pushing hungry teeth onto my neck, biting till hot colors explode behind my closing lids.

My hand followed the long curve of her lower back until my fingers sank deep into soft flesh. I slipped my strongest finger into the soft division, finding the crook of her tailbone. I pulled her back up to my mouth. She made a soft moan of affirmation and the warm sigh of stability. The sound every man on earth longs for on lonely nights when he swears to God it will never be offered. The tone that says *I'm here, take me with your heart. Take anything you want from me. Take me to the end of this rope to see what will kill me.*

I don't know how we came to find ourselves in bed, but there we were, bound to one another like jungle vines on the tops of tall trees. Suddenly, I *was* Zeus foraging into my new world. An elegant dance partner followed me everywhere, up into the silver web of the stars. Aladdin's carpet caught in a sailor's wind, we swept; I couldn't be certain we would return to this very bed. Muscles stretched, arguing for forgiveness.

Her breath was gasoline; fire could break out at any moment. Colors thundered behind my closed eyelids as her nails dug further into my back. Her lips found me over and over again. My hands squeezed with exhaustion as her sighs made me feel as light as a kite. Bound but free. She was telling me to be free. Free to love her anyway I wanted.

Ripples turned into waves as we pushed ourselves deeper into the universe. Our bodies never loosened from the wrangle; I flipped her onto her stomach, and she crossed her wrists at the curve of her lower back. I captured them in my grip like a saddle horn. The voice of Sade filled our ears somehow as if Bacchus himself slipped past, flicking on the CD. I dug my teeth into the back of her neck as she moaned for more.

Her body tightened and convulsed. She flipped; her hands clamped into my flanks as teeth tore at my earlobe. Hot breath pushed my hair, a soft voice rushed, pushing me into reserves. Her grip tightened while her breath heaved, fiercely without resolve. She was telling me she wanted me to take her even further out, feel the unyielding depths. Crash the boat. Drown her old self; wake up in a new skin. We pushed ourselves through the crashing waves without fear.

I felt her soul release, and we deflated into one another. I woke up with her body completely wrapped in my arms, her lips pressed into my chest. I wasn't out of breath, but my lungs were pulling hard like a fresh kill out on the savannahs—her breath, saliva, sweat, energy, surrender, exhaustion, and my exhaustion. We were a heap of it all.

She was draped like a woman who had just outwitted Sherlock Holmes. The one subject he just couldn't iron out. Scratching his chin after having just used all the lead in his pencil.

I'm not hired help anymore, I tell myself. You gotta get up to get down. Get ugly to get pretty, like Willie Nelson.

The phone rang and we untangled so she could go into the other room. I grabbed her hand like I was going to confess something. She squeezed mine harder.

"No need for that," she explained. "We both know where we are now." She let loose my hand and strode through the doorway. Her body just doesn't need words; it's a gift from the gods.

I laid back on the warm bed, looking around her bedroom. A tiny purple velvet pillow sat on a shelf by the window. I looked closer and found a decorated dried chicken foot lying across it. Curious, I went to it and picked it up. Multi-colored threads bound a small patch of hair to it, and it matched my hair. A vivid image of the red-faced seductress from my dream state flashed, and the drumming returned to my chest. She walked through the door carrying a walkie-talkie and set it on the dresser. I looked at her and returned the foot to its pillow of rest. She came to me, and her still warm breast softly pushed into the top of my ribs.

"Were you there the other night?" I softly asked.

"Did you want me there? If you did, then I was with you."

We stared into one another. That ancient hazelnut held me in place. Truth is impossible; it'll forever need words to empower it. Love never needs a single utterance, just perception and ritual.

The radio on the dresser squawked.

"Black car, and one white van on site," Big Dan clumsily announced.

She looked back at me and smiled. "Showtime, big boy."

"You?" I asked.

"My half-brother, Ferdinand, is in town inspecting the family's cargo business. I must ensure he and some others arrive at their destination on time."

"Later, if I'm not killed?"

"This bed is now yours too. Meet me back here, Mr. Man."

"If I'd known, I would have brought my toothbrush."

"All you need is being delivered."

"Delivering new life?" I asked.

"Oh, you have no idea."

"Have you seen my costume?"

"There isn't a need to hide your pretty face in the streets any longer."

"Yeah, and why's that?"

"A visit was made on your behalf," she said. "The assistant director of the C.I.A. is brother-in-law to our 'personal' senator if you know who I mean."

"The Limo? Wanda?"

"That one. Seems it would be easier to cover the butt of an ex-New Orleans Police Officer than to prune down the reputation of a political family tree. You are now immune to police retaliation. Except there is one thing. It seems a rogue hired hand is out there. Protection for the state's attorney general. I'm sure you've found him lurking."

"Big fella. Nautical clothing?"

"That's him. Seems he has gone into hiding. Our resources haven't spotted him around for some time now."

"Resources, huh? Is he connected with shipping? Connection with your clinic?"

"We don't closely oversee that clinic, I've told you. It falls under the jurisdiction of the other half of the family, Ferdinand."

I felt relief shoot into my heart on that subject once again. I could finally scratch her from a connection to Charlie now.

"What is that side of the family involved in?"

"International shipping is all I know."

"Your mother doesn't call the shots?"

"No. When her mother disappeared, Mother was shipped off and placed on an allowance. Her father remarried my mother's half-sister. That's where Ferdinand, our half-brother, or whatever the fuck he is, fits into the picture. He now controls the family fortune on that side. He loathes Mother and me and would love to see us disappear from the face of the earth for the fortune she's built."

"New Orleans Port?" I asked.

"Yes, and most of the East Coast."

"Did he put the Dixie Mafia onto you?"

"Probably, and I'm not in the mood for this conversation at this moment. You have an appointment to uphold, Fremeaux. People are counting on you again."

She didn't use my first name; she meant it's time for business. I went to put on the clothes that I was wearing before Mother Nature tore them from my body, and gather weapons. She walked me to the gate and kissed me.

"A fish doesn't always make a feast," she said.

"I can turn a potato into a casserole, baby." I smiled and turned into the sun.

CHAPTER TWENTY-SEVEN

I looked to see if Hubris's pink and lavender umbrella was up. I felt like a little taunt, but instead, I caught Monsignor's staff closing the trunk of a limousine as he was being escorted into the backseat. "Getaway?" I jested.

The Quarter was bare for now. The revelers were back at work as the city prepares for the next big convention. Hopefully, it was low-brow as some shit was about to hit the fan on my end of town, and it was easier to sweep shit under a carpet of drunken debauchery than anything else.

I look around the busted streets and reminded myself that Charlie was dead; this was our home. Home to the beautifully troubled, doing the best that we possibly could. I held up the radio.

"Xandi, Don Lee, is everyone in place?"

"We're here with the Porsche and the two shitbags," Xandi returned. Don Lee quickly returned with his affirmation.

"Dumaine?" I asked.

"Yes," Don Lee said. "In their designated places now."

"Four blocks away," I answered.

"Glad you're back with the living," Xandi said.

I spotted the silver Porsche parked in the middle of the block; I could hear the engine at idle. I saw a black Ford Ranger up near Esplanade, a black trunk in the bed of the truck with two women sitting atop it. Xandi approaches me from the street corner.

"Is the mother in that trunk?" I asked.

"That's her. Gagged and a little beat to shit."

"Couldn't help yourself, huh?"

"Do unto others, Fremeaux."

I noticed she didn't comment on my lack of a costume. No need for concealment. Did she already know? Or could she just not seem to care about such trivial matters? I move to the driver's window and kneel on the ground.

"Dirty deeds done dirt cheap, eh, Otto?"

He looked at me with that fucking thick brown mole, looking like it wanted to talk shit to me. Looks like something Stephen King uses as his muse. Up close, the thin hairs and thick wrinkles looked like they could easily be the brain center of Otto.

"Oh, it's you. I've seen you in uniform, foot cop. Well, my friends on the force are gonna take you out, you're nothing to us."

The kid's top lip was paper-thin, but the bottom one looked like he was storing potted meat inside of it. When he talked, everything moved out of sync, making him look like a goddamned sock puppet. The genetics of this family should be genetically realtered in a lab somewhere.

"I'm not a cop anymore, Slick. Just think about the Monopoly board, all you gotta do is pass go. You'll collect your money and ya skanky-assed momma."

"Fuck you, Fremeaux. We'll be back."

I looked past the mole and the afflicted lips to Big Dan, who was buckled tightly to his seat.

"You fill him in?" I asked.

He affirmed with a head nod and his three-ring smile.

"Otto, give this car all it's got. I need that limo disabled. The front tire needs to be shoved into the engine. When it's over, you'll walk over to the black truck, and we will drive you and your mother back to Mobile. You can then make a phone call and tell all your cop buddies just what some bad ole ex-cop made you and your mommy do."

"I don't have to call, Paw Paw, they've been watching you?" "Well, where are they now, just when you need 'em most?"

He gulped air. "This ain't over, asshole."

"Just make a clean run, Otto. Make ya daddy proud."

I stood and looked around the neighborhood. Just a few folks out straggling through the streets. It was Wednesday, Billy Delle would be spinning *Records from the Crypt* on WWOZ later. Everyone was going about their usual daily lives while we were out here about to fuck some shit up.

I maneuvered the soon-to-be crime scene and saw Don Lee walking in from the Marigny. Xandi has at least ten walkie-talkie-toting folks sparsely planted at street corners. I happened to know there was a mild lunatic in the hotel window above the scene. She had her shit covered.

Don Lee approached.

"Leda called, she said you'd be out of costume. I wasn't sure it'd be true."

"She doesn't fuck around."

"She never has. Who ya think is gonna be in that limo?" Don Lee asked.

"The wrong person," I returned.

We moved around the corner out of sight while our special forces concealed their walkie-talkies, wandering the block like the average tourist.

"Movement. Gates opening," a voice reported.

The drive chain on the black iron gates was bouncing when I peeked around the corner.

"Big Dan, get the car in gear," I commanded.

The limo pulled out from around the back of the house and pointed toward Barracks. A one-way street headed toward our trap.

"Be ready, folks. As soon as it happens, stay put and keep watch on the house. I need to know how many heads peep out at the scene of the crash. Store a memory of the faces, if there are any to record. Xandi and I will approach the limo seemingly to help the crash victims. Big Dan, we're counting on you and Otto to do his job."

"The black car drove off the driveway, turning right onto the street. Just as it began to reach the intersection, our lady crossed through the intersection, causing the car to come to a complete stop. I heard the engine of the Porsche rev, and the tires squeal. Then the harsh sound of crashing metal.

"Go," Don Lee told me.

Smoke and the smell of gasoline filled my nose as I went to the Porsche first. I bent to Big Dan; he was conscious, as was the kid. I looked into Big Dan's eyes; I saw our agreement. Big Dan unbuckled, turning to put the kids' neck in his grip. The kid's face turned to horror, shock red, as his oxygen cut off.

"Can you snap it?" I asked.

The kid slumped. I pulled the knife I used to kill Demortiers from the towel it was hidden in. Don Lee had placed Charlie's crow costume behind the driver's seat, and I slipped the murder weapon in with it.

Big Dan quietly wandered off down the block as if he was headed to pick flowers for his momma. We'll catch up later.

I saw Xandi knocking on the windows, asking if everyone inside was ok. I met her and found the doors locked. I pounded the windows myself, but to no avail. The windows were so blacked out that nothing revealed their contents. I went to the windshield and motioned to the driver. He wasn't budging, and no one else would either. I gave a thumbs up to the driver, signaling that all we wanted to do was help. I wanted him in a state of ease and not to be on the defensive in any way. He held a CB mouthpiece in the air, signaling he would handle the situation. He simply shook his head and began placing a sun visor over the dashboard, blocking any outside viewing. I motioned for Xandi to come to me.

"We have to get to the passenger."

The two ladies in the back of the truck jumped out. One laid a tire iron in the grass next to the truck, and they both jumped in the cab and drove away from the scene. Xandi went for the tire iron and returned it to me. I began pounding on the windows to no avail. Bulletproof. I tried prying at the doors. Just then, Agent Freeman arrived in an unmarked car and got out.

"I'll take from here, Fremeaux."

"I'm too close now."

He pulled his gun and held it to the side of his leg.

"Fremeaux, I have orders to have you move on. I am asking you to move on."

I could see the seriousness of his gaze. I realized I was possibly in the middle of something bigger than I could have imagined. I pictured a hand flushing a solid gold toilet high up in a penthouse somewhere.

"What the fuck is happening?" I asked the sun.

Just then, a wrecker arrived on the scene, and we all moved across the street. Four fellas jumped from the tow truck and proceeded to attach chains and pull the wrecked limo onto the towing bed. Directly, it sped away, leaving a wrecked Porsche, a dead kid, and a stunned audience.

Agent Freeman motioned for me to walk down the block with him.

"I'm just following command, Fremeaux. As you know, this place will soon be crawling with cops about that kid you left in the other vehicle. Someone's cornering you from somewhere, Dowd will shoot you just for being you. I'd disappear for a while, Fremeaux."

"I've killed people for this!" I mumbled angrily to myself.

Deflated, I went upstairs to the room in the hotel to ask the airwaves for a huddle. I noticed there weren't any sirens yet. I listened to footsteps accumulate in the hallway as I watched another tow truck arrive on the street below. In the same fashion as with the limo, the Porsche was quickly hauled away with the dead body inside.

"Well fuck me," I said, fogging the glass pane. "As if nothing ever happened."

As our little band of wounded angels piled into the room, I was wondering what in the hell just happened. Xandi closes the door behind us all.

"Is there anything anyone has heard tell? I don't know what we just witnessed."

"Were they ready for us?" A voice asked from inside the room.

"It's obvious they can self-heal. Took no time in cleaning up our mess," Big Dan grumbled.

"Is there still the white van? Has anyone spotted it leaving?" I asked.

It's still in there, the neurotic voice from the room reported.

I looked across the way. "Xandi and I are going in there when we get new bearings. Something's going on over there as we speak, I can feel it."

"Does anyone need to be anywhere? If so, do what ya need, we will need to reconvene here in a couple of hours to be ready to cover us." Xandi explained.

No one left. A sandwich list was put together, and a call was made to the Verde Marte. Closure is all these folks are looking for. They want to put their effigies in the closet for good. Sleep without seeking answers from the dark.

We're too close to rest, one voice said.

No more motherly pain! If we can make a difference, then I say kill the bastards for what they've done, another voice chimed.

"Let's do it, folks," I said. "For the unrested souls of your girls."

I looked out the window again.

"Xandi?" I said.

She came to the window. The grey man was turning the corner at Dumaine and headed back into the Quarter.

"Maybe his handler was in the limo?" I said.

Xandi went to speak with one of the younger women in the room and returned to me. The young lady exited the room.

"My cousin Clementina. She will keep up without leaving a scent."

I looked at her.

"What happened to me the other night?

"A good time."

"I'm not talking about the dancing and the ecstasy."

"Soul cleansing," she said.

"Why is there a chicken foot by Leda's bed with my hair attached?"

"Like all of us, Leda wants to light your path."

"Safe, huh? Was my soul captured?"

"Only you have say so over your soul's destination."

"Only me? Not the universe?" I asked.

"You'll hafta ask the universe for that answer."

"I wasn't aware you and Leda were acquaintances?"

"We're all acquaintances under the stars and through the clock."

"Even after death?"

"Forever, baby. Flesh is only a temporary costume."

"There is no straight answer in voodoo," I concluded. She gave me a devilish smile.

"I'll be back," she said and went out the door. I watched her walk out onto the street and on toward the ninth ward. I wondered if she was going to consult a crystal ball.

I peeked up through the trees to get a crack at the bluish-grey sky and wondered if Zeus had tried slipping in unnoticed again.

"Who's in the house?" I asked the universe. Nothing but a light breeze brushed the leaves. I'd have to wait and find out, I guess. Sandwiches arrived, and we chewed our way to nightfall. I noticed Don Lee didn't come up with us. I felt out of place with a passel of his friends I'm not familiar with.

"Has anyone talked with Don Lee?" I asked

"He said he had to be somewhere and would be back in a jiff," a voice answered.

As odd as it sounded that he'd take off without touching base with me, I somehow made it feel like it should be a normal part of the program. Is the universe telling me to stay calm? *¿Tranquilo, amigo?*

The land was starting to shadow when the drums returned to my chest. I looked off to the sky over the river again, wondering if Zeus's telltale sign could be seen, but I found a faint rainbow instead. The good earth was calling again. Becca, maybe? Or the dark side of the good earth, illuminating a siren call? Either way, both signs are manifestations of unwelcome weather.

I surveyed the house and the block. There's gotta be a way to those grounds from behind. I took out to Esplanade Avenue to find the way through the backside.

CHAPTER TWENTY-EIGHT

The limbs of the live oaks drooped down over the busted concrete, making it seem like the city itself didn't want secrets of any kind to be discovered. I remained conscious of foot placement as I peer down walkways looking for a way through. I couldn't afford a trip up, can't commit a crime if your knees are busted. I judged an approximate location and hopped over a wooden gate. Fences, tops of walls covered in broken wine bottle spikes, darkened windows, I navigated it all like a virus. The perfect bloodstream was here somewhere. I found loosened boards behind wilting Azaleas, and bingo, I quietly muscled through the first obstacle. I crept along, two backyards down, and I was discovered. Called out by a cockatoo in a huge fuckin' cage on a back porch.

"Ohh, another one. Another one. You're not gonna make it. You're not gonna make it. They won't like it. Won't like it. Call Monsignor. Call Captain Dowd. Call Monsignor. Call Captain Dowd."

I laid flat on the ground, hoping no one was home to check on the bird's declarations. I reached to turn down the volume on my walkie-talkie. The fucking bird was on repeat. I guessed I wasn't the only dumbass who's searched for this route. I remained silent and still. I could see their back wall was ten or twelve feet high. We would need to plan assistance from the ground up to get all of us over as quickly as possible.

That motherfucker had been listening to backyard secrets. Was a fuckin' eavesdropping bird admissible in a courtroom? Hell, I could use one of these. I couldn't believe the bastard hadn't gotten itself assassinated. Then I thought about how the bastard was going to announce our return. I couldn't kill an innocent creature of God, just like that, could I? He was just doing what he had been praised for. We'll hafta work with it. *Fuck, fuck, fuck, fuck me!* After lying like a dead man for fifteen minutes, I slinked backwards with a plan of attack to the hole I came in on.

Don Lee returned with a backpack and walked to me.

"I have them here now."

"What?" I asked.

"All the body parts."

"Okay?' I said, confused.

"Leda said you needed them here?"

"Leda? I didn't communicate anything to her."

I looked out the window and wondered just what the hell to make of those lost days in her apartment. Forty-eight hours of unconsciousness. No dreams to recall, not even Becca. The pull of puppet strings returns to my thinking.

"Thanks, Don Lee," I said, playing along with the universe. "We're about to go in," I told him.

"You sure about this?"

"I'm tired of cat and mouse. If the right people are in there, we're putting an end to this crap. Once and for all."

"What if all the right people are missing?" He asked.

"Take names and kill whoever is hanging around hover there."

"Well, okay, big boy. Let's go make a deal," he said.

"Just be aware. There could be young girls being held captive in there, you never know." I reminded.

"They need us if that's the case."

"Yes, they do, Don Lee. There was some kind of transference from the church to here the other day, and I watched the Monsignor get into a limo this morning as though he was en route to outta town. Something's up in the city of disbelief."

Don Lee nudged my ribs; I looked down at the street. Ruthie was walking by the gates of the driveway, as her ducks confidently flanked her. She stopped to place a brown paper bag on the ground. She removed two black voodoo candles, set them at each gate post, and lit them. She bowed her head for a moment, then shuffled on out of sight. Don Lee gave me the catfish frown of *beats the shit out of me* look.

The door opened, and Xandi returned with Big Dan and Booker Lot in tow.

"We're armed to the teeth, y'all ready?" she demanded.

I looked at Don Lee.

"You keeping watch?" I asked.

"Hell no, Paw Paw. I've been waiting too fucking long to bust this door in."

"It's about to go dark, we can jump the fence down there in the corner. One at a time, we can make the hump. I gotta warn ya'll, there's a fuckin parrot that's going to announce us. Gotta go as fast as we can. And we'll need two strong men to volunteer to vault us over a wall. Shall we hit it then?" I asked.

From the door, Xandi answered, "No more waiting, fellas, let's go."

I explained to Mrs. Havisham that we had our earpieces and that if anyone entered the property, it would be imperative to report it. No one else would hear the transmission. She understood, as the rest of the group did.

"We gotcha from here," they agreed.

We scaled the narrow stairwell one behind the other. Xandi was below us at the halfway mark when the narrowness of it all gave me a thick sense of claustrophobia, as dizziness and dimming of the lights swept my ability to see straight. The walls seemed to reach out for me.

As I moved down the steps, Xandi's body stretched and warped, becoming translucent for a second. What seemed like a body-shaped water bubble peeled and detached, something of her broke away and brushed in my direction. I could only guess it was aura, as the old mystics would call it. I could see it, but at the same time, I couldn't. It was there, and it wasn't, but I felt its humidity brush me as it ran into our past. I quickly turned my head following it and found Big Dan looming high above me with yet another circus freak grin, his head blocking the dim overhead light bulb. I peered around his waist to make eye contact with Don Lee, and he winked. I would never be sure if he had seen Xandi shed, or if I was caught up in something stretching from the other night's shenanigans?

I looked back down at Xandi, rushing into the future as her spirit fled, chasing off into our past.

Have we been assuming the arrow of time points in the wrong direction? Does our future flow past us with its puzzled information in tow? Are we not running into a passing future? *Fuck me.*

The voodoo drums sounded off in my ears, and blood began another tickle. Where did it call me? From back there, or just ahead, just beyond the door?

Xandi grabbed the doorknob and looked back up at me; her pupils seem to glow. Did she know what was waiting for us out there? Were we headed into another big bang that has already happened, sprinkling its mystery as we ran toward it?

I turned to look at Don Lee, hoping I hadn't been talking out loud again. I was certain that kind of babble would have the others spouting humbugs about my behavior, especially Booker; he didn't know what the fuck we were up to.

I returned my gaze to Xandi below as the boom of the hollow drum pounded louder and louder with each foot landing. Xandi held the door as my perception grew dimmer and dimmer until the streetlamp caught my attention, and my spirit fell back into its place. Déjà vu warped my thoughts for a second. I almost believed I had trampled this stairwell before.

"We all want to imagine our futures to be filled with trophies and warm friendships, but that's rarely the outcome," she told me on the sidewalk. I realize this chain of action is going to carry me to my grave someday.

"It all starts with just a little voodoo?" I asked her glowing pupils.

"It *always* starts with just a little voodoo." She smiled.

With her aura protecting our backs, we traversed the busted concrete of Esplanade Avenue.

"Okay. Move slow and quiet till we hear the bird start his speech, then haul ass to the wall, and you two fellas will fling us up and over. When we're all over, you will need to haul ass out. Don't go back to the room. Run into the Marigny and disappear till you hear from someone.

Everyone nodded affirmation, making sure our earpieces were secure. Booker tightened the straps on his toolkit.

We climbed and crawled till the bird squawked.

"He's back. He's back."

The little fucker has a recall. I pushed Xandi up and over the wall. Within seconds, we were all safely on the other side.

"Y'all, hang tight behind this bush." Just as I spoke, the garage door broke, and I took quick advantage to hustle through a patch of crepe myrtles, getting myself hidden behind the HVAC. A late-season wasp nest hung just under a water faucet three feet from me. Wings vibrated with anger as the confused young wasps crouched for attack.

"Fuck, you're all I need right now," I whispered.

A white van pulled out in a hurry and rounded the curved driveway out of sight. I took my chance and ran like hell for the closing door. As I jumped-started, the wasps lunged in full pursuit of me. Three stung the back of my neck, and two on my left calf through my jeans. I had to fend them off as quietly as possible while getting fucking stung. I made it through the door, tripping the automatic system, and returning it to open. I swore I could still hear that fuckin' bird. Between that bird and Becca, my conscience jostled like a Jell-O mold on a shrimp boat.

I motioned to everyone to get a move on. We had firepower, so I wasn't concerned with anyone inside watching cameras ambushing us.

I found three doors and a stairwell leading up to an entrance door, one flight up.

One door was behind the stairwell; it had windows and was cracked open. Another one next to it on the opposite wall also had glass but was locked. The third was on the far wall, and it had no windows. A thick oak board braced it on our side, and a humongous padlock was attached. Two large flashlights sat on a board shelf next to the door, along with eight or nine plastic buckets smelling of piss and shit and vomit. Whatever was behind door number three was meant to stay behind door number three.

The others entered in procession as I closed the door behind Booker. I raised my finger to my lips and pointed to the lock. Booker went to work. Xandi tiptoed up the steps to check the door at the top of the stairs. It was locked.

Booker had the padlock popped quicker than I had expected. Big Dan quietly lifted the oak board out of its resting place. We opened the door to find another long, dark hallway leading to one more black door at the end, and another padlock. I motioned, and Booker went down quietly to do his work.

We finally opened the door into some dungeon, and there were twelve to fourteen bunks with half-naked female bodies curled on them. They seemed to be drugged, as they were reluctant to move or cause a scene. When the flashlight would highlight upper torsos, they'd raise a hand to cover sore eyes. Their other hands were cuffed to the bottom of the bunks.

It smelled like sex and confusion, and the noxiousness of blatant disregard. Booker's jaw fell agape with disbelief. Xandi went in further and began to touch the girls. When they realized it wasn't foul play, they began to answer in sobs. Xandi shushed them to inspect their faces and bodies for harm. She walked up to me.

"The girl at Charlie's murder scene is in that bunk there." She pointed to the corner farthest from us.

"Dowd," I mumbled. Next to her was one of the girls dressed as Wonder Woman. "Fuck me," I mumbled. "These motherfuckers are fuckin slick. I just hope her friend is still alive somewhere."

"Funny how Charlie's accuser was whisked away from the scene before the newspaper could get a picture of her," Xandi stated.

"No need for trial since Charlie was too dead to be tried," I said.

I could hear Don Lee's breathing. He was blowing with anger as we looked through such a scene. I know he must be picturing Mary Catherine. I didn't want to intrude on his personal relinquish, so I placed a hand on his shoulder and listened to him breathe.

Our earpieces reported.

"Gates opening, limo about to pull in."

We assured the girls of a rescue. Whether they were in a state of understanding, I'd never know. We quieted back through the doors, placing the oak boards and padlocks back in their resting places, and hid in the slightly open utility closet behind the stairs, waiting with ears open, clutching our guns.

The car was parked; the garage doors were closed. A light turned on inside their area. A voice called from above us to the people arriving.

"All clear, fellas."

It was a relief to know we weren't on any radar, but then again, I couldn't rule out silent hand gestures, so I remained at attention. I heard Booker Lot gulp, and I patted him on the shoulder to calm him. We listened to the male voices just outside our hiding place.

"I want the redhead again," a voice said.

"We'll have them all at some point. They're headed overseas in a couple of days." Another answered.

"We don't do nothin' till Ferdinand gets here."

"Is he staying the night here, or will we smuggle one out?"

"I don't know his plans; it's an unscheduled trip this time. He showed up outta da blue. Let's go up and have some drinks and wait."

We felt the five or six sets of feet pound the stairs just over our heads. We stood frozen, waiting for another sign.

Xandi was as cool as a spring flower. I could see the slow burn swelling in Don Lee's reddening eyes. Booker looked confused, and Big Dan stretched his signature smile, looking over to Xandi.

The drums taunted me again. She cut her eyes at me and smiled, knowingly. We were bumping together, as voodoo chants reached me through her silent voice. She put her weapon on a shelf, rubbed her finger into something, and swiped the backs of all our necks.

"*Con bu nay killy con con,*" she chanted. I watched the boys relax. We waited again.

"Another Limo coming in hot, folks." Our earphones told us. Tires squealed and stopped. Doors opened, and new sets of feet scuffled the concrete floor.

"Go on up," I heard Golda's fierce accent command. Two or three extra sets of feet climbed the steps above us. We listened as high-heeled shoes walked to the secret door and went quiet for a few seconds, then tapped the concrete floor back toward us.

After the others had left, the door hiding us suddenly flung open. There she was, inspecting our faces. I looked at Don Lee, and I saw trust. Xandi stood curiously. My face must've expressed someone who just got caught smoking pot with the teacher's pet.

"Theodore, relax. You won't need to take another life this evening, you're all with me now."

I honestly thought for a second I was in hot water for fucking the teacher's pet.

"You folks sit tight. I will send someone down in a bit. You will hear that door open over there. You will hear a girl being escorted up the stairs. You will wait two minutes, then come up. Everything will be set for your trap." She closed the door on us, and the heels climbed the stairs. I noticed she held an umbrella in her hand. The oddity of it struck me.

"Who's gonna die?" Booker asked.

"Fuck if I know," Xandi answered. "When we make our move, you slip out the driveway, Booker," she told him.

Relieved, he gave the thumbs up. I saw sweat slip back into his skin. Don Lee looked ready to cut a throat, and Big Dan held the carnival in place. I didn't know what to fucking think. *Our trap,* she said. I had no skin in this trip. Don Lee had more than I do.

Was all this calculated from the very beginning? Why the hell was Golda here? Had we been blazing a trail that had been pre-cut? Were the grey man and the Magpie upstairs?

Don Lee lowered his head, bracing his palms on the washing machine. His voice became low and dark, a conjured growl like the night we sat out by the dark river.

"Some people use the idea of tomorrow just to get through the night. When tomorrow dawns, it's already spent. Huffing and puffing, they'll turn into disparate revolutionaries demanding replacement of society's ideals with hasty dogma. Our world is swelling with this diseased revolutionary demand.

"The interstate between Birmingham, Alabama, and Huntsville is a strong study of this behavior. I've driven to Nashville a thousand times for country music articles, and that stretch of highway always fumes my soul. Cloggers, I call them, constantly pushing frustration out into the world.

"Three lanes. Count 'em, three fuckin' lanes of American interstate will clog down to twenty, maybe thirty miles below the speed limit. For miles, you watch the cars thicken, your gas pedal leg shakes, furious with anticipation. You swear to God Almighty that you'll soon stumble across a warped steel catastrophe: overturned cars, flashing lights, gobs of men in blue. Ambulances, fire trucks, dread in faces on the side of the road somewhere up ahead. But you drone on and on and nothing. Nothing disastrous ever arrives. The whole time, it was simply human self-absorption clogging this American artery. A goddamned unwillingness to be cordial. A refusal to merge. A refusal to grant basic needs. Indecency it is. The sheer indecency of it pushes good people to snap. Some people want the rest of the world to slow down to their beliefs.

"Hippie do-gooders covered in world peace and Grateful Dead bumper stickers are the worst, complete lack of regard for *other* people. Hippie indignancy is real, ya know. God's fuckin' busted toilet plungers if ya ask me.

"Triple-jowled women with death stares because they got themselves knocked up by the wrong men, three times too many.

"Nouveau Riche bulling through in shiny new Cadillacs, "My taxes pave this side too, buddy. Move around," complete horseshit.

"Ignorant rednecks of all colors driving trucks the size of a New York studio apartment refuse, because nobody tells a badass what to do.

"Frankly, I'm tired of all this bloated, self-absorbed revolution bullshit."

He paused, with reddened eyes, knuckles stone-white again.

"It's the simple farmers, teachers, firemen, not afraid of decency. They merge right, allowing the other man the courtesy of their freedom. You see it in their eyes and humble smiles as you pass. We wave the secret wave, as we drive and look upon one another through dirty windows, the wave that says, *We got ya back*, my friend, go forth and prosper."

Another set of feet began clomping down the wooden steps, crossing the garage floor. White returned to Don Lee's eyes as he continued in another lowered growl.

"Jumping in bed with a fruit tray and goddamned television cameras demanding world peace is a stunt only a fucking Momma's boy could resolve to." His knuckles finally relaxed as he picked up his gun.

"Fuck excuses."

We heard the secret door open, a few minutes passed, then boots and bare feet slapping the concrete floor, then they clomped the stairs back up to the second floor. We looked at one another, concerned. We waited our requisite two minutes and walked out into the garage to shake off the stiffness and confusion, checking our weapons. Halfway up the stairs, a fella in full combat gear, face concealed in military garb, machine gun pointed at an angle toward the ground, stood in the doorway. I sized him to be as big as Big Dan. Golda appeared.

"No need for weapons," Golda said.

I don't have a fucking clue what could be happening at this point. Drums deliver a mixture of *what the fuck*, and *goddamn*.

We entered the upstairs room. I've never seen wine velvet walls in my life. Looked like a place Elvis took his mistresses. Poker tables, two built-in bars. Gold shag carpet, and I think I could see an octagon waterbed in the back.

Four men were tied on their knees under a Caravaggio print; one of them was Gilleach. Dowd stood next to them. Next to Golda stood a man dressed as though he ruled a small country somewhere, and next to him was the fella who fits the fella in the Magpie outfit's size chart. The very one dressed to the nines on Bourbon Street in the middle of the day. Then the Governor, Harold Heralds.

"Fuck me," I whispered. "The ballot box is upside down."

In the shadows were four more of the military types. Faces covered, guns in a clutch.

"Where the fuck did they come from?" I whispered to Xandi.

As soon as we were all present, our walkie-talkies started up.

"Grey man is walking in the area."

Golda turned to Xandi, "You want him?" she asked.

Xandi looked at me, and I nodded to her and Big Dan. They went back out the door.

I assumed the dignitary was this Ferdinand asshole I've been hearing about. He was knee-deep into kidnapping girls for his oil cruises, and she is about to change the family dynamics by striking a deal between him and the Gov? I could only assume.

Why the fuck am I here? I could understand Don Lee getting some relief of heart, but me? I had no skin in this game. Was I to be witness to the justice performed on Leda's hit? Gilleach? If it was the girls, then my part was over. Maybe I was part of some sort of initiation.

"I'm in no mood to spend any more of my time, people," Golda said, pulling the pistol from Dowd's holster and opening her umbrella. She pointed the open end of the umbrella at the kneeling men in the eenie-meenie-miney-mo motion. There's a hole in the top where she placed the gun barrel. Without a facial twitch, she swung the umbrella to the head of the upper-crusted half-brother, or whatever the fuck he is, pulling the trigger. The little bastard's head popped like a cantaloupe. Brains, mucus, hide, and hair ruined the red velvet wall. The umbrella kept Golda as clean as a day in church. Staunch as Dirty Harry, she didn't flinch a bit with hesitation. No sign of remorse whatsoever.

The room tensed as she looked over at the half-naked girl. The boys in the shadows raised weapons.

Golda walked to Charlie's accuser.

"Sweetheart? You ready for your day in court?"

The girl frantically nodded, scared, searching for an ending.

"Take these handcuffs off her, please, sir."

The little fella I suspected as being the magpie man pulled some keys from his trousers and, with agitation, he removed her handcuffs. Golda pulled the girl to her side, placing the pistol firmly in her grip, and whispered something to her. The girl gripped it, as all fear left her body. She was instantly the tough chick you didn't want to fuck in the dark alley. Golda quickly lifted the umbrella, the gun boomed, and the wall splattered with Dowd's brains.

"Don Lee, the two men next to Gilleach, are guilty of your Mary Catherine."

I saw his face turn sober with disdain. He loosened his shoulders like a prize fighter pulling up his dukes. Years of agony and lost love piled in his eyebrows. Jaws clamped, lips tucked. A Pulitzer Prize writer had nothing to say for once. The umbrella raised; the gun barrel pushed into the hole. No prayer, no remorse. He spoke softly.

"For my dear sister, Abigail, and our Mary Catherine."

Blood and brains flew again as two other men slumped in sin. Don Lee's sage wrinkles reappeared.

She loosened the gun from his grip.

"Life is imperfection. If it were perfect, there would be only one philosophy, one religion, and no need for justifiable intervention," she told us.

She pulled the governor, the magpie, me, and Don Lee into the poker room.

"Did you bring the body parts, Don Lee?" He smiled.

"Harold Heralds, you all know." She faced the magpie man. "This is Sydney, our attorney general. Don Lee, the dapper young man I just defeated, is Ferdinand; he is the owner of the shipping company that is responsible for the disappearance of all the girls over the years. A story must be written for the papers and the public, as I intend to regain control of my family's business and remove the sexual corruption." She leered at them with the seriousness of a doctor giving vital health advice.

"Dowd has been at the forefront of this for twenty years, and your eyewitness just killed him in revenge. He was about to rape the poor girl again. Can you take the story from here, Don Lee, Harold, Sydney?"

"Yes, Golda. I would love to cover it from here on out." Don Lee answered.

She looked at Harold Heralds. "A phone call from the church to your state will happen soon. The confession is foul play. That covers your reason for being on the premises tonight when your police staff arrive. Understood?"

He also nodded in the affirmative.

"It is all in Don Lee's hands. Follow his story, and all will be on track in the public eye."

She locked her hawk's eyes on me, "Theodore, come with me."

All I could think about was the fact that she had been privy to Mr. Shit Happens and Becca's body parts as I followed her to the stairwell.

"As I'm sure you've gathered, my own family put a hit on my daughter. They wanted my stake in American business, the business I've hand-built. You've witnessed what ordinary folk do to one another, but what the super-powerful are capable of doing to their own is something your mind just can't fathom, yet. I had to do what I had to do."

"The man inside, our attorney general, and monsignor? They get away, scot-free?" I asked.

"International business means bargaining and sacrifice. The church sits at the table of world regulation. I will let you and Don Lee have your way with the monsignor and Sydney in the future. *When* it is feasible. Revenge isn't in my wheelhouse. I have a nest to protect. Preventing is what I do. If I do that properly, then there is no need for revenge. The mother eagle never leaves her nest unattended; the snakes come to her. That's what we do, destroy on site, and no time for chasing assholes."

"Why am I here?" I asked.

"Why were you tested? I needed to know you had the balls to be here. I wanted to know how you would weed through the bullshit," she said, void of humor. "Leda is building her nest. Would you fight for your cause, or say fuck it like the rest of the beer commercial halfwits amplifying in this society of ease?"

"Well?" I asked.

"I didn't shoot you, did I? Men break their backs digging for precious metals for two bites of food a day, for one last pull of fresh breath. The other men on the other side of that coin will push children to the ground for silly trinkets. As long as there is fear of death, there will be inequality. Inequality breeds jealousy, which leads to murder; that's where we stand tonight. Murder keeps the human world on tilt. I didn't ask my father to throw me away, but he did, and what I built, his other children wanted to take it from us. Murder for protection is one of the first stories in the bible." She stared. I agreed with a head nod.

"Did you hear a man was found dead on his boat early this morning?" she asked.

"I had heard of a casualty."

Her thick accent added more menace than I wanted to hear.

"Picture this, if you will. A young shrimper heads out to meet his father and brothers down in Grand Isle, daylight is just hitting the river's current, and the ripples glitter a little in the darkness. Flies begin to wash over his face. Thick wads of possessed flies. Bloated black-green, pus-filled flies. He swashes at them, but the mass of them thickens, making him feel queasy. He removes his hat to push the thick of them from his eyes.

"Far off, trapped in an inlet at the Chalmette curve of the Mississippi, a small vessel aimlessly drifts on the edge of the tree line.

The young shrimper veers in its direction. The closer he gets, the thicker the flies. They flick off his teeth as he clinches his lips. Suddenly, he sees a body and yells toward it. No movement. He speeds up a little, his heart pounds a little tighter. The body seems to have climbed high up the mast.

" 'Why, is there a gator onboard?' He may ask himself. The unfortunate man seems to be caught in midair. He throttles a little more, then he sees it. It's covered in a thick blanket of those hungry, nasty summer flies.

" 'Oh my God,' he may mutter to himself. A man is tied to the top of the mast, his guts and genitals are splayed all over the deck, and those filthy flies have laid maggots in the air-cured intestines and blood. The young boat captain pukes all over himself.

"That's what happens to a man who tries to bring harm to my daughter." Golda had deepened her voice and slowed her words.

"I would dig a hole to hell to cut Satan's throat if I had to. Nobody could escape my wrath, Theodore." She turned to look me directly in my eyes. There was a reptilian stare for a split second, then she swallowed, and a different Golda emerged. I got the message and nodded that I would be ready to do the same.

"But, for now, I must help Don Lee return these poor girls to *their* mothers in the best shape I can provide them. Leda is waiting for you in my car, so go to her. It's parked in front of Cosimo's."

By her stare, I knew that the dead fella she had just recanted was Bucknell; no more words were necessary. I could also see the line I was to walk, my place in the sun, so to speak.

I turned to move down the stairs.

"Fremeaux, there's one more thing."

I stopped looking back.

"You have unfinished business back in Mason City. You'll need to ensure it can never come back to bite you."

I returned to my escape through the garage and out to the street. The confusion of her knowledge pushed through my pipeline of disbelief and crawled into the La-Z-Boy, into Red Dertinger's lap. It was just Red and me that night, no one else should hold the knowledge of his demise but him and me. His grin stretched to the edges of my mind. I have come to realize carrots were being dangled in front of me the whole time, making me wonder what else I would be used for.

I looked up to our gang in the window above, nodding that all was in good hands. Like following a shooting star as it burns toward earth, my gaze returned level, and I could see clearly why my little band of street detectives never opened the right doors. She needed me to lead them to this back door. We were her alibi. She needed *me* to bring Don Lee. An open invite was simply out of the question. Now the Governor and Sydney were aware of other eyes on them.

Whatever her prior knowledge about the kidnappings, she could easily say was discovered by our investigation. We'd never know if Leda saw Becca's hand that night, and it was best if it stays that way. Just like the bunny on that night trail, all we could do now was raise our heads to heaven and say, *Becca! Becca baby, you knew better than that.* And just like that, we could tell ourselves that if she had been more cautious, we would never have ached for her pains. We were no longer guilty of neglect, and that was a tough nugget to chew, baby. People who sat and whined about life not being fair needed a bitch slap. There was no such thing as an easy ride, and if you found one, you needed a bitch slap.

I saw Clementina standing at the entrance of the park, keeping a lookout. Then the scream of agony, followed by guttural moans, suddenly filled the night air. I knew the sound of the showstopper. Xandi had been itching to use it, too, and now the grey man was down. She and Big Dan would be standing over a dying man. Warm satisfaction would fill their hearts. Justice had been served with cold, clamped steel.

Leda was sitting in the backseat, her back stretched tall and firm. She held a new look; something had changed since this morning, more dignified, if that was possible, enhanced. Even perfection can evolve through time. I closed the door behind me and found I had crossed my legs like Cary Grant at a picnic as we pulled away from the scene.

I thought about the idea that all the stress I had put myself through the last couple of weeks was needless. I'd lost a week's worth of sleep. I'd questioned a thousand years of philosophy. I took her hand.

"You met mother's half-brother, I see?"

"You mean the dandy that your mother shot in the head?"

She smiled and brushed my face with her free hand, turning herself so that she could push her back into my side, resting herself under my arm.

"He may look like a dandy, but he was a cold-blooded bastard. Others will be coming for us. They'll think an advantage has opened in the form of weakness," she said softly.

"Who will?"

"Peers, oligarchs, tacky dictators, the usual shitbags looking to add to their financial empire."

"We'll cut whoever needs it," I told her. She squeezed my hand tighter.

"There's a new dawn coming to America. We are providing seed money for Pete Roselle and big tech. We will turn pro sports into a year-round Christmas. Provide entertainment for the masses and triple our wealth. Every bit of novelty they can buy to put hope in their hearts will have to be shipped through our ports. We supply the trivial pleasures; they fatten our banks."

"Sounds symbiotic enough," I said.

"Depends on how slant you look at it."

"Do you and Golda control everything?"

"We only control energy. Us and a small group of sagacious souls, you could say."

She replaced the word *money* with *energy*, I noticed.

"We don't want to control people's fates; that's up to each individual and the government they elect. Although your constitution did make a mistake. Every man is created equal, but each must evolve on their own merit, not on novelty. We may plant the tree, or build the windowsills and ladders of success, but people must work to find their own place to land. If people choose a path of less knowledge, nesting themselves in the tall grasses, mistaking the curve of the snake's eye for a shadow's arch, then that's just too bad. Life must move on; novelty isn't merit. Work hard to land higher or perish; it isn't our responsibility to provide life maintenance."

She wiggled herself into my ribs tightly.

"We beat our own wings with our own strengths and protect the nests we build for ourselves. This has been since the first dawn."

I kissed the back of her head.

"We'll be leaving the country in a few days," she confessed.

"Where and why?"

"Monaco. Our wedding will be there. Are you wearing your big boy pants?" She smirked.

"The grass will never be as green under anyone else's bed, my lady."

"No one's got you chained, just so you know."

"You've got the chicken foot, baby."

She smiled. The car stopped. I told her mother's driver to stay put; I'd be the one to open her door for her. She moved herself from my ribcage, knowing.

I walked behind her in full admiration. Past the two-hundred-year-old brick walls coated with ancient blood, sweat, and mixed dreams. Past the broken revelations I'd conjured and relinquished over the last couple of weeks. Through new ghosts and renovated consciousness. My gut told me I wouldn't suffer the doldrums ever again.

Hell, I didn't like the looks of Ferdinand, either; I probably would have rubbed his ass out, too. I wanted to think Becca would find that peaceful bed for her and her mother's souls.

We spirited ourselves up to the bedroom, lips falling into themselves like crashing stars. We busted into the sheets, and we fucked, and we fucked, and we fucked. We fucked and fucked and fucked. We fucked for murder; we fucked for mercy. We fucked until everything fell dark.

CHAPTER TWENTY-NINE

Something tickled my soul. I rubbed the hoodoo from my eyes to find the sun peeking in on us like a shining spot of new hope. She lay almost underneath my side, and the soreness in every bone in my body told me my future might not be as coordinated as I had hoped. It felt like I'd been left on tumble dry all night.

I ran my hand down her soft, warm skin. She peeked through squinted eye slits, kissing my shoulder, and scooched over a little.

I sat up, looking out the window across Jackson Square to watch the new clown twist the morning's first balloon animal for a young mother and her child.

I stood to walk to the window for a closer look. The clown man still looked a little disheveled, a little too unfortunate. As though the barstool he had just given up still held ass heat. The mother seemed timid and nervous. The child wouldn't let her leave without a latex animal.

"Chase novelty to an early grave or choose merit for the coming generations," I mumbled from the words of Leda in the backseat of the golden Rolls-Royce last night.

From the very beginning of solid communication, philosophers had been trying to wrangle the nature of truth to guide mankind to a higher plane of life. The problem was the truth that lies in nature's rulebook, and our thrownness into this world. Like the tumbling dice, we were all looking to avoid the gutter and the grave. Truth was, we all got shit on from time to time; it was the avoidance of that truth where brute force showed itself on occasion, which had a domino effect. Philosophy ended with the push and the shove, so I'd stick with looking up to the god of *Not Yet* for now.

This new clown in town would push and shove the wrong person soon, and shit will fly again; those were just the facts, ma'am.

Knowledge ain't for the lazy, as Don Lee liked to chant in his drunken, exaggerated hillbilly vernacular.

After I returned home from all the ceremonies planned for us, I'd be making a trip back to Double Gobble Road to try and persuade a lost mother to let me help save a brooding, lost young soul if I could. Xandi and I could find somewhere in the clan to teach the young boy a trade or two.

"Don't forget, we leave soon. You'll be officially meeting my father in a little while. And a dog named Baptist," she sleepily told me.

"Your Father?"

"Yes, Theodore, I have one. He is a large Cajun man in South Louisiana."

"I knew there must be one, but I figured he'd be a European fella. Possibly a deceased one at that."

"I told you, Mother's true love was here. Remember?"

"Yes, I do now. What do you mean by 'officially'?"

"You've shared a beer with him a time or two, you just didn't know it. He was also with Mother last night, in a combat uniform."

"Okay, baby," I answered with a new mystery planted in my thoughts.

I scratched my noggin, meandering to the guest bathroom, I guessed for routine's sake. Turned on the light to splash cool water over my face while soaking in all the new shit flooding my old life.

Grabbing for the hand towel, I found myself face-to-face with the stark white bag of peanuts once again. I scanned the bright reds, yellows, whites, and greens. Peanuts sprinkled about the black table. The wrinkled bags. The deep forest lines. I maneuvered through the plush, manicured lawn and birdless trees below, wishing to avoid the mystery lady and her binoculars.

"Is that a frown today? I know, lady, it's a tightrope. Some of us can still traverse it well enough, though," I mumble toward her.

I heard Leda sigh from the darkened bedroom, telling me that she was in waiting. I looked directly into the binocular lenses.

"I know, I know, old lady, ball of confusion. Weary will be the choice you'll have to live with."

For a second, the floating hand felt like it was waving above my head, warning me to watch my back. It was a long fall from this patio I'm staring into.

To swindle or not to swindle, is that the question? I thought as I wondered about the invisible man behind the hovering hand.

I looked at the fella staring back at me from the mirror. I found it to be the face I carried before all this shit hit the fan. My skin was taut and smooth again. My eyes had brightened. The lady in my new bed has mended my throne and restyled my hair.

"We dine from the hearth, not from the microwave," I told the lady hiding behind the binoculars, as I turned out the light.

A Poe-like wind whistling from the front room caught my attention, so I walked that way. The light pink hue of sunlight was threatening to expose the wet bar through the balcony doors when I noticed one of the doors had popped itself slightly ajar.

I felt compelled to peek out into the square before shutting it back and locking us safe again, and to my surprise, Ruthie and her ducks were waiting directly under the balcony. She peered up and we stared at each other for a full minute.

Could Ruthie have magically unlatched the door from where she stood? I soon realized I *had* been summoned, so I did as I was called and went down to greet her.

We stood face to face. She smacked her lips as the older, larger duck flailed its glorious orange mouthpiece about, ending its intention, and pushed into the underside of Ruthie's right breast. She lowered her palm under the beak of her friend. It twitched and chewed sporadically, twisting its head until it eventually spat something into the palm of Ruthie's upturned hand. Ruthie held it up for inspection, then dried it against her breast and placed the small pebble into my palm, closing my fingers into a fist.

Her eyes were a cool, bleached pinkish green, like the inside color of fresh-cut watermelon rind, telling me to never let it become lost to indifference. I opened my palm and found a fresh, unpolished, misshapen pearl. I looked back into those cool pinkish-green eyes again, making me feel as though I was staring across a vast, calm sea. Her eyes said that I must trust myself, my family, and my neighbors. If I can do that, I can sail any treacherous waters that may come my way with ease.

I felt another presence above us. I could feel Leda inspecting my station. I didn't feel the need to look up to her; I knew she knew I was thinking about the strawberries, and she knew that I knew she was thinking about the champagne. We had become entangled in our time.

My new feathered friend stretched out tall and dignified, flapping her wings with bravado. She bellowed a brash and confident honk as if putting the final punctuation on the moment.

Ruthie reached to squeeze my elbow, her gravelly voice fired off like Evil Knievel's motorcycle.

"Anya's her name, and she believes we're all full of shit."

Ruthie and her friends of the fowl and game persuasion turned to re-enter the wild kingdom, forcing me to fully accept that New Orleans truly is an anything-can-happen-at-any-moment-of-every-single-Goddamned day kind of town.

"Amen, Anya. Aaaaymen, Sister Girl!"

Made in the USA
Coppell, TX
15 June 2026

81641466R00173